Praise for Brenda Jackson

"Leave it to Jackson to take sizzle and honor, wrap it in romance and come up with a first-rate tale."
—*RT Book Reviews* on *Temptation*

"Brenda Jackson is the queen of newly discovered love... If there's one thing Jackson knows how to do, it's how to pluck those heartstrings and stir up some seriously saucy drama."
—*BookPage* on *Inseparable*

"Welcome to another memorable family tree created by the indomitable Brenda Jackson, a romantic at heart."
—*USA TODAY* on *A Brother's Honor*

"[Jackson] proves once again that she rocks when it comes to crafting family drama with a healthy dose of humor and steamy, sweaty sex. Here's another winner."
—*RT Book Reviews* on *A Brother's Honor*, 4½ stars, Top Pick

"This deliciously sensual romance ramps up the emotional stakes and the action.... [S]exy and sizzling."
—*Library Journal* on *Intimate Seduction*

"Jackson does not disappoint...first-class page-turner."
—*RT Book Reviews* on *A Silken Thread*, 4½ stars, Top Pick

"Jackson is a master at writing."
—*Publishers Weekly* on *Sensual Confessions*

For additional books by
New York Times bestselling author Brenda Jackson,
visit her website, www.brendajackson.net.

BRENDA JACKSON

FORGED IN DESIRE

HQN™

HQN™

Recycling programs
for this product may
not exist in your area.

ISBN-13: 978-0-373-79000-5

Forged in Desire

Copyright © 2017 by Brenda Streater Jackson

This edition published by arrangement with Harlequin Books S.A.

For questions and comments about the quality of this book,
please contact us at CustomerService@Harlequin.com.

® and TM are trademarks of Harlequin Enterprises Limited or its
corporate affiliates. Trademarks indicated with ® are registered in the
United States Patent and Trademark Office, the Canadian Intellectual
Property Office and in other countries.

www.HQNBooks.com

Printed in U.S.A.

To the love of my life, my best friend
and the wind beneath my wings, Gerald Jackson, Sr.
I'm everything I am because you loved me.

To everyone who enjoyed reading about the Grangers,
this one is for you!

"Happy is the man that findeth wisdom,
and the man that getteth understanding."
—*Proverbs* 3:13

PROLOGUE

"FINALLY, WE GET to go home."

Margo Connelly was certain the man's words echoed the sentiment they all felt. The last thing she had expected when reporting for jury duty was to be sequestered during the entire trial...especially with eleven strangers, more than a few of whom had taken the art of bitching to a whole new level.

She was convinced this had been the longest, if not the most miserable, six weeks of her life, as well as a lousy way to start off the new year. They hadn't been allowed to have any inbound or outbound calls, read the newspapers, check any emails, watch television or listen to the radio. The only good thing was, with the vote just taken, a unanimous decision had been reached and justice would be served. The federal case against Murphy Erickson would finally be over and they would be allowed to go home.

As far as the twelve of them were concerned, the prosecution had proved, beyond a shadow of doubt, that Erickson was the leader of a ring of organized crime that had resulted in over a dozen deaths. The majority of them so brutal it had taken everything Margo had to sit there, trying not to show any emotion, while listening to endless testimony about the deaths in gruesome detail. There had even been a family of four that included two children. Innocent victims who just happened to be in the wrong place at the wrong time.

"It's time to let the bailiff know we've reached a decision." Nancy Snyder spoke up, interrupting Margo's thoughts. "I have a man waiting at home, who I haven't seen in six weeks, and I can't wait to get to him."

Lucky you, Margo thought, leaning back in her chair. She and Scott Dylan had split over a year ago, and the parting hadn't been pretty. He liked reminding her that, as a financial adviser on Wall Street making a high six-figure salary, he could take his pick of women and she should be grateful. When she'd felt the relationship had run its course, he hadn't wanted to end things and had made a damn nuisance of himself.

Fortunately, as a wedding-dress designer, she could work from anywhere and had decided to move back home to Charlottesville. And there was the bonus of being near her uncle Frazier, her father's brother and the man who'd become her guardian when her parents had died in a house fire when she was ten. He was her only living relative and, although they often butted heads, she would admit she had missed him while living in New York.

"What about dinner tonight?" a deep masculine voice whispered close to her ear.

Margo didn't have to turn to see who it was. Carl Palmer had made his interest in her known from the first. Because of that wedding band on his finger, she hadn't reciprocated.

She shifted in her chair to look at him. To keep others from overhearing their conversation, he'd leaned in close as if he was checking out the papers in front of her. Carl was handsome, she would give him that, but she was not a woman who messed around with married men. "I would think after six weeks you'd want to get home to your wife," she whispered back.

"Soon-to-be ex" was his quick, whispered comeback.

"Doesn't matter. Not interested."

Before he could give a retort, the knock on the door got everyone's attention. The bailiff had arrived. Hopefully, in a few hours it would all be over and the judge would release them. She couldn't wait to get back to running her business. Six weeks had been a long time away from it. Lucky for her she had finished her last order in time for the bride's Christmas wedding. But she couldn't help wondering how many new orders she might have missed out on while on jury duty.

The bailiff entered and said, "The judge has called the court back in session for the reading of the verdict. We're ready to escort you there."

Like everyone else in the room, Margo stood. She was ready for the verdict to be read. It was only after this that she could get her life back.

"FOREMAN, HAS THE JURY reached a verdict?" the judge asked.

"Yes, we have, Your Honor."

The courtroom was quiet as the verdict was read. "We, the jury, find Murphy Erickson guilty of murder."

Suddenly Erickson bowled over and laughed. He actually laughed, and it was the kind of laugh that made the hairs on the necks of everyone in attendance stand up. The outburst prompted the judge to hit his gavel several times. "Order in the courtroom. Coun-

selor, quiet the defendant or he will be found in contempt of court."

"I don't give a damn about any contempt," Erickson
snarled loudly. "You!" he said, pointing a finger at the
judge. "Along with everyone else in this courtroom,
you have just signed your own death warrant. As long
as I remain locked up, someone in here will die every
seventy-two hours," Erickson threatened at the top of
his voice while looking around at the members of the
jury, the prosecutors, the clerk reporter, the defense attorneys, media and all others in the courtroom. It was
as if his gaze didn't miss a single individual.

Pandemonium broke out. The judge continued to
pound his gavel, trying to restore order. Police officers rushed forward to subdue Erickson and haul him
away. But even then the sound of his threats could
still be heard.

Margo glanced around and saw everyone was just
as stunned as she. She breathed in deeply, trying to
control her racing heart. The judge finally established
order in the courtroom and began thanking the members of the jury for their public service. His words
were lost on Margo. Erickson's threats were echoing
too loudly in her ears.

CHAPTER ONE

LAMAR "STRIKER" JENNINGS walked into the hospital room, stopped and then frowned. "What the hell is he doing working from bed?"

"I asked myself the same thing when I got his call for us to come here," Striker's friend Quasar Patterson said, sitting lazily in a chair with his long legs stretched out in front of him.

"And you might as well take a seat like he told us to do," another friend, Stonewall Courson, suggested, while pointing to an empty chair. "Evidently it will take more than a bullet to slow down Roland."

Roland Summers, CEO of Summers Security Firm, lay in the hospital bed, staring at them. Had it been just last week that the man had been fighting for his life after foiling an attempted carjacking?

"You still look like shit, Roland. Shouldn't you be trying to get some rest instead of calling a meeting?" Striker asked, sliding his tall frame into the chair. He didn't like seeing Roland this way. They'd been friends a long time, and he couldn't ever recall the man being sick. Not even with a cold. Well, at least he was alive. That damn bullet could have taken him out and Striker didn't want to think about that.

"You guys have been keeping up with the news?"

Roland asked in a strained voice, interrupting Striker's thoughts.

"We're aware of what's going on, if that's what you want to know," Stonewall answered. "Nobody took Murphy Erickson's threat seriously."

Roland made an attempt to nod his head. "And now?"

"And now people are panicking. Phones at the office have been ringing off the hook. I'm sure every protective security service in town is booked solid. Everyone in the courtroom that day is either in hiding or seeking protection, and with good reason," Quasar piped in to say. "The judge, clerk reporter and bailiff are all dead. All three were gunned down within seventy-two hours of each other."

"The FBI is working closely with local law enforcement, and they figure it's the work of the same assassin," Striker added. "I heard they anticipate he'll go after someone on the jury next."

"Which is why I called the three of you here. There was a woman on the jury who I want protected. It's personal."

"Personal?" Striker asked, lifting a brow. He knew Roland dated off and on, but he'd never been serious with anyone. He was always quick to say that his wife, Becca, had been his one and only love.

"Yes, personal. She's a family member."

The room got quiet. That statement was even more baffling since, as far as the three of them knew, Roland didn't have any family…at least not anymore. They were all aware of his history. He'd been a cop, who'd discovered some of his fellow officers on the take. Before he could blow the whistle he'd been framed and sent to prison for fifteen years. Becca had refused to accept his fate and worked hard to get him a new trial. He served three years before finally leaving prison but not before the dirty cops murdered Roland's wife. All the cops involved had eventually been brought to justice and charged with the death of Becca Summers, in addition to other crimes.

"You said she's family?" Striker asked, looking confused.

"Yes, although I say that loosely since we've never officially met. I know who she is, but she doesn't know I even exist." Roland then closed his eyes, and Striker knew he had to be in pain.

"Man, you need to rest," Quasar said. "You can cover this with us another time."

Roland's eyes flashed back open. "No, we need to talk now. I need one of you protecting her right away."

Nobody said anything for a minute and then Striker asked, "What relation is she to you, man?"

"My niece. To make a long story short, years ago my mom got involved with a married man. He broke things off when his wife found out about the affair but not before I was conceived. I always knew the identity of my father. I also knew about his other two older sons, although they didn't know about me. I guess you can say I was the old man's secret." Roland tried shifting in bed and suddenly let out a deep moan.

"You okay, Roland?" Stonewall asked in concern.

Roland nodded. "I'm okay."

"You need to rest," Striker said.

"The sooner I finish telling you everything, the sooner I can rest."

"Then finish before we call the nurse to increase your pain meds," Quasar said, leaning forward.

"One day after I'd left for college, I got a call from my mother letting me know the old man was dead but he'd left me something in his will."

Striker didn't say anything, thinking that at least Roland's old man had done right by him in the end. To this day, his own poor excuse of a father hadn't even acknowledged his existence. "That's when your two brothers found out about you?" he asked.

"Yes. Their mother found out about me as well. She turned out to be a real bitch. Even tried blocking what Connelly had left for me in the will. But she couldn't. The old man evidently had anticipated her making such a move and made sure the will was ironclad. He gave me enough to finish college without taking out student loans with a little left over."

"Good for him," Quasar said. "What about your brothers? How did they react to finding out about you?"

"The eldest acted like a dickhead," Roland said without pause. "The other one's reaction was just the opposite. His name was Murdock and he reached out to me afterward. I would hear from him from time to time. He would call to see how I was doing."

Roland didn't say anything for a minute, his face showing he was struggling with strong emotions. "Murdock is the one who gave Becca the money to hire a private investigator to reopen my case. I never got the chance to thank him."

"Why?" Quasar asked.

Roland drew in a deep breath and then said, "Murdock and his wife were killed weeks before my new trial began."

"How did they die?"

"House fire. Fire department claimed faulty wiring. I never believed it but couldn't prove otherwise. Luckily their ten-year-old daughter wasn't home at the time. She'd been attending a sleepover at one of her friends' houses."

"You think those dirty cops took them out too?" Stonewall asked.

"Yes. While I could link Becca's death to those corrupt cops, there wasn't enough evidence to connect Murdock's and his wife's deaths."

Stonewall nodded. "What happened to the little girl after that?"

"She was raised by the other brother. Since the old lady had died by then, he became her guardian." Roland paused a minute and then added, "He came to see me this morning."

"Who? Your brother? The dickhead?" Quasar asked with a snort.

"Yes," Roland said, and it was obvious he was trying not to grin. "When he walked in here it shocked the hell out of me. Unlike Murdock, he never reached out to me, and I think he even resented Murdock for doing so."

"So what the fuck was his reason for showing up here today?" Stonewall asked. "He'd heard you'd gotten shot and wanted to show some brotherly concern?" It was apparent by Stonewall's tone he didn't believe that was the case.

"Umm, let me guess," Quasar then said languidly. "He had a change of heart, especially now that his niece's life is in danger. Now he wants your help. I assume this is the same niece you want protected."

"Yes, to both. He'd heard I'd gotten shot and claimed he was concerned. Although he's not as much of a dickhead as before, I sensed a little resentment is still there. But not because I'm his father's bastard. A part of me believes he's gotten over that."

"What, then?" Striker asked.

"I think he blames me for Murdock's death. He didn't come out and say that, but he did let me know he was aware of the money Murdock gave Becca to get me a new trial and that he has similar suspicions regarding the cause of their deaths. That's why when he became his niece's guardian, he sent her out of the country to attend an all-girls school with tight security in London for a few years. He didn't bring her back to the States until after those bad cops were sent to jail."

"So the reason he showed up today was because he thought sending you on a guilt trip would be the only way to get you to protect your niece?" Striker asked angrily. Although Roland had tried hiding it, Striker could clearly see the pain etched in his face whenever he spoke.

"Evidently. I guess it didn't occur to him that making sure she is protected is something I'd want to do. I owe Murdock, although I don't owe Frazier Connelly a damn thing."

"Frazier Connelly?" Quasar said, sitting up straight in his chair. "*The* Frazier Connelly of Connelly Enterprises?"

"One and the same."

Nobody said anything for a while. Then Striker asked, "Your niece—what's her name?"

"Margo. Margo Connelly."

"And she doesn't know anything about you?" Stonewall asked. "Are you still the family's well-kept secret?"

Roland nodded. "Frazier confirmed that today, and I prefer things to stay that way. If I could, I would protect her. I can't, so I need one of you to do it for me. Hopefully, it won't be long before the assassin that Erickson hired is apprehended."

Striker eased out of his chair. Roland, of all people, knew that, in addition to working together, he, Quasar and Stonewall were the best of friends. They looked out for each other and watched each other's backs. And if needed they would cover Roland's back as well. Roland was more than just their employer—he was their close friend, mentor and the voice of reason, even when they really didn't want one. "Stonewall is handling things at the office in your absence, and Quasar is already working a case. That leaves me. Don't worry about a thing, Roland. I've got it covered. Consider it done."

MARGO CONNELLY STARED up at her uncle. "A bodyguard? Do you really think that's necessary, Uncle Frazier? I understand extra policemen are patrolling the streets."

"That's not good enough. Why should I trust a bunch of police officers?"

"Why shouldn't you?" she countered, not for the first time wondering what her uncle had against cops. On more than one occasion he'd made that quite obvious.

"I have my reasons, but this isn't about me—this is about you and your safety. I refuse to have you placed in any danger. What's the big deal? You've had a bodyguard before."

Yes, she'd had one before. Right after her parents' deaths, when her uncle had become her guardian. He had shipped her off to London for three years. She'd reckoned he'd been trying to figure out what he, a devout bachelor, was to do with a ten-year-old. When she returned to the United States, Apollo remained her bodyguard. When she turned fourteen, she fought hard for a little personal freedom. But she'd always known the chauffeurs Uncle Frazier hired could do more than drive her to and from school. More than once she'd seen the guns they carried.

"Yes, but that was then and this is now, Uncle Frazier. I can look after myself."

"Haven't you been keeping up with the news?" he snapped. "Three people are dead. All three were in that courtroom with you. Erickson is making sure his threat is carried out."

"And more than likely whoever is committing these murders will be caught before there can be another shooting. I understand the three were killed while they were away from home. I have enough paperwork to catch up on here for a while. I didn't even leave my house today."

"You don't think a paid assassin will find you here? Alone? You either get on board with having a bodyguard or you move back home. It's well secured there."

Margo drew in a deep breath. Back home was the Connelly estate. Yes, it was secure, with its state-of-the-art surveillance system. While growing up, she'd thought of the ten-acre property, surrounded by a tall wrought-iron fence and cameras watching her every move, as a prison. Now she couldn't stand the thought of staying there for any long period of time...especially if Liz was still in residence.

Her forty-five-year-old uncle had never married and claimed he had his reasons for never wanting to. But that didn't keep him from occasionally having a live-in mistress under his roof. His most recent was Liz Tillman and, as far as Margo was concerned, the woman was a real work of art with the words *gold digger* written all over her. Margo knew her uncle was a smart man and would eventually figure that fact out for himself. But right now it seemed he was quite taken with Liz's looks and body.

"It's final. A bodyguard will be here around the clock to protect you until this madness is over."

Margo didn't say anything. She wondered if at any time it had crossed her uncle's mind that they were at her house, not his, and she was no longer a child but a twenty-six-year-old woman. In a way, she knew she should appreciate his concern, but she refused to let anyone order her around.

He was wrong in assuming she hadn't been keeping up with the news. Just because she was trying to maintain a level head didn't mean a part of her wasn't a little worried. She could still recall the threat Murphy Erickson had made in the courtroom that day. Each time she remembered it chills would go through her.

Her uncle walked over to the window and looked out. It had snowed earlier. He stood there for a long moment, just staring out at the snow. She'd known that taking on the responsibility of raising her after her parents' deaths hadn't been easy for him. Not that he had ever complained. He'd always been there for her, although at times, especially during her teen years, she'd thought he was a little too controlling.

"What are you thinking about, Uncle Frazier?" she asked, getting up and joining him at the window to look out as well. Light snow was expected in Charlottesville during the end of January, but the snow that had fallen earlier had been heavier than usual, just like the forecasters had predicted. In the distance she could see it covered the top of the mountains.

"Too much snow for you?" she asked. Margo knew how much he hated cold weather. The times he'd visited her in New York had been during the summer months.

He chuckled, something she liked hearing since he rarely did it. Sometimes she wondered about him, especially when he got into one of his pensive moods. It was as if he was trying to deal with some major regrets. What were they? Would he ever share them with her?

"I was just remembering a day similar to this one," he finally said. "There was a lot of snow. And your father talked me into going outside and building a snowman with him."

Frazier chuckled again. "Crazy me, I did it, instead of refusing and throwing my weight around as the oldest. Your dad had that ability to convince me to do something I really didn't want to do." He got quiet for a minute and then said, seeming thoughtful, "At least with most things." He paused a moment. "Anyway, we had fun that day, although afterward I caught a bad cold and had to stay out of school for a week."

Margo smiled. She loved whenever he shared fond memories with her. He and her father had been close at one time… At least that was the impression her uncle gave when he reminisced about their childhood. She knew something happened to the brothers as adults that had placed a wedged between them, and to this day she had no idea what it had been. She'd asked, but he refused to say. In fact, he dismissed her assumptions as untrue.

"I have to be honest—you had me worried there for a minute, Uncle Frazier."

He looked down at her. "About what?"

"The reason for your preoccupied expression. I thought you were about to break the news that you've decided to get married or something."

He snorted and said, "Not hardly."

His words, especially the way he'd said them, made Margo wonder if there was trouble in paradise. He'd been with Liz for over a year now, longer than any other woman. After he moved Liz into his home, Margo rarely visited him at the estate, and he knew why. It was obvious whenever she and Liz were in the same room that they couldn't get along. Heaven knew she'd tried, but it was as if the woman saw her as competition. Liz wanted Frazier for herself and didn't intend to share him with any woman. Not even a niece. How crazy was that?

"I'm glad you're going along with me about the bodyguard, Margo."

She frowned as she glanced up at him. Had she really agreed? In a way she guessed she had. The last thing she wanted was for him to worry needlessly about her. "I'll give one a try…but this bodyguard better be forewarned not to get underfoot. I have a lot of work to do. An order came in while I was sequestered and the woman will be dropping by tomorrow morning for measurements. Although it's a September wedding, I want to get started right away."

"Why the rush?"

"I'd like to take this summer off. Possibly visit Apollo and his family in London."

"That would be nice."

She wasn't finished yet. "And another thing, Uncle Frazier," she said, crossing her arms over her chest. "I think you forget sometimes that I'm twenty-six and live on my own and am very independent. Just because I'm going along with you on this, I hope you don't think you can start bulldozing your way with me."

He glowered at her. "You're stubborn like your father."

She smiled. "I'll take that as a compliment." Dropping her hands, she moved back toward the sofa and sat down, grabbing a magazine off the coffee table to flip through. "So, when do we hire this bodyguard?"

"He's been hired. In fact, I expect him to arrive in a few minutes."

Margo's head jerked up. "What?! You hired him without consulting me?"

"I saw no need. He came highly recommended, Margo. I understand he's good at what he does and that's what I want."

That wasn't what she wanted. She wanted to vet her own bodyguard. The last thing she needed was someone breathing down her neck, watching her every move and telling her what she could and could not do, which was exactly what the sort of man her uncle hired would do.

"And I hope you follow his orders, Margo. His job is to keep you alive."

She scowled at him. "Since he came so highly rec-ommended, I'm sure that he will."

Margo drew in a deep breath. She hated being a smart mouth; however, the thought of another man crowding her space for any reason—even to keep her alive—didn't sit well with her. She and Scott had lived in separate apartments and had tossed around the idea of moving in together. He was more for it than she was. During the weekends he had stayed over at her place, she'd been more than ready for him to leave on Monday morning. He never picked up after himself and depended on her to do practically everything. She'd begun to feel like his personal assistant rather than his lover.

She leaned back against the sofa. Her uncle moved from the window to take the chair across from her. "So what do you know about this person whose presence I have to put up with for no telling how long?" she asked. "Who recommended him, Uncle Frazier?"

There was a long pause. Hadn't her uncle heard her question? Just in case, she repeated it.

"Someone I know."

"So this person has used him before?"

"Not sure."

She lifted a brow. "Yet you've taken his word for it?" She could tell her questions were agitating him. She was ready to dig deeper when the doorbell rang.

"I hope that's him," her uncle said, standing quickly.

She stood as well. A part of her hoped it wasn't him. Why did she feel certain her life would be changing? Probably because it would. A madman was on the loose. A killer for hire. Did Murphy Erickson really think he would be set free from prison? If nothing else, these additional deaths were on his hands. Had the man forgotten that Virginia was a death-penalty state? Did he care?

Margo moved toward the door, her uncle right on her heels. She started to say something and decided not to waste her time. What was the point? Her uncle had arranged for her to have a bodyguard regardless of whether she wanted one or not.

Upon reaching the door, she turned to her uncle. "Like I said, I won't have him underfoot, Uncle Frazier."

"If it means keeping you alive, I don't care if he's underarm," he responded tersely.

She rolled her eyes before turning back to the door. "Who is it?"

"Striker Jennings."

Striker? What kind of name was that?

She turned to her uncle, who nodded and said, "That's him."

She wanted to see what kind of guy went by the name *Striker.* She stared through the peephole and, as if he knew what she was doing, he looked directly at her. The moment their gazes connected, something—she wasn't sure what—made her breath catch.

Her uncle heard it and quickly asked, "What's wrong?"

Margo drew in a deep breath as she pulled away. "Nothing." She was lying. Who was this man? Why did just staring into his eyes have such an effect on her? The thought that he would be sharing her space…for who knew how long…was rather unsettling.

"Well, aren't you going to let him in?"

Instead of answering her uncle's question, she opened the door. And there he stood. The man named Striker Jennings. Instead of focusing on his eyes like before, she took in the entire man. And what a man he was. He was tall, way over six feet. And he was big. Muscular in a dark business suit and looking totally professional and serious. Why was her gaze intrigued by his broad shoulders, bulging biceps and flat abs? And those heavily lashed, dark eyes, the same ones she had stared into just moments ago, seemed to say, "Go ahead and try me."

Try him? Margo swallowed deeply while thinking, How? With what? And for how long? She snapped back to her senses when her uncle came around to verify the man's identity and said, "Show me credentials."

Although the man gave her uncle a look that all but told him what he could do with the credentials he'd asked for, the man shifted his duffel bag into the other hand before pulling an identification card from his jacket pocket. She and her uncle looked at it. *Lamar Jennings.* So Striker wasn't his real name. And he worked for a Summers Security Firm. There was a nice picture of him, but the real thing standing in front of her was so much better. Almost too much. Far too pleasing on any woman's eyes. His nutmeg-colored facial features were way too mesmerizing. Way too captivating to even be considered merely handsome. Definitely riveting. She noted there was nothing soft about him and detected a hardness that would kick ass first and ask questions later.

Her uncle handed the ID card back to him. "Come on in, Jennings."

"Striker," he corrected him, not moving an inch. It was as if he needed to establish a few things up front and what he wanted to be called was one of them.

Her uncle didn't say anything, and she wondered if he would. Although he often accused her of being stubborn, Frazier Connelly could be just as stubborn.

Even more so. The two men stared hard at each other, and then, as if her uncle had decided it would be in his best interest to be the one to concede, he said, "Okay. Come in, *Striker*."

She stepped aside when he walked past her and she closed the door behind him.

"You come highly recommended," her uncle was saying, extending his hand out to the man.

"Do I?" Striker replied, accepting her uncle's handshake.

"Yes, and this is my niece, Margo Connelly. The woman I'm depending on you to keep safe."

He turned his dark, penetrating eyes on her. She could feel a deep stirring in the pit of her stomach when he extended his hand out to her. "Ms. Connelly."

Margo accepted his hand and suddenly an intense rush of desire tore into her. It took everything she had not to snatch her hand back. She'd never met this man before. Didn't know a thing about him other than that he'd been hired by her uncle. Yet she was attracted to him. She'd heard of sudden attraction but had never been the recipient of it, until now.

Even though he was impeccably dressed in a business suit, she detected a rough edge. And she suspected if the need arose, he could be lethal. As far as she was concerned, lethal and good-looking was one hell of a combination. She *was* a woman and there was nothing wrong with appreciating a well-muscled, nicely built man when she saw one.

"Mr. Jennings," she said, pulling her hand from his.

"Striker," he corrected her.

Instead of acknowledging his correction, Margo didn't say anything, not sure she could find her voice even if she'd wanted to. At that moment a semblance of heated desire fanned low in her stomach. On top of that, her mind was still reeling from the sensations caused from their handshake. She felt irritated wondering what in the world was going on here. Putting the *appreciation* thing aside, it was totally unlike her to be *this* affected by any man. Although she relished eye candy like any other female might, she'd never let a man bring out the lustful side of her. In fact, to be totally honest, she hadn't been aware she had one until now. She hadn't been involved with a man since Scott. And that had been her choice. Her passion was her work and it superseded any intimate feminine needs. She'd learned not to place any man at the top of her pedestal.

That decision had come about after her last two serious relationships had left a bad taste in her mouth. Her attitude was that she didn't need a man to be happy since all they seemed to do was disappoint her anyway. She liked her life just the way it was. Uninvolved, unattached and drama-free. At least it had been drama-free before the Erickson trial.

As Margo continued to study the man who'd entered her home, she had a feeling she was in a heap of trouble that had nothing to do with any assassin's attempt on her life.

CHAPTER TWO

STRIKER WONDERED WHAT the hell was happening as he dropped his duffel bag on the floor by the sofa. He couldn't recall the last time he'd felt instant attraction to a woman. But he had with this one and could still feel the heat from their handshake. Roland should have warned him that Margo Connelly was such a looker. The woman standing before him was so incredibly beautiful he'd almost gone speechless when she'd opened the door.

The moment he had gazed into her face he'd been sacked by an intense desire that had somehow infiltrated his mind. That wasn't good, especially when she was the woman he'd been sent here to protect. And, of all things, she was Roland's niece.

He scanned his surroundings, needing a few moments to clear his head, specifically to unblock his brain. Doing so was a whole lot safer than looking at her again. He'd seen enough already, liked too much of what he saw. Besides striking features, she had a nice body—curvy hips, nice thighs, and the shape of her breasts outlined beneath her shirt was pretty damn appealing. And when she'd closed the door he had gotten a look at her tight and shapely backside. His gaze was also drawn to her mouth longer than it should have been, a mouth that appeared as lush as any he'd ever seen.

He'd known he was in trouble the moment he'd detected her staring at him through the peephole. A funny feeling had settled in the lower part of his body. The last thing he needed was a woman arousing him.

"How long have you been a bodyguard?"

He had no choice but to look at her since she'd just asked him a question. She stood there with a defiant expression on her face. He immediately knew it would be one of those kinds of parties. She didn't want him there. Nothing personal. She just figured she didn't need anyone protecting her gorgeous ass.

"I'm not a bodyguard," he said, trying to keep his eyes trained on her face and not roaming the length of her body like they were tempted to do.

Her brow lifted. "Then what are you?"

Besides a man lusting after you at the moment... "I'm a protector. And my job is to protect you, Ms. Connelly, not guard you."

She crossed her arms over her chest. "And if I don't want to be protected?" she asked in a rigid tone.

"Then I strongly suggest that you rethink that position. On my way over here there was a newscast on the radio reporting that another person has been killed. The foreman of the jury. The same jury you were on, Ms. Connelly."

She gasped and for a minute it seemed as if she was about to pass out. Her uncle gave her his shoulder to lean on and led her over to the sofa to sit down. Striker watched the two and hoped the news had shocked some sense into her. What was that BS she'd been talking about not needing a protector? Even if this was the first she'd heard about the fourth killing, she had to have known about the other three. Had she assumed the killer would stop at three and call it quits?

"Jeffery Turner." Margo spoke up in a rather soft voice. Definitely softer than the rough words she'd spoken earlier. "He was our foreman. He was a nice man. Married. Father of four. Two in college. He and his wife had been married twenty-five years." She looked down at her hands and said, "Jeffery would shake everyone's hands each morning. For six solid weeks. He hadn't wanted to be sequestered any more than the rest of us, but he'd said it was the right thing to do. It was our civic duty."

She paused a moment and then added, "He kept a level head at all times. And when some of the other jurors wanted to act like children, Jeffery knew how to handle them. He had experience. How dare someone take his life? Take him away from his family? Who would do that?"

"The same person who wouldn't hesitate to blow you away if you don't have any protection," Striker said.

She popped her head up and stared at him. Her gaze was angry, so full of fury he could all but see smoke coming out of her ears. He was aware that only a portion of that anger was directed at him because of his flippant statement. The true target of her anger was a hit man she didn't know. But like he'd just told her, whether she wanted to hear it or not, she could be the assassin's next victim.

"I came here to protect you. With my life if I have to. However, if you don't want to be kept alive, just say so. I have other things to do, Ms. Connelly," he said in a hard tone, deliberately so.

"Of course she wants to be protected," her uncle said rather quickly. "She's just a little upset at the moment. Surely you can understand that."

Striker didn't say anything. If the man was waiting for him to say he understood, then he'd be waiting all night. Instead he said, "While she's trying to compose herself, I'll take the time to see just how secure this place is." He turned to walk out of the room.

"Wait!"

He turned back around to face Margo. "Yes?"

"And what if you don't think it's secure?"

"If it's not to my satisfaction, then I'll make it secure if I can. Otherwise, we'll relocate."

She crossed her arms over her chest again, giving him that defiant look he had already come to expect. "This is my home. It's also where I work. I'm trying to get caught up after being practically locked away for six weeks. I have a client coming to be measured in the morning. I have to—"

"You have to stay alive. I would think, Ms. Connelly, that would be your top priority."

"I agree with him, Margo," Frazier said. "I think you've exerted your rebellious side enough for one day."

"Uncle Frazier, I—"

"No, Margo. You either let him keep you alive or you can move back home."

"No," Margo said, shaking her head. "I won't move back home, Uncle Frazier. You know how things are with me and Liz."

"Then I suggest you let this man do his job and keep you alive," Frazier said. He then turned to Striker. "Go ahead and check out things. I'd like to have a private conversation with my niece."

Striker looked from Frazier to Margo, and then,

without saying a word, he turned and strode toward the kitchen.

Determined to put Margo out of his mind, Striker entered her kitchen. Whoa. Whose kitchen looked this neat and clean? Probably one that never got used, he thought, taking his cell phone from the pocket of his slacks and pulling up an app to take notes. His gaze moved to her back door. It looked sturdy enough, but of course he intended to make sure.

Moments later he'd verified that it was, but he wasn't a fan of all these windows, although he could see why she was. There was a beautiful view of the Blue Ridge Mountains outside those windows. Nice but risky. The mountains could cast shadows on the rooftops of those homes. The perfect place for a sniper to take aim. And he'd noted the house next door was up for sale and appeared empty. He would make sure the office monitored any activities there.

Striker removed his tie and jacket and placed both across a chair before keying in information on the phone. And he definitely didn't like that sliding glass door that led outside.

Walking over, he slid it open and stepped out onto a patio. Quality wicker furniture was arranged to take advantage of the view of the mountains. She had a nice-sized yard with hardly any trees or shrubs. That was a plus. He also noted the area where she kept her garbage can and barbecue grill, which was a dark corner of the yard. A motion light would do the trick not just there but at every corner of her home.

She lived in a fairly upscale community although it wasn't gated. The homes were commodious and spaced a good distance from each other. According to Roland, she designed wedding dresses, and from what he'd heard, she had made quite a name for herself.

He also knew Margo Connelly was loaded, yet she lived modestly. Empress Lakes was a beautiful community of homes, but he had expected her to reside in one of those upscale neighborhoods like Oakwood Heights or Tamaquan Manor. And why not open a shop somewhere? Why would she even want to work from her home, where strangers would invade her personal space?

Earlier, at the hospital, Roland had asked him to stay behind after Stonewall and Quasar had left. Striker hadn't wanted to hang back because he thought Roland had exerted himself enough already and needed to rest. But Roland had been insistent. For some reason, Striker had suspected there was more to the story regarding Roland's relationship to his niece.

Although his niece didn't know he existed, over the years he had kept up with her. He had attended the ceremonies when she'd graduated from high school and college, and he had even attended several of her games when she'd played soccer in middle school. He'd known that after college she'd gotten a job with a clothing design company in New York where she had worked for a few years before opening her own business. It was obvious that Roland cared a lot for his niece. What might have started out merely as a sense of guilt because of his brother's death had turned into affection. He was the doting uncle—unseen and unknown.

Striker had never thought of Roland this way. The Roland he knew was an ex-cop, ex-con and loner. He rarely let anyone into his inner circle. Besides him, Stonewall and Quasar, there was only Carson Boyett Granger. Carson was the attorney who had risked her life getting Roland a new trial, and she was married to Sheppard Granger, a man Striker would be forever indebted to for helping turn his life around.

Striker guessed it wasn't Margo's fault that nobody had ever told her about Roland. And before their conversation ended, Roland had again stressed that he wanted the secret to remain just that. Striker had given Roland his word. If Margo found out the truth it wouldn't be from him.

Striker had just reentered the kitchen and closed the sliding door behind him when Margo rounded the corner. He could only assume her private meeting with her uncle was over. He wondered how that had gone.

"Well, did you find anything, Mr. Striker?"

He stared at her, trying not to notice how good she looked in jeans and a pullover sweatshirt. When she'd opened the door, her striking features had taken him aback, but now it was her outfit…actually, her body in the clothes…that was grabbing his attention.

She was tall, but he figured at least five inches of that height were the result of those killer heels on the boots she was wearing. And she was curvy, which was why those jeans looked so damn good on her. There was no way she didn't turn every man's head when she walked by. It would be hard not to.

"Drop the 'mister,'" he said. "It's just Striker."

Margo frowned at the man, wondering why he was so touchy with his name. And why her large kitchen suddenly felt smaller with him standing in it. She was attracted to him but felt that, except for trying to keep her common sense intact, there was nothing she could do about it. When a woman was being protected with a man who had the build of "The Rock," Dwayne Johnson himself, there wasn't much hope for her.

He had removed his jacket and tie, and she saw that a dark brown leather shoulder holster held his gun. The holster had a side compartment she guessed contained extra bullets.

Of course, she should not have been surprised that he was loaded down with such weaponry. He had been hired to protect her, after all. But still, seeing it was a stark reminder of her predicament. Her uncle had talked to her and she had promised to cooperate with her protector. With Striker. "Okay, Striker. Did my kitchen pass muster?"

"Not really. That's a nice view out that window, but you're going to have to keep the blinds drawn most of the time. I also noticed several troubling areas in your yard."

"What?"

Glancing at his phone, Striker told her what he'd noted.

"I never had a reason to worry about any of that before."

"Now you do. I'll take care of it." Striker moved around Margo to go back into her living room and she was right on his heels.

"So how long have you been a protector?"

Not long enough, he thought to himself. He didn't want to think how different his life would be today if years ago he'd been there to protect the one person he should have been safeguarding. He wouldn't be carrying around all this guilt if he had. "Several years," he said, tossing the answer over his shoulder. He kept walking to check the front door to inspect the locks. She had an alarm system and that was good. He glanced around the room. Again there were too many windows. And she had stairs. There were also several rooms connected to her living room. He would check them out later after doing a walk-through upstairs.

"How many is *several*?"

He stopped walking long enough to look over at her and wish he hadn't. She was leaning in the doorway that separated her living room from the kitchen. In that lazy, carefree pose, she looked good. Too good. There was something about her standing there with her hair tossed around her shoulders that made parts of his body ache.

"About eight years."

"And what did you do before that?"

He could tell her that his past was none of her business. But he had no problem sharing what he did because that time—thanks to Sheppard Granger—had pretty much shaped him into the man he was now. He was alive when he could have been dead. And he was making something out of his life.

He looked her straight in the eye and said, "I was in jail serving time for manslaughter."

CHAPTER THREE

MARGO'S BREATH CAUGHT as she stared at Striker. Had he just admitted to being an ex-con? Was he joking? From the intense expression on his face, she had a feeling he was dead serious. Did Uncle Frazier have any idea that the man he'd hired had a criminal record? For manslaughter?

"How many rooms are there upstairs?" he asked, picking up his duffel bag and moving in the direction of her stairs.

She jerked her head around. "Wait!"

Striker stopped and stared at her. Had hearing that he'd served time freaked her out? It wouldn't be the first time that someone he had been hired to protect reacted that way to his past. Some saw it as an advantage, thinking that if he had a killer instinct, he had the ability to keep them safe. Then there were others who found it so repulsive they would ask Roland for someone else. Considering Quasar and Stonewall were ex-cons as well, that eliminated Roland's top three protectors. Hell, that would even eliminate Roland.

Striker, Quasar and Stonewall had met when they'd served time together. From the first, he and Stonewall had been destined to be enemies. Quasar, the youngest of the three by only a year, had pretty much stayed to himself. It had been rumored Quasar had come from a well-to-do family and had confessed to some white-collar crime to keep a family member from going to jail. The three of them had been released from prison within months of each other and had hooked up with Roland, who had started a security business. Since neither Striker, Stonewall nor Quasar had known a damn thing about security, Roland enrolled the three of them into one of the top tactical training schools in the country. In addition, Roland managed to hook them up for a full year with former Secret Service agent Grayson Prescoli, who had a reputation as being one of the best in the business after serving under three presidents. Although they'd initially lacked in-depth knowledge in security, what the three of them possessed was an ingrained ability to survive and a drive to safeguard and defend anyone left in their care.

"You want something?" he asked in a tone that came out a little harsher than he'd intended. He was tired of her just standing there and not saying anything.

"I want to know what happened."

Striker continued to stare at her. If she was asking for details, he wouldn't be giving them to her. Instead he wrapped it up in a sentence that, as far as he was concerned, said it all. "Life happened." At eighteen he'd been found guilty and sent off to prison. He'd lost people he'd cared about as well as a scholarship to play football at the college of his dreams. And he knew he only had himself to blame.

Evidently his answer stumped her, if her expression and lack of response were anything to go by. He continued up the stairs and left her standing there.

Margo watched Striker move up the stairs, momentarily distracted by how well his body fit a pair of pants.

He didn't just have a nice-looking tush; it was sexy and got sexier with his every step. When he was no longer in sight, she shook her head, trying to pull herself together.

His response to her question meant he had no intentions of telling her why he'd been sent to jail. Knowing it was for manslaughter was bad enough. Who did he kill? Why? She wanted to think it had been self-defense, but if that had been the case, then he wouldn't have been sent to jail, right? How long had he been confined?

The key thing was that he was no longer in jail. He had served his time and she had a feeling rejoining society and rebuilding your life after prison couldn't be easy. But it seemed like he was doing okay, and she wanted to believe he was good at what he did.

He looked to be in his early thirties, which meant he couldn't have spent too many years behind bars. But then, how many were too many? How old was he when he'd gone in? When she heard him moving around upstairs, she decided to join him there as well.

STRIKER STARED AT the huge bouquet of yellow roses sitting on the desk of what appeared to be the room she used as an upstairs office. Telling himself that knowing who sent them was all part of his security measures to protect Margo, he pulled off the card and read it.

We need to get back together, Margo. Call me. Scott.

Striker shook his head, thinking, *What a way to go, asshole.* He was more than a little rusty in the romance department, but even he knew that using a few endearing words would have made an impression. Instead this guy Scott had issued an order that he'd expected her to obey.

Had she? Margo didn't come across as a woman who would say "how high" after any man told her to jump.

According to Roland, Margo and this Scott guy had broken up and she'd left New York for Charlottesville. That had been over a year ago. Evidently Scotty-boy wanted her back.

"Just what are you doing?" Margo asked in outrage, rushing into the room and snatching the card out of his hand. "You had no right to read that."

Striker had heard Margo coming up the stairs but hadn't hurried to put the card back. Why should he? "As the man protecting you, I had every right."

She threw the card on her desk and rounded on him. "You're supposed to be protecting me from a crazy hit man. Not an ex-boyfriend."

"And while I'm protecting you, I don't want to have to deal with a boyfriend. Ex or otherwise."

Anger flared in her eyes. "You won't. Scott has a tendency of being overly dramatic."

"For your sake, that drama better not happen on my watch."

For a moment they just stood there, faced off. Why, of all things, was he consumed by her scent? A lush fragrance that was uniquely hers. It was undeniably woman. Oh, shit. Thinking this way wasn't good. He backed up and turned to leave the room.

"Where are you going?"

"To continue what I was doing before you came up here—check out the place."

He left her standing there and walked to another room. Her bedroom. It was the kind of bedroom he figured she would have. It wasn't all that frilly, but it was feminine as hell. She was neat. Nothing out of place, no clothes lying on the floor or shoes thrown around. She'd decorated the bedroom in yellow and light gray, with a bedspread featuring yellow roses and matching curtains. Apparently she had a thing for yellow roses. In that case, it made sense for Scott to take advantage of that fact by sending her those flowers. And, damn, how many pillows did she have on that bed? Looked like a dozen or so.

"Is this really necessary?"

He didn't turn when she entered. "Evidently it is or I wouldn't be in here. I use all of my time wisely, Ms. Connelly."

She placed her hands on her hips. "Margo. You want to be called Striker. I prefer being called Margo."

He nodded. "Okay, Margo." He moved to look into the master bath. When he returned moments later, he glanced around her room again. "I assume this is the room you sleep in."

"Yes. Why?"

"Where is the guest room that I'll be using?"

As far away from this one as possible, Margo thought. "I have a guest room downstairs."

"Not close enough."

She dropped her hands by her sides. "What do you mean *not close enough*?"

"Just what I said. The way things usually work is that a team of protectors will work in shifts to take care of a client. Since the demand for security is high right now, I'll be the one protecting you morning, noon and night. Even when you sleep. I want to be close enough that I can hear you breathe, and I won't be able to do that downstairs. What's in the room next door?" he asked, already striding into the hallway.

He wants to be close enough to hear me breathe?

The thought of any man, especially him, being that close to her at night made her go still. It then occurred to her just how underfoot he intended to be.

"Wait a second," she said, rushing behind him. He had already opened the door to the other room.

"A guest room, I see."

She didn't say anything. To be honest, this was her only guest room. The third bedroom upstairs— where she found Striker snooping—was where she kept her work supplies and managed the accounting books. The room downstairs was her workroom where she did all of her fittings and sewing. Its sofa could be made into a bed, and that was where she had intended to put him.

"This is a nice room with its own full bath. It will work for me after I move a few things around."

She released a resigned sigh. "I like the way the furniture is arranged."

"I'll put it back just as you have it when I'm all done."

"And when will that be?" she asked.

"Depends on that crazy hit man."

His words reminded Margo of the seriousness of the situation she was in. It just wasn't fair. This was what she got for doing her civic duty. As if he'd read her mind, Striker said, "At least you're alive. Can't say the same thing for Jeffery Turner."

Her thoughts immediately went to Jeffery and she remembered how the jurors had hugged each other before departing that final day. Each of them had tried to downplay Erickson's threats, but deep down, they'd all been shaken up by them. She could tell. Nancy Snyder had been the only one to ask the FBI agent whether they should be concerned, and the man had assured her that they shouldn't be. Well, undoubtedly that agent had been wrong.

When she saw Striker leaving the room, she followed. "Wouldn't sleeping downstairs make better sense for you?" She was attracted to Striker and she wanted to put as much distance between them as humanly possible. She wasn't used to a man sharing space with her, especially one who emitted sexual vibes with every step he took. She wouldn't be able to concentrate on her work with him around. She wasn't used to being drawn to any male this way and she didn't like it. Found it downright irritating.

He surveyed the hall before checking out the bathroom. It was only when he came out that he responded to her comment by asking a question of his own. "Why would you think me sleeping downstairs makes better sense, Margo?"

She'd told him to call her Margo, but, with the huskiness of his voice, the name flowed from his lips with such an incredible sexiness. "Well, because you'd be closer to the front door. To protect me if anyone tries to get inside."

He held her gaze. "My job is not to keep them from getting inside. My job is to keep them from getting to you. There's a difference."

Margo didn't see the distinction. "They can't get to me if they don't get inside," she argued.

"Not necessarily," he countered. "Good assassins can get to their victims without setting foot inside their homes. They can use high-powered rifles with infrared beams to hit any target they want. Hell, if they are desperate enough they can blow an entire house up."

That was the last thing she wanted to hear. "Then maybe I should leave town for a while."

"That's what he'll anticipate you doing. I understand Turner was on his way to the airport to get lost. He never made it there. We'll stay here until it's decided that it is no longer safe to do so."

Then, without saying another word, he walked off and left her standing there.

STRIKER FIGURED IT wouldn't take Margo long to follow him downstairs. He was now checking out another room, where it was apparent she did most of her work. There were several huge sewing machines, mannequins, a worktable and bolts of fabrics neatly arranged in the room. No clutter. There was also a sofa, the kind that converted into a bed. Was that where she assumed he would be sleeping? Hell, that sofa bed wasn't even big enough for half of him.

"You got a nice work area here," he said, deciding to give her a compliment since she was hanging in the doorway and not saying anything. Just watching him. Knowing her eyes were on him was unsettling. Especially when he knew she was actually checking him out. A man could tell. Why did the knowledge that she was practically undressing him with her gaze make him want to smile…at least halfway?

"Thanks," she said, coming into the room to stand by him but not too close. Did she think he would bite her or something? He couldn't help grinning at that. He'd been known to leave a passionate mark or two on women. Why did the thought of leaving one on her do things to him? And why did he enjoy breathing her scent?

At that moment his cell phone rang and immediately he recognized the tone. Pulling it out of his back pocket, he answered the call. "Yes, Stonewall?" He nodded and then said, "I heard and I'm here. I'm forwarding my notes. Have Bobby pick up everything on my list. As soon as possible. Not taking any chances." He then clicked off the phone and sent his notes to Stonewall.

Striker glanced over at Margo, and she looked at him expectantly, as if she was waiting for him to tell her about the call. Instead he asked, "Have you eaten yet?"

He could tell his question caught her off guard. "Have I eaten?"

"Yes, have you eaten? Almost dinnertime."

"No, I haven't eaten."

He nodded before calling Stonewall again to arrange delivery of their dinner from the Bullseye.

After he ended the call, he looked over at Margo. She was staring at him. "What?" he asked her.

"Is it a coincidence or did you know that not only is the *Bullseye* my favorite place to eat, but what you ordered is my favorite meal from there as well."

"No coincidence."

"How did you know?"

"From my research on you. And just like I know what you like and don't like, the places you like to frequent and other interesting tidbits, any hit man who has made you their target knows as well."

"But you don't know if I'm anyone's target."

"You're right. I understand there were sixty to eighty

people in the courtroom that day. Unless they catch this guy, there's no telling who will be the next victim. My job, Margo, is to make sure it isn't you."

CHAPTER FOUR

"So TELL ME some things about yourself, Striker," Margo prompted. They were sitting at the kitchen table eating her favorite meal and things had gotten quiet. Too quiet. She had dismissed the sounds of the two men moving around in and out of her house. Striker had introduced them as Bobby and Bruce, and they were taking care of the items that bothered Striker, like the darkened areas of her yard. Bobby was outside installing floodlights and Bruce was upstairs putting in security devices that Striker wasn't elaborating on.

"Why?" he asked, wiping his mouth with a napkin.

She ignored how her stomach clenched when she looked at his mouth. More specifically, those lips he'd just wiped. When had she ever been fascinated by the shape of a man's lips? But there was just something about the shape of his—namely, that cute little dent in the center.

She jumped when he leaned over and snapped his fingers in front of her face. "Hey, you're out there in la-la land. Come back."

Gripes. He'd caught her staring. "I was just thinking about something," she said, which wasn't a lie.

"About what?"

He would have to ask, she thought. She couldn't just come out and say *your lips*. Instead she said, "How much you know about me and how little I know about you."

He shrugged massive shoulders and her gaze followed the movement. Was there anything about this man that didn't get her attention? "It's part of my job to know all I can about you."

"Well, I don't like it."

He pushed his empty plate aside and leaned back in his chair. "There's nothing for you not to like."

And as if that settled it, he stood. She couldn't keep her gaze from roaming over him. There was no way he didn't have a strict physical fitness routine with all those muscles. She hated admitting it, but she had enjoyed his company during dinner, although he'd sat there, eaten his food and hardly said a word.

It had been a long time since she'd shared a meal with a man. Her uncle didn't count. To be honest, Scott didn't count either since, toward the end of their relationship, he'd begun spending more time with his clients than he did with her.

She smiled when she thought of Scott assuming he was doing her a favor by being her guy, with him making a six-figure salary and all. He hadn't known anything about her wealth.

"What's the smile for?"

She looked over at Striker. "Just thinking."

"Again?"

She frowned at him. "You got a problem with me thinking?"

He pushed his chair under the table. "If I ever have a problem with anything you do, Margo, you'll be the first to know, trust me." Then he said, "I recall you saying something about an appointment with a client in the morning."

She drew in a deep breath, refusing to let Striker unnerve her. "Yes, Claudine Bernard. We met for coffee last week to discuss the details of her wedding. She hired me and I need to take her measurements tomorrow. Luckily her wedding isn't until September, so I'll have time to make her wedding gown after all."

"You like doing that? Making wedding gowns?"

"If I didn't enjoy it, then I wouldn't be doing it, would I?" Okay, she'd gotten smart with him. Just like he'd gotten smart with her earlier. As if he realized this, a smile touched his lips. It was so quick that had she blinked, she would have missed it.

"I like you, Margo."

"Don't do me any favors, will you, Striker." At that moment her house phone rang and she looked over at him as she got up from the table. "It's my business line."

"I know. It's okay to answer it."

She frowned. Did he actually think she needed permission to answer her own phone? As she picked it up, he took out his own cell. She wondered who he was calling as he moved to go back up the stairs.

When she heard one of the upstairs doors close, she answered the call. "Designs by Margo."

"Yes, Margo. This is Claudine Bernard."

Margo smiled. "Yes, Claudine?"

"I lost my appointment book and just wanted to verify what time we need to get together tomorrow."

Margo nodded. "Our appointment is at ten in the morning."

"Great! I'll see you then."

When she turned back around, Striker was putting his phone away as he came back down the stairs. He glanced over at her. "So Claudine needed to reaffirm your appointment time, did she?"

Surprise lit Margo's face. "How did you know?"

When he just stared at her smugly, she scowled. "You listened in on my conversation," she accused.

"Damn right."

Furious beyond belief, she crossed the room to stand in front of him. "How dare you!" she screamed almost at the top of her lungs.

"Dammit, woman. Don't burst my eardrums."

"Or mine."

They both turned and looked at Bruce, who was standing in the middle of the stairs. He was smiling. Margo didn't appreciate being the butt of anyone's joke.

"Everything's all set?" Striker asked the man.

"Yes, both upstairs and downstairs. I just need to take care of the yard," he said, coming the rest of the way down the stairs. He looked over at Margo, smiled and said, "Nice set of lungs, Ms. Connelly." Then he moved toward the back door.

Alone again, Margo stared up at Striker. "I have questions and I want answers."

He shrugged. "Only if I feel like giving those answers to you, Margo."

Margo closed her eyes. Why did this man, of all men, have to be the one protecting her?

"Getting sleepy?"

She snapped her eyes back open. "I am not sleepy, Striker. Stop being a smart-ass."

"Okay," he said smoothly, all but admitting that he had been.

Striker had to fight back a smile. There was something about Margo that made him want to distance himself from her one minute and enmesh himself in her the next. Unfortunately, putting distance between them wasn't an option. Not when he was protecting her. Whether he liked it or not, until the hit man was captured, he and Margo were as entangled as any two people could be.

For some reason, he liked rattling her. Probably because doing so would keep her mind off her situation. Other women he'd protected would be all but hovering in a corner by now. At least those not brazen enough to think that *protector* also meant bedmate. Like that damn socialite who'd hired him when she discovered she was being stalked. She had invited him into her bed the first night. Of course he hadn't taken her up on her offer, but it was still damn hard making the woman keep her hands to herself. He'd been so glad when the police had finally captured the prick stalking her. He definitely couldn't see Margo behaving so inappropriately. Hell, she'd been ready to kick him downstairs to sleep on that tiny sofa bed.

"Look," he finally said, deciding he'd rattled her enough. "Let's go back to the table and sit down. You ask your questions and I'll decide if I want to answer them." His tone was deliberately clipped, letting her know up front what to expect.

He watched as she angrily strode back over to the table. If she'd known how much he appreciated seeing her backside just now, she wouldn't have done that. He followed her to the table and sat down. "Okay, Margo. Let's get it out. What are your questions?" Before she could open her mouth, he added, "And ask nicely."

She glared at him while adjusting in her seat, resting her hands beneath her chin with her fingers entwined. Why did he find her so damn sexy? So incredibly desirable. He was a glutton for punishment even thinking that way.

"First of all, I want to know what's going on. Here at my house? With my phone?"

He leaned back in his chair. That question was easy enough. "Bruce Townsend is a man-wonder, a technology whiz. He's in hot demand and usually works with an exclusive clientele. Summers Security has a good relationship with him, and he's been hired to install extra security in and around your home."

"Like tampering with my phones?"

"Yes. All your phones—house, cell or otherwise—are now linked to mine. I can listen in to all your conversations."

"And what if it's a conversation I don't want you to listen to?"

He held her gaze. "If you happen to get one of those, then I'll get off the line to give you the privacy you need."

He could tell from her mutinous expression she didn't like it, so he said, "Relax. If Scotty calls you, I promise not to listen in."

Her frown deepened. "His name is Scott, and he won't be calling me. I told him not to ever again."

Striker lifted a brow. "Oh? Is that the way it is? You accept his flowers but not his calls?" He shook his head. "Tsk-tsk. Margo, don't you know that's no way to treat a man?"

Her eyes filled with anger. "How I treat Scott is no concern of yours," she said in a loud voice.

"I've warned you about my eardrums. And as far as your ex-boyfriend goes, if he decides to get dramatic, then it becomes my concern. Need I remind you that you're the one who claims he has a tendency to get melodramatic? Okay, let's move on. Next question."

She got quiet. For a minute he wondered if she would even bother asking him anything else since it was apparent that she was pissed off with him now. But he should have known her silence wouldn't last. "I want to know about you, Striker."

He held her gaze. "All you need to know is that I am capable of protecting you."

She leaned in closer to him, her eyes still filled with anger. "You're wrong. That's not all I need to know. You will be here with me morning, noon and night. Underfoot. Listening to me breathe. Sharing meals with me. Risking your life for mine. So just knowing you're capable of keeping me alive is not all I need to know."

She paused a minute and said, "Earlier you said you'd been incarcerated for manslaughter. I need to know who you killed and why."

As far as Striker was concerned, she didn't need to know a damn thing. Drawing in a strained breath, he then decided that maybe she did. How would she handle it if he were to tell her? Well, he was about to find out. Still holding her gaze, he said, "I killed a cop."

He saw her throat move. Heard her stricken inhalation. "A cop?"

"Yes, a cop."

He could see the question in the depths of her honey-brown eyes. Desperation to know why he'd done such a thing was gnawing at her. He could feel it and decided to help her out. "Go ahead and ask."

She nervously licked her lips and he tried not to concentrate on the movement of her tongue. Not just the movement of her tongue but her tongue, period. She took him up on his offer. Not that he'd thought she wouldn't.

"Why, Striker?"

Hearing her question didn't do him in as much as hearing her say his name. Breathing deeply, he said, "I killed him because he raped my sibling."

Margo's stunned gasp filled the room, echoed off the walls. She threw her hand to her throat in disbelief and shock. "Oh my God! He raped your sister?"

Pain from years ago resurfaced, began surrounding Striker in a degree of agony he hadn't felt in some time. "I don't have a sister. It was my baby brother. Wade was thirteen and the bastard raped him."

CHAPTER FIVE

THROUGH THE FOG of her traumatized mind, Margo was aware of Striker gathering the plates from the table before walking into the kitchen. She sat there in a daze. Totally stunned. Horrified beyond belief.

A police officer had raped Striker's thirteen-year-old brother and Striker had killed him. Needing more answers and hoping he would give them to her, she slowly stood and strode after him.

Margo found Striker putting the dishes in the sink. She stood in the doorway not saying anything but watching him. She knew she'd lived a pampered life with private schools, a household full of servants and chauffeurs to take her wherever she wanted to go. But she had a feeling Striker and his family hadn't had such luxuries. She could only wonder about his childhood. His teen years. His life before he'd been sent to prison and the life he had now.

He was moving around the kitchen as if he hadn't unloaded all of that on her just moments ago. But he had. And then he had left the room. Was she supposed to act like he hadn't told her anything? Fat chance of that happening. The enormity of what he'd shared with her had her head spinning. She might have lived a sheltered life, but that didn't mean she couldn't recognize an injustice when she heard one.

After a minute he sensed her presence and glanced over at her. The expression on his face all but told her he wouldn't be entertaining any more of her questions. But hadn't her uncle always said that she didn't know when to stop being a nuisance even when it was for her own good?

She nervously bit her lower lip and then asked, "If the cop did that to your brother, then why were you sent to prison?"

He continued to stare at her, and then, as if he knew she wouldn't let up until he answered, he said, "Because the law felt I should not have taken matters into my own hands. I should have called the authorities." He chuckled derisively. "Yeah, right, go to the cops. Honestly? Like another cop would go against one of their own. I got fifteen years instead of life, so I guess I should be grateful. Especially since I only had to do seven of those years."

She nodded. "And your brother? Wade?"

Striker broke eye contact with Margo. He should have known that particular question was coming. Didn't she know when enough was enough? But it was his fault for even answering any of her questions and for telling her anything about his past life in the first place. Why had he felt the need to unload? To cleanse his soul? And with her, of all people? He'd told himself he hadn't wanted her to be afraid of him. Afraid that he was a mass murderer or something.

"Striker?"

And why did it do something to him whenever she said his name? That didn't make sense. He hadn't known her, hadn't even heard of her, until today. Yet Margo Connelly was getting under his skin. Why? It wasn't like he lacked female company. Far from it. Hell, he had been in Deidra McClure's bed when he'd received that call from Roland to come to the hospital. Deidra was like every other woman he'd messed around with before; the only thing between them was sex.

He turned and tried concentrating on Margo's face and not her body. She looked so damn feminine standing there even when she was obviously upset. Upset on his behalf. That very thought was why he finally said in a firm voice, "Make this your last question, Margo. After this don't ask me anything else about my life—past, present or future." He paused for a moment and then asked, "Now, what do you want to know about Wade?"

She nervously licked her lips again and the gesture made his stomach clench. "How is Wade? I know what happened was years ago, but how is he now?"

Taking a calming breath, he tried dismissing the pain he always felt whenever he thought of Wade…no matter how much time had passed. "Wade was the defense's star witness. It took a lot for him to get on the stand. His testimony about what that bastard did to him is why I got a lesser sentence. But Wade was just a kid and he needed extensive counseling after what happened to him. Unfortunately, there was no one there to make sure he got it."

Striker paused a moment and then said, "The day before I was to be transferred to Glenworth Penitentiary, I got word that Wade committed suicide by hanging himself. Mom found him when she went into his bedroom to wake him up for school. It was the day before his fourteenth birthday."

There. Now he'd told her all the gory details about his family. Well, not all of them. She didn't need to know that his mom died a year later. With one son in jail and the other one dead, she'd gotten depressed and refused to eat and take her blood pressure medication. In the end, hypertension had done her in at the age of forty.

Glancing over at Margo, he saw her expression had gone from shock to empathy. Hell, the last thing he wanted was to start a pity party. He didn't need her or anyone's sympathy. Although the first couple of years in prison had been the hardest, he had survived. While locked up behind bars, he had met Sheppard Granger.

Shep, as the other inmates called him, was a lot older than most of them and was serving time for murdering his wife. It didn't take long for anyone who hung around Shep to know just what sort of man he was: a natural-born leader—a positive one. Before being sent to prison he was the CEO of a major corporation, Granger Aeronautics. While in prison Shep had become a father figure for most of the younger inmates, a mentor and confidant. He gained the respect and admiration of many. Instead of being resentful for being locked up for a crime he didn't commit, Shep used his time in prison to the inmates' advantage by implementing such programs as Toastmasters, Leaders of Tomorrow and both the GED and college programs. Because of Shep, Striker's life had changed forever. Shep's encouragement had given Striker a reason to become a better person in spite of all that he'd lost.

The back door opened and Bruce and Bobby walked in. "Everything's all set," Bobby said, smiling. "I installed motion lights around the front and back of the house."

"And you'll get a signal on your phone as well," Bruce added. "So you won't be caught off guard. I understand that Stonewall and the others are also monitoring the property from the office. And I took care of everything else you requested in here."

He nodded, giving Bruce the eye not to go into more detail. "Good. I'll see you guys out."

Leaving Margo in the kitchen, he walked Bobby and Bruce to the door. He glanced to where she stood and could see her staring at them. He kept his eyes on her as he locked the front door behind the men and proceeded to set the alarm.

"What are those other things you requested Bruce take care of?"

He held up his hand. "Please, no more questions. You've asked too many already." *And I've told you more than I should have.*

She placed her hands on her hips. "I have a right to know."

Striker rolled his eyes. They were back to that again, were they? "Listen, Margo," he said in a voice that indicated he'd all but lost his patience with her. "Instead of asking questions of any real significance pertaining to your situation, your questions involved getting into my business. Your nosiness cost you and I'm not answering any more of your questions."

Satisfied, he saw her anger escalating. An outraged Margo he could deal with. A compassionate one he could not. "And I need your schedule for tomorrow. I know about your appointment at ten with Claudine. What else is there?"

She narrowed her gaze. "No more questions, Striker. You've asked too many of them already," she echoed. And then she strutted to her workroom and slammed the door shut.

Striker felt pressure seep into the back of his neck and he reached up to rub a knotted muscle there. Only for Roland would he put up with this kind of BS. If Margo thought she was calling the shots, then she was wrong.

Deciding it was time she knew that, he went after her.

MARGO JERKED AROUND when her workroom door flew open. Striker stood there with a fierce frown on his face, his arms across his chest and his legs braced. He was mad. So what? That was his problem and not hers.

"You have an issue with knocking?" She figured her words infuriated him even more, and from his expression, she saw they had.

"You stormed off like a child," he snapped.

"Because you thought you could treat me like one," she snapped back. "Do I look like a child to you?"

His eyes slowly moved over her and she felt heat flare in every inch of her body. "Well, do I?" she all but yelled, thinking he had inspected her enough. Her heart was thumping so hard that she could actually hear it.

"No. There's nothing about you that resembles a child, but you're certainly acting like one."

Margo refused to go tit for tat with this man. If he wanted to throw his weight around, fine. She would simply ignore him. Sitting down to her desk, she focused on her computer screen.

Seconds ticked by and, out of the corner of her eye, she saw him watching her. She refused to look over at him for fear she would be tempted to check him out the way he'd checked her out moments ago.

"Stay away from the window."

She wouldn't give him the satisfaction of a response.

"And I still need your schedule for tomorrow."

She'd lifted her head to tell him once again she didn't intend to give him anything when her cell phone rang. She looked at it for a second.

"Do you recognize the caller, Margo?"

It was a local number. "No. But it could be a potential client."

"Do *potential* clients have your cell phone number?"

Now that he'd asked, she shook her head.

He nodded. "Go ahead and answer it," he said, pulling his own phone out of his pocket and speed-dialing a number.

Drawing in a deep breath, she clicked on her phone. "Yes?"

She heard someone breathing, but no one said anything. "Hello," she said.

When the person still didn't say anything, she looked over at Striker, who silently mouthed for her to hang up. A chill ran through her as she did so. "Wrong number, you think?" she asked.

"Possibly," he said, checking the caller's number on his cell phone.

Margo didn't think Striker sounded convincing. "So who do you think it was?"

Before Striker could answer her question, his cell phone went off. "Yes, Stonewall?"

Margo wondered if that was the man's real name or a code name or nickname, like Striker.

"Okay. Thanks." He then clicked off the phone.

"Well?"

He glanced over at her. "Well, I'll leave you alone

to do what you came in here to do. Remember not to go near the window." He closed the door behind him.

Striker walked over to the sofa and sat down. With his gaze holding steady on the closed workroom door, he speed-dialed Stonewall's number. "Did you trace where the call came from?"

"Yes. It came from one of those prepaid phones. And the caller was at the Leesburg Mall."

"And the name of the person who purchased the phone?"

"Not sure we'll be able to narrow that down since the phone was a burner, paid for with cash. But we're still checking things out anyway. Don't be surprised if it was a wrong number."

Striker drew in a deep breath. "Might have been, but for some reason, I don't think so. Although we could hear the person breathing on the other end, they didn't say anything."

"Could have been they were surprised to hear her voice since she was not the person they were calling. Not everyone has manners enough to apologize when they misdial a number."

Striker knew that was true, but there was something about the call that bothered him. The caller had held on too long for a miscall. "Still, let me know what you find out."

"I will. I understand Margo Connelly is a beauty."

Striker didn't have to wonder where Stonewall had gotten his information. When Bobby had seen Margo he had smiled all over himself. "She is that," he said, knowing Stonewall had been waiting for him to state his own opinion. "And she's Roland's niece."

Stonewall chuckled. "Are you reminding me or yourself of that?"

Striker frowned. There was no way he could forget. "I thought I'd remind you just in case." He knew Stonewall could appreciate a beautiful woman just as much as any man.

"Don't worry, I won't forget. Besides, I'm still trying to get a date with Joy."

Striker shook his head. He'd been with Stonewall at that charity event the night Stonewall and Detective Joy Ingram had met. He had picked up on all that sexual chemistry between the two. But he just couldn't imagine his friend dating a cop. "Good luck with that."

CHAPTER SIX

"GOOD MORNING, STRIKER."

Striker raised a brow. He'd timed it so he was standing on the landing the moment Margo walked out of her bedroom. Was her greeting, which she had delivered with a smile, an indication that her attitude from yesterday had improved? "What has you in a good mood?"

She proceeded down the stairs ahead of him. When she reached the bottom stair, she said over her shoulder, "I'm always in a good mood when I start work for a new client."

So that's what has her all smiles? "I guess that means for you ten o'clock can't get here fast enough," he said, following her into the kitchen.

"You're right. And it also means we need to talk," she said, moving to the counter to start the coffee.

"About what? And, by the way, I ordered breakfast."

She turned to him, surprised. "What do you mean you ordered breakfast?"

"First, what do we need to talk about?"

Margo's frown indicated her annoyance. "I like cooking my own breakfast whenever I'm in the mood to eat breakfast, which isn't every day. Only when I'm hungry. This morning I'm not."

He nodded. "Well, I prefer not cooking my own, and

I'm in the mood to eat breakfast *every* day. I happened to be hungry this morning, so if you're not, I'll eat yours."

She scowled before turning back to the coffeepot, and Striker wondered what had happened to that better-than-yesterday attitude she had earlier. Was it something he said? Surely she wouldn't get upset because he'd ordered breakfast.

She turned back, glowering at him. "How do you know what I'd want for breakfast? For all you know, I might be a cereal girl."

"Are you? A cereal girl?"

"Sometimes."

"To each his own. I am not a cereal guy and ordered a little bit of everything. Eggs, sausage, bacon, pancakes, grits and biscuits."

"All of that?"

"Like I said, I'm not into cereal. So, what do you want to talk about?"

Margo was trying to keep her cool with Striker. She had told herself upon waking this morning that she intended to be polite and try not to cause problems. Especially after what he'd shared with her yesterday about why he'd been sent to prison. She couldn't help but admire his overall attitude after what he'd gone through. Had it been her, she would still be bitter or, at the very least, still carrying a chip on her shoulder.

And then there was that call last night that had rattled her, set her nerves on edge and made her wonder if she was the assassin's next target. Four people had been killed already, one of whom she had spent six weeks with. And now he was gone. Dead.

Fingers snapped in her face and she jumped. "Stop doing that!"

"Then stop zoning out on me. Are you okay?"

She glared up at him. "Of course I'm okay. Why wouldn't I be?"

He shrugged strong shoulders. "No reason. Did you sleep well last night?"

"Yes," she lied. She had tossed around a lot and it had taken her longer to get to sleep than usual. "What about you, Striker. Did you sleep well?" She poured a cup of coffee and poured one for him as well.

"Thanks—and, yes, I slept well." Striker knew she wasn't aware that Bruce had installed devices not only in her bedroom but in every room, which picked up every sound, movement or conversation. Striker's concern for her well-being and the high level of security this job required made this level of personal surveillance necessary.

Striker had heard her showering and getting dressed for bed. He'd even lain in bed in the guest room and listened to her breathing when she slept. Although she claimed she slept well, he knew she had not. He'd known each and every time she'd tossed and turned, fluffed one of her pillows. That led him back to what he'd asked earlier. "What do we need to talk about, Margo?"

She sat down at the table and sipped her coffee as she looked at him over the rim of her cup. "You."

"What about me?" Striker had a feeling he wouldn't like whatever she was about to say.

"I need you to disappear when my client arrives."

"Disappear?" Had he heard her right?

"Yes. The last thing I want is for anyone to know I have someone following me around and—"

"Protecting you."

Margo blew out a breath in frustration. "It's not that I don't appreciate you protecting me, but I'm running a business. The last thing I want is for Claudine to think she's not safe here."

"For all intents and purposes, she may not be. And just how am I supposed to disappear?"

She nervously licked her lips, causing his stomach to knot and his sex to get hard. The thought that he was sitting here lusting after Roland's niece didn't sit well with him. But, damn, she looked beautiful this morning. She had soulful eyes and he wondered if they darkened during an orgasm.

"Just become scarce upstairs until she leaves," she said, as if what she was asking wasn't out of the question. "I'll take her measurements, she'll look through my fabric book to pick out the material she prefers, and I'll work up a few sketches for different designs based on what she wants. Think of it this way—the fewer distractions, the quicker she'll be out the door. *You* will be a distraction."

The room got quiet as he took a sip of his coffee and she took a sip of hers. He figured the silence wouldn't last for long. A minute later she proved him right.

"So, will you do it? Disappear for a little while?"

He took another sip of coffee, set the cup down and stood. "No."

Margo tried telling herself not to get angry. That he was not trying to be difficult per se, that he was just determined to do his job. But the bottom line was that she was mad. Why couldn't he bend just a little?

"You are interfering with my job," she said, standing, pushing her hair back from her face. It angered her that he seemed unaffected by her words. And then he walked off to pour another cup of coffee. "Are you listening to me?"

After pouring his coffee, he returned to his chair and sat down. "You remember yesterday when you said you resented me treating you like a child?" he asked her.

"What about it?"

"You're behaving like one again."

She inhaled deeply, willing herself to calm down. "Why can't you give us some privacy? What would it hurt?"

"Possibly you. And I won't take that chance."

There was something—the tone of his voice, the look in his eyes, the finality of his words—that told her something was going on here she didn't know about. Something she felt she should. "What aren't you telling me, Striker?"

He broke eye contact with her when he took a sip of his coffee. "What do you mean?"

"Why are you so protective?"

He gave her a look that said she'd just asked a stupid question. "Protecting you is my job."

But it was more than that. She was sure of it. Did it have anything to do with that call that came in last night? The one she'd assumed was a wrong number? What if he knew for certain that it hadn't been? He hadn't mentioned anything about it this morning. Was that intentional? Convenient? Necessary? Would he tell her if there were new developments in the case? Although he was pretending otherwise, deep down, she knew he was intentionally keeping her in the dark about something.

She walked over to the coffeepot to pour another cup, feeling his gaze was on her. She knew she was frustrating him. She supposed most people who hired him to protect them were only too happy to do as he said and didn't give him any lip like she was doing. But, then again, she hadn't hired him. He and his protection had been forced on her by her uncle.

Returning to the table, she sat down with her mug in hand and asked, "So, what do you suggest?"

He lifted a brow. "About what?"

She hated when he acted dense. "About how we will handle questions about us?"

He leaned back in his chair. "About us?"

"Yes. Since you won't disappear, how do I explain your presence at my house so early in the morning and the fact that you're making yourself at home?"

He shook his head, seemingly amused by her question. "Why do you feel you have to explain anything? This is your house and what you do and who you invite, no matter what time of day it is, is your business."

"Yes, but—"

"But nothing. You don't owe anyone an explanation. But if you think you do, then tell Claudine, or anyone else who wants to know, that I'm the man you're sleeping with."

Striker was certain Margo would choke on her coffee. Had he known his words would get her all rattled, he would have thought twice before saying them. "What's your problem? You're twenty-six and you act like you've never had a lover before."

She frowned at him. "That's not the point."

"Then what is the point? What about Scotty?"

Her frown deepened. "Like I told you, his name is Scott. And my relationship with him is not up for discussion."

"Suit yourself. But I still don't see why you think you need to explain my presence to Claudine or anyone else. Do you know the woman? Did she come referred by someone you know?"

"No, but my business cards are everywhere and I run ads in several bridal magazines. She was one of several people who left messages while I was sequestered. That was *before* all this drama began with Erickson. The only reason I was able to take her on as a client and not some of the others was because she won't need her wedding gown until September. The others either wanted them earlier or they wanted me to make the bridesmaid dresses as well. So if you're thinking she's connected to anything, then—"

"I didn't say that she was."

Her phone rang, and Margo immediately jerked at the sound. She looked over at Striker, and he nodded, pulling out his phone as well. She then pulled hers out of the pocket of her skirt and expressed a sigh of relief when she saw the number. Smiling, she said, "It's Uncle Frazier."

As if he hadn't heard her, he hit a number. She glared at him. "This is a private call, Striker."

He shrugged. "Not yet it's not." He pointed his head toward the ringing phone she still held in her hand. "Aren't you going to answer that?"

She glared at him but quickly answered. "Good morning, Uncle Frazier."

"Margo! You okay? What took you so long to answer the phone?"

She peered over at Striker when she said, "I was preoccupied in the kitchen. What's up?" She was glad

Striker clicked off the call and placed his phone back in his pocket.

"I was just checking on you. How are you faring with Striker?"

Deciding she definitely needed privacy to answer that one, she was leaving the kitchen when Striker called out, "Only go where I can see you."

She stiffened at Striker's order and moved across the room to stand with her back to him. "I don't know how long I can handle him here," she whispered to her uncle. "He's breathing down my neck and watching my every move." *Keeping me awake at night remembering how good he looks in his suit with those muscular shoulders and broad chest.*

She heard Striker's phone ring and refused to turn around. "Margo, we covered all that yesterday," her uncle was saying. "Striker's job is to keep you alive, and before I left yesterday you said you understood that."

"I do, but—"

Suddenly she felt heat directly behind her and swung around to find Striker standing right there, an intense look on his face. She immediately knew something was wrong. "Uncle Frazier, I'll call you back."

Margo clicked off the phone. "Striker, what is it? What's wrong?"

"The assassin has struck again."

Her heart nearly stopped. "B-but it hasn't been seventy-two hours since the last time," she said, feeling weak in the knees.

"Apparently, he's decided to play by a different set of rules."

WITH HANDS CUFFED behind his back and chains on both of his legs, Murphy Erickson was led into the room by armed guards. He looked at the three men standing around the room. Federal agents. Men he despised and who probably despised him just as much. He had eluded them for years and had brought some of their fellow agents into his network, paying them well for their treachery.

The feds thought capturing him and putting him behind bars would be the end of it. Unfortunately, they'd found out it wasn't—the last laugh would be his. He was showing them, shoving it in their faces quite nicely, that in jail or out he was still calling the shots. His loyal comrades were out there carrying out his orders.

"Unless you're here to tell me I'll be set free in a few hours, I have nothing to say to you bastards," he said, knowing his words did more than piss them off.

"Sit down, Erickson," one of the men ordered, and before he could tell the man to go to hell, he was shoved into a chair by one of the guards.

The federal agent who had ordered him to sit down leaned over the table, facing him. "You're getting on our last nerve, Erickson."

Erickson chuckled. "All of you can go fuck yourselves and your damn nerves."

"Call off your assassin."

"Not until I'm free. Like I said, everyone in that courtroom that day will die unless I walk out of here. And please don't ask me to give a damn about the families of the victims because I don't give a fuck about anyone but myself. Remember that. And, by the way, since it seems you guys are taking your time about giving me my freedom, the every-seventy-two-hours rule is no longer in effect. He can kill whenever he feels like it."

"You're a low-down, dirty bastard," one of the agents said, losing his cool.

"Your mama," Erickson tossed back and then added, "How is the lovely lady, Agent Flynn? I understand she likes living in Florida."

At the surprised look on the agent's face, Erickson laughed. "That's right. I know about all of you and your families. Don't tempt me to add their names to my hit list. I suggest you work out a deal. I won't go along with anything where I don't walk out of here a free man. Until then, the killings will continue."

CHAPTER SEVEN

"I THOUGHT YOU weren't hungry," Striker said, watching Margo dig into the breakfast that had been delivered. It was a good thing he'd ordered as much as he had.

"I wasn't at the time, but I have a tendency to over-eat whenever I'm nervous."

In that case, considering her size and curvaceous figure, she must not get nervous too often, he thought. "You have no reason to be nervous, Margo. I won't let anything happen to you."

That call from Stonewall only verified what he'd assumed. The assassin wasn't an amateur. They were definitely dealing with someone who knew how to stay one step ahead of the law. So far none of the security cameras mounted around the crime scenes had picked up images of the killer. It made one wonder how the assassin knew when and where to make his hit. The feds weren't happy they hadn't captured the man, and the local authorities were dealing with a city on the edge of chaos.

"He asked me out."

Striker raised a brow. "Excuse me?"

She shrugged her shoulders. "I said he asked me out. Carl Palmer."

Carl Palmer had been the assassin's latest victim.

Another juror. Striker frowned. "The news reports said he was married."

She released a deep breath. "He was…which is why I wouldn't go out with him, although he claimed he was getting a divorce. Men lie a lot."

Had she caught her Scotty lying? "Some do and some don't."

She pushed the empty plate aside. "And some like to be evasive."

Did she think that was what he was doing because he refused to tell her everything she wanted to know? She had the right to think whatever she liked because it wouldn't change a thing with him. He looked at his watch. "You sure you're still up for Claudine's visit this morning?"

"Yes, now more than ever. I need to stay busy and keep my mind occupied."

He understood. An idle mind was not good. Five people were dead and two of them had been jurors. How many others would lose their lives before the assassin was apprehended? "You want some more?" he asked, indicating her clean plate and the food he still had on his.

She gave him a wry smile. "I thought you were the one who liked eating a big breakfast. I feel bad that I ate most of it."

"Don't. As you can see, it wouldn't hurt me to miss a meal or two."

Margo thought he had to be kidding. Striker Jennings was in great shape. Too great. The man had a body that would make any woman drool. He even had beautiful hands. She couldn't help noticing them when he was spooning food off his plate onto hers. At one point her gaze had been practically fixed on them. When had calloused fingers become sexy?

She then thought of something she hadn't asked him but wanted to know. "Are you married?"

He looked at her over the rim of his coffee cup. "Where did that question come from?"

"Just answer, Striker."

He didn't say anything for a minute. "No. I'm not married and never have been."

She nodded. "Do you have a steady girlfriend?"

"Why? Are you interested in applying for the position if there's an opening?"

She rolled her eyes. "No."

"Then why is it any concern of yours?"

Margo wondered what type of woman could handle all that alpha-ness. All that testosterone. "I just want to know."

He put his cup down and stared at her for a minute. Then, as if he'd made his mind up about something, he said, "No, I don't have a steady girlfriend. Just unsteady ones. And that's the way I like it. No promises and no entanglements."

"So you're one of those men who specialize in bed partners only." It wasn't a question and she made sure he knew that.

"You shouldn't be so nosy, Margo."

She shrugged. "I can't help it. You're such an interesting character."

Striker's cell phone rang and he quickly pulled it out of his pocket. He recognized that ringtone. "Why are you calling? Shouldn't you be resting?" From Striker's earlier conversation with Stonewall, he knew Roland had been released from the hospital with instructions from his doctor to get some rest.

"How is she, Striker?" Roland asked.

Striker knew Margo was listening to every word he said. "Okay. And I told you I would handle things."

"And I know that you can, but I heard about the recent hit. Do you think we need to move her to another location that might be safer?"

"Not yet. Stonewall is my backup and, thanks to those security measures Bruce put in place, Stonewall is keeping an eye on things from where he is."

"It's a good thing I called Bruce in," Roland said. "According to him, the security system she was using was a joke. Anyone could have disarmed it with no problem."

"So I heard." Striker had been told the same thing from Bruce. "I'm ending this call now, Roland. Get some rest, will you?"

"I will. Carson wouldn't let me go to my place to recuperate. I'm at Sutton Hills."

Sutton Hills was the Grangers' estate that encompassed over two hundred acres near the foothills of the Blue Ridge Mountains. "Talk to you later, Roland. And do like I said and get some rest." He clicked off the phone and waited for the questions he knew were coming.

"Who's Roland?"

If only you knew. "Roland Summers is my boss."

"Sounds like he's more than that. I can tell that he's someone you care about."

Striker lifted a brow. She'd deciphered that after eavesdropping on his conversation? "Yes, he's more than my boss. He's a friend. A good friend."

"What's wrong with him? Is he ill or something?"

Taking a sip of his coffee, Striker felt his neck get warm. She was asking too many damn questions. "What makes you think that?"

"You told him to get some rest. What's wrong with him?"

There was no way he would tell her that Roland was recuperating from a gunshot wound. Instead he said, "He's a little under the weather."

"In that case, why would he take the time to call? He doesn't think you can handle this assignment?"

Striker frowned. "Roland knows I can handle things. Once in a while he likes to be kept in the loop. My goal is to keep you alive."

She leaned over the table. Something flashed in her eyes he hadn't seen before. Fear. "That's it, isn't it?" she asked him quietly. Almost too quietly, to the point he had to strain to hear her. "You know for certain I'm on the assassin's list."

He sighed. "You were in the courtroom that day, so you've always been on his list, Margo."

She slanted him an annoyed look. "You know what I mean. You think I might be next."

Striker wondered where in the hell she had gotten that idea. The last thing he wanted was for her to feel frightened. A frightened person had a tendency to let fear control them and the first thing to go was their common sense. A lack of common sense could bring on mistakes. Costly ones. What he wanted was for her to be alert and cautious.

"Hold on, Margo. All I know is that two jurors have lost their lives, but I don't know anything about you being next. All I'm doing is taking precautions. Don't start freaking out on me."

She stiffened. "I won't."

"Good." He checked his watch, deciding to change the subject. Hopefully Claudine would be on time and keep Margo occupied while he talked to Stonewall. He'd gotten his friend's text request that he call. Had it been of major importance, Stonewall would have called him instead of texting, but Striker couldn't help wondering what Stonewall wanted.

He moved over to the coffeepot to pour another cup. "So, Margo, since you've asked a lot of questions of me, I have a few for you."

What on earth did he want to ask her? Margo wondered. She twisted in her chair and studied him while he poured his coffee. Even from the back the man was very impressive. She'd never been a woman who enjoyed checking out a man's backside until now. He was definitely a hottie by any woman's standards. Her heart nearly skipped a beat when he shifted to reach for the container of sugar. Heat she'd tried keeping at bay was now flooding her. All she could do was sit there, totally mesmerized by him. No man should be as handsome as Striker or as ornery. Or was it that she had the ability to bring out the touchiness in him?

Moments later he rejoined her at the table.

"Why would you want to ask me any questions?" she asked him.

"Trust me, I have my reasons."

She couldn't help wondering what those reasons were. There was only one way to find out. "So what are your questions?"

Margo couldn't help staring into his eyes while

thinking how gorgeous they were. Her gaze shifted from his eyes to his mouth. Not for the first time, she thought he had a pair of lips that were downright sensuous.

"It's not that this isn't a nice community, but you're wealthy. Why not live in one of those pricey penthouses in Cumberland Landing? And why are you self-employed and not running one of your family's foundations?"

Margo pushed her fingers through her hair while thinking it wouldn't be the first time someone had asked her that. "I went to college to become a fashion designer and I enjoy what I do. I worked with a major designer in New York for a while, but all the politics it took to move ahead turned me off. I like being my own boss and answering to no one. I guess you can say I work better by myself."

She took a sip of her coffee and continued, "And this house suits me just fine and is just what I need. It's my belief that just because a person has money, there's no reason to flaunt it or use it unnecessarily." That was one of the reasons she'd canceled her memberships at several of the country clubs. She'd discovered that some people with money could be total snobs.

"And what did Scotty think of you being loaded?"

"*Scott,*" she said, placing emphasis on the name he was intentionally getting wrong, "didn't think anything about it because he didn't know. I never told him my financial worth. I saw no reason to do so. It wasn't about my money but about me." At least it should have been, she thought. However, with Scott, it was about *his* money and how appreciative she should be that he made so much of it.

"Do you think the two of you will get back together?"

Margo couldn't help wondering why Striker would want to know if there was a chance she and Scott would get back together. But then, he might think he had a right to ask since she'd just finished delving into his personal life. "No. There's no way Scott and I will ever get back together and he knows my position." And he hadn't liked it. Scott quit women. They didn't quit him. His ego had gotten more than bruised, but, as far as she was concerned, that wasn't her problem. She had refused to take any more of his chauvinistic ways. In addition to that, he had begun spending less and less time with her.

Margo was spared finding out what Striker's next question would be when the doorbell rang. He quickly stood and eased into his jacket. At least with his jacket on it wouldn't be so obvious that he was wearing a gun. "I'll get that," he said.

She was right on his heels. "I think I'm capable of opening my own door, Striker."

He stopped walking and Margo almost ran into him. He glanced down at her with that deep, dark scowl. "Too dangerous for you to do that. Stay right here while I open the door. And I suggest you figure out how you intend to introduce me."

CHAPTER EIGHT

"HI, I'M CLAUDINE BERNARD and I have an appointment with Margo."

"I know," Striker said, looking at the young woman who stood on the doorstep with a perky smile on her face. "Come in. She's expecting you," he said, closing the door behind her.

Margo quickly materialized by his side. "Claudine, it's good seeing you again." And then she turned to him and smiled. "Thanks for opening the door for me." To Claudine, she said, "I'd like you to meet my good friend Lamar."

Striker fought back a frown when Margo deliberately introduced him as Lamar instead of Striker. He reached out and shook Claudine's hand, ignoring the way the woman was looking at him. Margo might have introduced him as nothing more than a good friend, but he could clearly see the wheels turning in Claudine's head.

"If you'll follow me, Claudine, we can get started with those measurements."

"Alright. It was nice meeting you, Lamar."

"Same here." He watched the women disappear into Margo's workroom and close the door behind them. He couldn't very well follow them in that room, not when Claudine would be undressing for measurements. But he could certainly make himself comfortable right here on the sofa where he had a good view of that door. He decided to use that time to call Stonewall.

His friend answered on the first ring. "What's up?" Striker asked.

"Just need to bring you up to date on a few things. First, we still haven't figured out who actually made that call last night. But we checked the phone records and it seems that Margo's number is the only one that's been made from that phone."

"And when was the phone activated?" Striker asked.

"A couple of days after Erickson was sentenced."

Striker rubbed the back of his neck. There had to be a connection. "Is there anything else I need to know?" he asked.

"One other thing. I understand the FBI has asked for the assistance of one of the nation's top psychic investigators to work on the case."

"A psychic?"

"Yes. They're hoping the person they're bringing in will be able to assist them in some way. Right now the authorities don't have a clue about anything. It's obvious they're up against a professional who seems to be one step ahead of them. They don't even know if they're looking for a man or woman. So far they haven't received any good leads."

Striker nodded. There was no doubt in his mind, and, he suspected, in a lot of other minds as well, that Erickson had people on the inside who were on his payroll. Spies. Traitors. Collaborators. Each hit was too tidy and tight for there not to be. "Thanks for the updates. Need I ask how you know so much?"

"No."

Striker chuckled. Although Stonewall and Detective

Joy Ingram might not have gone on their first date yet, evidently they were talking. It was obvious she'd become his unofficial contact in the police department.

After ending the call with Stonewall, Striker glanced at Margo's closed office door and thought about all the questions he'd asked her before Claudine arrived. Mainly about her relationship with Scott Dylan. The one question he'd wanted to ask but had known better was when she'd last had some hot, mind-blowing sex.

He shook his head, knowing he had no right to even wonder about such a thing. But his curiosity would get the best of him each and every time he looked at her body, especially her mouth. The woman was pure sex on legs.

Suddenly he realized he didn't hear any sound or movement behind Margo's closed office door. He quickly pulled out his phone and speed-dialed the number connected to the audio monitoring device Bruce had installed in each room. Striker relaxed when he picked up conversation. That meant everything was okay.

Striker was about to click off the phone when he heard his name mentioned. He raised a brow. Since he was the topic of their conversation, part of him felt he had every right to listen in. But, then again, he knew that he didn't. Doing so would be invading their privacy and crossing a line. It took everything he had to deny his curiosity, but he clicked off the phone.

MARGO PUT ASIDE her sketch pad. Every gown she designed was unique, and Claudine had given her full details as to what she wanted. Margo had offered Claudine advice on the best types of fabric to use to get the most stunning effect. That was the part of Margo's job she enjoyed the most, when she would pull out her pad to make sketches based on her clients' wants and desires. They'd gone through a number of them before Claudine selected one they thought would flatter the woman's curvy figure, especially with the alençon lace she wanted. The only thing they hadn't decided on was the material to use for the lining. Claudine wanted additional time to look around before making a decision.

"He's hot."

Margo raised a brow. "Who?"

"Your Lamar. Who else?" Claudine asked, laughing.

My Lamar? Margo thought. Now, that was truly a laugh, although she could see how Claudine thought Striker was hot. But hers? Not hardly.

"How did the two of you meet?"

Margo hadn't expected the question and knew she had to come up with an answer quick. She decided to go with how she and Scott had met. "At a party."

"Have the two of you been seeing each other long?"

"No, only a few months."

"I can see the two of you getting married one day."

Married? It was a good thing she was already sitting. Otherwise, Margo was certain she would have fallen flat on her face. "Trust me. Getting married is not anything I want to do."

"Oh."

Margo hoped she hadn't offended Claudine since it was obvious that getting married was something Claudine wanted to do. "What I meant is that marriage isn't for everyone."

"Yes, but I'm sure you'd feel differently if someone like my Stan came along. He is simply wonderful."

So she'd heard. *Plenty of times today*, Margo thought. The woman had been singing Stan's praises since she arrived. It was Stan this and Stan that. It was apparent Claudine thought her fiancé was the perfect man. "Yes, you're probably right."

"I know I am. When I met Stan, marriage was the last thing on my mind as well. I bet in another month or so, you'll begin thinking of marriage."

Don't hold your breath for that to happen, Margo thought, but to Claudine she said, "Maybe."

Claudine laughed again. "No maybe about it. I have a feeling I'll be hearing about your wedding by the end of the year. This is February, so you have ten months to work on him."

It was apparent to Margo that Claudine was a romantic. Margo didn't want to burst the woman's bubble. Although she couldn't speak for Striker, she could definitely speak for herself—she didn't have a romantic bone in her body. At least that was what her boyfriend in college had claimed. Brock Ford had been the romantic one and loved watching television while holding her hand. And he would often text her sappy romantic messages during the day. She had fancied herself in love with Brock until she'd discovered his true reason for romancing her. He'd found out about her family's wealth and decided marrying her would assure him part of that wealth. That was the main reason she'd never divulged anything about her family's wealth to Scott.

Now she was back in Charlottesville and focusing on doing the things that made her happy. And she was determined never to forget the lessons she'd learned from both Brock and Scott. They were different but life-learning lessons just the same. She had dated a few times since returning home. Most of the men she considered nothing more than friends who were her escorts to various charity events for the Connelly Foundation. The last thing she wanted right now in her life was any serious involvement. She refused to ever get tangled up with a man who wanted her money or thought she wanted his. Until she met someone who truly knew the meaning of love and commitment, she'd rather not bother. If Claudine thought her Stan was such a man, then Margo was happy for her.

"I need to run," Claudine said, interrupting Margo's thoughts as she stood. "I'm meeting Stan for lunch and I don't want to be late. That's the one thing he's a stickler about—timeliness."

"Okay, I'll see you out," Margo said, standing as well.

"How long will it take to make my gown?"

"If everything goes as planned, your dress will be ready in twelve weeks. Maybe sooner. I only take on one client at a time, so your gown will get my full attention."

"That's great. I've hired this photographer who wants to take a ton of photographs of me before the wedding. I'm glad my dress will be ready for him to do so."

When they opened the door, Striker was standing right there. Margo frowned up at him. "Yes, Lamar?"

"I started a fire in the fireplace and was about to knock to see if you wanted me to order lunch."

"Oh, how thoughtful of him. Eating in front of the fireplace is so romantic," she heard Claudine whisper behind her.

Whatever. "Thanks for getting the fire started and,

yes, ordering lunch now is fine. Claudine is leaving and I was about to see her out."

"I can do that," he quickly said, offering Claudine his arm. "I'm sure you want to finalize your notes from today's meeting, Margo."

Margo tried keeping the glare from her eyes when she said, "Yes, of course, Lamar. Thanks for being so thoughtful." Turning to Claudine, she said, "You'll call and let me know if you come across any material you see that you like for your lining?"

"Yes, most definitely."

Margo then watched as Striker walked Claudine to the door.

"I'M GOING TO let you introducing me as Lamar slide."

Margo glanced across the table at him as they ate lunch. "I assume that's your name since it's on your driver's license. If you don't like it, then change it."

"Trust me. I would if I could." He knew Margo was annoyed at him for how he'd handled Claudine. "You do know pouting won't get you anywhere, don't you?" he said, before taking a huge bite of his sandwich.

She narrowed her gaze. "You could have compromised my relationship with a client."

"How?"

"You were wearing a gun."

He rolled his eyes. "Since I was wearing my jacket, how was she supposed to know what I had underneath it…unless she copped a feel. Were you expecting her to do that?"

"Of course not."

"Okay, then. You're getting all worked up for nothing. You need to just chill."

When she didn't say anything, he shook his head. Getting up from the table, he stretched his body before tossing the trash into the garbage container. He then leaned a hip against the counter and watched her.

Striker let the silence stretch between them, knowing he wouldn't have to wait too much longer. She jerked around and glared at him. "Just what are you staring at?"

"So, you can talk? For a minute there I thought that maybe you'd lost your voice."

She clenched her teeth so hard he swore he could hear her doing so. Instead of their working relationship moving forward, it was going backward, real fast. "Look, Margo. Don't you think at some point we need to reach an agreement to get along? You can't keep fighting me at every turn. Whether you like me or not, whether you like the situation you've been placed in or not, I'm not going anywhere. My job is to protect you and I intend to do that, regardless of how you feel about it."

"Fine. And you need to not be so unbending and show flexibility with some things. I'm aware of the danger I'm in, Striker, and I do appreciate you protecting me, but do you have to be so dogmatic?"

"Am I?"

"Yes."

Okay, maybe he was. He had given Roland his word to protect her and he took his promises seriously. "Alright, let's agree on a truce," he said. "I promise to try to be more flexible if you'll stop resisting me all the time. Agreed?"

For a long moment their gazes held and then she said, "Yes, I agree. Considering everything, I know

I need to be protected, but that doesn't mean I have to like it."

"You're right. It doesn't." He didn't say anything for a few moments and then added, "Trust me, Margo, I know exactly how it feels to get your freedom taken away."

She frowned. "No. Don't compare my situation with yours, Striker. What I'm going through is nothing compared to what you had to endure all those years. I can't possibly imagine."

She was right. She couldn't. But neither would he lessen what she was dealing with. "So, from here on out, we're good?"

"We're good," she said, standing and sliding her chair under the table.

Striker covered the distance separating them. "Let's shake on it," he said, offering her his hand.

She looked at his hand. "Shake on what?"

"On our truce."

"Really? Is that necessary?"

Striker forced a smile to his lips. She was hesitating and a part of him knew why. He wasn't made of stone and remembered what had happened the last time they shook hands. The moment their hands had touched yesterday, a pang of intense desire had shot through him. He'd felt it and had known she'd felt it as well. "I believe a person's word is their bond, and we need to shake on it."

"I said I agreed to a truce, Striker."

"I know you did. But why are you against sealing the deal with a handshake?" He knew he was playing with fire, but he didn't care. A part of him enjoyed pushing her buttons.

She lifted her chin. "I am not against it."

"Then let's do it."

Narrowing her gaze at him, she took the hand he offered.

CHAPTER NINE

JUST LIKE IT HAD YESTERDAY, an intense rush of yearning tore through Margo the moment her hand touched Striker's. But unlike yesterday, now she did not want to snatch her hand back. She needed to know, to understand, why there was this powerful desire whenever they touched. If she was truly honest with herself, she would admit the desire was also there whenever she looked at him.

While she had dated a few times, she hadn't been intimate with a man since her breakup with Scott; however, she doubted that could be it. Sex between her and Scott hadn't been all that frequent and it definitely left a lot to be desired. Could it be that Striker was such a dominant male in looks, build and sexuality that all that raw desire oozing from him had an effect on her whether she wanted it to or not?

She wasn't pulling her hand from his, but why wasn't he ending the handshake? And was she imagining it or was the air surrounding them suddenly charged with an electric awareness? The man and woman kind? A mere touch from Scott had never affected her like this. Not only was she fully aware of this man, but she was responsive to the intense heat he generated.

She continued to hold his gaze. Call it woman's intuition, but she had a good idea of what he was feeling. And the look in his eyes was definitely telling her what he was thinking. The gaze roaming over her was blatant, sexual and bold.

Her nipples tightened to hardened buds. When had they ever done that? Definitely not whenever Scott was looking at them the way Striker was doing. He was arousing her as no other man had before.

Margo felt a gentle tug on her hand and realized he was slowly easing her toward him. Now was the time to yank her hand free, but for some reason, she couldn't. And when he tightened his hold on her hand and continued to stare down at her with a gaze that almost took her breath away, she felt her senses infused with mind-numbing desire.

He shifted his stance to lean closer to her and began lowering his head toward hers. He started nipping lightly at her mouth. She could no longer deny what was taking over her mind and her body. Nor could she dismiss the hungry throb of her lips that wanted to be fully taken by his.

The tiny nips continued. Was he intentionally trying to drive her crazy by playing with her mouth instead of giving her a full, heated kiss? Surely he could hear her tiny moans, the way her breath was being forced from her lungs. Then finally with a confidence that shot arousal through every part of her body, he fully covered her mouth with his.

Margo felt his tongue enter her mouth, glide slowly around before finally touching hers, capturing it and proceeding to suck on it. She'd barely gotten the chance to familiarize herself with Striker's taste when his phone rang. Muttering a curse, he released her mouth to answer. Margo drew in a deep breath while thinking she should be thankful for the intrusion; it had shocked some sense into her.

She needed to get away from him, escape into her workroom, try to forget all about that short—yet satisfying—kiss and begin work on Claudine's wedding gown. She wanted to be any place but here when Striker ended the call. But the tenseness in his voice and his glance her way told Margo the call was about her, so she decided for the time being to stay put. He was no longer saying anything. Just nodding every so often while keeping his gaze firmly on her.

The call lasted a few moments longer and then he said, "Okay, keep me posted," before clicking off the phone.

"What was that about?" she asked, taking the chance he might tell her that it wasn't any of her business.

He rubbed his face as if he was frustrated about something. "An arrest has been made."

She threw her hand to her throat. Surprised. Elated. "They got the assassin?"

He shrugged. "The federal agents think so."

She studied his expression and saw the definite lack of jubilance. "But you don't?"

"Let's just say I choose to err on the side of caution. I'm willing to wait it out and see."

Wait it out? For how long? Did that mean he had no intention of packing up and leaving based on the assumption she was now safe? "So, what do you suggest we do now?"

He rubbed his face again. "The final decision will have to come from your uncle, but I suggest we continue as planned until we know for certain they have the right guy."

Continue as planned? Margo wanted to ask exactly how long that might be, but she didn't. Instead she began backing up, needing time by herself to think. And give herself a good scolding for letting him kiss her.

"Fine. I'll go along with whatever you and my uncle decide. In the meantime, like you suggested, I will err on the side of caution. Now I need to go online and order the materials for Claudine's wedding gown. And before you remind me, I know to stay away from the window."

And then she turned and hurried out of the kitchen.

STRIKER FOLLOWED HER as far as the living room and stood by the sofa. From his position he could see her sit down at her workroom computer. It was only then that he crossed to the fireplace and stared at the flames. What the hell had happened in her kitchen? The desire he'd felt for her had shocked him to the core. And when he'd kissed her, he hadn't wanted to stop. The kiss had packed a wallop but had been way too short.

When had a woman—a woman he was protecting— made him lose control? What was there about her that whenever he touched her, something inside of him would snap, make him even more aware of her as a woman? A woman he wanted.

With that admission, he drew in a sharp breath, clenched his jaw and tightened his hands into fists at his sides. He needed to start thinking with the right head and not the one that wanted like hell to get inside of her. It wasn't that kind of party, especially with her. He needed to rope in his horny thoughts and con-

centrate on what he promised Roland he would do—
protect her.

Needing to see her again, he walked back to the
sofa and stared into the workroom. She hadn't moved.
And at that moment, as if she felt his gaze on her, she
looked up from her computer. Damn. He felt it again.
Desire so intense it was like a living element, stirring across his skin, being inhaled through his nose
and getting absorbed into his body. That was the last
thing he wanted or needed, and he immediately broke
eye contact with her and walked into the kitchen for
another cup of coffee.

What the hell had happened to bring on this turn
of events? They had been at odds until agreeing to a
truce. In this case, a cease-fire between them might
not have been such a good idea after all. Once their
hands had touched to shake on it, some sort of dam
had broken and it was on. He didn't want to think what
would have happened had he not gotten that call, and
was thankful for the interruption. By rights, he should
have known better. But deep down, he knew why he'd
done it. He'd needed to see if the desire he'd felt when
he touched her yesterday had been real or a figment
of his imagination.

It had definitely been real.

He was trying to hold on to his sanity where Margo
was concerned. The last thing he needed was to let her
become his passion. Something he thought he couldn't
do without. He thought of something else that used to
be his passion. Football.

It had been his dream to one day play for the NFL.
Chances were he would have done so, but he hadn't
followed his mother's orders about Wade. She didn't

care how much he loved football, didn't care how much it had become his passion. She felt that the important thing was for him to look after Wade while she worked nights. Not wanting to miss any football practices, he'd thought that he'd found the best solution. In the end, he'd lost his brother because he had refused to give up something that had become a passion of his. Never again would he let something like that happen. Roland had entrusted Margo to him…just like his mother had entrusted Wade to him. Although his mother never blamed him for anything, he'd always blamed himself.

Striker knew that he and Margo needed to talk. Set things straight. What had happened in her kitchen couldn't happen again. No touching. No kissing. Yes, definitely no kissing. He was here to protect her, not lust after her. And the last thing he could do was let her get under his skin and start thinking foolish thoughts about her. Hadn't he promised himself years ago to never get attached to a woman? If he ever fell in love, he'd be risking losing her the same way he'd lost others that he'd loved.

Raising the coffee cup to his lips, he was about to take a sip when his phone rang again. He pulled in another frustrated breath when he saw the call was from Frazier Connelly.

"This is Striker," he said into the phone.

"Striker, this is Frazier. Not sure if you've heard, but the authorities got their guy, which means your services are no longer needed."

Striker shook his head. He'd been afraid Connelly would think that way. "An arrest means nothing, Frazier. Too early."

"The FBI just ended a news conference. They seem confident they have the right guy."

Don't they always? Striker thought angrily. He could clearly recall men he'd befriended while in the slammer, who were innocent. The situation involving Sheppard Granger quickly came to mind. Shep had been locked up for fifteen years for killing his wife, and the real murderers had still been out there killing others.

"I feel confident the FBI knows what they're talking about, so I'm relieving you of your services and—"

"You didn't hire me, Frazier. Roland Summers did and I stay put until he says otherwise," Striker cut in.

Frazier got quiet for a minute and then snapped, "Fine. I'll talk to Roland to let him know my position."

"Yeah, you do that. Good-bye." Striker clicked off the phone.

Certain Margo had heard his cell ring, he went back into the living room. She was watching him. Did she know the caller had been her uncle? Needing to talk to her, he was walking toward the workroom when his phone rang again. This time it was Roland.

"Yes, Roland?"

"The FBI thinks they have their guy."

'So I heard," Striker said, still holding Margo's gaze.

"I want you to stay put," Roland said.

"Connelly just called to relieve me of my duties."

"That's not going to happen," Roland said angrily.

"I basically told him that and he wasn't too happy about it, so expect a call from him."

Striker noticed that Margo had finally broken eye contact with him to resume working on her computer. "Do you know what I think, Roland?"

"What?"

"That you and Connelly need to get together and work things out. Reach an agreement. It's obvious that although there're ill feelings from all the shit that happened years ago, the two of you strongly agree on one thing, at least."

"What's that?"

"Keeping Margo safe."

MARGO DREW IN a deep breath as she tried concentrating on keying information into her computer. Striker was staring at her. She knew it because she could feel the intensity of his gaze. Why couldn't she forget about that kiss? The feel of his mouth against hers? His tongue sucking on hers? Why even now was her entire body still tingling from head to toe?

If the call hadn't come in, would he have kept on kissing her or would she have eventually stopped him? For some reason, she doubted it. She'd barely gotten a taste of him but had enjoyed what she had gotten and ashamedly admitted she had wanted more from Lamar "Striker" Jennings.

Something he'd said earlier piqued her memory as well as her curiosity. He wasn't overly fond of his first name. Why? At the time he'd said it, she'd been too annoyed with him to question him about it. But at some point, she would. And then there were those two phone calls he'd received. He'd been looking at her while talking on the phone. It was times like this that she wished she had the ability to read lips. Had he received more news about the man that had been arrested? Was there confirming evidence he was the assassin the authorities had been looking for?

She felt a presence beside her and jerked around,

finding Striker standing next to her chair. She placed her hand on her chest to still her heart. Her pulse was racing like crazy. She hadn't heard him enter her office. "Striker, you scared me."

"Sorry, I didn't mean to, but we need to talk. Your uncle Frazier wants to relieve me of my duties here since an arrest has been made. However, Roland agrees that I should stay awhile to make sure they got the right man."

"So what's the verdict? Do you stay or leave?"

"Connelly will be talking to Roland. Hopefully Roland will convince him why it's important that you're not left unprotected, even with the recent turn of events."

"Okay, let me know what's decided." She didn't want to think of the possibility that the wrong man had been arrested and the real assassin was still out there, getting ready to kill again.

She turned back to her computer, and when he continued to stand there, she glanced back up at him. "Is there anything else?"

"Yes."

"What?"

"You know what, Margo, but in case you need me to spell it out for you, we need to talk about what happened between us earlier in your kitchen."

"Oh, that," she said, hoping to make light of what he was referring to and dismiss it. "It was nothing."

Striker looked at her. "It *was* something. And we need to agree that whatever it was has no place here. My job is to protect you and nothing more."

"That's fine because you won't get anything more," she snapped. "You keep your hands and lips to yourself and I'll do the same. Now, if you will excuse me, I have work to do."

A part of Margo was angry, but another part knew she should appreciate his directness and his willingness to not dismiss what had happened like she'd tried to do.

When he didn't walk off, she looked up at him.

"Is there anything else, Striker?" she asked curtly.

"No, I guess not. However, I'd like to hear your thoughts on what happened in your kitchen. Our kiss."

She shrugged. Why did he care about her thoughts, since he'd already decreed how it would be between them? But he was standing there, undoubtedly waiting on a response, so she said, "I prefer not to talk about or think about it. In fact, I want to forget that anything happened. You've told me your position and I agree. What happened should not have happened. To be honest with you, I don't even know why it did."

He looked at her strangely. "You don't know why it happened?"

She rolled her eyes. "I'm not dim-witted, Striker. I knew yesterday that we were attracted to each other. But I also know that we're both adults and I honestly didn't expect…"

When she didn't finish, he asked, "Didn't expect what?"

"I didn't expect the attraction to almost get the best of us. I don't understand that. I guess we should be glad we were saved by your phone before things got too far out of hand."

"Yes, I guess we should be glad about that."

He then turned and walked out of her workroom, leaving her to believe that, deep down, he wasn't glad about it any more than she was.

CHAPTER TEN

Upon hearing Margo moving around in her bedroom, Striker swung his feet over the side of the bed to sit up. After talking with Roland, Frazier had agreed for Striker to stay on with a firm understanding that if there weren't any more killings they would assume—like everyone else—that the authorities had arrested the right man.

It had been four days since the arrest was made and so far there hadn't been another murder. That could be good news or it could be that Erickson was just fucking around with everyone and had deliberately framed an innocent man.

According to the media, the murder weapon was found in the man's car with his prints all over it. But the suspect, who had a prior criminal record, was claiming his innocence, saying he'd bought the gun from someone on the streets, not knowing it had been used in five murders. So far the man hadn't been able to provide any alibis for where he was at the time of each killing. The feds were so convinced they had their man they weren't trying to look elsewhere. And at the most recent press conference they'd pretty much told everyone they felt it was safe to resume living their lives normally.

For some reason, Striker had a gut feeling something

wasn't right with how things were going down, but it was nothing he could put a definite finger on. He'd constantly reminded himself that protecting Margo was just another job. No big deal. Whenever he got the word from Roland that it was okay for him to move on, then he would. Without looking back.

Without looking back...

Could he really do that? He would admit that lately his mind had entertained thoughts of how things might be once this ordeal was over and she no longer needed his protection. He could ask her out on a date. Take her to a nice restaurant. Enjoy a glass of wine as he got to know her better. Striker rubbed a hand down his face, knowing he was losing his mind if he thought any of that was possible. He and Margo weren't even in the same league. She was an heiress and he was an ex-con. But what was that saying about opposites attracting? And although he wasn't a rich man by any means, he wasn't a broke Joe either. He worked hard and over the years had made good investments. However, that wasn't the point. The real deal here—one he couldn't lose sight of—was that when this assignment was over, he would go back to his world and leave Margo in hers. He knew that and accepted that. Then why was the kiss—which had been way too short—constantly on his mind? And why had he gone to bed each night since that day wishing that instead of playing around her mouth, nibbling around her lips, he had just gone for the gusto and crushed her mouth with his in a full-contact, hot and heavy, wet-tongue, tonsil-touching kiss? One that would have lasted longer, and had her groaning, purring and shuddering in his arms? He had a feeling that moment was now a lost opportunity. All he had to do was close his eyes to imagine them standing there, body to body, mouth to mouth, with his hands plunged in her hair while his mouth seduced hers. Thoroughly. Possessively. The Striker Jennings way.

It was apparent that short, unfinished kiss had created a tense environment for them. Definitely for him. Being around Margo was pure hell. They ate breakfast, lunch and dinner together, but other than that they pretty much ignored each other. Or they tried. She seemed content to disappear into her office to work on that wedding gown. He, on the other hand, had kept busy by playing games on his cell phone, doing exercises and reading.

A number of packages Margo ordered had arrived, and only after he checked out each box had he given the okay to keep them. That had annoyed the hell out of her. But like he'd told her, he wouldn't take any chances.

A text came in on his phone. It was from Stonewall and the text simply said,

Nothing new to report.

In a way, that was good news. He and Margo had been together inside her house for almost a week and they were about to go stir-crazy. Cabin fever was getting the best of them, and their moods and attitudes were beginning to take a nosedive. It was hard trying to ignore the sexual tension whenever they were around each other. More than once he'd caught her staring at him and vice versa. The lust between them was mindboggling, and there was nothing he could do about it.

Hmm, maybe there was. Now that Quasar had finished up his last assignment, Striker could ask him to relieve him for a few days. But deep down, he knew he couldn't do that. He'd given Roland his word to protect Margo. Not that Quasar wasn't capable of doing it, because he was. But Striker didn't want another person protecting Margo. So here it was, the beginning of a new day, and just like he did every morning, he needed to get his shit together before facing her.

First off, he needed to clear his mind of all those dreams he'd had last night. The ones where he'd jumped her bones a number of times. Best sex dreams he'd ever had. So what if he'd thought about being inside her body? Had imagined her calling out his name during one hell of an orgasm? His thoughts in the wee hours of the morning were nobody's business but his own.

Standing, he headed for the bathroom.

FULLY DRESSED IN jeans and a pullover sweater, Margo took a moment to collect herself before opening her bedroom door, knowing what she would find on the other side. As usual, Striker would be there, leaning against the wall, waiting on her. And like always, she would fight to ignore the surge of desire that consumed her upon seeing him first thing in the morning. Why did he have to look so good and why did seeing him continually bring on flickers of longing and need?

And why couldn't she forget about that kiss? It wasn't like it had been her first, and she doubted seriously it would be her last. Why was she thinking that Striker's short kiss ran rings around Scott's long ones? Whoever thought all kisses were the same hadn't kissed Striker. She didn't want to compare him to Scott but couldn't help it. Scott was a chauvinist and would never apologize for being one, especially when he saw it as a quality a woman should admire.

Margo had a feeling Striker didn't have a chauvinistic bone in his body. A woman was his equal and
he would protect her with his life and not try to deliberately play on her fears like Scott had done. But,
on the other hand, the one thing Striker and Scott did
have in common was their stubbornness. Today she
was prepared for a fight after telling him she needed
to leave the house. The thread that had been delivered
for Claudine's gown wasn't the exact color she wanted
and she knew of one local craft store that had what
she needed. She would use the truce they'd shaken on
a few days ago in her favor. He had agreed to be flexible, hadn't he?

She would break the news to him over breakfast.
Regardless of how he chose to handle things, she intended to go to that store, with or without him. As far
as she was concerned, she'd been locked inside this
house long enough and needed to breathe in clean,
fresh air. The forecasters predicted a hard freeze at the
end of the week, and she wanted to at least spend a few
hours outdoors while the weather was halfway decent.

Opening the door, Margo saw Striker standing there
as always. How did he always time it to exactly when
she would be walking out of her bedroom? If she didn't
know better, she'd think he had ultrasonic hearing or
something.

His body looked hard and muscular leaning against
the wall. Feminine awareness invaded every part of her
and she couldn't help the primal reaction of her body
kicking in right then. She was well aware of the exercises he did each day. She knew he was putting her
treadmill and stationary bike to good use every night
before he went to bed. He also jumped rope a lot. More

than once she had glanced out of her workroom and seen him doing so in her kitchen, which afforded him a lot of room.

The moment their gazes met, acute recognition passed between them, stirring something hot and carnal in the pit of her belly. She couldn't help but admire the way he filled out a pair of jeans, and that T-shirt looked real nice on his chest. And those tattoos that ran up the length of his arms were interesting and made him look so formidable but in such an appealing way. For a minute her breath wobbled in her throat. She should still be upset with him because of the way he'd all but terrified the delivery guy yesterday when he'd dropped the packages off at the back door as usual. Not only had Striker almost shoved a gun up the man's nose, but he had searched through all the boxes before letting her accept them.

"Good morning, Striker."

"Good morning, Margo."

Their usual greetings were exchanged before she moved toward the stairs. Desire clawed at her as he followed. Just knowing he was a few steps behind her had more heat curling in her stomach. When they made it downstairs, she turned to him and said, "We need to talk."

"Before or after breakfast arrives?" he asked.

Before she could answer, a text came over Striker's phone. He checked it. "Our breakfast is on the way. We'll talk while we eat," he said.

"Alright."

Walking into the kitchen, she headed straight for the refrigerator to get the orange juice while Striker moved toward the counter to put on the coffee. She thought about how they'd gotten into a comfortable routine in the mornings over the last few days.

While getting glasses out the cabinets, she looked over at him. His powerfully built body seemed to fill her kitchen. The muscular definition of his abs and biceps were so well outlined she couldn't help but stare for a second.

Not taking the chance he might notice her ogling him, she quickly got the glasses, filled them with orange juice and headed for the table.

STRIKER LEANED FORWARD against the kitchen counter, trying to hide the physical evidence of his desire for Margo. Having a hard-on was a bitch but couldn't be helped. She was wearing a pair of tight jeans, a pullover sweater and flat shoes. The woman looked good this morning like she did every morning. And if that wasn't bad enough, then there was her scent—the scent of a woman—that was arousing him like crazy.

Moments later, after getting his body under control, he poured their cups of coffee and carried them over to the table. There was a knock at the back door. Automatically, he pulled his gun as he moved toward it. Although he was expecting the delivery of their breakfast, he never took any chances.

"Is that necessary, Striker?" he heard Margo ask behind him.

He wasn't in the mood today. Sexual tension was eating at him, and it was taking all he had to contain it.

He glanced over his shoulder. "What does it matter when I pull out my gun as long as it's to protect your sweet ass?" he snapped.

Refusing to engage in a verbal sparring match with

Striker, especially when it was quite obvious he was in a foul mood, Margo drew in a deep, controlled breath and then stared beyond him to the sliding glass door.

Moments later she watched a man enter carrying bags. From the aroma she knew it was their breakfast. But the man who entered her kitchen was not Cisco.

"Good morning," the man said, flashing a huge smile.

"You're not Cisco," she said, studying the man who was just as tall and muscular as Striker. His straight black hair that fell to his shoulders and chestnut-colored skin gave his handsome features an exotic look.

"Cisco is on another assignment. I'm Quasar Patterson. I'll be the one delivering breakfast from here on out."

"Thanks for bringing our breakfast, Quay, but it's time for you to leave," Striker said, noticing the way Margo was checking out his friend and getting annoyed by it.

Quasar broke eye contact with Margo and glanced over at Striker. "Kind of touchy this morning, aren't you, Striker?"

"Go to hell."

Quasar laughed. "Sounds like you might already be there." And then he opened the door and left.

"Honestly, Striker, did you have to be so rude?"

Striker stared at her. If she knew how he, Quasar and Stonewall spoke to each other at times, often using more profanity than not, she wouldn't make that accusation.

"Yeah, yeah, whatever," he said, unloading the contents of the bags. "He can handle it."

"That's not the point."

"And just what is the point, Margo? At least the one you're trying to make?"

"That you were rude."

"You said that already. In my line of work, it doesn't pay to be nice. And has it occurred to you that I'm not a nice person?"

"If you're trying to convince me of that, then you're doing a good job."

No, he wasn't trying to convince her of that, but for some reason, today he couldn't help it. But then, like he'd told her, he wasn't there to be nice. He was there to keep her safe. His mood came with the territory, especially when she was a woman playing havoc with his damn libido. And that wasn't good. After placing all the containers and utensils out on the table, he sat down, ready to dig in. "So what do we need to discuss?"

"I need to go to the store."

"No, you don't."

"Excuse me?"

Already digging into his meal, he said, "Tell me what you need and I'll have Quasar pick it up."

Margo scowled. "What I need is not anything that Quasar can pick up for me, Striker."

"He can pick up anything, even feminine hygiene products, if that's what you're alluding to."

Margo nearly choked on her orange juice and she felt her face redden. She couldn't believe what he'd just said. "For your information, that isn't it. I need to pick up a different shade of thread for Claudine's gown. The one I ordered doesn't match the way I thought it would."

"Then order some more."

"If I do that, I wouldn't get it until Monday. There aren't any deliveries over the weekend, and I refuse to lose two days of work waiting on thread. I'm going to the craft store after breakfast with or without you."

He didn't say anything, and Margo saw the way his jaw ticked as he stared across the table at her. He was mad, but she didn't care. She needed that thread, and like she'd told him, she would leave to go get it with or without him.

Striker was about to open his mouth and tell her that hell would freeze over before he let her go anywhere without him, and that her pretty little ass wasn't going anywhere. But then he quickly decided getting out of her house for a short excursion might not be such a bad idea. It would relieve some of their stir-craziness.

"Fine," he snapped. "We'll go get your thread. Tell me the name of the store so I can set things up."

"Set what up?"

"A plan to make sure my security team has our backs."

"Okay."

He dug into his breakfast, thinking, hell no, it wasn't okay. As far as he was concerned, nothing would be okay until his assignment of protecting her was over.

DR. RANDI FULLER stared at everyone gathered in the huge conference room as she paused before saying the words she knew they would not want to hear. But she said them anyway. "You have the wrong man in custody."

Everyone looked at her like they didn't believe she could say such a thing, and she understood why. Everything fit. They had recovered the murder weapon with the suspect's fingerprints all over it. The man didn't have an alibi, he had a criminal record, and he fit the description from the only eye witness they had. However, regardless of all that, she was convinced she was right.

"While we respect your opinion, Dr. Fuller, I think you're wrong. We're all convinced that we do have the right man."

She held the gaze of FBI special agent Tommy Felton. This wouldn't be the first time they had worked together on a high-profile case. And it wouldn't be the first time they'd disagreed and he had refused to consider what she had to say. The last case had been a human-trafficking ring. If the Bureau had taken her findings seriously then, they could have captured the leader of the group. They hadn't and the man was still out there somewhere. It seemed her presence always reminded Agent Felton of that. It didn't matter one iota to him that the reason she was here was because, with the use of her psychic abilities, she'd helped law enforcement around the country solve a number of cases that had been at dead ends.

"And why do you think we have the wrong man?" police chief Hal Harkins asked, ignoring the glare Felton shot his way.

At least someone was willing to listen to reason, Randi thought, shifting her full attention to the chief of police. She would have to give it to Chief Harkins—he and his team of detectives *had* taken her abilities seriously. Her approach to solving a crime was different than those of a number of other psychics. She didn't just depend on her psychic abilities but also an in-depth knowledge of the case. That method was more readily accepted by the skeptics, especially those who believed their way was the only way. She had the ability to speak as both a behavioral analyst and a psychic investigator. If the people she worked with preferred thinking of her as a BA rather than a PI, then so be it.

It didn't matter that at the age of twenty-seven she'd already assisted various police departments around the country in solving close to fifty cases, most of them unsolved murders, rapes and missing persons. She'd garnered national attention when she had helped federal agents rescue a well-known senator just moments before he was to be put on a plane to Libya for his execution by ISIS.

She knew Chief Harkins wanted to believe in her. He and a couple of his detectives had accompanied her to the five crime scenes, had made sure she had all the court records at her disposal and had set up her interview with Gus Pickett, the man who'd been arrested and tagged "Erickson's assassin."

"As you know, Chief Harkins, I spent most of yesterday with Gus Pickett. I had put together a psychological profile of the assassin based on where he decides to kill his victims, what evidence he willingly leaves behind and the time of day each hit was made. After my interview, as well as my visit to the crime scenes, several things stood out, which convinces me that Pickett's not the person you are looking for. There are several inconsistencies."

"Such as?" the chief asked.

"The assassin is a habitual coffee drinker. That's the only real evidence he leaves behind—coffee cups wiped clean of fingerprints."

"What are you getting at, Dr. Fuller?" Felton all but

snapped at her. "Are you suggesting Pickett doesn't drink coffee?"

"What I'm getting at, Agent Felton, is that Gus Pickett only drinks his coffee with cream. Coffee residue on the cups left at the murder scenes did not show traces of cream in the coffee."

"And how do you know what he puts in his coffee?" Harkins asked, curiously.

She glanced over at him. "I gave him a cup during our interview session. When I offered him some sugar, he said he only uses cream in his coffee. And another thing. Pickett is almost a neat freak. He would not have left those cups behind, littering the place."

"We know why they were left behind, Dr. Fuller." Another special agent spoke up, a tinge of annoyance in his voice. "His motive was quite obvious. He wanted to toy with us. He dropped hints and got caught."

Randi knew she was wasting her time trying to convince them of any theories other than those they'd come up with. These were Felton and his boys. FBI old-school. Although they could support behavioral analytical findings in most situations, since the FBI used them to crack a lot of cases, she knew when it came to psychics they were nonbelievers.

She placed her report on the table. "Here is my final evaluation as both a psychic investigator and behavioral analyst. I suggest everyone read it and weigh in on my recommendations, especially the one where I'm requesting an interview with Erickson."

"Trust me, you don't want to interview Erickson," Harkins said, rubbing his face. "The man is an asshole."

"I've dealt with assholes before. No problem," she said, forcing herself not to look over at Felton. "My report pretty much covers everything, including a psychological profile of the person you should really concentrate on finding. The real assassin is still out there."

"The real assassin is just where we want him. Behind bars," Felton snapped, tossing her report to the other side of the table. "We got our man."

Randi forced a smile. "In that case, my services here are no longer needed. Good day, everyone."

She walked out the door, thinking that when the shit hit the fan like she knew it would when the real killer resurfaced, at least she would be on a much-deserved vacation.

Glendale Shores was an island owned by her family that was the most beautiful of the Sea Islands off the South Carolina coast. And she couldn't wait to get there.

CHAPTER ELEVEN

"I THOUGHT YOU only came here for thread."

Margo suddenly felt heat on her neck, and she knew why. Striker was breathing down it. She wished he would back up a little and not stand so close. However, even when she turned around, he made no move to do so. He was determined to stick to her like glue. "Yes, that was my original plan, but I saw other things I needed."

He glanced around, the way she'd seen him do several times since they'd set foot inside Sandy Lee Craft Shop. There wasn't a single person who those sinfully dark eyes hadn't sized up, analyzed and scrutinized.

"At least I'm in the checkout line."

"Lucky me," he said sarcastically.

"You really are. I've never come here and been out in less than an hour. I could spend all day in here."

He peered down at her, seemingly bewildered. "Why?"

"Look around. What do you see?"

"Stuff. Too much stuff. All over the place."

Margo couldn't help but grin. She'd gotten practically the same response from her uncle when she'd talked him into coming here with her one day. It had been the first and last time he'd done so.

After the cashier rang up her purchases and Margo

paid for them, Striker walked her to the car. Like in the store, he studied their surroundings and stuck close to her. Too close for comfort, as far as she was concerned.

He'd told her that her uncle had decided to keep Striker on as her protector for another week. If no additional killings occurred, they would assume the right man was behind bars. She certainly hoped so.

"Can we go someplace for lunch?" she asked him.

Striker shook his head as he pulled out of the parking lot. "No. Quasar is bringing us lunch."

"He wouldn't have to if we stopped and grabbed something."

"No."

"Why are you being difficult, Striker? What happened to you agreeing to be more flexible? Bend a little?"

"I did bend. You got a trip to that craft store, didn't you? Don't push your luck with me, Margo."

On some days she could ignore his attitude. Today was not going to be one of them. This was her first time out in a week, and she was in no hurry to go back home. "I have a taste for a hamburger."

"No problem. I'll have Quasar bring us one."

"There's a hamburger place ahead on the right. What harm would it be to stop?"

"I could be placing you in danger. For some reason, you refuse to accept that you still might be."

How could she not accept it when he was with her practically 24/7? Striker's presence was a constant reminder of how her peace of mind had been stolen the moment Erickson made his threat at the trial. If at any time she was tempted to downplay the danger, all she had to do was remember those five innocent people whose lives had been taken away from them.

She looked back over at him. "But you will admit they might have the right guy since there haven't been any more killings?"

"That doesn't necessarily mean anything, Margo. The real assassin could be in hiding somewhere."

"Until when?"

"Who knows? Personally, I think he's waiting for the best time to hit again. I'm sure the feds are trying to figure out what orders Erickson gave the assassin. I understand Erickson isn't talking and the man they arrested is claiming his innocence. Erickson sees this as nothing more than a game to show he's still in control. People's lives mean nothing to him."

"That much was proved during his trial, which is why he got the sentence he did." Moments later Margo was surprised when Striker pulled the car into the parking lot of the hamburger place she'd told him about. He proceeded to the drive-through lane. She smiled. For the second time that day he had been flexible. Grudgingly or otherwise. "Thanks, Striker. They have the best burgers."

"So you say."

STRIKER WONDERED IF he needed to have his head examined for giving in to Margo's request. His only saving grace was that she'd been right. This was the best burger he'd ever eaten. He'd decided to park so they could eat in the car. They were in a good area, and he had a clear view of their surroundings.

Still, sitting here in a parked car with her felt too personal and intimate. Like they were on a date or something, when that definitely was not the case. Hadn't he given himself a get-real talk this morning that he and Margo would never date? So why was he thinking such things?

Probably because they were here and for the time being they had called a truce. And there was the possibility that if the right guy was in police custody, then his days with Margo were numbered. More than anything, even if it was for just a short while, he wanted to get to know whatever he could about her. He wasn't sure why that was important to him; he just knew it was.

Striker had a feeling that if he didn't take advantage of the time now, he would one day see it as a missed opportunity. One he would regret.

With that thought in mind, he decided to get the conversation going by asking, "How did you find out about this place?"

She looked at him. "Uncle Frazier. Once in a while he loses the shirt, tie and Armani suits and replaces them with regular duds and lives like the rest of us."

Like the rest of us? Had she forgotten she was practically an heiress? "So the two of you come here often?"

"A few times but not often. We haven't done anything together since he hooked up with Liz."

Striker recalled the woman's name from when it had come up before. It had been during a conversation she'd had with her uncle that first day. He'd picked up then the same thing he was picking up now, that Margo and this Liz person didn't get along. The dislike in Margo's voice was obvious. "I gather Liz isn't one of your favorite people."

"Hardly. She sees me as a threat."

"A threat?"

"Yes." And then as if she'd realized she might have said too much, Margo quickly asked, "What do you think about the fries? Aren't they delicious?"

"Yes, they're good," he said, popping one into his mouth. He had watched her eat and, as usual, had gotten turned on from merely seeing her chew her food. There was something about her mouth that he found so damn desirable.

"It was nice to get out. I almost hate going back."

He looked over at her. "What happened to you wanting to jump into working on Claudine Bernard's wedding gown?"

"I'm sure that even you would admit getting out of the house for a while is a relief."

He would have to agree it was nice. Cabin fever was the pits, especially when his mind was centered on lust.

"So, Striker, what do you enjoy doing in your spare time when you're not working? Any hobbies?"

"No hobbies, although I love taking my bike out."

"Bike as in motorcycle?"

"Yes. I have a Harley."

"Ride it often?"

"Every chance I get." No need to tell her that on a day like this he would have ridden it on a long stretch of highway, loving the feel of the wind whipping his face.

Margo removed her sweater, and the blouse she was wearing showed a lot of her cleavage. He could tell she had firm breasts. The kind he would just love to press his face in the middle of before swiping his tongue across the nipples.

Once he had agreed to take her to that craft store, she had raced upstairs and changed her shoes to a pair of boots. They complemented her outfit. They complemented her. She complemented them. He doubted there was an outfit that she didn't look good in.

"Why don't you like the name *Lamar*?"

He shifted his gaze from her chest to her face. There was nothing in her expression to denote she had noticed his interest in her breasts. "What makes you think I don't?"

"You said so. Were you lying when you said it?"

"No." He then took a sip of his iced tea.

"Well then, why don't you like it? I think it's a nice name."

Striker watched while she sipped more of her milk shake and had to shift in his seat to relieve the pressure of his erection against his zipper.

"Well?" she asked, licking her lips as if she was enjoying her milk shake and was oblivious to all that lust torpedoing through his body.

"Well, what?"

"What's wrong with the name?"

Wasn't it his plan to be the one asking the questions? To appease his curiosity and use this opportunity to find out more about her? Then how had she turned things around on him and asked him about his hobbies and now about his name? Was there ever a time she thought that perhaps she asked too many questions? Apparently not.

"I don't like the name because Lamar was also my father's name," he finally said.

She blinked, confused. "You had a problem being named after your father?"

If only she knew just how big a problem he had with it. "Yes. My mother named me after him for spite."

Gathering up their trash to put into a bag, he continued, "He refused to marry her when she told him about her pregnancy. And on top of that, he refused to give me his last name. So she thought she would get even by giving me his first name."

"Oh. You and Wade didn't have the same father?"

"No. Five years later Mom met and married Ray Jennings. He adopted me and gave me his last name. He was also the one to nickname me Striker. For obvious reasons, he didn't like the name *Lamar* any more than I did. And before you ask, the reason he decided on Striker was because as a kid I was good at football but lousy at baseball. The pitcher would strike me out nearly every time."

She chuckled. "I can tell from the sound of your voice that you and your stepfather are close."

Striker couldn't repress the smile that touched his lips. "We were. Ray Jennings was a good man. He treated Mom like a queen and provided for his family. Unfortunately, he was taken away from us too soon."

"How?"

"Car accident. He left for work that morning at the water plant and never came home."

"How old were you?"

"I was fourteen and Wade was nine. We took his death hard. Like I said, he was a good man."

Deciding he'd told her more than she needed to know, he checked his watch. It was one in the afternoon. He wasn't looking forward to returning to her place any more than she was. Although he would never admit it to her, he was enjoying this time sitting in the car and talking to her...although he did have an ulterior motive for doing so. He couldn't help noticing that away from her house she seemed more relaxed and at ease. However, it was up to him to make sure neither of them let their guard down, even if the authorities thought it was a closed case.

Still, they could risk a little more time out here. He eased back the seat to give his legs more room. He had backed the car in to get a clear view of what was happening in front of him. The lunch crowd was still coming, even more than before.

He glanced over at Margo. She was finished with her milk shake. He was glad of that since he wasn't sure how much longer he could have sat there watching her mouth on that damn straw, wishing it was his lips. His mind was filled with all kinds of naughty thoughts. Thoughts he was better off not having. So he decided to go ahead with his questions.

"So, Margo, you've managed—and quite nicely, I might add—to once again dig into my business, so it seems fitting for me to dig into yours. Fair play and all that."

She looked at him warily as she shifted in her seat as if to get comfortable as well. "Depends on what you want to know."

He would start with what was really burning inside of him. Namely, her relationship with Scott Dylan. Why he was so curious about it he wasn't sure, but he would admit inwardly to envying any man who'd been privy to her smiles. Her kisses. Her bed.

"I want to know about you and Scott Dylan. What happened? After almost a year together, why did the two of you break up?"

CHAPTER TWELVE

MARGO STARED AT STRIKER. What gave him the right to think he could ask her anything? But then, hadn't she been doing that for the last fifteen minutes? Drilling him for things she'd wanted to know about him. She would be the first to admit that she probably knew more about him than he knew about her. Although he hadn't wanted to, he had shared a lot with her, and she had a feeling there was more he wasn't sharing. But why did he want to know about Scott?

"Ask me about something else, Striker."

"Why?"

"Because I don't want to talk about Scott."

"Why not?"

When she didn't say anything, he added, "Okay, I get it."

She lifted a brow. "You get what?"

"The reason why you don't want to talk about Scott. The breakup was painful for you."

Did he really think that or was he just fishing? Should she let him believe what he liked or should she straighten him out on the matter? She preferred the second option to straighten him out. "Trust me. My breakup with Scott didn't cause me any pain."

"So why did the two of you break up? You're not the kind of woman a man would easily give up."

Was that meant to be a compliment? If so, it caught her off guard. Trying not to appear overly pleased by his assessment, she asked, "And why do you think that?"

He took another sip of his iced tea before responding with his own question. "Have you taken a good look at yourself in the mirror lately?"

"I do every day after I get dressed."

"Well, you evidently don't see what most men would. And don't ask me to expound because that will take us away from our topic of conversation. So why did you and Scott break up?"

Should she answer his question? Doing so would keep the conversation going and therefore prolong their outing. It was a beautiful day, the first week in February, and she'd desperately needed to escape the confines of her home, especially with him in it. She was convinced that being around him in such close quarters was damaging her brain cells. More than once, while sitting across from him sharing a meal, she'd ached for a repeat performance of what had gotten started in her kitchen. That kiss they'd shared had been everything she'd imagined and more. And it had given her a pretty good idea of just how skillful he was when locking lips with a woman. And his taste… The sampling had been too short but oh so sweet.

It didn't take much to recall the heat that had surrounded them, remember how just touching his hand had brought out combustible energy of the most erotic kind. Granted, the confines of this car were still generating heat, but it wasn't like it was back at her house. Here they had people around and a lot of traffic driving by.

"Margo?"

Had she been sitting there all this time just staring at his mouth? "Yes?"

"Why did you and Dylan call it quits after a year? Tell me."

Margo swallowed deeply. She heard a gentle plea, rather than a direct order, and that did something to her. This wasn't the first time she wondered how someone could be so dominantly aggressive one minute and then filled with such tenderness the next. How could Striker Jennings have such an unsettling effect on her at times? Was she letting her guard down because the police thought they had their man? Although she considered the risk to her to be at a decreased level, she was well aware that Striker was viewing it just as elevated as before.

"The reason I thought it was best to end things with Scott is because the relationship was going nowhere. He thought his work was more important than me."

There, she'd told him. Not the full story but enough. Now they could talk about something else. Like the weather. The championship game of football that would be played this weekend. The new president. But from the way he was looking at her, she had a feeling he wasn't ready to move on to another topic.

"He was a financial adviser, right?"

She lifted a brow. She hadn't told him that, so she could only conclude he'd done some digging on his own. "Yes. And I'm not going to waste my time asking how you knew."

He shrugged. "Part of my job to check out everyone in your life."

"Scott is not in my life. We should be concerned about an assassin, not Scott."

Instead of commenting on what she'd just said, he asked, "It's typical for financial advisers to work long hours, isn't it?"

Now it was her time to shrug. "Apparently so. Scott and I spent a lot of time together in the beginning. But then he started hosting all these dinners with clients and potential clients. They spent more time with him than I did."

"Did the two of you not talk about it? Did you not tell him how you felt?"

Margo scowled. Did Striker have a side gig as a relationship counselor or something? "Of course I told him how I felt, but he figured since I had a man making a six-figure salary that I should be smiling all over the place."

"The two of you were together for almost a year. Yet you never told him about your wealth. Why?"

Margo released a long, dramatic sigh. "Our relationship was not based on money but on mutual respect for each other." Or so she'd thought. "The issue never came up. He knew I had an uncle living in Virginia and that my parents were deceased. That was all he needed to know."

Striker disagreed. There was no way he would ever be seriously involved with a woman for almost a year without knowing everything there was about her. Both mentally and physically. Especially a woman like Margo Connelly. And she was not a woman a man could neglect. What was wrong with Dylan? What had he been smoking? "So he refused to change his ways and spend more time with you?"

She frowned at him. "Look, Striker, I wasn't this needy person who required a man's attention 24/7. However, I felt that if you're claiming to be my boyfriend, the least you can do is spend time with me on occasion. After a while he didn't even do that. He was too busy, going out of town or going to important dinners."

"Why didn't you go with him out of town or to these dinners?"

He could tell from the tilt of her chin that his question had hit a nerve. "I was never asked."

He stared at her. A part of him knew it took a lot to make that type of admission. What woman would want to admit that the man in her life had neglected her? He felt the hand that was holding his cup of tea tighten. Scott Dylan was an asshole, just as he'd thought reading the tone of Dylan's message on the card accompanying those flowers. What man in his right mind wouldn't want a woman like Margo by his side, every chance he got? The answer to that question came easily. A man who had a chick on the side.

Striker wondered if Margo had even thought of that possibility. He couldn't see her not doing so. She certainly didn't come across as being the kind of woman a man could easily fool. Although she wasn't saying, he had a strong feeling she suspected such a thing, which was probably the real reason she'd dumped the bastard. Emotions swelled within him that he wasn't used to feeling. The thought of any man treating her so shabbily pissed him off. "So why keep those flowers he sent?" he asked.

"Why not? He paid for them out of that six-figure salary he liked boasting about. They were pretty and I saw no reason to take out my irritation about Scott on a beautiful arrangement of flowers."

"He's trying to get you back," Striker said, wanting

to reach out and touch her hair, push a wayward strand away from her face, but knowing he couldn't do so.

"Yes. He got offended that I called it quits in the first place. He thought I should have been grateful for any amount of time I got to spend with him."

She paused a moment and then added, "Scott knows my position. Before I left New York, he made a nuisance of himself. I guess no woman had broken things off with him before. He didn't take that well and his ego got bruised. I had to threaten to go to the authorities if he kept it up."

"Kept what up?"

"Making an ass of himself."

"In what way?"

She shook her head. "Not important."

He wondered why she wouldn't say. Was it really not important as she claimed? What had the man done to make her threaten to go to the authorities? Had she ever confided in her uncle about it? For some reason, he doubted it.

"I have another question," he said, finishing off the last of his tea and squashing the cup to toss in the trash bag.

"No more questions about Scott, Striker. As far as I'm concerned, he's a closed subject."

For her sake, he hoped so. Not caring at the moment that his thoughts were too territorial, he knew Scott Dylan was the last man he would want to see her with again. "Okay, no more Scott Dylan questions. This one is about you. How did you develop an interest in designing wedding gowns?"

Striker could tell from the smile that touched her

lips that she had no qualms about answering that particular question.

"After my parents' deaths, Uncle Frazier sent me to a school in London. A man named Apollo Colter was my bodyguard, and I got to know his wife, Joan, and his son and daughter, Paul and Arian. Joan was a seamstress and I would sit and watch her work. I knew before leaving London to return to the States that I wanted to be a fashion designer. Deciding to concentrate exclusively on wedding gowns came later when I helped out a college roommate."

She smiled as if remembering the time. "Sharon was getting married the month after we graduated, and the woman she'd hired to design her gown became ill. So I stepped in. I had fun designing Sharon's wedding gown, and it got rave reviews. Sharon's father was a top executive on Wall Street and he bragged about my work. I got a job offer from a top clothing design firm in New York. I worked there for a couple years before deciding to go solo."

"Why not open a shop somewhere instead of working out of your home? It's not like you can't afford it."

She shrugged. "Uncle Frazier asked me the same thing," she said quietly. "I often work odd hours when designing a wedding dress. Late nights and early mornings. I feel more comfortable working at my house than staying late anywhere else. When I'm through for the night, instead of getting in my car and driving home, all I have to do is go upstairs, shower and go to bed. I guess the ideal place would be a shop that also had living quarters attached."

Striker was about to ask Margo another question, one specifically about her uncle's girlfriend, when his phone rang. From the ringtone he knew it was Stone-wall. "What's up?"

Intense anger boiled up inside him. "Got it." He didn't even take the time to put his phone back in his pocket. Instead he tossed it on the console. Without looking over at her, he slid his car seat back up, started the ignition and said in a tense tone, "Buckle up, Margo."

"What's wrong, Striker?" she asked, quickly snapping on her seat belt.

He pulled out of the parking lot. "Just what I suspected. The real assassin is still out there and he's struck again. Twice."

The color drained from her face. "Twice?"

"Yes. He made a hit on another juror, as well as one of the prosecuting attorneys."

Striker pulled into traffic, and when he came to a light, he glanced over at her. "You know what that means?"

He saw the tragic look in her eyes before she shook her head.

"That you're going to be stuck with me until that bastard is caught."

DR. RANDI FULLER watched the monitor. Her plane to South Carolina would take off in thirty minutes. She had returned home to Richmond from Charlottesville, staying just long enough to have a quick visit with her family, water her plants, gather up her mail and repack. Now she was on her way to Glendale Shores.

This would be one vacation she needed. She should have known better than to get involved with the Erickson case, given that Special Agent Tommy Felton was in charge of the investigation. She had hoped his attitude toward her had changed, but it hadn't.

She was about to grab a candy bar when her cell phone rang. She pulled it out of her purse. "Dr. Fuller."

"This is Chief Harkins, Dr. Fuller. You were right. We were holding the wrong man. The assassin struck again, less than an hour ago, killing two people. Both had been in the courtroom that day."

Randi pressed a finger to her temple. More senseless deaths. Anger spread through her. She'd tried warning the authorities, but they hadn't listened. "And why are you calling me, Chief Harkins? I told you that you had the wrong man but you didn't believe me. None of you even took my findings seriously."

There was a pause on the line and then the chief of police said, "I apologize for that, and we will now, Dr. Fuller. As for what we need you to do, I'd like for you to consider returning to Charlottesville and working with us to apprehend the real killer. The feds have their way of doing things, and the Charlottesville Police Department has theirs. My main concern is keeping the people in this city safe."

There was another pause and then he said, "Since news of those two killings hit the airwaves—after we had all but guaranteed the people we had the right guy in custody—this department and the feds are dealing with egg on our faces."

"Serves you right," Randi snapped.

"Yes, it does. So will you give us another chance and assist us?"

Randi nibbled on her bottom lip. Why should she assist them? It wasn't like she owed the Charlottesville Police Department or the FBI anything. But she did owe it to the people living in fear, who would continue living that way until the real assassin was caught.

"Dr. Fuller?"

She sighed. "The only way I'll consider helping is if I'm given a private office at police headquarters where I can work. That way I can concentrate solely on the case and everyone around me. Your people, doubters or otherwise, will see how I operate and gain more confidence in my abilities. I refuse to work out of a hotel room like before."

"That won't be a problem," Harkins said quickly.

Randi didn't tell him all the reasons she wanted to be located at police headquarters. She was convinced someone on the inside—probably more than one person—was working with Erickson and the only way she could expose those involved was to be in the thick of things.

"And another thing I want is to interview Erickson. He holds the key to everything. I need a guarantee that I'll get the chance to speak directly with Erickson. Alone. I need to get into his head. He might send off vibes that will tell me something about the person he hired to carry out these killings."

There was a pause. "I don't know if I can guarantee that, Dr. Fuller."

She frowned. "Then call me when you can. I'm at the Richmond International Airport and my plane leaves in less than twenty minutes. I intend to be on it unless you can assure me that I'll get *everything* I've asked for."

Harkins didn't say anything for a long moment. Then he said, "Okay. I give you my word that you'll get everything you've asked for…including a chance to talk to Erickson. Alone."

"Then I'll help." She heard his sigh of relief.

"Thanks. I'll send an unmarked police car to Richmond to pick you up from the airport."

CHAPTER THIRTEEN

"HERE, DRINK THIS."

Striker watched as Margo accepted the glass from him with trembling hands. He wished he had something stronger to give her, but wine was the only alcoholic beverage she had in her house.

He recognized that look in her eyes. It was the same one he saw in others, those he'd been hired to protect, when it finally hit them that their lives were in danger. Oh, they'd known it all along, but it was only when the shit got real did they finally get it. Margo was having one of those *I got it* moments. She took a sip. "Thank you," she said shakily, handing back the glass.

"No, keep it. You may want it later."

She lifted a troubled brow. "Why? Is there more than what you've told me?"

As if that hadn't been enough? "I haven't heard anything. Those other calls were from your uncle Frazier and from Roland."

She nodded. "Did you assure Uncle Frazier that I'm okay?"

Striker leaned back in the chair. "As best I could. He thinks you should move back home on his estate for a while."

She looked intently at him. "And what do you think?"

"Not my decision to make," he said, knowing how true that was. Her uncles, one known to her and the other unknown, would battle it out and decide. Striker knew from talking to Roland that he didn't agree with Frazier's suggestion. Striker agreed with Roland. Although Striker understood Frazier's concerns, the man needed to let Roland and his men do their job.

Striker tapped his fingers on the table a few times before asking her, "Do you want to go live on your uncle's estate?" He'd asked her that same question before and she'd been adamant she did not. He wondered if the recent series of events had given her a reason to change her mind.

"No. I'd rather stay here. I have work to do."

While he appreciated her efforts to keep as much normalcy in her life as possible, there was something she needed to understand. "If things get too risky for us to remain here, Margo, we will leave. And if that time comes, I hope you'll agree to put your life ahead of some wedding gown you were hired to make."

When she didn't say anything but merely took another sip of her wine, he felt the need to push the issue. When and if the time came, the last thing he'd put up with was any drama. "Margo," he said in a tone that conveyed that he expected her response.

"Alright, alright, enough already," she said with lips he noticed were trembling with anger. But he knew that anger was directed not at him but at the situation. It was ludicrous. He would agree with that. It was insane that the authorities had led everyone to believe they were safe after making that arrest. Someone's head was going to roll over such a monumental screwup.

Margo stood and began pacing. Just like he understood her anger, he also understood her frustration. Of course she would have known the female juror since they'd been sequestered together for six weeks. From what he'd heard, she'd been shot down while leaving the grocery store. How had the assassin known where the woman was? Had he been watching her? Security cameras around the store had revealed nothing. The workers and other customers hadn't noticed anything either, until they'd heard the shots fired. The assassin's new weapon was a high-powered rifle. Would he use the same gun from here on out?

Once Striker had gotten word of what had gone down, he had driven Margo home in record time. It was only when she was safe inside that he'd told her the identity of the female juror who'd been gunned down. Visibly shaken, Margo had crumbled in a heap on her sofa. It had taken everything within him not to go to her, pull her trembling body into his arms and hold her, comfort her and assure her that everything would be alright.

He drew in a deep sigh, knowing he couldn't go there and it wasn't even wise to think it. The shit had just gotten real for both of them. Deep down, a part of him had hoped the authorities had arrested the right guy. If they had, his time with Margo would soon be over. As much as he'd dismissed the idea earlier, he had thought more than once of possibly continuing a relationship with her after this. But these two recent hits had been a mental wake-up call for him. They had to get away from the personal and back to the professional. In order to do his job effectively, he had to reinstate the client–protector relationship they'd had before.

He watched as Margo continued to pace, and for a minute he considered telling her not to wear out the

kitchen floor. But he figured she wouldn't appreciate
his brand of teasing right now. And, frankly, given the
situation, he didn't feel like giving it. He didn't need
to rattle her any more than she already was. Besides,
he enjoyed seeing her pace. Definitely appreciated the
sway of her hips, as well as the bounce of her breasts.
He shouldn't notice such things at a time like this, but
what man wouldn't? She was a beautiful woman with a
great body that he craved more each and every day. But
hadn't he just decided to do away with the personal? Hell,
some things couldn't be helped, and a man's ingrained
ability to desire a woman was one of them. As long as
he didn't act on that desire, he was okay.

Suddenly, she stopped pacing and turned to him.
Striker froze when he saw something in her eyes that
he hadn't expected. "Talk to me, Margo. Get it out. Tell
me what you're feeling," he encouraged, while fighting
the urge to go to her and kiss those tears away.

STRIKER'S WORDS BROKE through Margo's anguish and
she drew in a deep breath. Maybe getting out what she
was feeling wasn't a bad idea. She could remember all
too well the perky blue-eyed blonde, who'd been married less than a year.

Nancy Snyder didn't mind letting everyone know
how much the separation from her husband bothered her.
In fact, one of the last things Nancy had said to Margo
was "I have a man waiting at home, who I haven't seen
in six weeks, and I can't wait to get to him." And now
Nancy was gone. Shot down in cold blood.

She stopped pacing to stare down at the floor. And
then there was Horace Amos, one of the prosecuting
attorneys. She'd seen him in the courtroom, heard him,

admired how he and his team had expertly and auda-
ciously proved without a shadow of a doubt just what
a heartless, cold-blooded killer Murphy Erickson was.
Now Horace Amos was dead. She couldn't help but
wonder who would be next. Her?

"Don't even think it, Margo."

Striker's sharp words made her jump. She saw in
his features a startling intuitiveness of what she'd been
thinking. How had he known? "How can I not think
it, Striker?"

She watched him push his chair back to stand. "Because I'm here and I won't let anything happen to you."

Margo sensed the truth in his words. She wasn't sure
how he would manage it if an assassin was hell-bent on
killing her, but a part of her believed he would. Over
the past week, she'd had moments where the reality of
what was happening had hit her hard, and this was one
of those times. And, for whatever reason when one of
those moments intruded, caught her off guard, it was
always Striker's presence that would bring calm to her
turbulent world…even if he had to go so far as to in-
cite her anger to do so.

He'd also incited her desire for something that was
as forbidden as it was yearned for. Okay, she would
admit it. And whether he knew it or not, she could
read him as well. Kind of. Enough. In the week they'd
spent together, she'd tried her best to figure out what
made Lamar "Striker" Jennings the person he was.
Much still remained a mystery. He was intentionally
keeping foggy certain aspects of himself and his life.
But what she was seeing clearer with each passing day
was that he was fighting the same longings, the same
desires that she battled. Margo knew he kept his dis-

tance, took great pains never to come close to her. And he definitely went out of his way not to touch her again.

Yet today, while sitting in a parked car and sharing a hamburger, they had talked. Although at times it had seemed more like an interrogation than a conversation, at least they'd communicated. She'd learned a little more about him and he'd certainly gotten to know more about her. Typically she was fairly easy to get along with unless someone tried getting into her business. She was overly protective of her privacy, but more than once she had let her guard down with Striker.

As she watched, he moved around the table with his hands shoved into the pockets of his jeans. For such a tall and built man, he had the ability to move with an ease that could take a woman's breath away. He had shaved that morning, she was sure of it. Yet she could see the dark stubble covering his entire jaw. Why did such a thing not only make him look dangerously serious as well as dangerously sexy? But nothing detracted from that sensual look, not even the holstered gun strapped to his shoulder.

He stood there watching her, not saying anything. He really didn't have to. The look in his eyes said it all. He was fighting this pull between them just like she was. For some reason, she felt the need to speak. To address what he'd said. "I know you won't let anything happen to me, Striker."

He nodded, as if satisfied by her response. Then he asked her, "Do you know how to shoot a gun?"

She actually got shivers at the question. "Heavens, no. Apollo tried teaching me and I couldn't even hold one in my hand. The thought that such an object is capable of taking a human life petrified me. If given a gun, I'd probably end up shooting myself. Pepper spray works just fine."

He shook his head. "Glad you told me that. I won't ever give you a gun for any reason."

It wouldn't bother her in the least if he didn't. She would leave the burden of protecting her solely on his shoulders, and roaming her eyes over him, she thought, *Those shoulders are massive.* He was standing there, staring at her, blatantly allowing all that manly heat to penetrate her space. Causing her heart rate to increase, shivers to ripple up her spine and quivers of need to infiltrate her very being.

"Don't look at me like that, Margo."

She swallowed. There was no need to ask what he meant. If there was any semblance of lust in her eyes, it was his fault. There was only one response to his deep, husky voice. "I can't help it, Striker."

He had taken a step toward her when his phone rang. The shrill sound should have shattered the moment, but it didn't. Not really. She stood there, as if glued to the spot as he continued to hold her gaze while pulling his cell phone out of his pocket.

"What?" he barked into the phone. Then in a mild tone, he said, "Everything is fine here."

Margo drew in a deep breath. Honestly? Did he think that? How could he when she was about to go up in flames thanks to his deep, penetrating gaze? She figured now was the time to escape into her workroom. To save herself before she was beyond rescuing.

She turned to leave.

"No. Don't go anywhere, Margo." She turned back around and saw he'd ended the call. He slowly strode toward her.

When he came to a stop directly in front of her, she swore she could hear the beat of his heart. "I think I should go, Striker," she said in a voice she was trying to keep calm.

"And I think you should stay," he countered.

Without saying anything else, he reached out his hand to her. She knew what it meant to let him touch her. Didn't Striker know what this could lead to? Was that what he really wanted? Did she? Granted, they had kissed before, but to cross this line again could cause problems if things between them went sour. Like her ability to trust him, listen to him or follow his orders when she should.

Considering all of that, she should be the sensible one and walk away, think of the danger surrounding them. She should concentrate on the fact that a killer was still out there and she could be his next intended victim. However, at that moment none of that mattered. The only thing she wanted to think about was a kiss that had ended too quickly, and that they needed to pick up where they'd left off.

Margo did the one thing she knew she shouldn't do and placed her hand in his.

STRIKER FELT IT the moment their hands touched—a yearning so acute it had parts of his body aching. Inwardly he was calling himself all kinds of fool, especially when just moments earlier he had decided to back away from the personal and concentrate on the professional. However, for a reason he couldn't quite understand, he was tired of backing away, didn't want to fight the intense attraction, the mind-blowing desire between them. At that moment he refused to consider the consequences or the possible outcome of his actions. If he crossed the line with Margo, if they had sex, how could they go back to just a protector–client relationship? The only thing he knew with certainty was that he wanted to kiss her. And he wanted to do it now.

He gently tugged on her hand and pulled her toward him, until their bodies were pressed close. That was when he released her hand to encircle her waist, gazing down at her. She had tilted her head back and it was as if she was offering her mouth to him. And, dammit, he intended to take it.

He didn't care if his phone rang; he wouldn't answer it. This time there would be no interruption. Nothing, he decided, would intrude into what was about to take place. Not a damn thing. With that thought firmly embedded in his mind, he tightened his hold around her waist, eased her even closer and lowered his head.

Striker took her mouth with the hunger he felt in every part of his body, immediately reacquainting himself with her taste. Without hesitation, his tongue skillfully and proficiently slid from one side of her mouth to the other, licking, exploring and tasting her with a yearning that stirred sensations that had never been riled before. A strong, primitive force had taken over his mind and his senses, pushing him to take as much of her mouth as he could while convincing himself that doing so was the only way to satisfy the raging desire coursing through him.

And the way she was kissing him back was fueling his fire and overwhelming him in a way that was totally earth-shattering. Why did the shape of her mouth seem perfect for his? Her taste was a total erection builder. Margo was storming his senses, igniting his fire. Stroke for stroke.

It was with great reluctance that he finally pulled his mouth away moments later, knowing he was leaving his taste with her just like she was leaving hers with him.

"Mercy." Margo breathed the word from a mouth that had just been thoroughly kissed. Talk about finishing what had gotten started a few days ago. Striker had left her breathless. The man had a startling sensuality that sent intense pleasure all through her. When had something like that ever happened to her before? She was convinced never.

Drawing in a deep breath, she took in his scent. Not only did he look good and taste good, but he also smelled good. Striker had the scent of a man. A man she wanted more of. And from the size of the erection that had been pressing hard against her middle a moment ago, he wanted more of her as well. The very thought had a heated effect on her.

It was then that his phone chimed with an incoming text and she appreciated it hadn't done so sooner. An interruption was the last thing she would have wanted when their mouths had been busy feeding off each other. But now she considered it a blessing. It would give her a chance to regain her senses. In fact, she tried looking everywhere but at him since she knew for certain he was staring at her.

"Margo?"

Hearing her name forced her to look at him. "Yes?"

"That was Quasar. Dinner is on the way."

"Alright." She nervously rubbed the front of her

jeans. "I guess I'll get back to Claudine's gown. Thanks for taking me to get that thread."

When she made a move to walk away, he reached out and grabbed hold of her hand. Intense desire shot all the way up her spine with his touch. "You okay, Margo?" he asked her.

She nodded. "Yes. I'm fine. I got just what I wanted, Striker," she said honestly.

Pulling her hand from his, she quickly walked toward her workroom.

ERICKSON LAY IN the bunk and stared up at the ceiling. The ultrabright fluorescent bulb nearly blinded him, but even that couldn't stop the smile that touched his lips. Did those bastards think a maximum-security cell could stop him from making sure things went off as planned? And was that crap they called food supposed to torture him? If that was what the fucks thought, then they had a lot to learn about him. It would take a lot more to break him, and in the end, his retaliation would cost them all. It was already costing them. They were running scared now.

He had intentionally given them four days to assume they had the right man. He'd seen the smiles, the gloating, the we've-got-you-now-bastard looks. Now shit was all over their faces, and what was really pissing them off was that they had no idea who they could trust. It was now obvious that someone on the inside was part of his network. For all they knew, it could be more than one person. And they were right. They would be surprised to learn who his people were. They would find out in due time that he knew every single thing about what was going on. He liked seeing the bastards sweat.

Pretty soon they would give in to his demands and he would get out of here. He would be free but not without a purpose. He had a lot of people he had to settle a score with. Not just those in the courtroom that day, but those responsible for his arrest in the first place. Traitors. Those he thought he could trust. They could try to run, but they could never hide. He intended to teach each and every one who thought they could betray Murphy Erickson a lesson they wouldn't forget. Ever.

CHAPTER FOURTEEN

"ARE YOU PLANNING on going to bed tonight?" Striker asked, leaning in the doorway of Margo's workroom. Seeing her reminded him of the kiss they'd shared earlier and just how much he'd enjoyed it. Knowing that was the last thing he should be thinking about, he glanced around the room. Aside from the sofa, the room had a couple of rectangular tables holding bolts of fabric, and some kind of lacy material was draped over several mannequins.

Margo placed the scissors down. "What time is it?"

"Past midnight."

She drew in a surprised breath and pushed a lock of hair away from her face. "I hadn't realized it was so late."

She'd kept herself busy. In a way, Striker saw that as a good thing. Margo was only human and, given the fact that two more people had lost their lives, he couldn't help wondering how she was *really* doing. It had to be driving her crazy knowing someone right this moment could be planning an attempt on her life. At least she had him protecting her. According to Stonewall, all security agencies in the city were booked solid. People were freaking out, and a number were arming themselves. Off-duty cops had been called in to maintain order, and additional federal agents had been called in as well.

Striker and Margo had eaten the dinner Quasar delivered, and afterward she had quickly fled to her work-room and hadn't been out since. He had taken a seat on the sofa that provided him a good view into her work-room while he was watching the news reports on the television.

Frazier had called earlier to talk to Margo. Roland had also called and would be talking to Stonewall about moving Margo to a safer location. Striker had warned Roland that would not go over well with his strong-willed niece.

Word had leaked to the press that the psychic inves-tigator who had been brought in had warned the feds and local police days ago they had the wrong man, but they hadn't listened.

Margo stood and stretched her body. Striker wished she hadn't done that when he felt his body immediately respond. He couldn't stop his eyes from roaming all over her; it was such a turn-on seeing a woman in a pair of skintight jeans and a tank top. Although she looked sexier than any woman had a right to look, she also ap-peared tired. He knew all her exhaustion wasn't due to working on that wedding dress. Although she might not ever admit it, she had to be under stress. There was no doubt in his mind that she was using her laptop to keep abreast of what was going on around the city. Knowing her name might be on some hit man's list had to be nerve-racking. A lot of women in her predicament would have caved under the pressure by now.

He couldn't help but admire her spunk, strength and fortitude, though he wondered if perhaps the reason she was still up past midnight, when usually she was in bed by nine, was partly because she was afraid of sleeping alone tonight.

Okay, Striker, you would look for any reason, any poor-ass excuse to keep her in arm's reach. He blamed it on the kiss he couldn't forget about. At some point he had to get a firm grip on the situation between him and Margo. Never before had he gotten involved with a client because things could get messy. He knew that, yet he couldn't get a handle on things when it came to her.

"Time for you to call it a night, don't you think? It's already another day," he said gently, when she made no attempt to leave the room.

He couldn't ignore the wary look on her face. "And then what, Striker? There were twelve of us on that jury and three alternates. So far three of us are dead. I can't help but wonder who will be next."

"It won't be you. I thought you believed that."

"I do, but I don't want it to be anyone."

He hadn't realized until that moment just how much she tended to think about others first, more than herself. For him that shed a little more light on the situation involving her uncle's girlfriend and why the thought of staying at the Connelly estate, even when her life could be in danger, was something she refused to do.

Striker had a feeling it wasn't the fact that she couldn't handle this Liz character but instead Margo's belief that if she did move back and drama ensued, it wouldn't be Margo whom Frazier would ask to leave. Although Striker didn't too much care for Frazier Connelly, he had a feeling he wouldn't put any woman, girlfriend, live-in lover or otherwise before his niece. Chances were Margo knew that as well and was actually doing Liz a favor…although Striker doubted Frazier's girlfriend saw it that way.

"Excuse me. You're standing in the doorway, Striker. Blocking it."

"Oh." So he was. He was thinking seriously about suggesting that she try squeezing by him. The thought of her doing such a thing had every cell in his body vibrating in desire. Deciding that wouldn't be a good idea, especially since he was pretty damn hot for her already, he slowly moved away from the doorway. "Sorry."

"No problem."

Except there *was* a problem, and it was one that had nothing to do with the threat of a hit man. It had everything to do with the two of them staying under the same roof together after sharing one hell of a scorching kiss. He knew her taste. He knew how she felt in his arms with their bodies pressed together. How his hard erection felt snuggled close to her middle. She'd almost made it past him when, for some reason, he reached out and snagged her hand. He wasn't sure why he'd done it. Was it because he knew that, once she got to her bedroom and closed the door, he wouldn't see her again until morning? Or was it because he needed her touch…desperately? Or could the reason be that once she was behind that closed bedroom door, he would get an earful of the sounds she'd make—stripping off her clothes, showering, putting on her bed clothes and sliding between the sheets. The hot and steamy visuals flowing through his mind would keep him hard all night.

Just as he'd expected whenever they touched, a surge of desire ripped through him, and from her expression, it had torn through her as well. Striker was well aware of all the dynamics that made up such an intense attraction—that could make all sorts of wicked, naughty and sinful thoughts go through a person's head. But more important, he understood how such magnetism could exist between him and Margo. It had to do with opposites attracting. And they were as opposite as opposites could get.

"Striker?"

He looked into her eyes and wished he hadn't. "Yes?"

Margo watched Striker's brows furrow as if he was trying to decide whether to let go of her hand or not. Little did he know she didn't have a problem with him holding her hand. Her problem was him standing there like he wasn't sure what his next move should be. Honestly, it really shouldn't be that hard to figure things out. If he was in doubt and needed a little coaxing, then she had no problem doing so. Because—bottom line—she was tired of avoiding him. Tired of yearning for something that was right here and accessible. Tired of wondering if another kiss could possibly be as good as the last one.

"Are you going to stand there all night or are you going to give in to what we both want right now?" she asked him bluntly, and this time she was the one tugging on his hand to bring him closer to her.

He didn't hesitate in coming. Margo wondered if she would regret any of this tomorrow. Possibly. And chances were she would try to figure out why she was giving in to her attraction to Striker after she'd fought so hard not to do that very thing. But she was a goner with him standing there, looking sexier than any man had a right to, while holding her hand and staring at her in a way that had the nipples of her breasts hardening against her top. There was no way he couldn't see the effect his touch was having on her. Just like she could clearly see what hers was having on him. A huge erection was something most men couldn't hide and he was no exception.

"This isn't right, you know," he said, releasing her hand and taking a step closer to wrap his arms around her waist.

She could feel the hardness of him pressed against the juncture of her legs. "What isn't?" she asked, trying to keep her voice at a normal pitch instead of a breathless whisper. "The fact that we like copping kisses off each other whenever the mood hits?"

He was studying her mouth in a way that had blood running fast and furious through her veins. "Copping kisses isn't why I'm here," he said gruffly. "My job is to—"

"I know what your job is, Striker. Trust me. You've made that pretty clear. Just chalk the kisses up to us sharing fringe benefits."

The last thing she wanted was for him to get all honorable when she was feeling pretty indecent right now. He wanted to continue to fight her, block this desire, this connection being forged between them. She understood, since she'd tried doing that same thing. But now she was willing to put fighting on the back burner. They had agreed on a truce, hadn't they? Besides, as far as she was concerned, they had some unfinished business to take care of.

He snorted. "Yeah, at the risk of Roland kicking my ass if I step over the line."

She tilted her head back and met his gaze. "And who's going to tell your boss anything? You certainly don't seem like the kiss-and-tell kind. Besides, why would this Roland care when it's just another job for his firm? The way I see it, unless I complain about your services, there shouldn't be any ass-kicking going on."

She intended to say more, but he began lowering his head, and before she could catch her next breath, his mouth took hers hostage.

STRIKER HUNGRILY FED off Margo's mouth like the greedy bastard that he was. It was a kiss meant to rob her of her senses, drain strength from her body and show her he was doing a lot more than just copping a kiss. He was branding her. He'd deliberately started off this way with a deep tonguing that had her moaning. After a while he would slow things down and tease her mouth, nibble from corner to corner and lick it all over. Then he would go for hard and deep all over again.

She was wrong to think this was just another gig for Roland's firm. Margo didn't know him being here was personal. Probably as personal as it could get for Roland. But at the moment he wanted to eradicate Roland from his mind and enjoy this kiss. This woman. Her taste.

Why was he enjoying her so much? He'd never gotten personally involved with a client he'd vowed to protect before. Even when the women had come on to him and wanted to blur the line, he'd been firm and wasn't having it. Then why was he having all of this and then some from Margo Connelly? How could any woman's kiss make him feel like he was in one hell of a sensuous daze? A daze that was quickly headed toward something he needed to put a stop to right now? The red-hot passion was all too quickly igniting flames of desire. He was feeling it with every stroke of his tongue and with every countering stroke of hers.

The ringing of a phone intruded, and he inwardly muttered a curse. However, this time it wasn't his phone responsible for the untimely interruption but hers. He broke off the kiss. Who would be calling her at this hour? And why? She'd spoken to her uncle earlier, so who else would be calling? Was it a suspicious call like the one she'd gotten last week?

As if she remembered that particular call as well, she nervously licked her lips before pulling the phone from her jeans pocket. From the expression on her face, he had a pretty good idea who the caller was, even before he'd made the connection with his phone.

"Scott? Why are you calling me?"

"I've been listening to the news. Are you okay?"

Striker frowned. Had he known Margo had been part of the jury and was in danger? From the look in her eyes, she was wondering the same thing.

"Why wouldn't I be okay?"

"Because of that crazy man going around killing folks in your town. It's all over the news. I heard his intended targets are people who were in the courtroom of some trial, but I think you should leave Charlottesville just to be on the safe side. He might get trigger-happy and start shooting innocent bystanders."

So he didn't know she'd been part of the jury but had called out of concern. Maybe Scott Dylan wasn't as big of an asshole as Striker had thought. He quickly dismissed that assumption upon hearing the man's next statement.

"I'd be glad to send you money for a flight but only if you make your destination my doorstep. I miss you, Margo. I need to see you. It's been a year. You can't be making too much money designing those gowns. I got another promotion recently and—"

"I don't need your money, Scott."

Striker shook his head. So the asshole still didn't know how wealthy Margo was. Striker knew he should hang up the phone and let them talk privately. After all, Scotty was her concern, not his. But something made him hang on. He refused to think it had anything to do with jealousy.

"Of course you need my money," Scott said. "Granted, you've never asked me for anything, but you've always known it was there if you needed it."

With a price tag on it, no doubt, Striker thought as he leaned against the desk in the room. What a wuss. Didn't he know most women didn't appreciate a man making them feel dependent?

Margo shot him a dark frown before saying to him, "This is a private call. Do you mind?"

Instead of answering her, he merely gave her an even darker frown.

"Margo?" Scott interrupted, reclaiming their attention. "Who are you talking to? Is someone there with you?"

"That's not any of your business, Scott," she snapped. "You aren't supposed to call me anyway."

"I have every right to call you. I didn't break things off with you. You broke things off with me."

Striker shook his head, wondering if the man had actually heard what he'd just said. Was Dylan such a simpleton that he didn't realize that when a woman broke off with a man, it meant the man no longer had a right to call? Shit, it meant he'd lost any rights.

"And I broke things off for a reason, or have you forgotten that?" Margo said angrily.

Instead of answering her question, Scott said, "I want to know who is there with you, Margo."

"That's none of your business, Scott."

"You are my business. You need me."

Striker thought he should go ahead and release the line before he was tempted to tell the prick a few not-so-nice things. Dylan was Margo's problem, and by rights, Striker knew that he should stay out of it and let her handle her business. Scott Dylan wasn't a threat. Not a real one. Striker decided there was no reason he should be listening in on her call. He was about to get off the line when Dylan's next words stopped him.

"You just won't forgive me for what I did, will you, Margo?"

Now, that piqued Striker's interest. What had he done? Whatever the deed, it was obvious from the daggers Margo was shooting over at Striker that she didn't want him to know. Too bad. There was no way he would release the call now.

"I don't want to discuss it," Margo snapped at Dylan. "Stop talking about it, will you?"

Probably because she doesn't want me to hear it, Striker thought.

Too bad Dylan didn't do as she asked. "I was wrong for getting that guy to scare you like that. I hoped you would get rattled enough to move in with me. He was just supposed to make you afraid of living there alone. How was I to know he would take it to that level?"

WTF? Striker straightened from leaning against the desk. What exactly had the man done to scare her?

He glanced back at Margo, and she deliberately looked away. "Look, Scott, I have to go."

"Why? And who's there with you? Why won't you tell me?"

Striker couldn't hold his anger anymore. "Because she doesn't want to tell you, so fuck off."

There was silence on the other end, and then in an incensed voice Dylan asked, "Who the hell are you?"

"If Margo wanted you to know, she would have told you. Now, don't call back disturbing us tonight or any other night. Forget you have this number."

Striker clicked off his phone and then, to make sure Margo didn't say anything else to the man, used his phone to remotely end her call to Dylan as well.

She stood there, glaring at him, obviously furious. "You had no right to say anything."

Maybe not, but he would deal with the consequences later. What he wanted now were answers. "Just what in the hell did that person Dylan hired do?"

CHAPTER FIFTEEN

MARGO CROSSED HER arms over her chest, angry with Scott for talking too much and totally upset with Striker for having the audacity to listen. How dare he invade her privacy like that? Did he think those kisses they'd shared had given him some rights? Well, she had news for him. No man had rights where she was concerned. "I'm not telling you anything, Striker. You had no right to—"

"At the moment I don't give a damn about any rights," he snapped. "What did he do? You either tell me or I'll report him to Roland and let him explain that bit of information to your uncle."

She dropped her hands. "That call has nothing to do with the reason you're protecting me."

"Doesn't matter. I'm sure Frazier would love to know what Dylan did to you. Once your uncle finds out, I doubt he'll last in that cushy, six-figure-salary job that he thinks so much of."

"What Scott did is not my uncle's business. Nor is it yours. I handled it."

"How? By running back here to Charlottesville?"

Margo crossed her arms over her chest again, livid. "That is not why I moved home."

"Then why did you? Can you explain that?"

"I don't have to explain anything."

Striker was about to tell her just how wrong she was about that when his phone went off. He recognized the ringtone. For Stonewall to call this time of night meant something was up. "What's going on?"

"The lights are still on there. Why haven't you and Margo gone to bed?"

"Why are you interested?" Now was not the time for his friend to get nosy.

Stonewall laughed. "Quasar said he's been picking up on a lot of sexual tension over there. If things are getting too hot for you, let me know and I'll send in a replacement."

Striker rolled his eyes. "You can kiss it, Stonewall. And tell Quasar to mind his own damn business." He rubbed his face and saw Margo head toward the door, but he eased over to block her from leaving.

"I need to go upstairs, Striker," Margo snapped.

"Not until I go up there with you. You know the rules, Margo."

"Can the two of you argue some other time?" Stonewall cut in to say. "There's a reason for my call."

"You mean it wasn't to harass me?"

"Not this time. Janice is working the monitors and noticed a car—black sedan—slowly driving by Ms. Connelly's place twice tonight. At first we assumed it was an unmarked police car, but now we aren't so sure. We're waiting for someone from police headquarters to call us back."

The hairs on the back of Striker's neck stood up. "Call me if anyone sees that car again or if anything else looks suspicious."

"Will do."

Striker ended the call. He realized Margo was studying him. She hadn't even pretended not to eavesdrop. "Now, Margo, where were we? Oh yeah, you were about to tell me just what that guy did to scare you."

She crossed her arms over her chest. He wished she wouldn't do that. It placed too much damn emphasis on her breasts. And they were breasts he recalled his chest rubbing against whenever they kissed.

"What did Stonewall want? What's going on?"

Leaning in the doorway, he placed his arms across his chest as well. "If you don't answer my question, I won't answer yours."

She glared at him. "Play your games by yourself, Striker. Move out the way so I can go upstairs."

He was about to move out of her way when his cell phone went off. It was Stonewall again. "You got something?"

"Yes. I just heard from police headquarters and that car wasn't one of theirs or the feds. I need you to kill all the lights in the house for at least an hour. We want to see if that black sedan does another drive-by. Someone might be checking to see if anyone's awake."

"Okay."

He hung up the phone and looked at Margo. There was no way he could avoid telling her what was going on now. He saw the way her eyes widened as he relayed Stonewall's message and could all but hear her heart thumping in her chest. "Who do they think it is?"

"They aren't sure. Stonewall is on it, so don't worry about a thing."

She lifted her chin. "I'm not worried."

Yes, you are, he thought and decided not to point out how she'd begun fidgeting with the hem of her top and showing a little bit of skin, which he didn't mind seeing. "We need to turn off all the lights for a while. And it will be best if we stay down here instead of going upstairs."

When he reached for the light switch, she intercepted and then snatched her hand back. He figured she'd felt the same tingling sensation that he had when they'd touched. "What did you do that for?" he asked her, frowning.

"Why are you turning off the lights down here? I thought you said we needed to stay down here. Why not go up the stairs and turn those lights off first?"

He shoved his hands into the pockets of his jeans to deflect the tingling sensation he still felt. "If someone is watching the house, from the outside it will appear as if we've gone to bed for the night when we turn the lights off on the first floor and then upstairs. We'll use the flashlight on our cell phones to come back down here and sit for a while."

"Sit?"

"Yes, sit and talk. You still need to tell me what that guy did."

"I'm not telling you anything, Striker."

She followed him out the room and he decided not to argue with her. He would get the information out of her no matter what it took.

THE HOUSE WAS completely dark as if they were tucked away in bed. The only light was from one of the lamp-posts that lined the street, its soft illumination coming through the window.

Margo was sitting on the love seat, and Striker was stretched out on the sofa. So far he hadn't brought up

Scott, and she was grateful for that. But she had to assume he would at some point. He'd been too adamant earlier about finding out. She had put the episode behind her and didn't want to talk about it again. Like she'd told him, she had handled it. And regardless of what Scott thought, there could never be anything between them again. Some men just didn't know when to let go, and she was finding out that Scott was one of those types.

Margo heard Striker ease up on the sofa into a sitting position. "Ready to talk?"

She rolled her eyes. "I have nothing to say."

"I need to know what that guy did, Margo."

She wanted to scoff at those words but couldn't. There was something in Striker's voice, she couldn't say exactly what, that seized her and wriggled through her defenses in a way she wasn't prepared for. "Why? So you can tell my uncle?"

"No, I won't tell your uncle unless I feel there is a security need for me to do so."

"I told you I handled it."

"But you should not have had to."

That much was true. But Scott had underestimated her. He hadn't really known her. He still didn't know her. "I'm a big girl, Striker. I can take care of myself." *Except in a situation like this*, she thought, *when there's a crazy man out there who wants me dead.*

"What did he do? Tell me." He swallowed. "Please."

That last word was softly spoken, but she heard it whether he'd wanted her to or not. There was a deep sense of care and concern in that single word. If their roles were reversed, she knew she'd be just as insistent because she would care as well.

"Okay, I'll tell you." She paused a moment to collect her thoughts, to recall memories she'd rather leave in the past. But she was bringing them into the present for him. "Scott had been trying to get me to move in with him for a while, and I kept refusing. He couldn't understand why, since he figured it would save me a ton of money in the long run. On the other hand, I couldn't understand why he would want me to share space with him when he wasn't paying much attention to me anyway. Eventually I realized it was all about control. He wanted me to be the dependent little woman who needed him."

She paused a moment and then said, "I began getting phone calls in the middle of the night." *Similar to the one I got last week*, she thought. "The person wouldn't say anything, but I knew he was there. I could hear him breathing."

"Did you report it to the police?"

"Yes, but all they did was file a report and tell me to get my number changed. I did. I thought that would be the end of it. But that wasn't the case."

"What happened next?"

She closed her eyes. To some it might have been a harmless prank, but she hadn't seen it that way. "Scott must have told the guy how terrified I was of snakes, so he put several in my car. They weren't poisonous, but I had no way of knowing that. The guy claimed the plan was for me to see one of them the minute I opened the door. I didn't and had driven a block when all those snakes seemed to come out of nowhere."

Margo doubted that she would ever forget that day. "I freaked out, nearly hit a post and jumped a curb before bringing my car to a stop and rushing out.

Luckily there hadn't been much traffic on the road. I don't want to think about what could have happened if there was."

"How did you find out who was behind it?" She could tell Striker was trying to hold back his anger.

"My college roommate, Sharon, whose wedding gown I made, is married to an FBI agent. As a favor, Walter checked out a few things after the local police claimed they had more serious crimes to investigate. It was easy enough to trace who'd recently purchased that many snakes. When Walter paid Freddie Siskin a visit, he confessed. Said he was a college friend of Scott's and was doing him a favor by scaring me. Scott claimed he hadn't known about the snakes, and that all Freddie was supposed to do was make those phone calls."

"You knew Siskin?"

"No, never met him. I still haven't met him. I let Walter and my attorney handle everything. I had no desire to see a man who could be so despicable."

"And you didn't press charges?" Striker's tone was furious.

"No. Scott agreed to pay for the damage to my car. Since there were no injuries, I didn't get the police involved. I just wanted Scott out of my life. He wanted to make it up to me, but I refused to let him. Then I decided it was time to move home, which I had been thinking of doing anyway."

Striker was quiet for a minute, and then he said, "I hope I never get the chance to meet Scott Dylan."

Even with the dim light shining through the window, she could see the tightness of his jaw. "Why?"

His dark eyes stared at her. "Because if I ever do, I plan to pulverize his ass."

"I told you I handled it."

"And just how did you handle it, Margo?" he asked in a voice she could tell had reached its boiling point. "You just said you didn't press charges."

"No—instead both Scott and Freddie Siskin agreed to give a specified amount to my favorite charity."

"And what charity is that?"

"The Foster Child Foundation. When I lost both my parents I was lucky to have Uncle Frazier. Other kids aren't that fortunate. This particular foundation provides college scholarships for kids in foster care."

"How much did they have to pay up?"

"One hundred thousand dollars each. And they had only thirty days to get the funds together. It was either that or acquire records as felons."

As far as Striker was concerned, she still had let them off too damn easy. What man would do something like that to a woman he claimed to care about? Like he told her, he hoped his path never crossed with Dylan's. He'd meant what he'd said about what he would do. And the crazy thing of it was that the man expected her to take him back after all that bullshit. How would Dylan handle it if he ever found out Margo was loaded and hadn't really needed his six-figure salary anyway?

Margo shifted on the sofa, and Striker's gaze moved over her. She was now sitting cross-legged on the love seat. "How much longer do we have to just sit here?" she asked.

He glanced at his watch. It was close to two in the morning. They'd been sitting down here for almost an hour now. "It shouldn't be too much longer. They want to see if that same car drives by again."

"Is that what assassins do? Scope out where the person lives before making a hit?"

"I wouldn't know." He was lying because in a way he did know. While in the slammer, one of his fellow inmates had been an assassin for a drug lord. The man claimed his method of elimination was dependent on the target. Of course, Striker wouldn't tell Margo that. She had enough to be stressed out about already. Although he agreed they needed to take precautionary measures, he was hoping the car was a false alarm.

At that moment his cell phone went off. It was Stonewall. "Yes, Stonewall?"

"It's been an hour and nothing has happened. Go on to bed and we'll continue to keep an eye on things over the monitors here. If anything develops, we'll let you know."

"Okay." He then clicked off the line.

"Did Stonewall say we can go to bed now?"

Why did she have to make it sound as if they were sharing a bed and not sleeping in separate rooms? "Yes."

"Good."

He moved across the room to turn on the lights and then glanced back over at Margo. She had eased from the sofa and was stretching her body again. He stood there, almost spellbound, and watched her. He couldn't breathe. Could barely swallow. At that moment he almost forgot his name. He couldn't help it and was all but shivering at the sensations racing through him. Evidently she didn't know how good she looked stretching her limbs like that or she wouldn't be calling attention to herself. Or maybe she did know and was being coy about it.

Striker dismissed that notion immediately. The one thing he did know about Margo was that she didn't have a coy bone in her body. A few nosy ones and a couple of flippant ones that went along with that luscious mouth, but there was nothing coy about her.

His nostrils flared when he picked up her scent, the same one he'd been inhaling all day. How could she still smell so good at this hour?

"I thought we had to keep the lights out."

"That car probably won't return tonight, so it's okay. But if you prefer, we can keep them off," he said, flipping the switch and throwing them into darkness again. And then he began moving toward her.

When he came to a stop in front of her, she tilted her head to look up at him. "What's going on, Striker?"

When he didn't answer but reached for her hand, she asked in a strained voice, "What do you think you're doing?"

He felt it just like she did—sexual attraction that had the ability to overpower them, send spikes of heat through their bodies even when they didn't want it to. When they couldn't fight it. This time it was more intense than ever. Hell, even his balls were on fire.

He eased in a little closer, so close their bodies touched. Their hands were still joined, their fingers entwined, and what felt like electrical shock waves were traveling all through their limbs. He felt a deep thumping in his chest from the forceful acceleration of his heart.

"Striker, what are you doing?"

She posed the question again. He figured Margo needed to pay better attention since she should know by now what usually followed the hand-holding. "I'm about to kiss you, Margo."

Pulling her even closer into his arms, he lowered his mouth to hers.

CHAPTER SIXTEEN

PROTECTOR OR SEDUCER? Which one was the real Striker Jennings? Margo wondered. She had a feeling the answer was both, although it was the seducer who was winning her over right now. He'd already demonstrated just what an experienced kisser he was. Now he was taking all that skill to a whole other level.

Her knees had nearly buckled the moment his tongue had entered her mouth. Then, without wasting any time, he'd begun mating his mouth sensuously with hers. She closed her eyes, feeling whatever strength she had left drain from her body. Resisting him was clearly not an option at this point.

She had come to know his taste that first time and had savored it with each kiss since. But now she wanted to do more than just savor. She wanted to consume it in a way that would be downright scandalous. When had Margo Connelly ever done anything shocking? Disreputable? Outrageous?

Never. Until now.

The instant his mouth had come down on hers, he had captured her tongue and held it hostage while he sucked on it. And he was doing so in a way that had her heart pounding and the juncture of her thighs throbbing. How in the world were they supposed to hold off the bad guys when they couldn't hold off each other?

And then there was the way he was embracing her, deliberately letting her feel his long, hard erection pressing against her belly. The feel of that swollen shaft sharpened every sense she had, and little by little she was caught up in a wave of desire so thick she was becoming disoriented. They were wearing clothes, but they might as well be wearing nothing at all. Heat was consuming her, and she knew it had to be consuming him as well.

Instead of completely ending the kiss, Striker released her tongue to begin nibbling around her mouth, corner to corner. Then he took the tip of his tongue and licked where he'd nibbled, causing a drugging rush of need to swamp her.

"Striker?"

"Hmm?"

"Where will this lead?" She wanted to know. Had to know. Especially when she was standing here and letting him touch and taste her in a way no other man had done before.

Margo was well aware how his hands had been working her backside. When had a man kneaded her butt cheeks like dough? Pressed them closer to the fit of him. Included them in this process, and this was a process. If his intent was to drive her insane, make her lose her senses, then he was doing a real good job at it.

Then she noticed they were moving. He was leading her backward toward the sofa. When the backs of her legs brushed against the sofa, he released her mouth only to begin gently sucking on her lower lip. She could hear herself moan. He had quite a knack for making her do that.

When he finally pulled back, it was to stare down at her, his lips still wet from their kiss. "You want to know where this will lead, Margo?" he asked in a deep, husky voice, as he removed his holster carrying the Beretta and placed both on the table.

He was looking at her in a way that was so incredibly hot, she could barely breathe. The best she could do was nod in answer.

"It leads here." And then he lowered her to the sofa.

STRIKER KNEW BETTER. He, of all people, knew this shouldn't be happening, yet he wasn't of a mind to stop it. He didn't want to think about how things would be in the morning. After all the heat and lust had worn off. How their protector–client relationship would have taken a hit it could never recover from. Still, knowing all of that meant nothing right now. Not when he eased Margo on the sofa and followed her there, straddling her body.

They were still clothed, but he wasn't sure just how long that would last. Not when he wanted to strip every single stitch off her. Not when he wanted to taste her all over but especially between the legs and then slide inside of her.

"I want to pleasure you," he finally said, not able to remain silent any longer.

He could see the shocked look that appeared on her face. "Why are you surprised by what I just said?" He definitely needed her to explain.

She licked her lips as she stared up at him and said, "I've never had a man tell me that."

"No?"

"No. Not that I've had a lot of sexual encounters. I'm not in the habit of sleeping around for the sheer fun of it."

If not for the fun of it, then what? he wondered. As long as it was safe sex that both people wanted, then he didn't see a thing wrong with it. Especially if you didn't intend to get serious, which was against his policy. And that was him. He didn't believe in getting serious about a woman. Too complicated. What if he let a woman down by not being there when she really needed him…like he'd done with Wade? Dealing with the guilt of failing one person was enough. He didn't want or need to take on another.

"It doesn't matter how many lovers you've had, Margo. What matters is making sure pleasure is shared. I can't wait to show you what I mean."

The blush that touched her features suggested her other lovers had never been so blunt. "Can I ask you something?" He leaned in and licked around her lips with his tongue. He loved her taste.

"What?" she asked in a near groan.

Striker figured if his licks were getting to her, then how would she handle his brand of foreplay? When time slipped by and he'd been so into licking around her mouth that he hadn't answered, she repeated her question. "What? You had something to ask me."

He leaned back and looked down at her mouth. It was wet. He liked that look. "Yes, I have something to ask you. Are you into oral sex?"

MARGO'S MOUTH DROPPED OPEN. Shocked, she looked up at him. What man would ask a woman a question like that? Evidently the same man who had no problem telling her he wanted to pleasure her. She'd certainly never had such conversations with Scott or Brock.

"Do you have an answer for me or are you trying to decide, Margo?"

She released the breath she'd been holding. "Truth is, I—I—"

He lifted a brow. "You what?"

This was really getting out of hand, she thought. Why weren't they just going at it? Why so much discussion? Doing so should be cooling the flame, but for some reason, talking to him about sex was actually stimulating the fire. "I've never engaged in it before."

He looked at her strangely. "By *it* you mean oral sex, right? And not sex?"

Why had his voice gone to a deep, raspy tone, one that was like a sensuous stroke down her spine? "Of course I've had sex before," she said, nonplussed. If he was waiting for her to reveal anything she and Scott had done in the bedroom, that wouldn't be happening. Although she was certain Striker had pretty much figured out at least one thing they hadn't done.

"Why all the questions about that, Striker?"

"About oral sex?"

"Yes."

"Because before I get inside of you I want to taste you all over."

At that moment Striker didn't want to think about the fact that good ol' Scotty had dropped the ball, big-time. Damn, it was hard to keep his chest from expanding, because he intended to pick up the dropped ball and run with it. By the time he finished with Margo, she would know what she'd been missing.

Starting now.

He leaned closer and homed in on her mouth, taking it with a hunger that had an intense degree of lust spreading through his body. When she began returning his kiss, he could actually feel his erection swell even more.

When he broke off the kiss, he whispered against her lips, "I want you, Margo." He felt she needed to know that.

He gazed at her wet and swollen lips and the desire-filled eyes staring back at him. "And I want you too, Striker."

A smile touched his lips. And he continued to smile when he eased off her to stand and to pull her up with him. "You are one sexy lady," he said, brushing his fingers along her wrist and feeling her tremble. "Do you know how often I think about seeing you naked?" he said, bringing her hand up to his mouth so he could kiss it.

"No."

"Every damn time I hear you in the shower."

She looked at him strangely. "You can't hear me in the shower."

"Yes, I can," he said, using the tip of his tongue to lick around her wrist.

"No, you can't. My bathroom doesn't share a wall with your bedroom, so there's no way you can hear me."

He released her hand to pull the tank top over her head and tossed it aside. "Okay, then, I can't." He wasn't about to argue with her. Not when he had better things to do.

"Striker?"

"Hmm?" She was wearing a skin-tone lace bra and through all that lace he could see her nipples. Hard, tight and protruding.

"I asked you a question, Striker," she said in a voice that was rising in anger. "How can you hear me in the shower?"

He needed to get her mind off what he'd said and knew this would be one sure way to do it. Reaching out, he cupped her breasts, loving the way they felt in his hands. Thick. Full. Firm.

"Striker?"

He leaned in close to release the clasp of her bra and then eased the straps from her shoulders. Perfect. His tongue thickened just looking at them. And when he took the pad of his thumb and rubbed a turgid nipple, she said his name again. This time between breathless gasps.

Instead of answering her, he leaned toward her chest and eased a nipple between his lips and began sucking on it. He felt her stomach clenching against him and knew he was boosting her desire, making her want him as much as he wanted her. He was getting her wet.

He didn't want her just wet; he wanted her drenched. When he released her right breast, he immediately shifted his mouth to the other one, giving it the same intense attention.

"Oh, Striker!"

He pulled back. He wasn't ready for her to come yet. He had a lot of other places to taste. Lowering his body to his knees, he removed the flat shoes from her feet. She placed her hands on his shoulders to keep her balance while he did so. His shoulders burned where her hands touched.

"I could have taken off my own shoes," he heard her say.

"I wanted to do it." Didn't she know that when a man

undressed a woman he covered all bases, from head to toe, and especially those areas in between? Her red nail polish was a total turn-on and complemented a pair of pretty feet. He appreciated a woman who liked looking good in her clothes, under her clothes, in her shoes and out of them.

"Now for these," he said, reaching up to gently grab the waistband of her jeans. "They have to go." He couldn't wait to see what color panties she was wearing, what style. He had a feeling it didn't really matter. They would definitely look good on her.

Another thing he noticed was that she had a pretty flat stomach that was attached to a gorgeous pair of hips. Her navel was a cutie as well, and he couldn't resist leaning in close and copping a lick. Then another. And another.

"Striker?"

"Hmm?" He hoped she wouldn't tell him to stop because he enjoyed the taste of her skin. He finally pulled back and looked up at her and smiled. "You like that?"

"Yes, I like it a lot."

He thought about how much he loved her honesty while he slowly eased down her zipper, and when he saw a flash of red, his erection hardened even more. Red panties on a woman was like seeing fire. Something inside of him—probably the desire to bury his head between her legs—made him quickly pull her jeans down past her hips, curvaceous thighs and gorgeous legs. After she'd stepped out of them and stood there in her red lace bikini-cut panties, he felt his balls nearly explode. She was so friggin' hot.

"When will I get the chance to take off your clothes?"

she asked, and he could tell she was nervous about being on display. He would remedy that soon.

"Right now, it's all about you," he said, tugging the panties down her legs. Those mesmerizing dark eyes staring down at him made him wish he could make it all about her every day.

Striker drew in a sharp breath and knew he had to pull himself together and stop thinking such foolish thoughts. There could be no *every day* with her, and for him to even think otherwise was as crazy as it could get.

He leaned back on his haunches and stared at the juncture of her thighs. She had a gorgeous-looking sex. Those womanly folds were plump, ready to be divided and conquered. Or should he say divided and taken. In his frame of mind it was the same thing. He couldn't wait to taste her. "You look amazing."

MARGO WASN'T SURE what she could say to that. No man had ever been in awe of her there, and no one had ever said they thought she looked amazing. Scott would give her compliments, but they couldn't compare to some of the things that came out of Striker's mouth.

And talking about his mouth…

He was staring at her and licking his lips. This was where she could only imagine what would happen next since she had no experience of a man going down on her. She had heard her college roommates whispering about men doing it to them. She'd only listened, unable to add a thing. But she'd definitely taken something away. Curiosity.

Now she was about to get her curiosity appeased. But was she ready for Striker Jennings? Could she handle this? There was no doubt in her mind the man was intensely sexual. He probably had the ability to make a woman scream, and she never screamed.

She then recalled what he'd said about hearing her in the shower. Was her bedroom bugged? Had he been listening to everything she did without her knowing it all this time? Was bugging her bedroom one of the security measures the tech guy Bruce had done? One that Striker had refused to elaborate about? If he thought making love to her would make her forget about him invading her privacy that way, he was wrong. But for now she was more than willing to concentrate on other things, like how Striker was making her feel.

Not sure what was in store and wary of how much she could handle, she was about to take a step back when he reached out and grabbed hold of her hips. And the moment he touched her, she knew she would see this through. Margo wanted to know what all the mystery was about when it came to oral sex, and more than anything, she wanted Striker to be the one to show her.

He looked up at her. "And now for that pleasure I promised you."

He leaned closer and began placing small nibbles around her womanhood. The same kind of nibbles he'd nipped around her lips earlier. But this area seemed more sensitive. More in need. And when he took his hands and opened her and eased closer to insert his tongue inside of her, she nearly buckled to her knees. She had to place her hands on his shoulders to remain standing.

There was something about his tongue moving inside of her, lapping her up one minute and then sucking on her the next. She felt sensations ripple through her entire body, and the moans that poured from her lips couldn't be helped. The man was eating her alive. He tightened his hold on her hips and drove his tongue deeper. She wasn't sure how that was possible, but feeling was believing.

And then the pleasure he'd told her about began mounting inside of her, making her whimper, making her entire body tremble before an orgasmic blast detonated inside of her.

"Striker!"

She screamed, and her hands dug into his shoulders, but he wouldn't let up. Nor did he let go. With no control, she felt another orgasm shoot through her. It was only then that he let her go, as he gently eased her back down on the sofa.

"I want to get inside of you, Margo."

In a near daze, she lay on the sofa just as he'd placed her. Naked and spread-eagle, she watched him nearly rip off his clothing. He tossed his shirt near the love seat, missing it by an inch as he kicked off his shoes. He didn't waste any time unzipping his pants and lowering them down strong, muscular legs. Now that he'd undressed, she saw more tattoos on his body and thought the artwork was beautiful, especially the one she got a brief look at when he turned to pull a condom from his pants pocket—a fierce-looking dragon with fangs resting between his shoulder blades.

"I thought that I would be undressing you," Margo said as she paid close attention to how easily he sheathed himself in a condom.

"Next time. I need you too much now."

Her breath caught when she saw the size of his erection. Holy cow! And he thought she was amazing? He was male perfection. Extraordinary. Striker was definitely striking.

He moved toward where she lay on the sofa, opened and ready. He settled on her body and immediately took her mouth. But she felt the head of his massive manhood probing at the entrance to her womanhood.

And when he slowly began sinking inside her, on instinct she adjusted her body to wrap her legs around him. "We're going slow and easy at first," he said as he began gently thrusting back and forth inside of her. "And then we finish fast and hard."

All she could do was nod. Too many sensations were tearing into her with every thrust he made. How was that possible on the heels of two climaxes? Her nails sank into his shoulder blades, and she wrapped her legs tighter around him, crossing her ankles at the base of his back. She held on as his thrusts started coming fast and hard.

He was looking down at her. She hadn't known making love to a man could be this perfect. This right. Her inner muscles clenched him, milked him. Needing to give as well as take.

Margo couldn't handle the sensations anymore. She could no longer hold them at bay, and when he whispered close to her ear, "Go ahead and let go, baby," she did. Never had she screamed so loud. And he kept thrusting, kept pounding, kept moving in and out of her. Then his body buckled and he became overtaken with the same climax. It felt as though her body, her soul, had been forged with his in their shared desire. She had been captured by pleasure and satisfied beyond a shadow of doubt.

And when he shifted their bodies and rolled with her onto his side, she became overwhelmed. Her orgasms tonight had been so spectacular. And she could only thank Striker for that.

"We'll take a nap," he whispered in her ear while drawing her even closer to his side.

A nap? Margo figured it had to be past three in the morning. She yawned as he held her tenderly in his arms. A nap might not be such a bad idea after all.

THE DRIVER OF the black sedan pulled the car to the shoulder of the road, killed the ignition, opened the door and got out, inhaling the crisp mountain air before pulling the coat tighter. It had taken just a couple of drive-bys to get a feel for the best time to make a move. All the plans were falling into place rather nicely.

Looking up into the night's sky, he was sure that snow would be falling by morning, although the moon and stars were out in full force. All in all, it was a beautiful night, and Margo Connelly needed to appreciate such nights while she could. When the time came, she would be taken care of.

A chuckle permeated the night's air. This would be fun.

CHAPTER SEVENTEEN

A SERIES OF kisses scattered around his mouth woke Striker, and he slowly opened his eyes. A deep, drugging rush of desire filled him when he met Margo's gaze. He'd never been awakened quite like this and had no complaints.

He forced his gaze from hers to glance around the living room and saw the scattered clothing. His and hers. They'd never made it upstairs. After making love on the sofa a couple of times, they'd settled in with her stretched out on top of him. He'd grabbed a blanket from one of her closets to cover their nakedness from the cool temperature of the room.

"Good morning, Striker."

She was smiling, and that combined with those kisses meant there were no morning-after regrets on her part. "Good morning, Margo."

"I need to go to the bathroom, and your leg is holding me down," she said, brushing another kiss across his lips.

"Oh."

Their legs were entwined, so he shifted and released his leg's hold on hers. As soon as he did, she got up, stretching her naked limbs before grabbing the blanket to wrap around her body.

"I'll be back in a second, and when I return, be prepared to discuss why you thought it was okay to invade my privacy by bugging my room. I haven't forgotten what you said last night about listening to me shower."

That was not a conversation he wanted to have with her. Easing up, he looked at his watch. "Shit." He hadn't realized it was that late. When was the last time he had slept past eight in the morning? It didn't matter that it had been close to five before they'd settled down to get some sleep. He needed to get a grip and keep in mind that he wasn't here for a damn sleepover.

"We need to get a move on and get dressed. Quasar will be arriving with breakfast shortly."

When she dashed out of the living room to use the bathroom, Striker rubbed his face and inwardly cursed himself out. He'd let his guard down and crossed the line with a client. But not with any client. His boss's niece. He'd known better, yet he'd done it anyway. A sexual attraction between a man and woman was healthy. But this particular attraction could get them both killed if he didn't stay on top of things.

He quickly stood, reached for his clothes and began putting them on. His gun and holster were a glaring reminder of why he was here.

His cell phone rang. "Yeah, Quasar?"

"Anything special the two of you want for breakfast this morning?"

"No. The usual is fine, but hold off coming for another hour."

"Why?"

"We're just getting up."

"Oh, I see."

Striker didn't like the sound of that but decided not to ask his friend to elaborate. "I'll see you when you get here." Clicking off the phone, he contemplated a shave and a shower.

"I'm back."

He glanced over at Margo as he strapped on his Beretta and holster. She was standing there wrapped in a blanket that really wasn't covering much of her naked body. "I just talked to Quasar. He's going to give us time to shower and dress before coming with breakfast."

"Good. I'm hungry."

He watched her discard the blanket as she picked up her clothes. Since he'd become Margo's protector, getting an erection was one of his prominent pastimes. And now that he had firsthand knowledge of how it felt to be inside that body and just how that body tasted, he could see himself staying hard. Forcing his gaze off her, he knew he had a problem. A definite problem.

"So is my bedroom really bugged, or were you just joking about that?"

He hadn't been joking, but now was not the time to have that conversation. He figured she would be royally pissed about it. "We can't discuss this now, Margo. An hour will be up before you know it."

"Fine. Just don't think I'm going to forget about it."

"Whatever," he said. Her hair was mussed. Why did he like it that way?

"I'm ready to go upstairs now, Striker."

Could the reason he liked her hair be his recollection of riding her hard while running his hands through it, tightening his hold on a few locks?

"Striker?"

He blinked. "Yes?"

"I said, I'm ready to go upstairs now."

"Oh, okay." It was his routine to precede her wherever she went for safety measures. Damn, he needed to stay focused and accept that for him and Margo there couldn't be any more make-out sessions. Somehow they needed to get their footing back on level ground and remember the reason his presence was required in the first place. He was here to protect her. He wouldn't fail her like he'd done with Wade. That meant during breakfast they needed to have a real serious talk. And during that conversation he would admit to bugging her room. He was well aware there was a pretty good chance all hell would break loose with that confession.

She followed behind him as he moved up the stairs. "How long will it take for you to finish showering and dressing?" he asked when they reached the landing.

Easing up close to him, she said in a flirty voice, "It depends on whether or not you plan to join me, Striker."

Why did she have to go there and make his already aroused body even more stimulated? Her words alone could stroke him, make him fantasize about sharing a shower with her. He had to hold tight to what little control he had left. It might be a good idea to get Quasar to cover for him while he took a few days off. He needed space from Margo to get his mind back under control and hope that his body would follow suit.

"I got a few calls to make."

"Oh."

He tried not to notice the disappointment in her eyes. "I'll be standing right here when you're finished."

SCOTT DYLAN CLOSED the door behind the woman he let out of his house. She'd shown up last night for a booty call, and he'd been more than happy to oblige. But now with the early morning and the presence of a new day, he was still angry about his phone conversation last night with Margo.

He was about to go into his kitchen when his cell phone rang. Picking it up off the table, he already knew who it was. Freddie Siskin, his roommate from college. "What the hell do you want, Freddie?"

"I dropped by early this morning and saw Wanda's car. She's a pretty good lay and gives damn good blow jobs, so why are you in a bad mood?"

Freddie was right. Wanda did give good blow jobs, and Freddie probably knew that firsthand. Wanda got around. It didn't bother him. She'd gotten what she'd come for, and he'd made sure he'd gotten what he wanted.

"Why were you dropping by?" Scott had heard Freddie had gotten laid off from his job at the bank. He hoped Freddie wasn't trying to hit him up for a loan. He and Freddie hadn't been the best of friends since that stunt he'd pulled with Margo involving those snakes. And then Freddie's lie to that FBI agent that Scott had known about it had prompted Scott to cool his friendship with Freddie.

"To tell you something I found out about your ex-girlfriend."

"Who? Margo?"

"Yes, that bitch, Margo."

Scott knew Freddie was still angry that Margo had threatened them both with jail time unless they donated all that money to her favorite charity. Criminal records were the last thing they'd wanted or needed.

"What about her?"

"She played you, man."

"What are you talking about?"

"I haven't gotten over how she made us pay all that money to some damn charity. Who does that, man? Give *that* much money away? She must be somebody who had a lot to give away. That's when I knew she had to be loaded and was just making those damn wedding gowns for the fun of it."

Scott shook his head. "Freddie, what point are you trying to make?"

"I'm talking about the fact that Margo Connelly didn't need your money like you thought. She was nothing more than a bored little rich broad who didn't even have to work."

"Where did you get a crazy idea like that from?"

"With no job, I have plenty of free time on my hands. So I did what you should have done when you met her and checked her out. A few searches online and it was easy. She's worth millions."

Scott frowned. Freddie had to be lying. But what if he wasn't? Scott rubbed his face, considering the possibility of the latter. He recalled how he'd wanted to make Margo dependent on him, make her need him. If what Freddie claimed was true, then Scott could imagine Margo laughing at his antics behind his back.

"You sure about this, Freddie?"

"Look her up your damn self. I'm telling you, man, the woman is an heiress. And she has an uncle who's wealthy as sin too."

Scott drew in a deep, angry breath. That was probably the uncle who'd raised her when her parents had died. Why hadn't she ever told him she was well-off? "I talked to Margo last night before Wanda showed up.

I called to see how she was doing since there's a killer on the loose in her town."

He paused and then added, "A man was there with her. He got on the phone and told me not to call her back."

"You need to do something, man."

"Do what?"

"Teach her a lesson for using you. Having her new boyfriend tell you off like that wasn't right. Do you want me to go take care of them for you?"

Scott knew Freddie didn't do anything without a purpose. "What's in it for you?"

"For starters, I plan to get my hundred thousand dollars back. She forced me to empty my damn savings account. Now I don't have a job and I'm barely getting by. She owes me."

Scott rolled his eyes. Although he was pretty damn angry with Margo right now, he refused to let Freddie talk him into doing anything he would regret later. "Get over it, Freddie. You fucked up with those snakes, and Margo wasn't responsible for you getting laid off at the bank."

"I won't get over it. Your ex-girlfriend is loaded and she played your ass. If you don't plan on doing anything about it, then that's your business. But I intend to get my money back. Every single cent."

He hoped Freddie was talking crap, but he had a feeling he wasn't. "Settle down, Freddie, or you'll get yourself in even more trouble than before. Let it go, man."

"I won't let it go. You shouldn't either. What we should do is kidnap her and make that rich uncle of hers pay to get her back."

Kidnap Margo? He hoped like hell that Freddie wasn't serious. Unlike Freddie, who was out of work and down on his luck, Scott did have a job—a good, paying one that he intended to keep.

"Meet me at Gritty's for breakfast so we can discuss it." He would try talking Freddie out of the crazy idea of kidnapping Margo. Kidnapping was a federal offense, which meant real jail time. No way would he be a part of anything so stupid.

STRIKER MOVED AROUND the room, pulling clean clothes out of his duffel bag while trying not to listen to the sound of Margo in the next room. She was humming, of all things. At least one of them was in a good mood.

He'd lied about needing to make some calls. There was no way he would step into a shower with her. He could guess what would happen. For the past week he'd lain in bed, listening to her shower and thinking of all the things he would do to her if given the chance to ever share the stall with her.

Removing his Beretta and placing it on the nightstand, he then called Stonewall. His friend answered on the first ring.

"What's going on, Striker?"

"I'm about to shower. Keep an eye on the outside, will you."

"I always do."

After clicking off the phone with Stonewall, he went about removing his clothes. He was about to head for the shower adjacent to the guest room when he heard the sound of Margo's voice. She was no longer humming but was talking. Had she called someone? She knew the rules. No outside contact without his knowledge. Had she called Scott after she'd all but sworn she was through with the man?

He stilled to listen carefully to the sound coming through the speaker Bruce had installed and realized she was speaking directly to him.

"Striker, just in case you missed all I said the first time, I am repeating myself. I'm not sure if you were being truthful when you said you could hear everything going on in this room, but if you were, then listen to this. I want you again. I want to take a shower with you. I want to taste you all over like you tasted me last night. I want to make sure you like it as much as I do. If you don't take me up on this invite, I'll assume you just lied about being able to hear me."

Blood rushed like crazy through Striker's entire body and then settled in his groin. He didn't blink. Could barely breathe. He stood there, unable to move. The only thing moving was his erection. It was expanding like nobody's business. *Oh, shit.* Where was his willpower when he needed it most?

He needed to fight his desire. He had to. But, dammit, the thought of a naked Margo in the shower waiting on him was too much. And she wanted to taste him all over…

He drew in a sharp breath, grabbed a towel and walked toward his bathroom. Inside, he glanced at himself in the mirror. The reflection staring back at him was of a man who'd made love to a woman last night and who still wanted more. All he had to do was close his eyes and he could inhale her scent, probably because it was still on him. He'd brushed his teeth yet he could still taste her on his tongue. And it was a tongue that wanted to taste her again.

Crap! He turned and, before he could talk himself out of what he was doing, called Quasar.

"What's up, Striker?"

"Make that two hours on breakfast."

Not waiting to hear what Quasar had to say, he clicked off the phone. Grabbing a couple of condoms, he headed straight for Margo.

STONEWALL HAD PICKED UP his coffee cup to take another sip when his office door opened and Roland walked in. Stonewall's eyes widened and he stood. "What the hell are you doing here instead of recuperating somewhere?"

Roland waved off his words as he settled in the chair across from the huge desk. "I had a doctor's appointment this morning, and he said I'm fine."

Stonewall frowned. "But I bet he didn't say you could return to work yet."

Roland leaned comfortably back in the chair. "And I haven't returned. Just dropped by to check on things."

Stonewall nodded, knowing it was more than that. "We've been busy. Everyone wants protection, even people who weren't anywhere near the courthouse that day. Craziness happening."

Roland nodded. "How's Striker?"

"Fine," Stonewall said, sitting back down. There was no way he would tell Roland what he and Quasar suspected about how Striker was really doing. So he asked, "How did you get off Sutton Hills without Carson's approval?" After Carson helped clear Roland's name, Roland and Carson had remained good friends, and when Carson married Sheppard Granger last year,

Roland was pretty much adopted into the Granger family like the rest of them.

"Wasn't easy," Roland replied. "Carson drove me in to the doctors and Shep followed. I suspected the doctor would give me back driving rights and I would need my car."

"And I'm sure the doctor expected you to leave his office and go straight home, Roland."

"This is home for me, Stonewall."

Stonewall knew that to be true. Roland pretty much stayed here 24/7, even though he had an apartment a few miles away. Roland had a room with a cot for any of his men who needed power naps between jobs, and all of them were well aware that Roland used it as much as they did.

"You don't think I can handle things here?" Stonewall asked.

Roland chuckled. "You know that's the last thing I think. I trained you all well. It's just that I was wondering how Striker was doing with Margo."

"You could have picked up a phone and called to ask, Roland. Need I remind you that you took a bullet less than a month ago?"

"No, you don't have to remind me."

"The police still haven't caught the dude who tried to hijack your car?" Stonewall asked.

"No, and with so much other stuff on their plates, they aren't looking. They have a much bigger fish to catch."

At that moment Quasar stuck his head in the door. "I'm about to leave to—"

When he saw Roland, Quasar frowned. "What are you doing here?"

"Visiting."

"Well, visit somewhere else. Shouldn't you be home recuperating?" Quasar asked him.

"I am home."

Quasar's frown deepened. "You know what I mean. You're supposed to be at Sutton Hills, where Hannah can keep an eye on you." Hannah was the Grangers' housekeeper and cook.

Roland laughed. "Hannah wants to fatten me up. She's always cooking. A man can get spoiled."

"Then go back and let her spoil you. We got things here," Quasar said.

"I can see that. So where are you headed?"

Quasar came into the room and shoved his hands into his pockets. "To deliver breakfast to Striker and Ms. Connelly."

Roland checked his watch. "Kind of late for breakfast, isn't it?"

Quasar tried keeping a straight face as he shrugged and lied through his teeth. "I was running late. They understood and said they weren't all that hungry." He decided not to glance over at Stonewall, who'd probably figured out why he'd fibbed.

Roland stood. "I'll follow you over there."

"Over where?"

"To take Striker and Margo their breakfast."

Now Quasar did give Stonewall a look that clearly said, *I don't think that's a good idea.* He knew Stonewall understood when Stonewall said to Roland, "You don't need to follow anyone anywhere. I think you should go back to Sutton Hills and get some rest."

"I told you I'm fine, Stonewall, so don't treat me

like some damn invalid. The doctor said I can drive and I'm driving."

Knowing there was no way they could talk Roland out of following him to Ms. Connelly's house without making Roland suspicious, Quasar said, "Fine. I'm ready to go."

To Stonewall he said, "Call Striker and let him know breakfast is about to be delivered."

Stonewall nodded. "Trust me, I will."

CHAPTER EIGHTEEN

MARGO OBVIOUSLY HAD guessed wrong about her bedroom being bugged. It was probably a good thing considering that flirty invitation she'd issued. When had she ever been bold when it came to a man? Never. And what about her resolve to keep things casual with men? But this wasn't getting serious. It was about having a little fun, and right now she felt the need to let loose a little, especially after such a passionate night with Striker.

As she opened the shower door and stepped inside the stall, vivid scenes of them making love last night began playing in her head. She regretted that the shower would wash away his scent—a scent that seemed to be entrenched in her skin.

She closed her eyes as memories continued to trickle through her mind the same way the spray of warm water was trickling over her body. She could clearly recall Striker on his knees with his head buried between her legs. And then there was the first time he'd eased himself inside of her. And he'd gone deep.

Margo was convinced it had been deeper than any man had ever gone. Had a year without sex done this to her? Brought her to this state? Made her a ball of wanton desire? No, it didn't have anything to do with abstinence but everything to do with Striker. The man was all alpha, all male and blatantly sexy.

She could tell from his attitude this morning that he'd expected her to have some regrets about last night and maybe she should. But she would have to be totally honest and admit she didn't. She had wanted him and he had wanted her. The big question now was what would happen next.

Striker didn't come across as someone who made irrational decisions, but she had a feeling he could overthink a situation. Although he had shared some things about himself, she knew there was a part of him that he was keeping off-limits. She didn't want to continue to pry, but there was so much about him that she wanted to know.

She decided not to dwell on what she still didn't know about Striker and concentrate on all those things she did. First up was just what an expert lover he was. The man had given her an orgasm not once but numerous times, and he'd moved inside of her in a way that made her want their bodies to stay connected forever.

Forever?

What kind of crazy thought was that? All she knew was that for a while last night, she had refused to remember Striker's purpose in her life and that a murderer was still out there somewhere. She had needed that time with him for some reason.

She jerked around and gasped when she heard the shower door open. There Striker stood. Completely naked. Totally aroused. "I accept your invitation, Margo," he said in a deep, husky voice.

She wiped water from her face to make sure she was actually seeing him. That he was really there. "So you've been spying on me?" she asked incredulously, finding it hard to ignite much anger when a totally masculine and very aroused naked man was sharing the shower stall with her.

"Not spying but protecting. I couldn't go to sleep at night if I didn't. I need to make sure you're safe at all times."

The thought that he'd been privy to her every sound and movement gave her pause, but it didn't keep her gaze from roaming all over him. All those firm muscles, perfect abs, broad, muscular shoulders, flat and hard stomach. And then there was that monstrosity of an erection between his legs. Large and jutting proudly from a dark thatch of curls. It was already sheathed, making it quite obvious Striker had come prepared to protect her in another way.

Even with the condom covering his shaft, she could see the thick veins running along the sides of it. And she could vividly recall all that solid thickness stretching her last night. Thrusting in and out while embedded deep within her.

"Ready to shower?"

His words made her swallow. She had a feeling that they would be doing more than showering. "Yes."

"Then pass me the soap. I want to lather you."

He wanted to lather her? It was bad enough whenever their hands touched. The thought of those same hands moving all over her body—like they'd done last night—had heat settling between her legs.

"Margo?"

"Um?"

"The soap."

For a minute there she'd gotten lost in his heated

gaze. Her eyes left his face to once again travel lower. The man was so well-endowed that her senses were beginning to unravel. They had gotten unstitched last night and she hadn't recovered. Now she doubted that she ever could.

Reaching behind her, she grabbed the bar of soap and handed it to him. Their hands touched and her body began shuddering. And that was when he made his move. He wrapped his arms around her as water streamed down on both of them.

"You're trembling, Margo," he whispered hotly against her ear, before licking it on the side.

That wasn't all she was doing, she thought. The man could touch her and she would go up in flames…even while standing under water. Then she felt his hands all over her, felt the soapy caresses move over her back, her buttocks and shoulders while blood pounded furiously through her body.

Then he took a step back to start on her front, first by spreading a warm lather over her chest. The moment his hands began stroking her breasts, using his fingertips to tease her nipples, she moaned. She was finding out that Striker knew how to take the word *steamy* to a whole new level. He had the ability to stir a sexual need inside of her she hadn't known existed until now.

When his hand moved lower and began lathering her stomach, an intense ache began curling between her legs. She felt her heart kick up several beats and found it almost hard to breathe. Had anyone told her lust could fuel desire to this extreme, she would not have believed them.

He was staring at her, with those dark, penetrating eyes, as if he wanted her to feel his own need in his every touch. He wanted her to know his own desire was driving what he was doing, Margo got that. She felt it.

And when he dipped his hand lower between her legs, she almost shot out of her wet skin. He had opened his fingers and was using them to spread her before inserting one inside. Her head dropped to his shoulder when he began rotating that finger inside of her, making every bone in her body tremble.

"Striker…"

He whispered in her ear, "I'm going to lift you up, and when I do, wrap your legs around me, Margo."

Effortlessly he lifted her off her feet and, as he'd told her to do, she wrapped her legs around him, nearly screaming in pleasure when she felt the hardness of his erection slide into her. He was supporting her backside with his hands and stepped away from the spray of water to the shower wall. She felt the cold tile at her back, but what really had her attention was Striker and how he'd begun thrusting in and out of her hard. She couldn't help but moan.

His mouth captured hers, the play of his tongue silencing her. He was deliberately going slowly around her mouth, licking and sucking areas with skill that made her want him even more than she already did. To retaliate, she clamped her feminine muscles around him and began squeezing, milking him until he was the one moaning. She had no problems showing Striker that two could play his game.

He jerked his mouth away and stared at her, holding her gaze as his thrusts increased, went deeper, pounded harder and pushed her beyond physical satisfaction of the most intense kind.

"It's crazy, but I can't get enough of you," Striker

said huskily, showing her exactly what he meant with each and every thrust.

Margo knew this was crazy, but at the moment it was necessary. When had a man making love to her become so crucial? And then he threw his head back and released a growl unlike anything she'd ever heard. But she felt it, all the way to the bone. Was she imagining things or had his erection just expanded inside of her? It made her feel so full of him. And that was when she lost it.

She screamed when an orgasm struck her, and she began trembling so much he had to tighten his hold on her. *Omigod.* This was unreal. She'd thought last night was pretty damn amazing, but today, right now in this shower, with her back against the wall and Striker relentlessly pounding into her, was definitely off the charts.

Margo screamed again, and in seconds Striker's mouth was there, taking hers, using his tongue to again kiss her in ways she hadn't known a woman could be kissed. She felt them moving as he edged them over to the spray of water. He slowly eased out of her and slid her body down his tall, hard frame, all while their mouths remained connected. If they were going to drown then, this was the best way to go.

STRIKER DIDN'T UNDERSTAND why he couldn't get enough of Margo's kisses or her entire body, for that matter. It was as if he was in a Margo Zone. It was crazy but so damn pleasurable. While inside of her he'd felt all her muscles and had loved each and every time they had squeezed down on him.

They needed to get out the shower, dry off and get dressed. He'd asked Quasar for a two-hour extension on breakfast and Quay was always on time. But for the life of him, Striker wanted to go another round with her. He reached up and turned off the water, thinking there would always be tonight. He knew this shower thing should be one and done, but he had a feeling it was just the beginning. And that wasn't good.

After opening the shower door, he grabbed the towels. His gaze roamed over Margo before settling between her legs. Studying the beauty of the curls covering her womanhood, he remembered how, last night, he'd parted her there, tasted her clitoris with his tongue.

"Let me help dry you off," Margo said.

Striker didn't have a problem with that, even though he was setting himself up for more torture. "Only if you let me return the favor," he said, thinking of all the scenarios that could lead to.

At that moment his phone rang. He picked it up off the vanity and saw he'd missed three calls from Stonewall. Damn, he hoped nothing had gone down while he was in the shower with Margo. He clicked on the phone. "Stonewall, what's up?"

"Your ass if you aren't careful. I thought you were going to take a shower."

"I did. Just getting out."

"That was a damn long shower, Striker, and I can guess why. I suggest you hurry and get dressed. Quasar is on his way."

Striker had figured as much. "Okay, Quasar is on his way. Why the rush?"

"Roland is following him over there."

"Shit. He shouldn't be driving around while recovering from a damn gunshot wound."

"Yeah, that's what I say. He showed up unexpectedly, coming straight from the physician's office. His

doctor restored his driving rights and, knowing Roland,
I'm sure that means he plans to hang around here a lot.
However, first on his agenda was to make sure Ms.
Connelly is okay. I suggest the two of you get dressed
and plaster innocent smiles on your faces when Roland
arrives. I think you know why I say the word *innocent*."

He was tempted to tell Stonewall to go to hell but knew
Margo was listening to his conversation and she probably wouldn't like it. Besides, Stonewall was right. He
needed to get dressed quickly. They both did. "Thanks
for the call."

He clicked off the phone and turned to Margo, who
was coming toward him with a towel. "Rain check," he
said, taking the thick velour towel from her. "We need
to get dressed ASAP. Quasar is on his way and he has
my boss with him."

"I thought you said your boss was just feeling under
the weather. Why didn't you tell me he'd gotten shot?"

Striker shrugged. "At the time I didn't want to go into
detail." No need to tell her the panic he'd gone through
when Roland had been shot. The thought of almost losing him was something he didn't want to think about.
For Striker, Quasar and Stonewall, Roland was like an
older brother. He'd been there for them when they had
no one else. Shep, who'd been inside with them, had suggested that, after they'd gotten out of the slammer, they
spend time with Reverend Luther Thomas, who dedicated his life to helping ex-cons get acclimated back into
society as easily as possible with strong, positive influ-
ences. They had met Roland through Reverend Thomas.

"I still want details," Margo interrupted his thoughts
to say. "So what happened?"

He released a resigned sigh and then answered, "It was an attempted carjacking."

"Oh. Did the police catch the person?"

"They haven't yet. I guess they're too busy trying to nab a hit man."

"Well, at least I'll finally get to meet your boss," she said as she continued to dry off.

Striker wrapped the towel around his middle while wishing she could finally meet Roland another time. Now, as far as he was concerned, was lousy timing.

"DR. FULLER, WE'RE GLAD you decided to rejoin us."

Randi glanced around the room knowing Special Agent Felton did not mean what he'd said. But she knew without being told that he had come under fire for not taking her findings seriously before. Most of the people in this room had. And because of their disregard, more lives had been lost. Now they would work with the devil himself if it meant catching a demented killer.

"So what additional clues do you have?" she asked Chief Harkins as she sat down at the table.

"As you've heard, the assassin struck down two people. Another juror and one of our federal prosecutors. We need to stop him before he hits again."

She shook her head. "Too late. He already has."

"What!" Harkins said, and he was out of his seat in a flash and checking his phone. "We don't know anything about another hit that has taken place. Are you sure?"

She nodded sadly. "Yes. I got a mental flash of another victim the minute I entered this room." She didn't tell them of the physical signs—the cold chills that had gone through her body or the fiery feel of the blood rushing through her veins. Not surprisingly, most of the people in the room looked at her with skepticism all over their faces. They still didn't want to believe her. They didn't understand how anyone could possess the psychic abilities that she did. If only they knew how hard she had fought against the powers that she'd inherited from her paternal grandmother.

At that moment both Special Agent Felton's and Chief Harkins's cell phones rang, and she could tell from the way the two men looked at her while they conversed that what she'd told them was being confirmed. Another person had been murdered.

Both men disconnected, and it was Harkins who spoke in an angry and disgusted voice to everyone in the room. "A news reporter who was in the courtroom that day just got shot down. He's dead."

He rubbed his face and then looked over at Randi. "You were right, Dr. Fuller. It seems the assassin struck again."

"So what do you need from us?" Felton asked in an annoyed voice.

Randi stood. "The first thing I need is for someone to take me to the crime scene."

A woman stepped forward and offered Randi her hand. "I'm Detective Joy Ingram, and I've been assigned to assist you any way I can."

Randi took the woman's hand, wondering about the strange vibes that suddenly passed through her. She forced a smile, deciding to analyze the strange aura later. "Thanks, Detective Ingram."

CHAPTER NINETEEN

MARGO WONDERED WHY Striker was so uptight about his boss arriving with Quasar. She could only assume the security firm had a no-fraternization policy. If they did, the last thing she wanted to do was get Striker in trouble, though what they'd done in the shower had been the kind of trouble she'd enjoyed. He definitely wasn't out of the woods yet for spying on her. She would have to think of a way to make him pay. Her mind was suddenly filled with a number of ideas. All of them were simply scandalous and all of them made her smile.

"What's that smile for?"

She glanced over at him as they entered the kitchen. "Want a list?" Before Striker could give her an answer, there was a knock at the back door. "Sounds like our food has arrived," she said.

She stepped aside, watched as he drew his gun in case her assumption was wrong. "Who is it?" He barked out the question.

"Quasar and Roland."

Striker moved toward the door and she knew to remain back until he'd verified their visitors. Once he had, he slid his gun back into the holster. Quasar walked in and he shot her a friendly smile, which she returned. "Good morning, Quasar."

"Good morning, Margo."

She then looked at the man with Quasar, presumably Roland Summers. He was handsome in a rugged sort of way and immediately reminded her of someone. There was something about the shape of his eyes and mouth.

Margo guessed he was in his late thirties or early forties. It was obvious he was the one in control, although Quasar and Striker seemed relaxed around him, making it quite obvious both men had a close working relationship with their boss.

Striker glanced over at her and said, "Margo, I'd like you to meet Roland Summers."

Margo crossed the room. Was she imagining it or was he studying her with keen interest? There was nothing sexual about it, but it was as if he was trying to figure her out. She extended her hand. "Mr. Summers."

He took it and smiled. "Ms. Connelly. And please call me Roland. I take it Striker is doing a good job keeping you safe."

She smiled. "Yes. I have no complaints. He's protecting me, and that's what matters."

At that moment Striker's phone went off. Margo was beginning to recognize the specific ringtones and knew it was Stonewall. The intense look that suddenly appeared on his face drew her attention.

Margo's heart began beating deep in her chest when he clicked off the line. "There's been another shooting, hasn't there?"

Her question got everyone's attention. Margo's heart almost stopped when a grim-faced Striker nodded. "A news reporter who was at the courthouse that day has been killed."

Wrapping an arm around Margo, Striker led her over to the kitchen table to sit down. "You okay?" he asked, concern lacing his words.

She patted his arm as if to assure him that she was. "Yes. I expected to hear what you said, but when you actually said it, I—"

"You looked like you were about to pass out." He would have understood if she had. Something had to be done. Somebody needed to make Erickson talk, make him call off his goon even if it meant hanging him up by the balls to do it.

She glanced around. "Where are Roland and Quasar?"

"Probably in your workroom. I believe Roland got a call from your uncle."

She threw up her hands in frustration. "That's just great! No telling what Uncle Frazier is instructing him to do with me. He probably got the company jet fueled up and is ready to fly me heaven-knows-where."

Striker came close to saying that might not be such a bad idea. "And what if he has taken those steps, Margo? Will you go?"

"Yes. Just as long as you're protecting me."

Striker drew in a deep breath. For the first time in his life, he felt he had a personal stake in the individual he was protecting. Deciding not to say anything, for fear of saying something he shouldn't, he sat down across from her and reached for the bags Quasar had placed on the table earlier. "Come on, let's eat. Our food is getting cold."

"Okay."

Breakfast looked good. After taking a sip of his coffee, he looked around the room to make sure Roland

and Quasar weren't nearby and then leaned over to say, "I'm starving. You nearly wore me out in that shower."

A chuckle erupted from Margo. "I did not."

"You did too."

Smiling, she placed emphasis on each word. "I. Did. Not."

He thought the smile on her face was priceless, and he wished it could stay forever and that she never had to worry again about a threat on her life.

"Hey, why not let us in on what you did or didn't do." Margo and Striker quickly turned to find Frazier Connelly standing beside Roland.

"Uncle Frazier! What are you doing here?" Margo said, getting up from the table to give her uncle a hug.

"I thought I was always welcome here."

"You know what I mean. I didn't hear the doorbell."

"I didn't use it. Roland was expecting me and met me at the front door."

"Oh," she said, glancing at Roland. Then she asked, "And where's Quasar?"

"He left," Roland said. "With all that's happened, he might be needed back at the office."

Frazier rubbed the back of his neck in agitation and then said, "We need to talk, Margo. This situation has gotten real."

She looked taken aback by her uncle's words. "I always thought it was real. You didn't?"

He bristled at her question. "Yes, of course I did, but I assumed the authorities would have caught the person by now."

She crossed her arms over her chest. "Well, they haven't."

"That is why we need to come up with another plan

for you. I don't think remaining here in this house is a good idea, and Roland agrees with me."

She looked past her uncle to Roland Summers and met his gaze. She knew her uncle's ability to persuade people to his way of thinking…although that talent always failed when he tried it on her. For some reason, she believed it would fail on Roland as well. He didn't come across as the type who would let her uncle—or anyone else, for that matter—sway him. If he agreed with her uncle, Roland must already be convinced.

She looked back at her uncle. "So what's the plan?"

"Let's sit down and talk."

Margo dropped her hands to her sides and sat back down at the table. "Fine. You all can join me and Striker for breakfast. I can't speak for Striker, but I don't mind sharing."

"Sorry," Striker said, taking the last bite of his sandwich. "I have nothing left. I was hungry."

Margo tried not to smile about why he'd been hungry. And she was glad her uncle hadn't pressed her about their back-and-forth banter.

"Eating breakfast kind of late, aren't you?" her uncle observed as he and Roland joined her and Striker at the table.

Margo refused to look at Striker as she said something partly true. "I worked really late last night on the wedding gown I'm designing and wanted to sleep in this morning. I'm glad Striker didn't have an issue with it."

"I understand that for safety measures the FBI wants to round up everyone who was in the courtroom that day and move them to an undisclosed location under protective custody," Roland said.

Margo nodded. "Why do I get the feeling that you don't like that idea, Roland?"

"Because I don't," Roland responded in a tight voice. "Something might go wrong and it would benefit the assassin if it does."

Margo arched a brow. "How so?"

Roland leaned back in his chair while meeting her gaze. "I'm sure you've figured out by now that this assassin isn't working alone. I believe there's a mole somewhere. In that case, the police and FBI are the last people I'd want to know the whereabouts of every person on the assassin's hit list."

Margo took a sip of her coffee and then said, "My uncle has this issue about trusting cops. It seems you do too."

"That I do," Roland said.

"Something the two of you have in common," she said, looking from Roland to her uncle and then back to Roland. "So what do you suggest?"

Roland rubbed his face. "I agree we need to get you out of here and to some place where no one knows where you are."

Margo nibbled on her bottom lip and then her gaze moved over to Striker. Although this was the first time she'd looked at him since the two men had sat down at the table, she knew he hadn't taken his eyes off her. She had felt his gaze just like it had been a physical caress.

"What are your thoughts about this, Striker? Since you're the one who'll be protecting me." There, she'd let everyone know she expected Striker to remain her protector.

He held her gaze long enough to convey he understood. "I agree with Roland's plan, Margo."

She nodded. There was no sense asking how long her life would be disrupted because no one knew. It could be for a few days or a few weeks. Hopefully, the authorities would do their job and capture the guy. The only good thing was that since Claudine's wedding wasn't until September, she didn't have to worry about not finishing her gown right away. But it did mean she would have to work through the summer instead of taking the time off like she'd planned.

She glanced back at Roland. "And are you sure no one other than your people will know where I am?"

"Yes, I can say that with certainty. And I believe you won't have to stay hidden long. The authorities will be working around the clock, following up on leads. I also understand that psychic investigator is back to help work the case. Maybe this time they will believe what she tells them."

Margo drew in a deep breath. "Make the arrangements, and I'll do what you suggest."

"Alright," Roland said, getting ready to stand.

"Wait," she said quickly. "I'd like to discuss something with you and Uncle Frazier." This should be a private conversation, but she had no problem with Striker hearing.

"What is it?" her uncle asked.

"Would one of you like to explain how you're related?"

RANDI WALKED AROUND the crime scene as she tried to pick up any mental details. Something *was* different here; she could feel it but couldn't decipher what that difference was. The coffee cup had been left behind like before, and the victim had been shot in the head.

It had been an accurate shot with the same rifle used in the last two hits, according to Harkins.

"Do you want to read the report on the victim?"

She paused. For a minute she'd forgotten Detective Ingram was still with her. Randi shook her head. "No, I like putting the pieces of the puzzle together myself. He was young. Under thirty. Hadn't been a reporter more than a couple of years. Got hired right out of college."

From the expression on Detective Ingram's face, Randi knew she'd pretty much given the detective all the facts on the victim without reading his profile. "All that info is correct."

Randi nodded. "The really sad thing is that he wasn't supposed to be at the courtroom that day."

Detective Ingram raised a surprised brow. "He wasn't?"

"No, and I bet that isn't in the report."

"Then why was he there?" Detective Ingram asked, clearly perplexed.

"Last-minute change. The reporter who should have covered the trial called in sick."

"Oh. And was he? Really sick?"

Randi chuckled lightly. It seemed the detective assumed Randi's psychic powers could tell her practically anything. "Now, *that* I don't know, but if he was, then being sick saved his life." She continued walking around a minute and then she suddenly stopped and closed her eyes.

"Is something wrong, Dr. Fuller?"

She opened her eyes. "No, nothing is wrong," she lied. *Yes, something is wrong.* She could feel it but decided not to say anything at the moment. However, there were a few things she would share with the detective.

"The killer is definitely a male. Right-handed. Loner. Already he's preparing to kill again."

"Think you'll solve this before he does?"

Randi looked over at her. "I never solve crimes, Detective Ingram. I use my psychic abilities to assist you guys. I'm merely an investigative instrument."

"I guess that's one way of looking at it."

"As far as I'm concerned, that's the only way to look at it."

CHAPTER TWENTY

IT WAS QUITE obvious Margo's question had caught Roland and Frazier Connelly by surprise. Striker studied the two men, noticing how quiet the room had gotten. He wondered how she'd figured things out and couldn't wait for her to tell them. He took a sip of his coffee, thinking things were about to get interesting.

"Uncle Frazier?" she asked, when no one said anything.

Connelly looked uncomfortable and loosened his tie. "Why would you think we're related?"

Margo smirked. "So, now you want to convince me you're not?" She switched her gaze to Roland. "Would someone tell me something?"

"How about answering my question, Margo? Why would you think we're related?" Frazier asked her.

Margo shook her head as a stilted laugh escaped her lips. "Have the two of you ever stood side by side and looked into the mirror?" Her statement made the two men glance at each other. Striker also took a good look.

When they didn't say anything, she said, "When Roland walked in the house with Quasar, he immediately reminded me of someone. And when I saw the two of you standing together I realized who it was. He favors Dad. And then I knew there was no way the two of you weren't related."

When the silence continued, she asked, "So what's going on? Is there some family secret that I don't know about?"

Frazier drew in a slow breath before he finally said, "I'm embarrassed to say you're right."

Striker could tell Connelly's comment didn't sit well with Roland. Taking offense, Roland turned to Frazier and snapped, "Don't make me tell you what you can do with your damn embarrassment."

Roland got up from the table, but Frazier said, "Please sit back down, Roland. You misunderstood what I meant. I wasn't saying you were an embarrassment but that my treatment of you has been."

Striker saw the surprised look on Roland's face. He wasn't sure what had Roland sliding back down in his chair—Connelly asking him to or his shock at Connelly's words. Striker glanced over at Margo, and he could tell from her expression that she was probably wondering the same thing.

Deciding coffee was in order, Striker silently went over to the counter and poured two cups, which he then placed before the two men. He knew Roland took his black and shouldn't have been surprised when Frazier did as well. Striker then sat back down. By rights, he knew he should leave since this was a family discussion. But since he knew the entire story anyway, he decided to stay put. Besides, Margo hadn't asked him to leave. Whether she realized it or not, the fact that she hadn't meant that she trusted him to a degree he found a bit overwhelming. He couldn't recall the last time anyone, besides the men he worked with closely, had displayed that much confidence in him, and it meant a lot.

"Will someone please tell me what's going on?" she asked in a soft voice.

"Yes," Connelly finally said. "It's about time you knew."

Margo studied the two men. Had she really tapped into some family secret? What she'd told them earlier was the truth. They favored each other. Had no one ever pointed that fact out to them? Had they met before Uncle Frazier hired Roland's firm?

"It seems," her uncle Frazier started off by saying, "that my old man lived a double life...which I never suspected. He was so dedicated to Mom and all. It was only when he died that Murdock, Mom and I found out differently. His attorney advised us that someone by the name of Roland Summers had been notified to attend the reading of the will, but he wouldn't tell us why."

He paused a minute before continuing. "We found out the truth when Roland walked into the conference room. My father had been having an affair. An affair that had resulted in another son. It was hard to believe. Hard to stomach. Mom was furious and I was furious right along with her and we treated Roland awfully."

Margo nodded. She could recall very little of her grandmother, who'd died of a heart attack a few years before Margo's parents' deaths. But she'd heard that Audrey Connelly had been quite a character. A pampered, spoiled and selfish debutante. On the other hand, she'd heard nothing but admirable qualities about her grandfather. She could imagine how his affair must have come as a shock. And to learn he'd had an illegitimate child had probably been too much for her grandmother. For any woman. But that was no excuse for the behavior she was hearing about now. It hadn't been Roland's fault. "How old was everyone?"

Roland took a sip of coffee and then spoke up. "I was eighteen and in my first year of college."

Frazier tacked on, "I was twenty-five and had recently taken over running Connelly Enterprises after Dad's early retirement. He'd always said he would step down and enjoy life when I could take over. Murdock was twenty-three and just finishing law school. He had married your mother the year before."

Frazier paused a minute and then said, "Mom didn't want to believe it and tried blocking what Dad bequeathed Roland, which was a sizable trust fund. I guess Dad anticipated she would make such a move and had hired some of the best attorneys to protect Roland's interest so she couldn't do a damn thing about it."

Frazier took another sip of his coffee. "Mom became bitter, broken and vicious toward Roland and his mother." He then turned to face Roland. "What I'm embarrassed about, Roland, is that I allowed her to do that. I also allowed her feelings to affect me. I saw accepting you as my brother as being disloyal to Mom."

Margo nodded. "What about Dad? Did he feel the same way you did?"

Frazier shook his head and smiled slightly. "No. In fact, Murdock took the position that I should have taken as the oldest. He felt Roland was not to blame for our father's indiscretions, and that Mom and I were treating him unfairly. No matter what Mom and I said, Murdock did not let us keep him from reaching out to Roland, establishing a place in his life as his brother."

Good for him, Margo thought. She'd always known her father was a special man, one who wouldn't let his mother rule him. She'd heard about her father standing up to his mother when she disapproved of his marriage to Margo's mother.

"I'm surprised Dad didn't tell me about you at some point," she said to Roland.

Roland hadn't said anything while Uncle Frazier spoke but had sat there listening, studying the contents in his coffee cup. Finally he glanced over at Margo and said, "He wanted to, but I advised him not to. Although Murdock wasn't ashamed that I was his brother, I didn't want to be the cause of any more trouble in the Connelly family. I figured he could tell you about me when you got older and could understand and accept things."

But that time never came because of her parents' deaths, Margo thought. She was suddenly filled with deep emotions. Roland Summers was her uncle. And just like her father had claimed him, she would as well.

"So, as my newest uncle, what's your take on all of this? Regarding how shabbily you were treated by the Connellys?"

Roland stared at her, and she couldn't help but smile.

"Yes, I am my father's daughter. Even Uncle Frazier will attest to that."

"Yes, I will," Frazier said, grinning, reaching over and tugging on a lock of her hair.

"As far as I'm concerned, it's all in the past," Roland said.

Frazier turned again to Roland and, with a serious expression on his face, said, "I can't undo how Mom and I treated you, but I can and will say I'm sorry about it. I was wrong to get angry with Murdock when he—" Uncle Frazier paused and quickly glanced at Margo "—when he helped you out that time. I don't blame you for anything." He stood from the table. "Will you accept my apology?"

Roland looked at Frazier's outstretched hand and then he stood as well and took it. "Yes, apology accepted."

Margo had a feeling there was more she didn't know. When had her father helped Roland out and what didn't her uncle Frazier blame him for? She'd discovered so much today that maybe it was best if she didn't push. It was obviously an emotional topic for her uncles. She wanted to savor this good news on a day that had brought so much bad already. And she trusted they would tell her in their own time.

Striker hadn't said anything. Considering his relationship with Roland, she wondered if he'd known. If he did that would certainly explain his intense desire to protect her and his reluctance to be intimately involved with her.

A part of her appreciated Striker for choosing that moment to speak up and get things back on track by asking, "So, what's the plan regarding relocating Margo?"

Both men sat back down. "Our family owns a ski cabin in Jackson Hole, Wyoming," her uncle Frazier said.

"That can easily be traced if it's listed anywhere as part of your family's assets. Until we know whether or not the assassin is working alone or with someone, I'd rather we didn't take any chances," Roland replied, rubbing his jaw in thought.

He looked over at Margo and Striker. "I'll have a plan in place within ten hours and will need the two of

you ready to move out when you're contacted. In the
meantime, stay on your guard."

STRIKER CLOSED AND locked the door after the two men
left. He turned and watched Margo remove all the trash
from the kitchen table. She wasn't saying anything, and
he couldn't help wondering what she was thinking. A
lot of stuff had been dumped on her today. And something of vast importance had been revealed about her
family. He had admired her attitude and easy accep-
tance of Roland.

"Need my help?" he asked her.

Without bothering to even look up at him, she said,
"No, I've got this."

Did she really? For some reason, he didn't think
so. He rubbed his cheek as he continued to watch her
and had a strong feeling that Roland had picked up on
something going on between them.

Surprisingly, the possibility of Roland figuring things
out didn't bother Striker. Although there was no set policy about getting involved with a client, Roland would
expect him to use his best judgment in such matters.
Given the degree of danger surrounding Margo's situation, Striker knew his mind should be focused on
keeping her safe and not having sex with her. But some
things couldn't be helped and it wasn't as if he hadn't
tried resisting temptation. The attraction between them
had been too strong not to give in to it. It was either
that or they'd have eventually driven themselves crazy
with lust.

Sometimes "one and done" was the best rule. However, with them it hadn't been a rule he'd stuck to…
considering what had happened in her shower this

morning. The memory of him taking her there made his erection swell. And each time she'd screamed his name had made him want to thrust into her even more. Made him want to brand her as his.

Damn it to hell. How could he even think of something like that? He didn't want to brand any woman. All he'd ever wanted was a good roll between the sheets with one. Yet, with Margo, things weren't the norm.

He couldn't fight this ache he was feeling for her. Nor could he deny that he wanted her even now—hell, even while sitting across from her at the kitchen table with her uncles. He'd studied her whenever she'd talked. More than once he'd caught his gaze lingering on her mouth, as he remembered how sweet it had tasted. Then his eyes had drifted to her chest, as he'd recalled how he'd sucked on her nipples. He doubted Frazier had noticed him staring, but he would be surprised if Roland hadn't.

Her frustrated sigh recaptured his attention, and he rubbed his cheek again. They had been sharing space long enough for him to know whenever something was bothering her. He should let it go and let her deal with it on her own, but for him that was easier said than done. "Do you want to talk about it, Margo?"

"About what?"

"Whatever is bothering you."

She paused and looked over at him, and the eyes staring back at him were soft yet troubled. He slowly crossed the room, took the garbage bag out of her hand and pulled her into his arms.

To hold her. To protect her.

At that moment Striker knew he was asking for trouble because he liked holding her too damn much. And he liked making love to her even more. Why hadn't he told Roland that someone else needed to protect her from here on out? Because he couldn't do that. And then she'd made it clear she wanted him to protect her if she was relocated elsewhere. Knowing she was willing to put her life in his hands had done something to him. It was still doing something to him.

There were times when a man had to do what he felt in his gut that he had to do. Even if that gut was filled with a need and desire that could render his senses off kilter. "You want to talk about it?" he asked.

She pulled back and looked up at him. "Talk about what? The fact that I have to leave my home and go into hiding to heaven-knows-where, or the fact that I discovered today that I have an uncle that I didn't know about."

He would listen to anything she needed to get off her chest. Since she'd asked, he decided discussing the issue of her uncles could prove more positive for her in the long run. And he wanted her to have a positive outlook. "Is having another uncle such a bad thing?"

"Of course not," she said, as if surprised by his question. "Uncle Frazier took my father's death hard, and I wish he could have shared that grief with my uncle Roland."

Her uncle Roland. It still amazed Striker just how accepting she was of Roland's place in her life. There were a number of things she didn't know yet; one was Roland's suspicion that the fire that had killed her parents had been deliberate. "Thanks to you, Margo, the healing between Frazier and Roland has started to take place, and that's a good thing."

She appeared to think about what he'd said for a

minute and then asked, "You knew, didn't you? That they were brothers."

Standing so close to her like this had his erection throbbing. An erection she had to feel—there was no way she couldn't. Instead of taking a step back, he tightened his arms around her and brought her closer. "Yes, I knew. Roland told me everything before I took this job."

"And you didn't tell me?" she said accusingly.

"I had no reason to tell you. You were just a job."

She stared at him, and he wondered what she saw in his eyes that made her ask her next question. "And now? Am I just a job, Striker?"

He could say yes, that was all she was and that sleeping with her, being inside her body, learning her intimate taste, meant nothing. That she was no different than any other woman he'd had sex with. But he knew that would be a bald-faced lie. It was different with her. Although he didn't want to dwell on what that difference was, it was there.

So he decided to be honest. "No, you're not just a job, Margo. Not anymore. You are more than that."

And because he knew how her mind worked, was familiar with those nosy bones in her body, before she could ask he said, "And the reason I don't see you as just a job is because last night was a game changer. I've gotten to know you." *Boy, have I gotten to know you.* "Now you're also a woman I want." There, he'd said it. She knew where he stood.

The smile she gave him at that moment was well worth his honesty. Striker knew he had to shift gears, make sure they remained focused on the real problem at hand. "Whenever Roland calls and gives the word, we need to be ready to go. There's no way you can set up shop where we're going, but I'm sure there are a few smaller items you might want to gather out of your workroom to take with you."

"Do you have any idea where we're going?"

He shook his head. "No, I don't have a clue. But Roland will make sure it's safe and not some place anyone could easily find. It's going to be important that no one knows your location."

She nodded. "At least you'll be there to protect me."

Yes, he definitely would be. And like he'd told her before, he would protect her with his life if he had to. But now those words were beginning to have more meaning for him.

He stared down into her face as his hands left her waist and slid down to cup her backside. Striker knew he needed to get a grip on his mind and not necessarily on her ass, but damn, touching her right there felt so good. And it was obvious from the look on her face that she liked him touching her there too.

"Do you think Roland suspects anything?"

Striker saw the way she was nibbling on her bottom lip. "About what?"

"That we slept together."

"Would it bother you if he did? What about Frazier?" he asked.

"No. We're adults."

"Then why did you ask?"

She shrugged. "I don't want to get you in trouble."

He couldn't help the smile that touched his lips. She was worried because of him. "Are you concerned about me losing my job?"

Her lashes lowered. "You did seem concerned about

Roland finding anything out before he arrived. I know you have a close relationship with him and all."

Striker used the tip of his finger to lift her chin. "And that won't change."

"How did the two of you meet?"

He no longer minded sharing how his close ties to her uncle came about. "When I got out of prison, it was suggested that I look up Reverend Luther Thomas. He was a former inmate whose sentence was overturned when they'd discovered he was innocent. He decided to dedicate his life to helping other inmates get acclimated to society. He was instrumental in making sure I finished my degree at Hampton and introducing me to Roland for a job. Roland had started his security company a couple of years before and made sure I got the proper training to be a protector. Our friendship started from there. I consider him the older brother I wish I had."

His gaze drifted over her face. He saw the look of desire that was still in her eyes and knew he should step back; otherwise he would be sweeping her off her feet and carrying her up the stairs to her bedroom.

"We need to pack," he said. "We'll probably leave in the dead of night. Will you be ready?"

She nodded. "Yes, I'll be ready."

THE LONE FIGURE lifted the cup of coffee to his lips as he gazed down at the list in his hand. So far each hit had been a piece of cake, and he knew things would continue that way. No witnesses and so far he'd only taken out intended targets. Not one bystander harmed, although it would not have bothered him in the least if one had been.

He glanced at his watch. The person he was waiting for was late. She was his contact at police headquarters and the only one who knew his identity. Normally he worked alone, but Erickson's hit list was a huge one, so a network had been implemented to stay abreast of what the feds and local police were doing.

He would admit she'd been rather useful so far. Thanks to her, he pretty much knew what was going on at police headquarters. He also knew all about that psychic who'd been brought in. It didn't matter to him. He had no reason to believe in some weirdo's abnormal abilities.

He and Erickson had a long history of working together. These weren't the first hits he'd done for the man, and if things worked out the way Erickson planned, they wouldn't be the last. He grinned at the thought that Erickson had things under control even from behind bars. There was no doubt in his mind that eventually Erickson would be set free. They would be stupid not to release him. But then, the feds and the local officers had shown him they weren't too bright. Since he was still a free man getting ready to take care of his next victim.

He heard the knock on the door. It was about time she arrived.

CHAPTER TWENTY-ONE

STONEWALL LOOKED UP when the office door opened. He'd been expecting Roland, although he'd wished otherwise. "I was hoping you'd keep driving to Sutton Hills after leaving Margo Connelly's place."

Roland walked into the room. "You would hope that. Do I need to remind you whose chair you're sitting in?"

With a chuckle, Stonewall leaned back in said chair. "You can have it back but only when you're physically ready. I prefer being out there where the action is instead of in here pushing papers."

"You've been doing more than pushing papers and you know it," Roland said, sitting down in a nearby chair.

Yes, he knew it, Stonewall thought. The only downfall in spending so much time here at the office was that he'd put his family as well as his social life on hold. His grandmother and sister understood how things went whenever it came to his work. So they weren't his major concern right now. Detective Joy Ingram, on the other hand, was. Although he talked to Joy often, they had yet to go out on what he considered a real date. And lately her work schedule was becoming just as hectic as his.

"I stopped by Granger Aeronautics and talked to Sheppard and Jace," Roland said, interrupting his thoughts. "Jace thinks he has the perfect place for Margo to go into hiding. It's a cabin Jace owns in the mountains near Shenandoah."

Stonewall wasn't surprised that Roland had already started putting plans into action. Sheppard Granger was a man of great integrity, for whom Stonewall had the highest respect and admiration. Jace was Shep's oldest son. Stonewall was convinced he would be dead now if it hadn't been for Sheppard Granger.

"I want things in place to move Margo into that cabin within eight hours, Stonewall."

Stonewall released a groan. He knew Roland had sat in this chair a lot longer than he had and was fully aware that what he was asking for would require a hustle on everyone's part. But they would get it done. "It's going to be important that we make sure no one knows where she's being relocated."

"And more than anything, we need to make sure that when the move is made, Striker isn't followed," Roland tacked on.

"All that will be taken care of. I'm hoping the authorities capture the bastard soon."

"There still aren't any major leads?" Roland asked.

Stonewall knew Roland was well aware that he spoke often to one of the female detectives working the case. "Nothing major."

"How are things going with that psychic?"

"Okay, from what I understand. I hear she's good at what she does and has a favorable track record."

"That's good." Roland stood. "I think I'll go lie down on the cot for a minute."

"Okay, you do that." Stonewall watched as he left the office.

LIZ TILLMAN SWEPT into Frazier's office with a frown on her face. "Honestly, Frazier, you need to do something with Goldwyn. He can be rather rude. I was in the middle of watching a very important television show when he interrupted to say you needed to see me immediately. When I told him I'd be there once the show was done, in a mean tone he told me you needed to see me immediately."

Frazier stood from behind his desk and for a minute he didn't say anything because Goldwyn, who'd been his trusted butler for a number of years, had been following his orders. "You won't have to worry about Goldwyn bothering you any longer, Liz."

Her frown turned into a huge smile. "Are you finally getting rid of that god-awful man, sweetheart?"

"Goldwyn isn't going anywhere, but you are."

Her smile quickly reverted to a frown. "What do you mean?"

"Because you are leaving. I want you packed and off the estate in less than two hours. If you dare to linger I'll call security to make sure that you don't. And don't take anything that you didn't bring with you."

Liz's frown was now replaced by shock. "Frazier? What is the meaning of this? What's wrong?"

When he didn't say anything but continued to stand there and stare at her, she straightened her spine and lifted her chin. "I'm being replaced, aren't I? Your niece told you to get rid of me and—"

"Leave Margo out of this."

Liz lifted her chin higher. "And why should I? She's a bitch and has never liked me. I tried to get along with her, but you can't blame me if she didn't accept my friendship. As far as I'm concerned, she should have stayed in New York. We were doing great before she decided to move back to Charlottesville."

Frazier crossed his arms over his chest. "You've said enough, Liz. I want you gone. You're no longer welcome here."

Rage, the likes of which Frazier had never seen before from her, covered Liz's entire face. "You're going to regret this." And then she angrily stomped out the room.

Frazier rubbed his face, hoping he'd seen the last of Liz. After what Goldwyn had caught her doing, Frazier knew she could no longer be trusted. He then switched his thoughts to what had transpired at Margo's house earlier that day and how she had so easily figured out things about Roland. Frazier had never thought that seeing them together would make Margo suspect anything.

He picked up the phone on his desk to call Striker and give him a heads-up, just in case Liz got it into her head to pay Margo a visit.

STRIKER CLICKED OFF the phone with Frazier a few seconds before Margo walked out of her workroom. He wondered if there would ever be a time he wouldn't get a stirring in his gut when he saw her. "Was that Stonewall?" she asked him.

There was no reason for him not to answer truthfully. "No, that was Frazier. He wanted to warn me that Liz Tillman might try paying you a visit."

Margo lifted a brow. "Why?"

"Apparently they broke up, and she feels you're responsible."

Margo dropped down on the sofa, shocked. "Uncle Frazier and Liz actually broke up?"

He studied her. "You seem surprised. Does that mean you didn't see it coming?"

She shrugged. "I had my issues with Liz, but I never tried influencing Uncle Frazier about her. She was his business. I figured sooner or later he would come to his senses and see the type of person she truly was. Did Uncle Frazier give you any details as to what happened?"

"No." And for that reason, Striker decided to have Stonewall run a background check on Liz Tillman. It was better to be safe than sorry.

"We need to talk, Margo," he decided to say. While she'd been in her workroom, he had used the separation to think clearly. In order to continue to protect her, he needed to stay out of her pants.

She slouched back on the sofa. "What about?"

He wished she didn't do that. Look so damn comfortable and beautiful at the same time. She was wearing an oversize blouse and a pair of black leggings. Both showed her figure, and already he could feel the area below his belt thicken. How he would manage to keep his hands to himself he wasn't sure, but it was something he had to do. He had no options regarding that.

"The need for us to keep our hands to ourselves."

She smiled. "Okay."

He was surprised she was so agreeable. What part of what he'd said did she find amusing? "Am I missing something here?"

"Why would you think that?"

She wasn't helping matters, he thought. If anything, she was making them more complicated. And if he was reading her right, she wouldn't make resisting her easy. "I have to do my job, Margo."

"Then do it. Why would I stop you?"

"Trust me. I won't let you stop me."

They stared at each other for the longest moment, and then, easing off the sofa, she said, "Great. Now I need to go upstairs. Think I'll lie down awhile. Take a nap. Want to join me?"

She had asked in that same sultry voice she'd used when issuing that shower invitation. Her doing so nearly knocked the wind out of his sail. Almost made him say, *Hell yeah, I'll go upstairs with you and lie down. But you better believe we won't be taking a nap. We will finish what we started in the shower this morning.* But he held his peace, although the size of his erection was growing by leaps and bounds.

"I will go up the stairs to do my normal check. But there won't be any funny business going on."

"So in other words, you won't let me take care of that?" she said, her gaze zeroing in on his erection.

Why at that moment did said erection begin throbbing? "That's right. I won't let you take care of it."

She shook her head sadly. "What a pity."

Christ. I am in trouble.

"If you're ready, I will escort you upstairs, Margo."

"I'm ready."

Once they made it up the stairs, Margo moved toward her bedroom door. Before opening it, she turned to him and smiled. "If you change your mind about joining me, Striker, just knock." She then opened the door, went into her bedroom and closed the door behind her.

He stood there and stared at the closed door. She was

deliberately tempting him, and he knew he couldn't take the bait. A lot was at stake, and making sure she was kept alive headed his must-do list. Why did she have to be such a challenge, one he couldn't seem to get a handle on? When he thought he had himself back in control where she was concerned, something would happen to make him lose that control all over again. He was tired of going back and forth with her when the one constant was his desire. It seemed stronger for her than ever and was growing like crazy.

Heaving a sigh of frustration, he moved away from the door.

LIZ TILLMAN DROVE through the gates of the Connelly estate. She still couldn't believe Frazier had ordered her to leave. Even while packing she'd expected him to walk into the bedroom they'd shared together, strip her naked before tossing her on the bed and having his way with her.

She couldn't help wondering what had made him end things between them. Had he found out about that private investigator she'd hired? She'd only been looking to get a little insurance, to make sure he stayed committed to her. She'd only been driven to do such a thing because she'd picked up on him distancing himself from her.

If anyone had told her she wouldn't be the mistress of the manor by now, she would not have believed them. At one time she'd all but had him eating out her hand. Then that bitch of a niece decided to move back to town.

She knew Frazier felt beholden to his dead brother to make sure his daughter was taken care of, but Margo Connelly was a twenty-six-year-old woman who could take care of herself. Frazier was so damn protective of her. The first time he'd picked up on friction between them, he had taken the bitch's side.

And now her plans to marry Frazier were ruined thanks to Margo. And there was no way she wouldn't believe everything was Margo's fault. Now she had nowhere to go and no money to spend. While she'd been Frazier's live-in lover, he'd opened a bank account in her name and had kept the funds pouring in to use however she liked.

Frazier had let her know before she pulled away that her bank account was closed. In other words, after she used what was in it now, she shouldn't look for any further deposits. Had he found out she had used some of those same funds to hire that PI?

As Liz moved toward the interstate, the more she thought about her situation, the angrier she got. She bet Margo was somewhere laughing. Well, Liz intended to have the last laugh. She would make Margo Connelly regret coming between her and Frazier.

CHAPTER TWENTY-TWO

WITH HER HEART beating hard in her chest, Margo leaned back against her bedroom door. Striker had finally moved away. He had stood outside her door for the longest time, probably trying to make up his mind about what he should do. Yes, she'd heard his words about them not making love again. He assumed that in order to protect her it had to be hands off. Well, he would find out soon enough how wrong he was. She had discovered since being around him just how strong sexual chemistry could be. And like him, she'd tried fighting it and had discovered doing so was a losing battle.

She had decided not to fight it anymore. The emotions she was feeling were all new to her, but she had accepted that, of all men, Striker could make her want to do things she'd never thought of doing in her entire life. Like being bold enough to invite a man to her bed, even when she knew the only thing between them was a strong attraction that neither of them could control.

Didn't Striker understand they had crossed the line and in doing so were now in each other's system? Granted, she couldn't speak for him and had no intentions of doing so, but she could definitely speak for herself. Making love with him had been so off the charts she doubted if she would ever recover. It took skill and unselfishness, and it was obvious Striker knew a lot about pleasure. About how to give it as well as receive it.

She drew in a deep breath. She'd thought she would be the last person to ever have such thoughts about a man, especially after the likes of Brock and Scott. But she was intuitive enough to know Striker was different. Besides, it wasn't like something serious was developing between them. They were enjoying the moment. At least she was, but she really couldn't say the same about him. She understood his wanting to keep her safe, but she was learning that when it came to an attraction between a man and a woman, desire could get the best of you. She was experiencing so many things being with Striker, things she'd never had to deal with before. Emotions. Desires. Needs and cravings.

Moving away from the door, she kicked off her shoes and eased her leggings down her legs before pulling off her top. Wearing just her bra and panties, she lay across the bed for her nap. Quasar would be delivering dinner in a few hours. Since they'd had a late breakfast, Striker had called him and told him not to worry about bringing them lunch. Instead she had offered to make sandwiches and tea. There was nothing like good old peanut butter and jelly in a pinch. Striker hadn't complained and seemed to enjoy the sandwiches as much as she had.

They had eaten in silence, but that hadn't stopped her from noticing how his mouth moved when he chewed or how he would lick his lips every so often. Both had been turn-ons for her, so she didn't have to wonder why she was so hot for him today.

Once he'd caught her staring, and for the longest moment he hadn't broken eye contact with her. And, during that long, sensuous moment of silence, something vital had taken place between them, whether he wanted to admit it or not. Their desire for each other wasn't normal. There was no way that it could be. A look from him could rock her body, kick her heart rate into overdrive and send all kinds of delicious thoughts running through her mind.

Margo wanted to talk to her uncle and find out why he had ended things with Liz. But for now she would take a nap. She hadn't gotten much sleep last night but wouldn't complain. Not when she had enjoyed the sexual activities she and Striker had shared. Shifting in the bed with her head against the pillow, she closed her eyes.

FREDDIE GLANCED AROUND his hotel room. The place was a dive, but at the moment this was the best he could do. He recalled the times he'd traveled for work and stayed at the best hotels around. Not anymore. When the bank had downsized, those making the most income were the first to get kicked out the door.

Scott thought he was wrong for being so bitter. But Freddie didn't give a damn what Scott thought since Scott still had his cushy job. Freddie hadn't gone to college for this. He was supposed to be employed for life. He'd sent in résumés, but no calls had come in, and he was tired of waiting. His funds had run out and he needed money. Bad.

So here he was in Charlottesville, Virginia, after borrowing the money to get here from his brother-in-law. He could recall the days when his sister and brother-in-law would come to him for money. And now he was crawling to them for a loan. On top of that, he'd lied and said the reason he needed money for the trip to Virginia was for a job interview.

What pissed Freddie off more than anything was Scott's attitude about the whole damn thing. When they'd met for breakfast at Gritty's, Scott had tried talking him out of his plans to kidnap Margo. That was why he hadn't told Scott anything about this trip. As far as Freddie was concerned, the less Scott knew the better.

Freddie checked his watch. He would go down to the restaurant, grab something to eat and strategize. He had contacted another college friend who lived in DC, who was also down on his luck. Mark Cramer used to have a good government job, but his gambling addiction had gotten the best of his good sense. Freddie's promise of big money had been the lure to bring Mark on board. To carry out his plan successfully, Freddie would need one more person, and Mark would know someone else who also needed money.

By the time Freddie left Virginia to return to New York, he intended to be a hell of a lot richer.

STRIKER RUBBED HIS FACE, wondering why he was torturing himself like this. He had heard Margo move around her room, had even heard her kick off her shoes. And heaven help him, he knew the exact moment she'd undressed. Who stripped down to take a nap?

He was imagining her lying on that bed naked, or wearing very little clothing, and wished like hell he could join her. She had issued an invitation, and he had turned her down. Was that a smart move or the actions of a fool?

He tried to switch his thoughts to something else, and the only other thing that infiltrated his mind was the memory of him and Margo that morning, in the shower, standing under the spray of water. There was nothing more arousing than a sexy, wet feminine body, all slick and smooth. He recalled how it had felt to run his hands all over her, soaping her up. And the driving need that had erupted within him when he'd seen the damp, downy curls covering her womanhood.

When he had lifted her off her feet, cupped her backside and tilted her hips before backing her up against the wall to thrust in and out of her, he had been consumed by a spike of desire. He'd been overtaken with lust of the most potent kind. And the pleasure that followed still had him quivering in the groin.

Inhaling deeply, he knew he had to pull himself together before placing a call to Stonewall. Since Striker had no idea how far he'd need to drive to relocate Margo, he planned to take advantage of her napping next door and take a nap himself. He would alert Stonewall to make sure the exterior was monitored while he caught a few winks.

"What's up, Striker?"

"Checking in. About to take a nap."

"This time of day? Um, sounds interesting."

Striker rolled his eyes. "Get your mind out the gutter, Stonewall."

"Whatever. We'll keep an eye on the exterior and buzz you if we see anything out the ordinary."

"Any more sightings of that dark sedan?" Striker asked.

"Not since last night, but we're keeping watch. I have a funny feeling about that car. And just so you know, we're getting another place ready for you and

Ms. Connelly. A cabin. I'll tell you where in a coded message."

Striker nodded. The thought of him alone with Margo in a mountain cabin for no telling how long could spell trouble. But he had no intentions of breaking his rule about not taking her again.

"Get some rest while you can. Chances are you'll be moving out tonight."

Striker nodded. "Did Roland go home when he left here?"

"No, he's here. Right now he's resting on the cot," Stonewall replied. "He still needs to take it easy, but you'll never convince him of that."

At that moment Striker heard sounds coming from Margo's bedroom and went on full alert. Moans. Groans. His ears perked up. *What the hell?* "Stonewall, I've got to go," he said quickly, knowing he sounded rushed.

"Something's wrong?"

The last thing he would do was tell Stonewall what he was hearing. "Nothing I can't handle."

Stonewall was quiet for a moment and then said, "We'll be calling later with specifics about tonight. We'll text coded messages."

"Okay." Striker then clicked off the phone and listened intently. Either Margo was in the throes of some hot dream or she was intentionally messing with his mind. He had a feeling she was deliberately setting him up, probably thinking he didn't have the ability to keep his pants zipped where she was concerned. Well, he had news for her. He was programmed to do without a lot of things he wanted. Things that could become his passion. That was the way of life for him. And when it came to his job, he took it seriously.

Granted, lust had overtaken his senses last night and this morning, but he was back in control now. He would admit she was a temptation, but he would fight it. He *could* fight it. And if it was a setup like he suspected, he would have to show her his resolve was better than most. The quicker she knew that the better.

With that dogged tenacity, he moved out the door. When he got to her bedroom door, he stopped. She was still making those sounds and was probably having fun doing so, figuring he would eventually come to her. Intent on catching her in the act, he opened the door, stepped in her room and froze.

Margo was lying in the middle of the bed, and it appeared that she was really sleeping. And it seemed those sounds she was making were from a dream. He wondered who the leading man was in what appeared to be the equivalent of a wet dream. He would like to think it was him, but for all he knew, it could be good old Scotty.

Striker tried not to let that possibility annoy the hell out of him. Thinking she deserved to have her dream in private, he was about to leave when he heard his name moaned from her lips. He drew in a sharp breath. So what if she was reliving memories of their time together while she slept? He could understand that happening. After all, the lovemaking had been good. Damn, better than good. But still, the fact stirred his insides and made him hard.

His gaze swept across the bed, and he wished she wasn't lying there in just her bra and panties. And he couldn't help noticing that her thighs quivered and her legs twitched whenever she moaned. Damn. Just what was he doing to her in the dream? Was his mouth between these twitching legs? Was his body between these quivering thighs? Inside of her? Was she on top of him? Was he on top of her? Who was riding whom?

The visual of any one of those scenarios made his erection press hard against his zipper. A degree of lust he didn't want to think about or feel took over his mind and senses. Where in the hell was that control he'd felt earlier? That determination not to touch her again? Both had been obliterated the moment she'd moaned his name.

Moving closer, he inhaled her scent before squatting down beside the bed. The movement brought her awake. She snatched open her eyes and jerked upright in bed, looking at him and then frantically glancing around. "What is it, Striker? What's wrong?"

His gaze roamed over her, and then, after a slight hesitation, he said, "You said my name."

She looked at him, confused. "I did?"

"You moaned it, actually. Must have been some dream you were having."

His words made her blush and her expression went from bemused to knowing. Pushing a lock of hair from her face, she said, "Well, yeah, it was. I invited you to join me, but you turned me down. So I had to dream up a few what-if scenarios."

He stared at her, fascinated. And those scenarios had made her moan and groan? Striker knew better than to ask the next question, knew he should stand and walk out the door. But he couldn't. Not when his gaze was taking in every inch of her. Not when he was remembering how her skin had tasted all over. How he'd wanted her last night and again this morning.

And he wanted her now.

Still squatting by her bed, he leaned in and asked, "Is the invitation still open to join you?"

Striker watched as she licked her lips. His gut tightened. His erection throbbed. Her hesitation was killing him. When he thought he couldn't last a moment longer, she finally spoke. "Yes, the invitation is still open, Striker."

CHAPTER TWENTY-THREE

MARGO COULDN'T BELIEVE Striker was really here. In her bedroom. Crouching beside her bed. Especially after he'd told her earlier that the intimacy they'd shared last night and this morning wouldn't be happening again. That he was putting back on his protector gear, a role that didn't include touching of any kind. Now he was beside her bed and was so close she could reach out and touch him. She wanted to. But more than anything, she wanted him to touch her.

He said she had moaned his name. And, yes, it had been some dream. They had been making love and it was the kind of lovemaking where she'd been having orgasm after orgasm. Nonstop.

"I want to be touched, Striker. I want to be touched all over." And she meant it. She had discovered that Striker had some real serious skills when it came to pleasing a woman. And he was looking hot, sexy and accommodating. As far as she was concerned, he needed to put those exemplary skills to good use. If he was going to break his own rule, he might as well break it real good.

"If I stay, Margo, I will do more than touch you."

Her mind was suddenly flooded with memories. Heated memories. Lustful memories. And if Striker wanted to add new ones to those already stored in her mind, she had no problem with him doing so. "The only thing I have to say to that, Striker, is go for it."

He stood, and she watched as he pulled the phone out of his back pocket and speed-dialed a number, then said, "Quasar, hold up on dinner. I'll call you when we're ready." And then he clicked off the line and put the phone on her nightstand.

The phone wasn't what held her attention while he'd been talking. She was eye level to his zipper, and the huge erection pressing against it definitely couldn't be missed. He was fully aroused, and so was she. Even if she didn't want him to know how much, her breasts were giving her away. They were tight and the nipples felt like hard pebbles pressed against her bra.

She looked up and met his heated gaze. "You have on too many clothes," he said in a voice so sensual it made goose bumps appear on her arm.

Margo broke eye contact to look down at herself. He actually thought that? Seriously? When all she was wearing were panties and a bra? She looked back at him. "I think you're the one wearing too many clothes... and stuff."

The stuff she was referring to was the gun and holster strapped to his shoulder. Although she thought he looked like the ultimate badass protector, weapons had no place in her bed.

"That can be remedied, trust me," he said, removing the gun and holster.

She did trust him. Not because she had no choice but because she wanted to. She knew where she stood with him. The man who wanted to be called Striker was a loner who only enjoyed *unsteady* girlfriends. Bed partners. He'd said as much. Now she'd become one of those bed partners. So what? She wasn't looking for a steady man any more than he was looking for a steady woman. Whenever she was tempted to think otherwise, all she had to do was remember Brock and Scott and the crap she'd put up with.

She jumped when he snapped his fingers in front of her face. "You're still with me, Margo?"

She looked at him. He had removed his shirt, and his fingers were tucked in his jeans, which meant he was about to remove them as well. "Yes, I definitely am."

He smiled, and she thought his sensual lips should smile more often. It did something to his overall features. Made them appear less hard and more handsome.

"I might as well get comfortable for the strip show," she said, securing a relaxed position in bed by sprawling on her side. "I don't want to miss a thing."

He chuckled. "You saw it all last night and again this morning. Nothing new."

"Let me be the judge of that, Striker Jennings." It might not be anything new, but, unless her eyes were playing tricks on her, it was definitely a lot bigger, she mused while focusing her attention on *that* part of him.

He moved away from the bed to stand in the middle of the room as if to make sure there was no obstruction to her view. She appreciated that. Glad he was so accommodating. And when he eased down his zipper, she could feel her heart beating like crazy in her chest.

"You okay over there, Margo?"

He would have to ask. "Stop teasing and get on with it." She was enjoying this playful side of him. Both playful and sexy. And she needed that right now. What was going on in her life was pure craziness, but at this very moment she could push all that to the back of her mind. As far as she was concerned, lying here watching him strip naked was a hell of a lot more fun than cowering somewhere in fear.

"Be careful what you ask for." And with those words, he kicked off his shoes and then slowly eased his jeans down past muscular thighs.

She arched up and watched the movement of his pants as they were lowered down his legs, and then she quickly snapped her gaze back to his middle, which was covered by black briefs. She swallowed thickly, thinking that she could claim an orgasm just by looking at him. Those briefs could barely hold him and the thought of all that jammed into his underwear was almost too much to handle.

She practically held her breath when he tugged down his briefs. She thought the same thing now that she had last night. The man was definitely packing it. And when he stood there naked she couldn't help releasing a sigh of pure feminine appreciation.

"Your turn, Margo."

Meeting his gaze, she shook her head. "If you recall, I said I wanted you to touch me."

With a stride that made her heart beat faster with every step he took, he moved toward her and the bed. When he reached it, his gaze roamed all over her. She saw the blatant spark of lust in his dark pupils. "I gave you a warning to be careful what you asked for."

STRIKER STARED DOWN at Margo, wearing just her bra and panties. How could any one woman stir such heated lust within him? Make him forget he needed to stay focused on her, but not this way. It seemed she had become an addiction he couldn't kick. An itch he just had to scratch. An ache for which there was no known relief but one, and he was about to use as many dosages of it as he could manage.

He stood there for a full minute just staring at her before he finally spoke. "Do you have any idea just how much I want you?"

She shook her head, causing a mass of hair to fan across her shoulders. "No, tell me."

"If I do, it might just scare you."

"How can I be afraid when I have my protector with me?"

Those words should have snapped him out of the haze. Instead they had the opposite effect. "And now your protector wants to get inside you. Pound hard. Harder. Relentlessly. And I want to suck your breasts until you think they were created just for my mouth. In other words, I want to give you a reason to really moan my name."

She smiled and replied, "So the Striker wants to strike?"

Hell, he wanted to do more than just strike. He wanted to devour her. Without giving her an answer, he reached down and flicked open the front clasp to her bra, making the twin globes tumble out.

Striker sucked in a deep breath. He thought the same thing now that he had when he'd seen them for the first time. They were absolutely beautiful. Unable to help himself, he leaned in and, using the tip of his finger, trailed a path from one breast to the other, before using the pad of his thumb to tease her nipples. He loved the way they hardened with his touch.

His hands traced a line lower to her panties and he leaned in closer to ease them down her legs. After tossing both bra and panties over his shoulder, he looked back at her. Totally naked. Starkly beautiful.

"So, Striker Jennings, what's next?"

His nostrils flared with her scent. "Next, I taste you all over, and then I get inside of you and—"

"And what if I want to taste you?"

He threw his head back. Imagining such a thing made a low growl erupt from his throat. Made his shaft throb even more at the very thought of what she was hinting at. If she were to put her mouth on him, he doubted he would be able to endure the pleasure. It would probably kill him, and then who would protect her?

"Not sure I could handle you doing something like that," he said honestly, not caring if it made him seem vulnerable.

"I'll make it pleasurable for you."

He didn't doubt that. The mere thought of just how pleasurable it would be had blood gushing through his veins. Instead of saying anything, he picked his jeans up off the floor to pull a condom pack out of his wallet.

Moments after sliding on the latex, Striker made the gesture that started it all by extending his hand to her. She took it, and immediately red-hot sensations shot all through him. He tugged on her hand and brought her close, almost plastered to his chest. The feel of her nipples pressing into his skin almost sent him over the edge right then and there.

He whispered close to her ear. "And now for the pleasure I'll always make sure you get."

CHAPTER TWENTY-FOUR

SHE DEFINITELY KNEW what to expect, Margo thought as Striker eased on the bed with her. The only thing she wasn't sure of was just how he planned to go about it. She'd discovered last night and this morning that he had an innovative mind. One filled with a number of erotic ideas. Whether he knew it or not, he was opening her up to a whole new world. One she'd never thought of embarking on before.

Thanks to Striker, sex for her was no longer out of sight and out of mind. Around him it was in her thoughts constantly. How could it not be when she was around such a handsome, buff and virile guy twenty-four hours a day? And then there were those looks he would give her when he thought she wasn't looking. The ones filled with heated lust, strong desire and powerful yearning.

His body straddled hers, and when he captured her mouth in his, she moaned on contact. He had the ability to take kissing to a level that was outside of her realm of normalcy. He was using the force of his tongue to release desire she felt in every part of her. It was evident that he wasn't holding anything back. Neither was she. She never knew how enjoyable kissing could be until Striker. The way his tongue was swirling around hers, dominating and plowing her with relentless strokes, she couldn't help but groan. He was immersing her in sensations so strong she was on the edge of passing out from sexual overload.

He unhurriedly ended the kiss but continued to lick around her mouth for a while before leaning back to stare down at her. She wondered what he was thinking. If the same sensations were overwhelming him like they were her.

"Mercy, Margo. You're beautiful from your head to your toes."

His words, spoken in a deep raspy tone, penetrated through the sensual daze that had overtaken her. She had no problem returning the compliment. "Thank you, and I think you're beautiful too."

She really meant it. Although she was well aware that men didn't think of themselves as beautiful, in Striker's case, there was no help for it. But if he preferred her using words like *handsome*, *striking*, *gorgeous* or *attractive*, then she would.

He smiled, and she thought the same thing she'd thought earlier. He didn't smile enough. Smiling made him even more beautiful. A part of her was glad she was the one who'd put the smile on his face.

His gaze shifted to her breasts. They hardened beneath his stare. Her breath caught when he lowered his head and captured a nipple in his mouth and began sucking on it. The suction was so intense she could feel a pull in the area between her legs from the force of it.

He went to the other nipple to give it the same torment, and within seconds she was moaning his name just like she'd probably done in her dreams. She was in such a sensual state of utopia that she hadn't realized his mouth was traveling down from her breasts until he'd lifted her hips to place her legs over his shoulders.

Before her mind could fully comprehend what he was about to do, his face was there, within mere inches of her womanhood.

"Damn, you're wet," she heard him say in a throaty voice just moments before he gave her a quick swipe of his tongue. Then another. "I love your taste, Margo. And my tongue wants a deeper taste than before."

Deeper than before? She wondered how that was possible when she recalled how deep his tongue had gone the last time. "Is that possible?"

He lifted his head from between her legs just long enough to grin at her, wink and say, "Trust me, it is."

When he lowered his head again, she felt him continue to lick her, using the tip of his tongue to greedily whip around those areas he was parting with his fingers.

"I love this here," he said, inundating her clitoris with several flicks of his tongue.

"Do you?" she asked, barely able to respond and wondering if her eyes were rolling in the back of her head. She felt her hips moving with each flick of his tongue and couldn't stay still even if she wanted to.

When he sucked her clitoris, she screamed his name. But he didn't let up. As if her clit was the most delicious thing he'd ever tasted, his fingers parted her even more and he used his other hand to lift her hips. She could feel his tongue actually going deeper, licking all the way and applying a hard suction to certain spots.

It was as if he knew just those areas of her body that would make her shatter. As if he was fine-tuning her for both their pleasure. How could any man possess both a fierceness and gentleness when making love to a woman?

Suddenly she couldn't think any more as her entire body exploded into what seemed like a million pieces, with each piece sensitive to his touch. Before she could get her second wind, he came up over her and entered her in one hard thrust.

She was pinned to the bed as her head thrashed from right to left and she felt an intensity of pleasure she hadn't thought was possible. She was convinced this degree of ecstasy could only come from Striker. He knew just where to strike, for how long and how deep. The man was perfection in the bedroom.

And then he took her mouth again. It happened again, this explosion more powerful than the last. She felt her entire body shaking from one end to the other. She clutched the bedcovers, trying to keep everything from spinning. Too late. It was as if her entire body had blasted off into outer space.

And like he'd said, he didn't let up. He kept thrusting, pounding, holding her hips steady to receive one hard strike after another. The most pleasurable strikes she'd ever received.

From her Striker.

She drew in a sharp breath that was quickly absorbed by his mouth. No matter how much they enjoyed pleasuring each other, he was not *her* Striker. She must never let such foolish thoughts enter her mind. Although he admitted she was now more than a job, she knew all she was to him was another bed partner.

He released her mouth to let out one huge guttural growl.

When she actually felt Striker getting hard inside her again, she blinked, thinking she had to be imagining things. But when he quickly pulled out of her and went to the bathroom, only to come back and put on another condom, she knew she hadn't imagined anything.

He eased back between her legs and entered her in one smooth thrust. He began moving, thrusting hard, like he hadn't just had an orgasm moments earlier. She released a needy moan when sensations began building inside her again. How was that possible? Striker Jennings had to be the most virile man she knew. What other man could do this?

Striker could. And Striker did.

STRIKER GATHERED MARGO into his arms and held her. When had he become such a greedy ass? It was as if every time he was inside her body he felt at home. He felt the need to take her to the heights he'd always wanted to climb.

While making love to her, he'd felt on top of the highest mountain. On top of the world. Parasailing across the damn Atlantic Ocean. How could any one woman make him feel that way?

He looked down at her. Her eyes were closed, and she was moaning and quivering. On the second go-round he hadn't planned to pound so hard. In fact, he'd established a moderate rhythm. His strokes had been gentle and undemanding. But she'd asked, said she wanted hard again, and he'd had no problem giving her what she wanted.

"Striker?"

"Yes?"

"What's happening to me?"

He knew why she was asking. "You're experiencing orgasmic aftershocks." Orgasmic aftershocks weren't all that abnormal after an intense orgasm or a series of them. Usually they only lasted for a minute or two. So far hers had lasted for over five minutes now. If a man hit a woman's G-spot at a certain angle, followed by the insertion of his finger inside of her for further stimulation, it could cause continuous surges of pleasurable sensations. And he'd deliberately made sure she received the full effect.

"It will wear off in a minute. How do you feel?"

"It's hard to explain." She glanced up at him. "I feel like you're still inside of me."

"I am."

"I mean you. Not your finger."

He smiled. "Next time I'll make sure I stay."

She finally stopped trembling and tried lifting her head, but it fell back against his arm. She must be drained. "Next time?"

Striker stared down at her. Had he said that? He hadn't meant to give her the impression there would be another time for them. When he inhaled her scent he knew there would be a next time. Somehow he would protect her as well as bed her.

"You're okay now," he said, sliding his finger out of her and then boldly licking that finger while she watched. "Delicious," he said huskily. "Now we'll shower, but not together. I don't want to wear you out too much. Besides, I need to call Quasar to bring our dinner and get an update with Stonewall with the relocation plans."

"So we still have to leave here?"

He shifted to face her. "Yes, but you understand why, right?"

She nodded. "Yes, I understand. I just wish they

would catch the person responsible, put him in jail and throw away the key."

"That might happen. I understand the psychic who they didn't listen to the last time has agreed to work with them again. If the authorities had taken her seriously before, then they would have known they'd been holding the wrong man."

She lifted a brow. "She's that good?"

"I hear she has quite a reputation and has worked with law enforcement before. Most notably, she worked with the feds to bust up a human-trafficking ring a couple years ago."

"Wow. I hope she uses her psychic abilities to bring an end to all the killings."

Striker pulled her closer into his arms. "So do I."

RANDI TURNED FROM the barred window when she heard a sound behind her. The person she'd been waiting for had entered the room. Murphy Erickson. He seemed surprised to see her, and, just like she had requested, he was alone and wearing no restraints of any kind. Other than the orange prison suit, there was nothing to show that he belonged inside these prison walls.

He looked over at her, and his lips lifted in a curious smile. "Well, who do we have here?"

Already she was picking up negative vibes and, in a way, that was a good thing. "I'm Dr. Randi Fuller, Mr. Erickson. A psychic investigator."

His eyes narrowed. "A psychic? I didn't ask to see you."

"No, but I asked to see you."

He glanced around, and when he looked back at her, his face had hardened. "We're alone. Don't know whose idea that was, but it was a stupid one. I could kill you. With my bare hands. What do I have to lose?"

"What you have to lose is whichever body part you want me to mutilate first. Just so you know, I am a fifth-degree black belt. If you try to attack me, I will hurt you to the point that you'll wish you were dead. In the end, you might very well be."

He stared at her for a minute and then chuckled. "You're kind of feisty, aren't you? I like you. But just so you know, I don't believe in your mumbo-jumbo stuff."

"I'm surrounded by skeptics every day, but it doesn't matter. In the end, I produce results."

He pulled out the chair at the table and sat down. "So what do you think you're going to get out of me?"

"Anything you want to tell me."

"There's nothing to tell. In the end, I produce results," he echoed. "We're up to how many dead people now?"

Randi stared at him. He was trying to use her own words against her. How could he talk about those people whose lives he'd help to end as nothing more than a means to an end? She wondered how one man could be so evil. The aura surrounding him was vile and full of dark forces. She could barely stand to be in the same room with him.

When had it all begun for him? Had it been when his mother's live-in lover had sexually molested him at ten? Or when his mother had whored him out as a teen whenever she needed a fix? Both scenes flashed in Randi's mind. She had to get past his upbringing since it was clouding the present.

"Why kill them? They didn't do anything to you."

Her words, as she'd known they would, put him on

the defensive. "They *did* do something to me. I don't care if some of them were no more than spectators in the courtroom. They were there to witness what they thought was my downfall. So I'm making sure it's theirs."

"Sounds so sinister."

"Call it what you like."

"You have inside help and they will be dealt with. You're not working alone."

A sudden thought of approval came into his mind, as if he was proud of the way he had pulled everything together, outsmarting both the FBI and local law enforcement. He would probably shield his mind if he knew just how easy he was to read. Normally, she would rely on the murdered victims to help her tune in psychically to their killers. In this case, she would use the one who masterminded these particular killings. She would tap into Erickson's thoughts to determine how he'd put such an elaborate scheme together.

"I know what you're doing," he said, leaning back in the chair.

"And what exactly am I doing?"

"Trying to engage me in conversation, hoping that I'll slip and tell you something."

Randi smiled. "No, actually that's not how I operate. I'm hoping your mind is trying so hard not to tell me anything that it does anyway. Telepathy, so to speak. But then, you don't believe in all that mumbo jumbo."

He was silent for a minute and then said, "I'm through talking to you."

She had begun to rattle him. "Why? Are you afraid

your mind might tell me about Wally Forbes? Or Mack Foster?"

His eyes widened. "How do you know about…?"

He stopped speaking, so she finished for him. "Those men from your past? Men who once deceived you? The very first men you ever ordered hits on? And the fact that you're using the same man to carry out the hits now?"

Erickson stared at her. "You read some damn report on me. That's how you got those names."

Denial was expected. "You think so? Think back, Mr. Erickson. Your name was never linked to their assassinations. You covered your tracks well."

"Then you're guessing."

"Am I?" When she mentioned him covering his tracks, something flashed in his mind. He was beginning to doubt himself.

"Stop! Stop this foolishness or you will die!" he yelled, coming to his feet.

"You better hope not. I just got a glimpse into something you probably need to know. You will die before I do."

She'd said it so matter-of-factly that Erickson paused a moment. "I don't believe you."

"Are you willing to take a chance on your life?"

He straightened his shoulders. "I'm getting out of here."

Images began flowing through Randi's mind. He was trying to block them but couldn't.

"I'm leaving. Like I said, I'm not telling you anything."

He went to the door, banged on it a few times, and

when it opened, several armed guards stood there, ready to handcuff him and return him to his cell.

Randi stared at the door. He might not think he'd told her anything, when, in essence, he had revealed so much.

CHAPTER TWENTY-FIVE

MARGO GLANCED OVER at Striker. "Where are we going?" They had left her house and were heading to heaven-knew-where. He hadn't said, and from the delay in his response, he didn't plan to either.

"The less you know the better."

She sighed, closed her eyes and leaned back against the headrest. Her body still felt invigorated. Amazing. It had been close to five hours since they'd made love and every so often she would get the most delicious reminders. He no longer had to touch her to set her body on fire. He could look at her, say something to her in a particular tone and she would be immediately turned on. How was that possible? Her entire body was reacting in ways it never had before.

Giving in to temptation, she opened her eyes and looked at him again. His eyes were on the road. It was dark, so she didn't bother trying to figure out their surroundings and location. She knew Striker had things under control.

Quasar had delivered dinner around eight that evening. And in a move she knew annoyed Striker, Quasar had stayed and eaten dinner with them. She found it almost amusing how Quasar spoke in codes that Striker clearly understood.

After dinner Quasar had left, only to return hours

later with a cargo van. After they put Striker's car in
her garage, automatic timers had been placed on the
light switches downstairs in her workroom and upstairs
in one of the bedrooms. That way the lights would give
the impression she was there.

In the dead of night they loaded up the van and,
with Quasar behind the wheel, they had driven to an
empty building where they had transferred the items
from the van into an SUV. Now she and Striker were
on the road alone. Already they had been driving for
close to an hour.

Her phone rang. Thanks to Bruce Townsend, technology whiz, the GPS on her phone had been disabled
to make sure her whereabouts could not be traced. It
was her uncle. "Uncle Frazier?"

"Yes. I'm just calling to make sure you're okay."

"I'm fine. We're relocating."

"Yes, I know." Striker clicked off the phone, giving
her a semblance of privacy, although he was privy to
her side of the conversation.

Since her uncle didn't ask where she was going,
she had a feeling that he knew not to ask. She thought
that now would be a good time to bring up the subject of Liz.

"I'm sorry about you and Liz, Uncle Frazier."

"Don't be. A few days ago Goldwyn overheard a
phone conversation between Liz and a private investigator. Seems she was hiring one to dig up *dirt* on the
family. Of course Goldwyn alerted me as to what was
going on."

Of course, Margo thought. Good old Goldwyn. He
was more than just a butler. He'd been her uncle's faith-
ful confidant for years. That was why she'd never wor-

ried about Liz. She'd known that sooner or later Liz would mess up and her uncle would see the woman for who she truly was.

"Just what sort of *dirt* did Liz think she could dig up on our family?"

"I don't know. She probably intended to use it as leverage if I never got around to proposing to her."

"She would have tried blackmailing you into marriage?"

"I believe that was her plan." He paused a moment and, as if he was through talking about Liz, then said, "I want you to promise me that you'll stay safe."

She smiled at Striker, whose eyes were on the road. "I'm being protected by the best." When Striker turned and gave her an intense look, she couldn't help noticing how the lines around his eyes were tight, as if he'd realized the depth of her faith and confidence in him. When he turned his attention back to the road, she said to her uncle, "I just hope everything is wrapped up soon. I have a wedding dress to complete."

"I hope so too. But if it's not as soon as you'd like, be patient and stay put until it's safe for you to return."

She talked to her uncle a few minutes more before ending the call.

"You and your uncle are close, aren't you?" Striker asked her.

"We've had our moments, trust me. But I wouldn't trade him for the world."

"Did he ever visit you in New York?"

"Once or twice. He preferred us meeting somewhere warm like Florida or the islands. Uncle Frazier isn't overly fond of cold weather and can barely tolerate Charlottesville's winters."

"So Scott never got a chance to meet him?"

She shook her head. "No. The one time Scott could have done so, he claimed he had dinner plans with a client."

"He claimed? You didn't believe him?"

"No." She paused a moment and then said, "I'm not stupid, Striker. I suspected another woman was involved, which was one of the reasons I broke things off with him."

Margo wondered how she had wasted almost a year with Scott. Putting up with his crap? She knew the answer. Because he hadn't mattered. If he had mattered, things would have been different. She would have felt the need to be honest with him about her finances. She would have demanded more of his time. She would have ended things when she first suspected him of cheating.

"But you never confronted him about it? The other woman?"

"No. I didn't see the need. I honestly didn't want him to think I cared."

"But you did?"

"I tried to. I wanted to believe he was different from Brock."

Striker lifted a brow. "Brock?"

"Yes, Brock Ford, a guy I dated my senior year of high school. The guy I thought was my Mr. Right until I heard about his plan."

"What plan?"

"To marry me after college to get his hands on my trust fund and secure a cushy job at my uncle's firm."

"How did you find out?"

"He bragged about it to the wrong people, thinking it wouldn't get back to me."

"Is that why you never told Scott just how wealthy you were?"

"Yes. I wanted the next guy to want me because I was me, not because I was some rich chick." She chuckled. "I went from bad to worse. Scott didn't see me as a rich chick but just the opposite. He saw me as one of those needy women looking for a well-to-do husband. So I guess you can say I've learned my lesson when it comes to men. I decided to never put them at the top of my priority list again. I don't need a man in my life to be happy. I can be happy all by myself."

STRIKER EASED BACK in his seat as he absorbed Margo's words. *I don't need a man in my life to be happy. I can be happy all by myself.*

Why did that bother him when for years he hadn't felt the need to have a woman in his life? He wasn't into casual relationships. He didn't want to let anyone down or not be there when they needed him. But whenever he spent time with Margo, the possibility of something more serious crept into his mind.

Could it be because they'd spent so much time together? It was going on three weeks now. Typically the same protector wouldn't be assigned to the same case from start to finish. They worked in shifts. But Margo's case had been different, and he'd known it from the beginning. He just hadn't realized at the time just how different it would be.

She had started growing on him, and he wasn't sure how he felt about it. Granted, they'd slept together and, more likely than not, would continue to do so. But that didn't necessarily mean anything. She'd made it clear just now that she was not looking for a serious relationship with any man because of Scott and that guy she'd fallen for in college. So why was he dwelling on it?

He had to admit he enjoyed talking to her, listening to her voice…even when she was asking him questions that really weren't her business. And he liked looking at her, even when she wasn't aware he was. They shared meals, practically all the time. He was getting used to it. He liked it.

Striker also knew that he and Margo enjoyed each other sexually. He especially liked it when after making love he kept his finger inside of her, giving her an extended sexual experience while watching her face as she had another orgasm.

So where would all this lead? He knew the answer without really thinking. Nowhere. And as far as he was concerned, there was nothing wrong with that as long as they both understood. They would enjoy themselves today and not worry about tomorrow.

She had her issues with men. Although he didn't have issues with women per se, he doubted he could ever become attached to someone that way. Especially someone he could love. Where their well-being was solely in his hands.

He'd screwed up once and wouldn't let such a thing happen again.

CHAPTER TWENTY-SIX

IT WAS NEAR daybreak when Striker and Margo made it to their final destination. She walked into the cabin, rolling her luggage behind her while taking in her surroundings. "This place is beautiful, Striker. Who owns it?"

He stood beside her. Stonewall had sent someone ahead to stock the refrigerator and pantry with food and start a fire in the fireplace. Since the location of the cabin was more than an hour's drive from Charlottesville, while they were here Quasar would not be delivering food. They wouldn't risk him being followed. For now they were on their own.

"Jace Granger."

Margo looked up at him. "Jace Granger? Where have I heard that name before?"

"Probably from the media. Jace is the oldest son of Sheppard Granger."

Recognition showed in her face. "Sheppard Granger. Isn't he the guy who was locked up all those years ago for killing his wife and was freed last year when the real killers were apprehended?"

"Yes. They are one and the same."

"It was sad how an innocent man could have been sent to prison that way."

"Happens all the time," he said, moving around the room and looking around.

"And Roland knows Jace Granger?"

"We all do." One day he would tell her just how well he knew the Grangers and how Sheppard Granger was the closest thing to a father figure he'd had in his life in years.

"Let's put our stuff away and I'll show you around," he said.

"You've been here before?"

He smiled, recalling the memories. "Yes, I have."

"With another client?"

Did he detect jealousy in her voice? Did she think he'd spent time here with another female client? "No, I was here as a guest of the Grangers."

He saw curiosity in her eyes and knew her nosy bones would soon surface and the questions would start. "Come on and let me get you settled. Then I intend to cook breakfast."

MARGO WALKED OUT of the bedroom after unpacking. Although she and Striker hadn't discussed sleeping arrangements, the fact that he'd placed his duffel bag in the same bedroom she would be using spoke volumes.

She'd gotten an idea of where they were when they'd passed a sign for the Shenandoah National Park. They had driven through miles and miles of wilderness and up the Blue Ridge Mountains. She'd been surprised by the look of the cabin they'd pulled up to. It wasn't rustic, but rather it looked more like a beautiful château in the mountains.

Striker had given her the tour of the place once they'd settled in. It had two stories with the second floor overlooking the first. The walls were made of stained wood and the downstairs was spacious, with an open concept. The large kitchen was meant for someone who loved to cook and the dining area seated a big family. The living room was enormous, with a huge fireplace on one wall and a wide-screen television on the other. Rugs scattered throughout gave the place a lived-in feel, while the silk plants that looked almost real added foliage that wasn't grown in this area. The greenery enhanced the inside scenery and complemented the outside. For convenience, a separate set of stairs led from the second floor down to a fully stocked wine cellar.

What she liked most was that the entire back wall was made of glass and provided a panoramic view of Streater Lake and the Blue Ridge Mountains. The sun had just been rising as she stood at the windows. It had been a beautiful sight.

She stopped walking and sniffed the air. Rounding the corner, she found Striker in the kitchen, standing at the stove fixing breakfast, with his back to her.

She just stood there, taking in all his male perfection. His stance drew her gaze to the width of his shoulders and all those rippling muscles that extended down his back. Muscles his shirt only enhanced. She wondered if Striker had any clue just how much he oozed raw, animal sexuality. The thought of just how well he could back up that quality in the bedroom sent shivers through her entire body.

"Are you going to stand there and stare at my backside or are you going to volunteer your services in the kitchen?"

Margo chuckled. Did the man have eyes in the back of his head?

"Oh, I don't know," she said as if she was definitely undecided. "I like looking at your backside."

He turned to her. "I liked seeing your backside as well. And I also like looking at your front, preferably naked."

The man had a way of sending blood racing through her veins. And since they'd taken the wall down between them, they weren't holding back in expressing their desire for each other. "You sure you want my help?"

"Yes, I'm sure…as long as you keep your hands to yourself."

Guilty. She did like touching him. Every chance she got. "I can only promise to try," she said, going to the cabinets for plates. As she set the table, she kept stealing looks at Striker. He was spooning eggs from the frying pan into a platter. The more time they spent together, the more he mattered to her. She believed he was a man with morals—something Scott had lacked. She could not see Striker preying on a woman's trust. He wouldn't establish unrealistic expectations between them. Even now she knew where she stood with him.

"You seem at ease in the kitchen. Who taught you how to cook?" she asked him when he'd placed all the trays of food in the center of the table and they'd sat down to eat. She didn't miss the pain that flashed across his face with her question. It had been quick, yet she'd seen it.

For a moment she wasn't sure he would answer. And then he held her gaze and said, "My mother taught me to cook."

"Well, she did a great job. Where does she live?"

Another pause. "She passed away years ago, not long after I began serving my time."

She didn't say anything as she thought about what he'd shared. Did that mean he had lost his brother and mother within months of each other? As if he read the question in her eyes, he tried forcing a smile on his lips as he said, "Your nosy bone need scratching again?"

She nodded, deciding not to back down if it would mean finding out what she wanted to know about him. "Yes, it needs scratching."

He sipped his coffee for a minute as if giving his response much consideration. Then he said, "Mom took Wade's death hard. Me being locked up on top of that was too much for her. She had a bad case of hypertension and needed to take her medication daily. With both her sons gone, she wasn't taking care of her health. One of the neighbors, Ms. Foster, called the police when she realized she hadn't seen Ma for a few days. They found her in bed. She had died in her sleep."

"Oh, no. How awful that must have been for you."

"Yes, it was hard not being able to attend her funeral. Her sister, my aunt Gussie, handled everything for me."

Margo felt the lump in her throat and fought back the tears in her eyes. The man sitting across from her had endured so much pain in his life. Undeserved pain. "I'm sorry, Striker. I am so sorry." She couldn't help the tear that fell from her eye.

"I didn't tell you that to get your pity, Margo," he said in a gruff tone.

She shook her head. "What you got from me, Striker, is not my pity but my admiration. Despite your past and what you've endured, despite everything you've gone through and what I know is probably just the tip of the iceberg, you've made something of yourself. You are a man to be admired. My protector."

As if her words had done something to him, he pushed his chair back, came around the table and pulled her into his arms. Before she could take her next breath, he leaned down and captured her mouth in his and immediately robbed her of her senses. He was being methodically slow, yet extremely thorough. It was a good thing his arms had moved to her waist to support her or she would have buckled over.

She closed her eyes to hold on to the little strength she had left, but he wasn't making it easy. He was taking his time to taste her and she couldn't help tasting him back. Every stroke of his tongue was making flames of desire blaze through her. But deep down, she knew it was more than that. At that very moment there was no doubt in her mind that she was falling in love with Striker.

That startling realization had her pulling back from the kiss with a sudden gasp. When she opened her eyes, she saw him staring down at her. How had she allowed Lamar Striker Jennings to get past her defenses? The bottom line was that he had. Yet she knew there was no future for them, and, in that moment, she was saddened. After this assignment with her was over, he would leave and not look back.

When he released her, she dropped back down in her chair, not able to stand on wobbly legs. He returned to his chair, and she watched as he resumed eating. Making a decision to try to pick up the conversation where they'd left off, before his kiss had all but rendered her mindless, she cleared her throat and asked, "So, where are you from, Striker?"

He smiled over at her as he bit into a piece of bacon, probably knowing what she was trying to do. "I was born and raised in Little Rock, Arkansas. I lived there until I was sent to Glenworth Prison in Kansas."

"Kansas?" she asked, taking a sip of coffee. "What made you decide to relocate to Charlottesville once you were released?"

He didn't say anything for a short moment and then he shared, "It's where Shep suggested I come."

"Shep?"

"Yes, Sheppard Granger."

Surprise lit her eyes, and before she could ask him to expound further, her phone rang. She picked it up and saw it was an unknown number. She glanced across the table at Striker.

He nodded. "Go ahead and answer it," he said, ready to listen in.

Margo clicked on her phone and said in a cheerful voice, "Hello."

"Margo Connelly?"

She met Striker's gaze, and when he nodded, she said to the caller, "Yes, this is Margo."

"You're just the person I want to talk to."

She didn't recognize the deep male voice. "May I help you?"

"No, but I'm willing to help you. I have something you want."

"Who is this?"

"Freddie. Freddie Siskin. Remember me?"

She couldn't stop her skin from crawling. "Yes, I

274 FORGED IN DESIRE

remember you. Why are you calling me? Do you want to make another donation to my charity?"

"No," he snapped. "I don't want to make another donation to any damn charity."

"Then I'm going to end this conversation."

"I wouldn't if I were you. I've got something you might want."

"If it's not a donation, then what is it?"

"A sex tape."

She looked over at Striker and saw the way his face had tightened. "Excuse me?"

"I have a sex tape of you and Scott doing the nasty. He gave it to me. If you call Scott for verification, I'll put it out on social media. I'm sure you wouldn't want that, being an heiress and all."

"I don't believe you." She wondered how Freddie had found out she was an heiress. And from the look in Striker's eyes, she knew he was wondering the same thing. If Freddie knew, chances were Scott knew as well.

"Then meet me somewhere so I can give you your own personal copy. Once you view it, you'll have twenty-four hours to contact me to make a deal. If it's something you don't want exposed to millions, then be ready to pay me off."

"That's extortion!"

"Call it whatever you like. Meet me today. And, remember, if Scott tells me you called him, then all talks are off. Besides, Scott is pretty pissed with you, which is why he gave me the sex tape. All this time he thought you were a struggling seamstress. Imagine his shock when I told him you're loaded. You used him."

"I didn't use him."

"You forced us to give our hard-earned money to some damn charity."

"You didn't have to accept the deal. Both of you could have gone to jail."

He snorted. "Just because of a joke I played on you? Look, I'm through talking. If you don't want me to put this sex tape on the internet, I suggest you meet me today."

Margo held Striker's gaze as he mouthed the words *stall him*. She nodded. "We can't meet you today. I'm not in town now."

"Too bad. I would suggest you make your way back to Charlottesville. I will call you in four hours with the location."

"But what if I can't get back to Charlottesville by then?"

"Then that will be pretty damn unfortunate. Like I said, I will call you back. If you report this conversation to anyone, then be prepared for the consequences."

Freddie hung up.

Margo clicked off her phone, and for the longest time, she just sat there. Shocked. Did Scott actually make a tape of one of their lovemaking sessions? A part of her wanted to believe that Freddie was lying. But what if he wasn't?

"Margo?"

She blinked and met Striker's gaze. There was nothing judgmental in the eyes staring back at her, and she appreciated that. If Scott had made a sex tape and given it to Freddie, she didn't want to think of the possible consequences. "Yes?"

"If given the chance, I plan to kick Freddie's ass right along with Scott's."

His words, filled with anger, conveyed his support, and at that moment she needed it. She felt like such an idiot for even getting mixed up with Scott.

"Don't blame yourself," he said, reaching across the table to take her hand in his. "Personally, I don't believe Freddie has anything. I think he's merely trying to play you. Get some money off you."

Even while her life seemed to be falling apart, she still felt desire with Striker's touch. "But what if he does have a tape? He offered to let me view it before I pay anything."

"I think he did it just to be convincing. It's just bait to get to you."

Striker's words gave her some hope and were filled with such understanding and support that a part of her wished she could curl up in his lap, lay her head on his shoulder and have a good cry. "But how can we do anything when I'm in hiding, Striker?"

A wicked grin stretched across Striker's lips as he ran his thumbs across her knuckles. "Just leave that up to me, Margo."

CHAPTER TWENTY-SEVEN

THAT NIGHT MARGO lay in bed beneath the covers, trying to put that phone call from Freddie Siskin out of her mind. It bothered her whenever she thought that Scott could stoop so low as to make a sex tape of them. More than anything, she appreciated Striker for taking control of the situation. His plan was truly ingenious, and she couldn't wait for it to unfold.

Striker, determined to help her relax, had suggested that they have a picnic for lunch and spend some time outside by the lake. It was one of those rare days in February when the sun had come out. While he packed up the food for their meal in a basket, she'd gathered the blankets.

Freddie's call could easily have ruined the entire day, but Striker had made sure it didn't. While sitting on the blankets they'd spread on the ground, they'd made easy conversation, and she managed to relax.

Hours later, when they'd returned to the cabin, he watched a basketball game on television while she prepared a dinner that consisted of pork chops and gravy, wild rice, green beans, corn on the cob and iced tea. He'd told her a number of times that he had enjoyed it. After they had worked together and cleaned up the kitchen, she had gone upstairs to shower while he checked around and locked up for the night.

She heard his footsteps coming up the stairs, and more than anything, she wanted to be held in his arms tonight.

He leaned in the doorway for a minute and stared across the room at the bed and her in it. For the longest time, their gazes held and he didn't say anything. Deciding to break the silence, she asked, "Everything looks okay?"

He nodded, pushed away from the doorway and came into the room. "Yes."

She watched as he took off his gun and shoulder holster and then slowly crossed the room to place both on the nightstand. As usual, seeing them was a stark reminder of the danger she was in. The assassin was still out there, and until he was captured, her life remained in turmoil.

"I got a call from Stonewall."

"Any new developments?"

"Nothing new regarding the Erickson case. But Stonewall has been in contact with Detective Ingram, and a sting for Freddie has been set up. Hopefully by this time tomorrow it will all be over."

Margo hoped so. More than once today she had been tempted to call Scott, but she knew doing so would ruin everything. Striker had asked her to trust him enough to let him handle things and she would. More than anything, she appreciated how he'd taken charge and known whom to contact. He'd reassured her that everything would be alright. And now, thanks to Striker, Freddie would be walking into a sting operation the police had been brought in on. Whether he knew it or not, he was more than a protector to her. He'd become her hero.

"I need to shower," he said, breaking into her thoughts.

"Alright." He headed for the bathroom. That gave her hope they would be sharing a bed.

Margo shifted positions in bed when she heard the sound of the shower going. She had gotten so used to having Striker around that she found comfort in his presence. A part of her couldn't help wondering how she would handle things when he was no longer her protector.

AFTER REMOVING HIS CLOTHES, Striker stepped under the warm spray of the shower and tilted his head back. The water drenched his face, body and skin. He drew in a deep sigh as the water washed away some of the day's stress, but it did nothing to rid him of all those sexual thoughts he was having of Margo in that bed. She was naked beneath those covers, he was sure of it. And for her not to suggest that he sleep elsewhere meant something, didn't it?

He cursed under his breath when he thought of that call from Freddie Siskin. Striker had meant what he'd told Margo about wanting to kick both Siskin's and Dylan's asses. What decent man would do something like that? Make a sex tape of his and his lover's intimate encounters and then give it to someone to expose her if she didn't pay up?

Although Striker didn't know Dylan, he couldn't see him being involved in extortion. Not only could he lose that job he thought so much of, but the bastard could end up in jail. That made Striker wonder if perhaps Siskin was once again doing something stupid without telling Dylan about it. If that was the case, it would be up to Dylan to prove his innocence if Siskin was arrested.

And Striker was sure Siskin would be caught. Everything had been coordinated with Stonewall and the police. Just like he said he would do, Freddie had called back in four hours and Margo claimed she had returned to town and agreed to meet with him the next day.

While Freddie thought he'd be meeting with Margo, it would really be an undercover police officer impersonating Margo. Since Margo and Freddie had never officially met, he wouldn't know the impersonator wasn't Margo. And just in case Freddie had seen a picture of Margo, the undercover police officer would be someone with similar features to Margo. The officer would be wired, and if there was any discussion of exchanging the tape for money, Freddie would be arrested. Margo's uncle had been apprised of what was going on, just in case he also received a call from someone trying to extort money. Stonewall was coordinating things with Detective Ingram, and Striker had no doubt they had everything in hand.

As he lathered his body, he remembered Margo in that bed. Why were all those flutters going off in his stomach? He knew the score. There never would be anything between him and Margo but this. For him it was a need that wouldn't go away. A need that had him wanting her every time he looked at her, picked up her scent or touched her.

But still, some inner part of him knew that although he enjoyed having sex with her, it was more than that. It had to be. And that was what scared the shit out of him. There was her smile that could light up a room, and then her frown that somehow had an alluring appeal. Even her nosy bones no longer bothered him because he accepted them as a part of her. On top of all that was her ability to care, sometimes too damn much. And she'd told him that she admired him, of all things. Other than Shep, no one else had ever told him that. He had felt her sincerity when she'd said it. He knew better than to let her opinion of him go to his head, but it had. She was becoming important to him, and that wasn't good. There was a war going on inside of him, and he wasn't sure which side he wanted to win. A part of him wanted to believe that, if given time, something serious could develop between them. He could prove to her that he was a better man than those two asses she'd been involved with in the past. He would appreciate her, treat her the way a woman should be treated.

But then another part of him was afraid to even consider such a thing. The voice of reason wanted to convince him that when his protector gig with Margo was over he should keep walking and not look back. Looking back would be too risky. He could end up losing both his heart and soul. The thought of actually loving someone and losing them like he'd done with Wade and his mother would destroy him.

After rinsing the soapy suds from his body, he turned off the shower and stepped out to towel off. Thoughts of making love to Margo again were consuming him. But he couldn't see how he could stop them. He was too far gone, too overcome with desire.

Wrapping the towel around his waist, Striker left the bath suite and headed to the bedroom…and to the woman he hoped like hell was waiting for him.

CHAPTER TWENTY-EIGHT

STRIKER WALKED INTO the bedroom, took a look at Margo in the bed and felt coiling sensations grip his erection. His gaze held hers, and at that moment there was no doubt in his mind she was waiting for him. Even from across the room he could feel the strong sexual chemistry flowing between them. It was so powerful his chest heaved from labored breathing. Tonight she lay there looking soft, feminine and very, very sexy while watching his every move. The thought that she wanted him just as much as he wanted her had him walking toward the bed. And when he got close enough, he dropped the towel.

He heard her sharp intake of breath. She'd seen him naked before, and she'd seen pure unadulterated evidence of his desire for her. So why did seeing him now cause such a reaction? "You okay?" he asked, pushing the covers aside to slide into bed beside her.

"Yes, I'm okay," she said, easing toward him when he reached out for her. "Now that you're here."

Just as he thought, she was naked, and that fired his libido even more. Pulling her into his arms, he felt her hands caress his back and shoulders. She paused when her finger touched an old scar on his arm, and she leaned in and kissed it.

"A motorcycle injury?" she asked, gently rubbing the scar.

He saw no reason not to tell her the truth. "No, it's a knife wound."

She pulled back and stared into his face. "A knife wound?"

"Yes, compliments of Stonewall."

"The same Stonewall who works for Roland and keeps you updated on things? Why would he stab you with a knife?"

He was in the mood to make love, not to answer questions, but he would tell her this much. "It happened when Stonewall and I were in the slammer together and—"

"Stonewall was in prison with you?"

"Yes, that's where Stonewall, Quasar and I met."

That seemed to shock her.

He knew she was trying to wrap her head around what he'd told her, probably wondering why her uncle would hire ex-cons. He wouldn't be the one to tell her that Roland had served time in jail as well.

Deciding he would kiss her before her next question, he leaned in and joined his mouth with hers, letting her feel his tongue inside her mouth. Hopefully that would take her mind off his past and put it on her need for him.

From the way she was returning his kiss, it was working. He had no problem succumbing to the primitive forces taking over his senses, making him not want to think beyond tonight.

At that moment he felt pushed to the limits, desperate. He wanted her with a degree of passion that only she could stimulate. He felt incredibly hot for her and needed to get inside of her, join their bodies, their minds and their souls.

Their souls?

He suddenly broke off the kiss, wondering where that thought came from. He wasn't sure and at the moment he didn't want to analyze his thoughts. What he wanted was to see her. Pushing their bedcovers aside, he exposed all of her naked body and licked his lips as his gaze roamed over her. Her body was one any man would appreciate. She had the most gorgeous breasts, and the hardened dark nipples appeared as delicious chocolate morsels that his mouth wanted to devour.

But then, the same thing could be said for the area between her legs. He loved tasting her there. He loved going inside of her, moving around, thrusting inside, pounding hard. Just seeing her like this, comfortable with the way he was looking at her, was making him crazy with lust.

Every inch of her body was a total turn-on. He was about to pull her back into his arms when she pushed him on his back. She straddled him with her breasts hovering over his face. Not one to let an opportunity pass him by, he reached up and grabbed hold of a breast and sucked a nipple into his mouth, needing her taste. He applied suction with the intensity he craved.

"Striker…"

Doing this to her breast was probably making her wet. That was a good thing because he'd make a damn feast of her later. He took hold of the other breast and continued the torment, loving the sound of her moans. Margo was a highly sensual woman, and he knew if he kept this up, he could make her come just from sucking on her breast. The thought was tempting.

He wasn't immune either and was greedily feeding a desire within him that he felt all the way to his toes. It was a desire he wanted to take to the next level with her. Now. But then she flipped the script and decided to take things in her own hands, literally. She reached down and took hold of him with a snug grip and whispered, "Now it's my time to taste."

He saw the heated lust in her eyes. Saw the greed and his erection throbbed. Just looking at her made him a near goner, and he had a feeling it would be him who would be coming all over the place.

MARGO SLID DOWN Striker's body until she was eye level with his spread legs and stared at the huge shaft that was within inches of her face. The first word that came to her mind was *magnificent*.

His shaft was standing straight up, surrounded by a dark thatch of curls. The head of it was big and smooth with thick veins running along the sides. This was the first time she'd seen a man's penis this up close and personal and she thought it should be a model for all others.

She had known how huge he was because she'd felt it slide inside of her, knew how her body had stretched to accommodate him. She also knew how it felt moving in and out of her and pounding into her hard. But still, each and every time she saw it, it did something to her. It made her want to do what she intended to do now.

"Margo?"

She licked her lips. "Yes?"

"You sure about this?"

Margo smiled. Oh, she was definitely sure. And to show just how sure she was, the hand holding him began moving as she slowly began stroking him from the tip of the head all the way down to his balls. She did so while watching the play of emotions on his face. She loved seeing how his eyes would darken with each stroke, how his breath caught whenever her thumb rubbed over the smooth head, and the sound of his moan when her fingertips traced along the protruding veins.

She lowered her head and rubbed his thick shaft against her cheek, loving the feel of it sliding against her skin. When had she become so bold and naughty? And why did being so mischievous feel so good when the man was Striker? The same man who was capturing her heart even when he wasn't trying to.

"You're killing me, you know."

The husky sound of Striker's voice made her smile. Made her attuned to everything male about him. His scent. The sound of him breathing. His strength. But, most of all, his ability to be a total turn-on. "No, I didn't know. In that case, I guess I need to put you out of your misery."

With that said, she slid him between her lips, taking him into her mouth. She stared up and looked into his eyes, seeing the glaze of passion in their dark depths. If he only knew just how empowering his heated looks were. When she heard him groan her name, she became even more sexually charged. She continued to pay homage to this part of him, enjoying every minute. And if the moans that continued to flow from his lips were anything to go by, she believed he definitely appreciated her effort.

Wanting Striker was easy. Wanting to please him was a desire that seemed to be a part of her. She felt the tremors that began moving through his body as she worked her mouth over him. The moment he reached out and grabbed her hair, fisting several locks, she tightened her grip on him and felt emboldened.

She was determined that by the end of the night Striker would realize that when it came to pleasure, he wasn't the only one who could dish it out.

STRIKER FELT HIS body beginning to shudder and knew he needed to end things. Margo might not realize just what she was in for if he didn't. But for the life of him, he couldn't. How could he when he was planted inside her mouth with her tongue stroking him, slowing and tantalizingly pushing him closer to the edge?

He intended to hold on to sanity as long as he could… but it wouldn't be easy. Not when her mouth on him felt so damn good. And seeing her head bob up and down between his legs, while blowing him away, had him fighting back the urge to lift his hips and move in sync with the way her mouth was stroking him. The heat of her tongue was destroying his willpower, and a groan of pleasure rumbled in his chest.

And then it happened. He growled out a series of expressive words as a mirage of explosive sensations ricocheted through his body, nearly propelling him off the bed. Somehow she wouldn't stop, didn't let up as she drew the very essence of his being out of him and then worked her tongue over him, lapping up anything she might have missed. He began murmuring words, not certain just what those words were or if they made any sense. For him it didn't matter. He'd just been given the blow of blows and his body was still reeling from the impact of what Margo had done.

Needing her with an urgency he felt in every part of his spent body, he reached down and gently cupped the back of her neck. He eased her up his body, fully aware that her tongue was now licking areas she passed along the way. And then with all the strength he could conjure, he switched their positions so she was on her back beneath him. He reached over to the nightstand to grab a condom packet.

"Striker?"

He paused and looked down at her. "Yes?"

"I'm on the pill, and I'm healthy. Unless you're not, you don't have to use one unless you really want to."

He didn't want to. The thought of not doing so, of being skin to skin with her, had him trembling inside. "I'm healthy, too, and as long as you're comfortable with me not using a condom…"

"I'm comfortable with it," she assured him.

Breathing heavily, he used his knee to ease her legs apart. He slid inside of her, loving the feel of his flesh touching hers. Pressing her into the bed as his weight bore down, he felt himself go to hilt. Lifting his head, he stared down at her while his heart raced a mile a minute. She looked up, returning his intense stare as her hands began softly stroking his back and shoulders. Her touch was sending him over the edge again as stirring sensations rejuvenated in his groin.

"Striker…"

Her inner muscles were clenching him tight, seemingly holding his shaft hostage. As far as he was concerned, that was an unnecessary move since he didn't intend to go anywhere. He was perfectly satisfied to remain where he was for now. Striker inhaled deeply, absorbing Margo's scent through his nostrils. Loving her aroma. Loving how she said his name whenever he was inside of her.

Loving her.

He went still when that thought flashed through his mind. He blinked and then stared back down at her. The woman beneath him. The woman whose body he was inside of. The woman whose life he'd been hired to protect. The woman who'd pushed it beyond that. The woman who had broken through all the blockades he'd erected.

Striker was shaken by the very thought that he had any feelings for Margo beyond what was necessary to do his job. He could try fighting it, blow off his concerns, find a solution to the madness or accept things as they were. But he knew the best thing was to deal with the issue of Margo and his feelings for her when he was in a better frame of mind. It had to be during a time when she wasn't around to muddy the water, hold his thoughts captive or make him believe in things that he really shouldn't.

He wouldn't accept his love for her, regardless of how difficult that might be. When he got some distance between and could think more logically, things would be clearer. He was sure he'd gotten lust confused with love. That had to be it.

Satisfied with that supposition, he began moving inside her, loving the way it felt. He began growling deep in his throat with every single stroke. His eyes were glued to her face, watching her expression each and every time the hard length of him slid into her body and then out again, over and over in repetitive strokes. She couldn't mask the unadulterated, raw emotions in the eyes staring unflinchingly back at him. It was a degree of desire and longing unlike anything he'd ever felt, and he was feeding off of it. It was driving his passion, his hunger, lust and need.

Suddenly, something shot through him, causing him to blink at the force that rushed even more powerful emotions through him. She said his name again, calling out to him in the most primitive way as if to beckon him to claim her as his. So he did. He leaned down and kissed her, needing his mouth to be joined with hers. Not wanting anything separating them. He wanted them to be joined from head to toe.

And when their lovemaking suddenly escalated to a fevered pitch, he felt her body shudder, almost uncontrollably, and he felt those tremors trigger his own orgasm. He blasted off inside of her, never wanting anything as much as he wanted to fill her with him at that moment. Wishing he could stay buried inside her forever this way.

He forced himself to snap out of those thoughts. Margo Connelly had somehow managed to wrap herself around him, every single inch, and right now he didn't see a single thing he could do about it.

And he wouldn't waste his time trying.

CHAPTER TWENTY-NINE

A SHORT WHILE LATER, Margo could still feel every nerve-pulsing sensation flowing through her as she tightened her legs around his finger, which was embedded in her. He had done it again, triggering her orgasm into after-shocks that had her shuddering in pure, piercing passion. The kind that you couldn't release until your body was ready to do so. His techniques in the bedroom were simply amazing. And she loved it.

Somehow he'd known when the last moan would flow from her breath, and his mouth was right there, capturing hers and kissing her with a need that mirrored her own as their tongues tangled greedily. She started moaning into his mouth as a spike of unrelenting desire began swirling around in her stomach.

He drew back from the kiss at the same time he withdrew his finger from inside her and, like before, she watched him lick the finger that was drenched with her juices. Then he pulled her tighter into his arms and held her, speaking to her in a soft voice, telling her how much he'd enjoyed her.

With all the strength she could muster, she lifted her hand to his cheek as her fingertips brushed across the sexy, dark stubble covering his chin.

Leaning down, he used the tip of his tongue to lick sweat from the side of her face before nibbling around her lips. She was amazed how much pleasure and passion he could generate, whether it was with his finger, tongue, hands or whatever he decided to use.

She would never forget the moment she'd felt his semen shoot into every part of her. It was the first time she'd made love to a man without any barrier between them, but for some reason, she had made the offer to Striker and he'd accepted. She had made the same offer to Scott, and he'd turned her down. At the time he'd all but accused her of having ulterior motives. As if she would deliberately set him up to be her baby daddy or something. She had found his way of thinking so ludicrous. That was the one time she'd come close to telling Scott that she didn't need his money because she had enough of her own. And that having a baby with him was the last thing she'd want.

"Ready to go to sleep now?" Striker asked, intruding on her thoughts while running his fingers through her hair.

She should be ready, but a part of her felt too wired. Too aware of him in every single pore of her body, especially the heat of his skin touching hers. "Can we talk?"

She figured that was better than asking for them to make love again. She could feel the crackle of sexual energy that was always in the air whenever he was near.

"Just as long as it's not about Siskin and Dylan. I've had enough of them for one day."

So had she. Margo knew what she wanted to talk about, something she just had to know. "Why did Stonewall stab you? And if the two of you were in prison, then how did he get a knife anyway?"

Striker knew Margo wouldn't let it go until he told

her what she wanted to know. One day he would learn to keep his mouth shut around her…unless he was kissing her. He decided to give her the short version. "It was a butter knife from the kitchen." No need to tell her that if the knife had hit its target and ruptured a vein, it would have been just as deadly as a butcher knife.

"Stonewall was already in prison when I got there. We clashed and over time became bitter enemies. One day things came to a head and we fought. End of story."

He shifted positions in bed to hold her while they slept, but he should have known that for her it wasn't the end of the story. She wiggled out of his arms and sat up to loom over him. "But the two of you are friends now."

"Yes. Stonewall, Quasar and I are the very best of friends."

"What happened to turn that around?"

Seeing he wouldn't be getting any sleep for a while, he propped himself up on his pillow and pulled her to him. "It's not what, Margo, but who. Sheppard Granger happened. He arrived at prison one day and changed everything. Don't ask me how he did it because I don't really know. All the inmates thought they were badasses, except when they were around him. He was much older and carried himself in a different way. It was easy to tell he was someplace he didn't belong and way out of his element, but he had decided since he was there he would make something positive out of it. He started these programs for us. Most of them were educational in nature. And more than once Shep stepped in to help fight for better living conditions and educational opportunities. He was a born leader."

Striker paused a moment before adding, "Shep became our liaison with the warden. Keeping peace when needed and telling us when we were wrong, teaching us how to pick our battles. Over time he became a father figure to not only the three of us but to a lot of the other younger convicts as well. I think we reminded him of his own sons."

Striker remembered how at first they'd all tried resisting Shep's overtures, no matter how positive they were. "Somehow he understood each and every one of us. Made us believe that no matter what crime we'd committed, there was a life waiting for us beyond that barbed-wire fence. That we didn't have to wait to make something of ourselves until *after* we served our time, but we could do it while incarcerated. I got an associate degree while in prison and finished up with my bachelor degree at Hampton University when I got out."

She lifted a brow. "You have a bachelor's degree from Hampton University?"

"And an MBA from the University of Virginia."

She stared at him for a long moment. "That's remarkable."

He shook his head and chuckled, pressing his nose to hers. "Why don't you go ahead and ask why I'm not working at a job that uses my degree? Don't try to pretend you're not curious."

She snuggled closer to him when he tightened his arms around her. "Okay, I admit that I'm curious."

He could understand. "I own a pretty good chunk of stock in several companies…including Roland's firm. The three of us—me, Stonewall and Quasar—own quite a number of shares. But we're satisfied with being silent partners and letting Roland run things."

He waited for her to ask something about Roland,

whether or not he had a past in prison, and when she didn't, he figured she hadn't thought that much about it yet.

"So that's why you have such a close friendship with the Granger family?"

"Yes. I owe Shep my life. He convinced me that retaliating by killing Stonewall wasn't the anwer. He helped me get on the right track to get out of prison and made sure I kept my head on straight to stay out. What he's done for us could never be repaid. I don't know any man who was more highly respected, and it was well-earned and deserved respect. He would have done anything for us, and usually he did."

Striker was proud that, last year, when Shep's sons' lives were in danger, he had been in a position to pay some of that debt back. He, Quasar and Stonewall had stepped up as protectors for Shep's sons. Not that he was going to tell Margo how he'd saved Caden Granger's life, risking his own. He'd done what any of them would have, and he didn't need Margo making a big deal out of it.

"Thanks for sharing all of that with me, Striker."

He looked down at her. For some reason, sharing it with her had felt right. "No problem."

"I guess we'll go to sleep now."

He saw the look in her eyes. "Do you really want to?"

She shook her head. "Not really. What about you?"

"No. I could claim it's my time to ask you some questions, since you've been drilling me with yours for close to an hour."

Margo chuckled as she snuggled closer to him. "Are you sure that's what you want to use this time for? To ask me questions?"

Striker drew in a deep breath, deciding, no, that wasn't how he wanted to spend his time. At least not now.

LIZ TILLMAN TIGHTENED her coat around her and then glanced at her watch. The man was supposed to meet her at ten. She didn't like coming to this area of town at night, but she was determined to teach Frazier and that bitch of a niece a lesson.

She quickly walked into the café, taking a seat at a vacant booth. She used to frequent places like this but that was in the old days. And definitely not since she had moved up in the world after deciding she wanted to go places. She had worked hard to overcome her past, and when she had met Frazier she'd known he would be her ticket to the life she'd always wanted.

She didn't appreciate all her hard work going down the drain because of one person. As far as she was concerned, Margo Connelly had coming what Liz had planned.

"Faye Matthews?"

She glanced up and was about to tell the big bruiser of a man standing at her table that he had mistaken her for someone else, when she quickly remembered that the name *Faye Matthews* was her alias. She plastered a smile. "Yes, I'm Faye."

He chuckled and gave her a look like he knew that wasn't her real name, before sliding into the seat across from her. "So what kind of job do you have for me, Faye?"

She nervously looked around before turning back to him. He had come highly recommended from a friend of a friend. She wasn't sure this was the place they should talk. It wasn't crowded, but most of the tables were filled. The last thing she wanted was to have their conversation overheard. However, she didn't want to go anywhere with this man. She felt safer inside the diner than outside, where the building was surrounded with dark alleyways.

She leaned over the table and said in a low voice, "There's someone I want you to get rid of. Here's a picture." She slid the photo over to him.

He took it and looked at it for a few minutes and then smiled, showing his crooked teeth and a sinister glint in a pair of beastly eyes. "What's her name?"

"Margo. Margo Connelly."

CHAPTER THIRTY

RANDI STUDIED THE notes on her computer screen. She was alone in the office Harkins had provided for her use and she was grateful for that. Her meeting with Erickson had been draining. More than once today, while doing her research, she had lapsed into what she'd long ago termed a deep state of concentration. For some reason, her psychic mind was treating this case differently. It was strange how strong the ambiences were, and she was determined not to take any of them lightly.

She knew about Erickson's sordid past. Most of it she'd decrypted from the time she'd spent with him. A part of her was glad he was finally behind bars for his crimes. But then there were murders he hadn't been convicted of. Murders he'd never even been linked to. In her mind she had seen the victims, and they were calling out to her. The only good thing was that about 80 percent of those murdered had been assassinated by the same individual, Erickson's personal hit man. And she hoped she would be able to stop him before he could kill again.

She looked up when there was a knock on the door. "Come in."

Detective Ingram walked in. "How are things going? Do you need anything?"

Randi shook her head as she leaned back in her chair.

This was the first she'd seen of Detective Ingram today. According to Chief Harkins, she'd been pulled to work another case. Randi got strange vibes whenever she was around Detective Ingram.

"Things are going fine," Randi said. "And, no, I don't need anything. In fact, one of the officers brought me a fresh pot of coffee a few moments ago. Guess it was obvious I'd be burning the midnight oil. Grab a cup. I'd like to go over a few things with you."

"Sure. Want me to pour you a cup as well?"

"Yes. Thanks." Randi looked back at the computer screen. The number three had been flashing through her mind most of the day. She had awakened at three o'clock this morning and had a hard time getting back to sleep. Then her mother had called to remind her that Randi's twin nieces would be turning three in a few weeks. When she had arrived this morning, the room she'd been given by Chief Harkins had been office three. What did all this mean?

"Here you are," Detective Ingram said, placing the cup of coffee on the desk.

"Thanks." Randi lifted the cup to take a sip and glanced over at the detective, who was about to do the same. Suddenly, a flash of one of the recent victims' faces nearly blinded Randi. "Stop!"

Randi's word startled Detective Ingram. "Why? What's wrong?" she said, moving closer.

Randi placed her coffee cup down and said, "Don't drink that."

Detective Ingram glanced at the coffee cup she held in her hand. She looked back at Randi, confused. "Why not?"

"It's tainted with poison."

CHIEF HARKINS DREW in a deep breath and glanced at the two women. For the second time since he'd been summoned, he asked, "And the two of you are sure you're okay? That you didn't drink any of that coffee?"

Detective Ingram shook her head. "No. I was about to, but Dr. Fuller stopped me."

The police chief nodded and then met Randi's gaze when she said, "No, I didn't drink any either."

Harkins's phone rang, and he quickly answered it. "What have you got, Bill?" Moments later he hung up his phone and said, "It's not that I didn't believe you, Dr. Fuller, but I had to follow protocol. That was the lab, and you were right. The coffee was laced with arsenic. A high dosage. Had either of you taken a sip of that coffee, you would have died."

He rubbed his chin thoughtfully. "Since no one knew Detective Ingram would be returning from that case she'd been assigned to work, I can only assume that coffee was meant for you. Do you recall the name of the person who brought the coffee to your office?"

Randi nodded. "You're right. It was meant for me. And the name of the officer was Ted Elliott."

Harkins addressed one of the officers in the room. "Bring Officer Elliott here immediately."

"Yes, sir."

The officer left and within a few minutes he returned with Officer Elliott.

"Yes, Chief?"

"Officer Elliott, I understand you delivered a fresh pot of coffee to Dr. Fuller earlier today."

Officer Elliott smiled proudly. "Yes, sir, I did."

When no one smiled back, his smile wavered. "Did I do something wrong, sir?"

"It depends. Did you make the coffee?"

"Oh, no, sir. Officer Blackshear made it. Then she got busy and asked me to deliver it for her."

Chief Harkins raised a brow. "Officer Alyson Blackshear?"

"Yes, sir."

Harkins turned to the same officer he'd asked to fetch Officer Elliott and said, "Get Officer Blackshear in here immediately."

"I saw her leave the precinct around an hour ago," the officer said.

"Then go pick her up for questioning," Harkins ordered. "And take backup when you do." The officer quickly left the room.

"Three," Randi said, getting everyone's attention.

Harkins asked, "What about three, Dr. Fuller?"

She met his inquisitive gaze. "There are three plants working with Erickson and the assassin. Officer Blackshear is one of them, but it might be too late to question her."

"Why?" Harkins asked.

"Because Erickson thinks she'll become a liability and wants to quiet her." What she didn't reveal was that she had a feeling Erickson was worried Randi would pick up on his plants' identities, and he was trying to make sure if she did that they wouldn't be alive to tell anything.

Nobody said anything for a minute. Then Detective Ingram asked, "You said there were three. What about the other two? Can you identify them? Do they know about each other?"

"No," Randi said somberly. "I can't identify anyone, and I have a feeling that although everyone's identity was to be kept a secret, it wasn't. Pretty soon the other two will figure things out, especially now that Officer Blackshear is dead."

"Dead?" the others in the room asked simultaneously.

Randi nodded. "Yes. I see her face, and now she's a victim like the others."

For the longest time, the room was quiet...and then Harkins's phone rang. He didn't take his eyes off Randi as he answered it. "Chief Harkins." He pinched the bridge of his nose, clearly frustrated. "I'm on my way."

He looked at everyone in the room. "An officer was shot down. A female officer."

"Officer Blackshear?" Detective Ingram asked when no one else did.

"Yes," Harkins said, rubbing his face. "And it appears she might have been killed with the same high-powered rifle used on the others."

STRIKER GLANCED OVER at Margo as he clicked off the phone. They had taken advantage of another beautiful day to eat their lunch on the patio outside. "That was Stonewall. The sting operation went down and you won't believe what happened."

"What?"

"When the female decoy arrived at the appointed place to meet Siskin, she was grabbed as soon as she got out of her car and shoved into another vehicle, one driven by Siskin's accomplice."

"He had someone working with him?"

"Yes. Two others. One shoved your double in and the other one did the driving."

"Please tell me one was Scott."

"No, it wasn't him. Neither the man who abducted the decoy nor the driver of the vehicle had any idea the woman wasn't you, and they told her everything, bragging about the fact that there really wasn't a sex tape and laughing at her and calling her stupid for believing Siskin's lie. It seems the plan all along was to kidnap you for ransom."

"Kidnap?"

"Yes. They delivered the policewoman to Siskin, who was just as clueless that the police officer wasn't you. By the time the decoy admitted to being a cop, law enforcement had surrounded the place. Siskin and his accomplices surrendered without a fight."

"So it's over?" she asked, sounding relieved.

"Yes. Siskin and the other men were arrested, and someone from NYPD has picked up Scott for questioning. Siskin claims the kidnapping was Scott's idea. If it was, then Dylan is in a lot of trouble."

At that moment Margo's phone rang, and he saw the caller was Claudine. "I need to answer this, Striker."

"Why?"

"I've been expecting a call from her. She was supposed to decide on the type of material she wanted for the lining of her wedding gown."

"Fine, but don't let her know where you are."

Margo nodded while clicking on the phone. "Claudine?"

"Margo, hi!" Claudine said in an excited voice. "I found the perfect material. Would it be okay for me to drop by later today to show you the sample?"

Margo glanced over at Striker, who was listening to her call. "I'm out of town now, Claudine."

"Oh." She heard the disappointment in the woman's voice. "When will you be back?"

Margo nibbled on her bottom lip as she said, "Hopefully in a week or two."

"Hopefully? Don't you know? Will my gown be finished in time for my wedding? Will you—"

"Your dress will be finished in time. I have until September, Claudine."

"I know that, but I don't want a rushed job done on my gown," Claudine snapped. "My wedding day will be all about me, and I want to be the most beautiful bride everyone has ever seen."

Margo rolled her eyes. "And you will be. I got this, trust me." Even while saying the words, she was hoping she was right. "I'll contact you the minute I get back into town. I can't wait to see the fabric you've found. Bet it will look beautiful beneath your lace," she said as a way to smooth Claudine's ruffled feathers.

"I think it will too," Claudine said, her voice cheerful again. "Just call me so I can drop by when you return."

"I will."

Margo clicked off the call and Striker asked, "Are all brides-to-be that pushy?"

She smiled. "Some are worse. I have some who would like to come to my house, pull up a chair and watch me sew every stitch. Like Claudine said, it's a day that's all about the bride, and they want to look beautiful, not only for the groom but for everyone attending. All my gowns are meant to give a wow effect, and hers won't be any different."

He nodded and smiled. "Come on. Let's go for a walk so I can ask you all those questions that I didn't get around to last night."

THE MAN HID his smile as he took in the crime scene, standing among other onlookers as if he was also curious. The uniformed officers were doing a good job holding people back while the detectives on scene worked to collect evidence. No doubt they were wondering how such a thing had happened and why.

Only he knew the answers since he was the one who'd pulled the trigger. Erickson had ordered the hit, thinking that eventually Officer Alyson Blackshear would be a loose end, one he was convinced couldn't be trusted not to spill her guts. Seemed Erickson had been right. Blackshear had taken it upon herself to get rid of that psychic after becoming scared the psychic would eventually finger her.

When Erickson had found out about the attempt made on the psychic's life, he'd been furious to the point that he'd ordered hits on two other informers who he thought were weak links like Blackshear. The man wasn't sure what had gone on during Erickson's meeting with that psychic, but for some reason, Erickson didn't want anything to happen to the woman. It was as if he was scared of her for some reason.

The assassin shook his head at the absurdity of that idea since he knew Murphy Erickson wasn't afraid of anyone. For whatever it was worth, the assassin had liked Blackshear and knew sooner or later they would have shared a bed. Too late now. He got paid to follow orders, not to ask questions. Erickson was running the show.

For now.

He'd heard a rumor that someone new was taking over Erickson's territory. He'd gotten word that sinister plans were being made to make sure Erickson didn't leave prison, and the last thing the assassin intended to do was get in the middle of some fucking turf war. All that shit might indeed be true, but for now he would continue to take orders from Erickson.

The assassin decided to move on. It wouldn't be a good idea to hang around for too long. The cops would discover Blackshear had a connection to Erickson as soon as they saw she'd been killed with the same gun as the latest victims. Eventually they would figure out she'd been a traitor and they'd wonder why Erickson had turned on her.

As he walked to his car, the assassin knew he had two other informers to take care of. Three deaths within twenty-four hours should keep the cops and feds scrambling for a while. Then he could turn his attention back to his hit list. Next up was a woman by the name of Margo Connelly. He knew she had left the city. But little did Ms. Connelly know there was no place she could hide.

CHAPTER THIRTY-ONE

MARGO COLLAPSED ON top of Striker's chest. There was something to be said about sex in the morning. Being awakened by a man kissing all over your butt cheeks, followed by sensual licks up your spine, could definitely grow on you. And when that same man flipped you on your back, buried his head between your legs and proceeded to make you his breakfast, it was absolute heaven.

"Ready to shower?"

She glanced over at him with drooping eyes before burying her head under the pillow. He had to be kidding. She doubted if she could move an inch. She was exhausted with a capital *E*. On top of that, she hadn't gotten much sleep last night. How many times had they made love? Too many to count but plenty to remember. Heated lust was not bad. In fact, it was something she was getting used to.

He pushed the pillow off her head. "I asked you a question, sweetheart. Are you ready to shower?"

Sweetheart? She felt a sudden tingle in her heart. He'd called her "sweetheart" last night as well. Usually, she didn't let a man's terms of endearment get to her, but Striker didn't come across as a man who would use such sentiments lightly.

She glanced over at him. "I'll pass for now. I could

use at least one more hour of sleep. Maybe two," she mumbled groggily.

"Okay. I'll do a few exercises, shower and make some calls. Maybe by then you'll be ready to play again."

Play again? She knew exactly what kind of playing he had in mind. The man had more stamina than anyone she knew. After the last time, she needed to get her second wind. "Maybe."

She heard him chuckle as he walked out the room. She drew the pillow back over her head. *Let him laugh*, she thought. She didn't care. Right now all she wanted to do was sleep.

AFTER A STRENUOUS hour spent working out, Striker took a shower. Coming back to the bedroom, he dressed while Margo slept. She still lay spread out on top of the bed, naked. He took the corner of the bedspread to cover her. Seeing her without any clothes was too much temptation.

Even covered up, she looked sexy. Her head was no longer hiding under the pillow and her hair was in disarray all over her head. She was sleeping peacefully, and, as far as he was concerned, she was the most beautiful women he'd ever seen. In clothes or out. Asleep or awake. Smiling or frowning.

He wondered if she could tell she'd been the first woman he'd ever ejaculated inside of. Knowing that she was the first had made him anxious. He had wanted to know how it felt to be skin to skin with a woman. But not just with any woman. With Margo.

Being inside of her without a condom had felt like heaven. His shaft had felt her wet heat, had nearly drowned in it. She had gotten wild on him, stroke for stroke. He was certain her fingernails had left marks on his back and shoulders, but he didn't care if they had. He had loved every minute of making love to her and didn't regret a single thing.

Striker checked the time. He had just strapped on his gun and holster when his phone vibrated in the back pocket of his jeans. He quickly left the bedroom to answer it, glad he'd had the presence of mind to place it on vibrate so it wouldn't wake Margo.

"What's wrong, Quay? You miss bringing us our breakfast?"

"No. I got plenty to do here. Charlottesville is getting crazy, man. It's been leaked to the press that the police-woman who was shot down yesterday was one of Erickson's insiders. It's also rumored there are two others, so they're all looking at each other with suspicion."

"Why is Erickson turning on his own people?"

"To be honest, I'm not even sure it's Erickson. Word on the street is that someone else is vying for the position Erickson held within the mob before going to jail. Nobody knows what's going on."

Quasar paused as if to catch his breath. "The mayor is holding a press conference at noon. The people are calling for some of the top officials to step down, including him. The citizens are running scared and don't think they can trust law enforcement."

Striker decided not to comment on the latter because he didn't trust them the majority of the time either. But then, Roland trusted them even less. "How's Roland?" he asked.

"We got him to go home last night, but he was back

today at the crack of dawn. Stonewall and I decided to leave him alone and let him feel useful."

"That's probably not a bad idea." He, Stonewall and Quasar had known Roland long enough to know that he used work as a way to deal with a lot of things that still haunted him.

"I heard about the guy who thought he was kidnapping Margo. Glad that he and the guys who were helping him are behind bars."

"So am I," Striker said, wondering if Dylan really had been involved.

Striker conversed with Quasar a little while longer before ending the call. He glanced at the closed bedroom door and moved in the opposite direction, heading down the stairs. Margo definitely needed her sleep. It had been one orgasm after another last night, for both of them. Each one more intense than the one before. But even more special had been the times when they'd lain there afterward, their gazes locked and their limbs entwined while trying to get their breathing back on track.

There had been something singularly profound about it. Something akin to sheer bliss. *Sheer bliss?* When had he ever experienced something like that in his life? When had he thought something like that even existed? Especially with a woman? He'd enjoyed women in bed before, but when it came to Margo, it went beyond mere enjoyment. He would admit, and not even grudgingly, that the time he'd spent with Margo, even considering the circumstances, had been pretty unforgettable. And maybe, quite possibly, if he had to do it all over again, he wouldn't change a thing.

He had a feeling Margo would sleep until close to

lunchtime. He might as well cook a pot of soup. Forecasters predicted the weather would take a turn and cold temperatures would be returning. Wood had been chopped for the fireplace and they had plenty of food on hand. There was even a generator in case they lost power.

Under different circumstances, he would love to be snowed in with Margo. Just thinking of all the possibilities made him hard. But he couldn't forget the reason they'd sought refuge at the cabin. A crazed killer was out there. And although they'd taken every single precaution to make sure that as few people as possible knew where she was and that they hadn't been followed, for some reason, he had a funny feeling about something he couldn't put his finger on quite yet.

He lifted his hand and looked at one particular finger and smiled. He now thought of it as Margo's finger since he liked having it inside her when triggering her aftershocks. He shook his head, knowing he needed to get his mind off what he would like to do with Margo anytime and every time he got the chance. Instead he would get started on that pot of soup.

PERCY WEAVER HAD a feeling his days were numbered. Ever since hearing about Alyson Blackshear and her connection to Erickson, he'd begun looking over his shoulder. Although he didn't know Blackshear and hadn't realized that, like him, she was on Erickson's payroll, all that mattered to him was that she was dead. And from what he'd heard, she'd been gunned down by the same assassin who was going around killing everyone who'd been in the courtroom that day.

Percy wondered what he'd been thinking to get in-

volved with Erickson in the first place. He knew the
answer, though. Greed. At least if anything was to
happen to him, his family would be taken care of. He
had set up everything to ensure they would live comfortably for the rest of their lives. With all the money
he would leave his wife, she could return to Italy, her
birthplace, and live lavishly rich. Or she could buy her
own damn island if that was what she wanted. And
just so the feds wouldn't try to confiscate anything,
he'd transferred everything into a Swiss bank account.

He glanced down at the package in his hand. It was
the final piece to the puzzle he needed to take care of.
To be on the safe side, just in case someone was onto
him, he had put a plan in place, one he hoped would
work. The package in his hand was a fake. He'd hired
a courier to make sure the real thing got to its intended
destination.

He stepped out of his office and the first person he
ran into was Special Agent Felton. Damn, just his luck.
It seemed the man had been too visible lately, asking
questions and making Weaver wonder if perhaps Felton
was onto him. The last thing Weaver needed was to start
getting paranoid. Felton had no reason to suspect him of
anything. As far as Felton was concerned, Weaver was
one of the good agents.

"Going someplace, Special Agent Weaver?" Felton
asked, noting the package in his hand.

Why had Felton called him by his full title today,
not *Agent Weaver* or just *Weaver*? Was it deliberate?
"Yes. My wife wants me to mail this off to her parents in Florence." Just in case he was stopped for some
reason, the package was addressed to Leigh's parents

in Italy, just like he'd told Felton. Inside the package were souvenirs Leigh would send to them on occasion.

"That's nice of her."

Weaver forced a smile. "I have a nice wife."

"Yes, you do," Felton responded, looking at him strangely. "Tell Leigh she hasn't invited me and Harriet to dinner in a while. The four of us should get together."

"I'll make sure I tell her that. Now, if you'll excuse me, I'm in a hurry to get to the post office before they close."

"Okay. I'll see you tomorrow."

"Sure thing."

Weaver left the FBI building and kept glancing over his shoulder as he walked to his car in the parking garage. He had opened the door and slid in the seat when a text message came across his phone. He checked it. It was a reminder from Leigh to pick up a dozen eggs on the way home.

He put on his seat belt and started the ignition. The moment he did so, he heard a strange sound. When he realized what the sound meant, it was too late. Within seconds, the car exploded.

"PACKAGE FOR J. B. SWEET."

Manning Carmichael looked up from the stack of papers to stare at the young man standing in front of his desk. "I'll sign for it."

"I was instructed to make sure J. B. Sweet gets it."

"And she will. I'm her personal assistant. I can take care of it."

The courier shook his head. "Sorry, pal. I got strict orders to hand this to J. B. Sweet and only J. B. Sweet.

No one else. I got a big tip to follow those orders, and I intend to earn every cent."

Manning rolled his eyes, thinking this guy better be glad he was in a good mood today. Otherwise, he would tell him just what he could do with his delivery. "Fine, have it your way." He smiled. At least it would give him the chance to interrupt whatever was going on in his boss's office. Her husband, Dalton Granger, had arrived over an hour ago and hadn't left yet. Knowing those two, Manning's imagination was running wild as to what was going on behind the locked office door.

He pressed the intercom and couldn't hold back the chuckle at the annoyed voice who answered, sounding breathless. "What is it, Manning?"

"Sorry for the interruption, Jules," he lied, "but a courier is here to deliver a package that he claims he can only put in your hands."

He heard the expletives that came from Dalton and the giggles from Jules as she tried shushing her husband. "Okay, give me a minute and I'll be right out."

Manning clicked off the phone and looked up at the courier. "You might as well take a seat. It will probably be more than a minute."

Fifteen minutes later the door to J. B. Sweet's office opened and Jules Bradford Granger walked out. Manning figured that most people were surprised to learn that J. B. Sweet was a woman. Since a majority of people preferred having a man handle their investigative work, Jules had come up with the ingenious idea to use her first and last initials as well as her mother's maiden name for her business; hence the moniker *J. B. Sweet*.

"Hello," she greeted the young man with a huge, bright smile.

Manning shook his head, knowing the effect Jules had on most guys. Manning would be the first to admit his boss and good friend was gorgeous. The young man was all but drooling and couldn't keep his eyes off Jules while she signed for the packet.

"Thanks!" the courier said, smiling like a dimwit.

"No problem."

The young man walked out of the office, whistling like Jules had made his day.

Jules studied the packet and then noticed Manning was staring at her while shaking his head. "What?"

Manning was surprised she had to ask. He figured she must not have noticed her hair was all mussed up, making her look like a hot, sexy goddess.

"Pardon me for saying," he said, leaning back in his chair, "but since you and Dalton are married, can't the two of you take it home?"

Jules smiled as if she didn't have one shameful bone in her body. Then she reached out and playfully pinched his cheek. "Oh, Manning, yes, we could and eventually we will. If you're feeling jealous, then I suggest you seriously start looking for a partner."

She tucked the packet under her arm, went back into her office and locked the door behind her.

CHAPTER THIRTY-TWO

"I LOVE IT HERE," Margo said, as she and Striker took an evening stroll around the cabin. He had taken her hand in his as they walked down a wooded path. The weather had turned somewhat cold, but the wool jacket she was wearing kept her warm. And then there was Striker's heat that seemed to flow through her, keeping her warm as well.

"But I wish I was here for another reason," she added. Although if she had been there for another reason, she wouldn't be here with Striker walking by her side.

"It is nice, isn't it?" he agreed, and when they came to a bench, he said, "Let's sit a spell. That's a beautiful view."

She sat beside him and followed his gaze to the meadow below. In the center of it was a huge geyser with water gushing upward toward the sky. It was simply breathtaking. The cabin was a place of peace and solitude, a place she had escaped to…to hide. For how long she still wasn't sure.

When she had finally awakened that day, it had been past noon. She had gone downstairs to find Striker sitting on the sofa, as if he'd been waiting for her. That had prompted her to cross the room and curl up in his lap, wrap her arms around his neck and kiss him. She was certain that particular kiss would have led to something a lot more intimate if her stomach hadn't decided to growl. That was when he'd picked her up in his arms and actually carried her into the kitchen and set her down in a chair at the table. He then proceeded to serve the meal he'd cooked—the most delicious vegetable soup she'd ever eaten, along with the tastiest turkey-and-cheese sandwich on wheat bread. Afterward, he suggested they put on their jackets and walk around the property for a while.

"Did I tell you how much I enjoyed lunch?" she asked him.

He chuckled. "Yes, you did. Twice, in fact. Glad you enjoyed it."

At that moment his phone rang and Margo didn't have to wonder who was calling. She'd gotten pretty used to the ringtone.

"Stonewall? What's up?"

Margo could tell from the expression that appeared on Striker's face that it wasn't good news.

"Okay. Keep me updated." Striker clicked off the call.

Margo stood, concerned. "Striker? Is anything wrong?"

He looked over at her and nodded. "According to Stonewall, there was a car explosion and the person inside the vehicle was an FBI agent. Even though it's not his usual MO, the authorities think it's the work of the assassin again."

She raised a brow. "Had the agent been in the courtroom that day?"

Striker shook his head. "No."

Margo frowned. "I don't understand. Why would Erickson want him dead? What's going on?"

Striker rubbed his face and said, "I think it's a foregone conclusion Erickson had insiders' help in carrying out this crazy plan of his. It's believed the dead agent was one of Erickson's men."

"An FBI agent?"

"Yes. A cop was also killed yesterday." Striker then told her about the female police officer and how it was believed she was also connected to Erickson.

"Do you think Erickson has abandoned his plan to kill everyone who was at the courthouse and has new targets? His own people?"

"Not sure how Erickson's mind is working right now. Until we know what's going on and why, we stay in hiding and stay alert."

JULES BRADFORD GRANGER watched her husband as he slid back into his pants. Manning had left for the day, and by rights, she should have, too, but she and Dalton were still here. They had a perfectly good bed at home, but for some reason, he liked the sofa in her office. "I need to put an end to your drop-in visits, Dalton."

He glanced over at her as he straightened his tie. "Why?"

She was about to give him a list of reasons when her cell phone rang. She smiled, recognizing her sister's ringtone. "Shana? How is my nephew?" Her sister, Shana, was married to Jace Granger, Dalton's brother. The third Granger son, Caden, was married to his childhood sweetheart, Shiloh.

"He's fine. Starting to sleep through the night and that's a good thing. Jace and I wanted to know if you and Dalton would like to join us for dinner. Caden and Shiloh will be here, and so will Dad and Mona and Sheppard and Carson."

"Um, what's the occasion?" Jules asked, leaning back against her desk as she continued to watch her husband re-dress.

"The architect dropped off the final house plans, and Jace and I can't wait to show them to everyone."

Jules heard the excitement in her sister's voice. Shana and Jace had made the decision to build a home on Sutton Hills, the Granger estates. Sutton Hills encompassed over two hundred acres near the foothills of the Blue Ridge Mountains. A thirty-minute ride from Charlottesville, the area consisted of the most beautiful land anywhere.

Each of the three Granger sons had inherited ten acres. Caden and Shiloh were thinking about building a home on the Granger estates at the end of the year. However, Jules and Dalton weren't in a hurry. They enjoyed living in their condo in town, which was close to restaurants, nightclubs and a number of other hot spots they frequented. "Dalton and I would love to come to dinner. Do you need us to bring anything? I'm still at the office and can make a pit stop if you need me to."

"You're still at the office? Then you'll probably be delayed because of the explosion. A lot of the streets are closed, which means there's a lot of traffic in town."

Jules raised a brow. "What explosion?" She noticed her words got Dalton's attention, so she put her sister on speakerphone.

"It seems that an FBI agent's car was rigged to blow up the moment he started the ignition," Shana said.

"And I heard he was someone working the Erickson case."

"Was he in the courtroom that day?"

"No. And that has people wondering why he was murdered."

Already Dalton had crossed the room to turn on the television to the news channel. "Okay, Shana, Dalton just put on the news. Let me see what's up."

"Dalton is there with you?"

"Yes, he's here."

"Hmm. Interesting," Shana said. "Jace mentioned he never returned to work after lunch. Now I know why."

Dalton gave Jules one of those I-don't-care-who-knows-I-enjoy-fucking-my-wife kind of smiles. "Whatever. Dalton and I will see everyone later."

Jules crossed the room to stand beside Dalton and watched the newsbreak.

"This is Connie Moore reporting live near the FBI building in downtown Charlottesville. If you're just tuning in, we are reporting the car bombing of an FBI agent. The victim has been identified as Special Agent Percy Weaver. It is believed that Agent Weaver's death was the work of the same assassin who has been targeting those involved with the Murphy Erickson trial. Agent Weaver was working on the Erickson case, but law enforcement is wondering why Weaver was targeted when he was not in the courtroom the day the jury reached a verdict."

The hairs on the back of Jules's neck stood up. *Percy Weaver.* Where did she know that name from? She frowned, trying to remember.

"Hey, baby, you okay?" Dalton asked her, reaching out and caressing her bunched brow.

"I know that name, Dalton. Percy Weaver. Or I've seen it somewhere. Recently." She slowly turned and stared at the package on her desk. The one that had been delivered that day. "That's it! He sent me a package."

"Who?"

"Percy Weaver," she said, quickly moving toward her desk to pick up the package. She looked over at Dalton. "Yes, that's it. This package is from a Percy Weaver."

Dalton crossed the room to her. "Do you think it's the same person?"

"I'm not sure, but there's only one way to find out," she said, tearing open the package. Inside was a letter addressed to her that was taped to another smaller package. She opened the letter and read it out loud.

Ms. Sweet, I read about you in the newspapers and admired the way you handled the Sheppard Granger investigation. I am sending this package to you with instructions not to open it...unless you know for certain that something has happened to me. I am a special agent for the FBI and if I am killed, make sure you take care of this and get it to the right people. Be careful who you trust in the Bureau and in the police department.

I am also enclosing a sealed envelope containing a letter to my wife, Leigh. Please make sure she gets it. Thanks. PW

Jules handed the letter to Dalton, who quickly read it. "He's right, Jules. You need to be careful who you trust."

Jules nodded. She was a former police detective and knew that not everyone in law enforcement was honest.

She wondered what category Percy Weaver fell into.
More than anything, she wanted to know what was on
the disk he'd sent her.

"I'll call Marcel." FBI Agent Marcel Eaton was a
family friend who'd worked with Jules's father, Ben
Bradford, when Marcel and Ben had been police officers in Boston. And more recently, Marcel had been
the FBI agent who'd worked on the case that had resulted in Sheppard Granger's exoneration.

Dalton nodded. "Contacting Marcel is a good idea."

LEONARD SMALL WATCHED the news program and sweat
broke out on his forehead. He should have seen it coming, should have known Erickson couldn't be trusted.
First Alyson Blackshear and now Percy Weaver. He
hadn't known either Blackshear or Weaver personally and definitely hadn't known that, like him, they'd
been on Erickson's payroll. Erickson took great pains
to make sure none of his informers were aware of each
other.

Now Blackshear and Weaver were dead and rumors
were going around that they'd been Erickson's informers, killed by that damn assassin. If that was true, why?
Was Erickson now turning on those who'd assisted him
in pulling off the hits he'd ordered? Small admitted
he'd been paid well, but what good was money when
you were dead?

Speaking of the dead, Small knew of one man who
would be glad if something happened to him, and that
was Jerry Franklin, who worked in the technology development department of the FBI. With Small dead,
Franklin wouldn't get blackmailed into sharing all his

high-tech creations anymore. Like the one used at the courthouse that day.

Small stood and walked to the door. He had a plan. If he was targeted, then he would make sure he wouldn't be the only one going to the grave.

CHAPTER THIRTY-THREE

JULES GLANCED AROUND her office. After listening to the tape that Percy Weaver had sent, Jules had contacted Marcel, who had contacted Special Agent Felton and police chief Harkins, in turn. Harkins arrived with Detective Joy Ingram and another woman, Dr. Randi Fuller, who was a psychic investigator assisting on the Erickson case. From what Marcel had told Jules and Dalton, Dr. Fuller had fingered Officer Alyson Blackshear and had also said there were two others working on the wrong side of the law with Erickson.

Special Agent Percy Weaver had been one of them, and he'd confessed as much on the tape. He'd also named the third person involved, Leonard Small, who was a US marshal assigned to the courthouse where Erickson's trial had been held. According to Weaver, Leonard Small wasn't aware Weaver had known about him. But for security measures, Weaver had made it his business to know who else might have been working on the wrong side of the law. Small was the only person whose identity Weaver had managed to obtain. He did not know anything about the assassin or Officer Blackshear's role.

After listening to the tape with the others, Agent Felton had ordered that US Marshal Small be picked up immediately and taken to FBI Headquarters for questioning.

On the tape Weaver had also stated how the assassin was tracking who'd been in the courtroom that day. Security had been stepped up due to the high-profile nature of the case, and additional screening procedures had been implemented. In addition to the standard metal detectors and X-rays, everyone's hands were swabbed for traces of explosives.

"So, let me make sure I understand all of this," Jules said, addressing everyone in her office. "They were actually using the swab to apply noninvasive, long-lasting tracking matter onto the person's skin, specifically, the back of their hands?"

"Yes," Marcel said, nodding his head. "It's been rumored such a substance was in development at our headquarters in DC. If that's true, I want to know how US Marshal Small got his hands on it."

"If what Weaver said on that tape is true, and I have little doubt that it's not," police chief Harkins said, "that means the assassin knows the whereabouts of every single person who was in that courtroom, and probably within a pretty accurate longitude and latitude. So, in essence, it doesn't matter that people are in hiding since the assassin has the ability to track their locations."

"Is there no way to get this substance off their hands, since it's obvious that regular soap and water won't work?" Jules asked, leaning against her desk.

"I've already made a call to our lab to find that out," Felton said. "I told them this is urgent. We have close to ten people from the courthouse that day who agreed to the private protection we offered. They are at an undisclosed location and are depending on us to keep them alive."

"Not to mention those who refused police protection," Detective Ingram tacked on.

"We need to get word out immediately," Harkins said, pulling out his phone. "Unfortunately, we don't even know where some of those people are. Some went into hiding and we can't contact them to tell them the assassin knows their location."

"The group under police custody is okay for now, since the assassin knows nothing about the package sent to Ms. Sweet," Dr. Randi Fuller said, grabbing everyone's attention. "Right now, his main focus is another member of the jury. A woman. She went into hiding, not realizing the assassin can find her."

Everyone had gotten quiet as they thought about what Dr. Fuller had said. It was Harkins who finally asked, "Do you know who she is, Dr. Fuller?"

Randi shook her head. "No, my mind can't outright identify her, but from the flashes I'm getting, she's hiding somewhere in a cabin in the mountains, somewhere near Shenandoah."

"Aw, hell!" Dalton Granger's outburst had everyone shifting their gazes to him.

"What's wrong, Dalton?" Jules asked her husband.

"My brother Jace owns a cabin in the mountains near Shenandoah, and I understand he loaned it out to someone, a bodyguard who's protecting a woman who was on the jury."

"We need to know if it's the same woman, Dalton," Marcel said. "I assume she's being protected by one of Roland's men." He'd gotten to know Roland Summers and several of his bodyguards last year when Jules's and Dalton's lives had been in danger.

Dalton pulled his phone out his jacket. "I'll find out from Roland right away."

Marcel chimed in with, "I thought Roland was re-cuperating from a gunshot wound."

"He's supposed to be recuperating. If he's not at the office, then Stonewall will answer."

A few moments later Dalton clicked off the phone. "According to Stonewall, the woman being protected is Margo Connelly, and Striker Jennings is her body-guard. Stonewall will get word to Striker immedi-ately."

"Margo Connelly?" Harkins asked, frowning. He looked over at Detective Ingram. "Didn't we foil an intended kidnapping of her just yesterday?"

"Yes, sir, we did."

"Kidnapping?" Jules asked, looking at Detective Ingram.

"Yes, she's the Connelly heiress," Detective Ingram answered. "We were informed of a blackmail plot against her. We used one of our female officers as a double. Turns out the threat of blackmail was a decoy, and they really intended to kidnap her and hold her for ransom. The kidnappers snatched the under-cover officer, and when they took her to a warehouse, we made our move. The three men are in jail and a possible fourth has been picked up in New York for questioning. They've been turned over to your agency, Felton."

"Sounds like this Margo Connelly is pretty popular these days," Felton said, shaking his head while thinking that maybe it was time for him to retire after all. He had suspected something was going on with Weaver but had figured the man was having marital problems or something. Boy, had he been wrong.

At that moment, Felton's cell phone rang. Expletives followed, alerting everyone that the news Felton was getting wasn't good. He clenched the phone while staring up at the ceiling. Then he barked into the phone, "Don't move any bodies. I'm on my way. Don't notify the press of anything yet, and there better not be another leak to them."

"Bodies?" Detective Ingram couldn't help asking.

Felton glanced over at her as he headed for the door. "Yes. Small is dead. Looks like the assassin got to him before we did. But the worse of it is that Erickson was found dead in his cell."

"What?! What happened?" Harkins asked, incensed.

"Prison records show Small paid him a visit, claiming it was official business, and he had documents to prove it, which I'm pretty sure will turn out to be fake. I'm not releasing any information to the press until I get there and see what happened for myself." Then Felton was out the door.

"We'll start warning the jurors we can contact to stay on guard, even if they're in hiding. The assassin knows where everyone is. But, based on Dr. Fuller's vision, the number one priority is Margo Connelly. This could be our chance to stop the bastard red-handed. We need to get our men out to that cabin immediately," Harkins said, heading for the door as well. "Detective Ingram, you and Dr. Fuller can come with me. We'll take a police chopper to the cabin."

"DAMMIT, STRIKER, PICK UP the phone," Stonewall snarled angrily, while rubbing the top of his head. "Where the hell are you?"

"You still can't reach him?"

Stonewall looked up to find both Roland and Quasar standing in the doorway. "No, and it's not like Striker not to answer. I need to let him know about the tracker on Margo."

"Come on. We'll keep trying to reach him in the chopper," Roland said.

"What chopper?"

"The one owned by Connelly Enterprises," Roland said, strapping his gun and holster to his shoulder. "It will get us to the cabin quicker."

Quasar looked at Roland as he strapped on his own gun and holster. "I guess it won't do us any good to ask you to stay behind and let us handle things, will it?"

"No. Not when Striker's and Margo's lives are in danger," Roland said, looking from Quasar to Stonewall. "And by the way, Frazier Connelly will be our pilot."

Quasar and Stonewall exchanged looks with each other but otherwise said nothing as they followed Roland out the door.

STRIKER WAS CONVINCED Margo was trying to drain every ounce of strength from his body. She was only supposed to dry him off, but instead she'd taken things a hell of a lot further. She had tortured him with her hands and mouth, and he'd become putty in them both.

One thing was for certain—they'd spent more time taking care of each other's sexual needs than showering. They'd stayed in the shower for over an hour mak-

ing love. It had been one orgasm followed by another.
Each one more powerful than the one before. The moment he had stepped out the shower to grab a towel,
she'd taken it from him and proceeded to practically
lick him all over.

When he hadn't been able to take it anymore, he'd
picked her up off her knees and carried her into the
bedroom, dropping her in the center of the bed and
joining her there, making love to her once again.

Striker knew he needed to screw his head back on,
but the only thing he wanted to screw was her. Again.
If that wasn't fucked up, then what was? He glanced
over at her, sprawled on the bed beside him as naked
as he was. Never had any woman rocked his world like
Margo was doing.

He looked at the clock on the nightstand and grimaced. It was eight o'clock at night already? That meant
they'd spent the last two hours all into each other. Literally. "You are trouble, Margo Connelly. You do know
that, right?"

She didn't even try hiding her smile, which made
her appear even sexier. He should hate it whenever she
smiled like that because it always did something to
him. Made him appreciative that he was the man getting it, and, damn, he got a tightening in his stomach
whenever he did so.

"Only because you say so, Striker Jennings. Just
keep in mind that before you came on the scene, my
sexual experience was at an all-time low. I guess you
can say I'm making up for lost time."

"And trying to kill me in the process. We need to
set some ground rules."

"You said that over dinner."

Yes, he had and he'd meant it at the time. This wasn't a pleasure trip, although it seemed they'd turned it into one. The reality of the situation was that they were in hiding for her safety. A crazy man was out there and there was no telling who was next on his hit list. More than once Striker had let his guard down to enjoy his time with Margo, mainly because he knew at some point his job of protecting her would come to an end. He tried not to think about it. He refused to think about it. This had been three weeks he would never forget. Could never forget. He would remember every single time his mouth closed over hers, each time he stripped her naked, showered with her. And when he made love to her. That kind of pleasure was meant to stay with a person for a lifetime, and there was no doubt for him that it would.

But the bottom line was that Margo Connelly was not his future. She deserved more than someone who was mired in remorse and shame, still on a guilt trip that wouldn't end. But a part of him wondered if perhaps the trip never came to an end because before now there had never been anyone in his life worth ending it for.

He noticed Margo had gotten quiet. Not surprisingly, she had drifted off to sleep. Just as well since he tended to get more done when she wasn't awake. Margo did a good job of claiming his attention, intentionally or not, and he wasn't sure just what he could do about it. He hadn't known her for a long time, but she had gotten to him in a way no other woman had. Now he knew why and refused to deny it any longer—he loved her.

Striker rubbed his face but not in frustration. Only because he knew it was a do-or-die situation. He could no more deny loving her than he could refuse to take his next breath. He had never loved a woman. When he was younger, in his teens and a star football player, he'd assumed he had plenty of time to do so. Instead he had enjoyed playing the field. Then a few weeks after graduating high school, when he was looking forward to the fall and utilizing that football scholarship he'd gotten to Ohio State, his world as well as Wade's had come to an end. It would be fair to say the world of the entire Jennings family seemed to end, given the physical and mental toll on his mom.

When he had been released from prison, getting seriously involved with any woman had been the last thing on his mind. Getting his life back together had been the top priority. Women had only entered the picture when sex was needed. He understood that and made sure they understood it. It should have been that way with Margo, but he could no longer think of what they'd been sharing as sex only. For him it was a lot more than that. And because of that, the job—protecting Margo—was more important than ever.

Striker needed to check in with Stonewall. He'd left his cell phone on the bathroom vanity before stepping into the shower. Easing away from Margo, he untangled their legs and stood, telling himself not to look at her or he'd never leave the bed. He slid into jeans and a T-shirt before strapping his gun and holster on his shoulder. He crossed the room to the bathroom. When he picked up his phone and tried dialing Stonewall, he discovered he couldn't make a call. What the hell was going on? Somehow, reception was being blocked. He felt the hairs on the back of his neck stand up. Something definitely wasn't right.

He was about to check if any text messages had managed to get through, when suddenly there was an explosion.

CHAPTER THIRTY-FOUR

MARGO DID HER best to ignore the pain throbbing through her entire body as she tried lifting herself off the floor, only to fall back down again. What was going on? What had happened? There had been some sort of blast. She had been in the bed asleep and now she was naked on the floor. And where was Striker?

She tried saying his name but the sound lodged in her throat. He had been in the bed with her. Hadn't he? With eyes stinging of smoke, she quickly looked around. From the moonlight shining in through the broken window, she could see the room was in total shambles. Dragging herself to her knees, she ignored the fact that she was stark naked and began feeling around on the floor. Striker had to be here somewhere. What if he was injured? Unconscious? Or even…

She fought back a wave of hysteria, refusing to consider it. *Please let Striker be okay.* The thought that he might not be okay made her heart seize. All was quiet as she crawled around on the floor in the darkness. Her stomach began to roil when she couldn't find Striker anywhere. *What if he was on the other side of the bed and—*

Suddenly she was pulled into big strong arms. She would have fought if she hadn't recognized those arms. His manly scent. "Striker!"

He quickly put his fingers to her lips. "Shh," he whispered, drawing her even closer, while rubbing her naked skin with his big hands, as if he was trying to determine if she was all in one piece.

"I'm fine, Striker," she said, softly. Unlike her he was clothed. When had he put on clothes? He must have dressed and left her sleeping. "What's going on? What happened?" she asked, trying to talk above the loud security alarm that had begun blasting when the window had been blown out.

"Someone is firing missiles in here. We need to get someplace where there aren't any windows," he said, tugging on her arm.

"No," she said, pulling back. "I'm not going any-where naked."

The next thing she knew, he was pulling something over her head. From the scent and warmth of the material, she knew he'd removed the T-shirt off his back to put on her. It barely covered her thighs, but she loved the way it felt against her skin.

"Where did you put your shoes?" he asked her.

"On this side of the bed somewhere," she said, fol-lowing his lead by speaking in a low voice. She could tell he was feeling around on the floor.

"Got them." He proceeded to help her put them on.

"Where are we going? There are windows in every room in this house."

"Underground. To the wine cellar. The bastard ex-pects us to run outside just so he can use us as target practice."

"It's the assassin, isn't it?" she asked.

"That's my bet."

Her head was spinning. "But how did he know where to find me? We made sure nobody followed us."

"Evidently someone talked."

"Who?"

"Don't know, but I intend to find out. At least Stonewall and the team know something's going on."

"How do you know that?" she asked, hearing rather than seeing him doing something to his gun.

"The cell reception's been blocked. Stonewall would have tried checking in with me by now, and when he couldn't reach me, he'd know something was going on."

"Do you think that whoever is firing those missiles is responsible for blocking your phone?"

"Probably. I was about to check for any text messages when the explosion happened. I lost my balance, and my phone fell into the toilet. It's no good to me now."

"And I left my phone downstairs on the kitchen table," she said. That was where they'd been, finishing up dinner, when he had swept her into his arms and carried her upstairs.

"What about the security alarm that's going off? Won't the police be notified and respond to that?" she asked.

"They should, but the assassin might have blocked that like he did the phones. We can't wait for anyone to show up. Come on."

He took a firm hold of her hand as they crawled toward the door.

FOR THE TIME BEING, Striker pushed to the back of his mind the realization that he'd literally fucked up. If he'd been alert, chances were he would have known what was about to go down. Instead of protecting Margo, the only thing he'd cared about was how it felt being between her legs. And now he had placed her life in danger.

But he was determined to get them out of this alive. Afterward, he would have plenty of time to call himself all kinds of fool for desiring her so much.

For falling in love with her so completely.

When they reached the door, he released her hand to grip his revolver. Based on what he could determine, the missile had been fired through the bedroom window. The bastard was probably using one of those illegal handheld missile launchers. Striker's plan was to get Margo to the wine cellar, where she would be safe. Then he intended to find the bastard and make him regret ever making Margo a target.

Easing the door open, he could see the glow from the ceiling lights they'd left on in the kitchen and living room below. At least he'd had the damn good sense to keep the curtains drawn. Only once, when Margo had complained of not being able to see the beautiful view outside, had he given in and kept them open for a few hours. It had been against his better judgment, but it had been worth it to see the smile on her face.

Striker rose to his feet and brought Margo up with him. "I doubt if anyone has gotten inside, but I'm not taking any chances. Evidently that first missile was to let us know he's here. He's probably giving us time to think about that for a minute or two. And that's where he's making his second mistake." His first mistake was even thinking he could take Margo's life.

Pressing against the wall with Margo, whom he tried keeping behind him, he eased them toward the second set of stairs that led to the cellar. He had checked out the wine cellar the first day and saw it was stocked with several bottles of water as well.

It was only when they reached the stairs that he moved her in front of him to protect her back. "Watch your step. It's a long way down," he told her, releasing her wrist, grateful for the emergency lights that shone near the floor to illuminate the way. "Lock the door behind you and stay put until I come back for you."

She grabbed hold of his arm, frowning. "Why? Where are you going?"

"To take care of business, like I should have been doing all along. Now, please do as I told you."

She stared at him, and it was as if she was seeing into his very soul. "Take care of yourself, Striker, and come back for me."

He didn't say anything for a moment and then he leaned down and kissed her forehead, thinking he would love her forever. "I will. But I don't want to worry about you. The person I'll be dealing with is a killer, and I need to concentrate. Stay focused."

She nodded. "I understand, and I will do what you said. You just make sure you keep your word and come back." She tilted her mouth for him to kiss her.

He lowered his mouth to hers. Kissing was the last thing they needed to be doing right now, but he figured it was the only thing he wanted to do before he left to make sure her life was never threatened again.

He loved kissing her, loved the way she would respond, contribute and share a part of herself with him. But, knowing he had to go, he broke off the kiss. Instead of saying anything else, she licked her lips, which was her way of letting him know how much she'd enjoyed his taste. She turned and quickly walked down the stairs to the cellar. He held his breath when she opened the door, went inside and closed the door behind her. He heard the lock click in place.

It was only then that he released the breath he'd been holding. Turning with his gun in his hand, he was determined to put an end to the assassin's killing spree once and for all.

THE ASSASSIN TOOK a sip of his coffee as he leaned against a tree. *Nice place*, he thought, looking at the huge cabin. Too bad by the time it was over he would have destroyed most of it.

By now the police would have discovered Leonard Small's body. What pissed him off more than anything was that Small had been expecting him. That was no fun. He liked having the element of surprise on his side. It was no fun when the person knew they were about to die.

He took another sip of coffee, smiling when he thought about how easy it had been to block any calls coming in or going out of the cabin, thanks to a device he'd acquired on the black market last year. He'd also been able to block the police notifications when the security alarm went off. So if they were waiting for the police to respond to the alarm, they were in for a rude awakening.

It was obvious the woman wasn't at the cabin alone. A hysterical female on her own would have run out of the cabin hollering and screaming and giving him a chance to get a good shot on her.

He checked his watch, thinking he'd given the people inside the cabin a good twenty minutes to ponder

what they needed to do. It was time to give them another scare. If they still refused to come out, then he
would shoot a flaming ball inside the cabin. He would
either burn them out or burn them up. Either way was
fine with him.

ADRENALINE SEEPED OUT OF Striker's every pore as he
crawled out the bathroom window. It had been a tight
squeeze and he'd scraped his upper arm on a piece of
glass. That scratch, along with the night's chill, was an
unwelcome reminder that he was shirtless. But the last
thing he'd wanted was for Margo to be naked. Hell. The
fact that she was wearing his T-shirt without a stitch of
clothing underneath was bad enough and sure to raise
a few brows when they were rescued. And he wanted
to believe they would be. Like Striker had told Margo,
Stonewall would have figured they were in danger by
now. In the meantime, he would show the crazy assassin that, when warranted, he could be just as crazy.

He was glad Margo hadn't given him any grief about
staying locked in the wine cellar until he returned. He'd
seen a degree of trust in her eyes and he didn't intend to
let her down. Her life depended on it. And because she
was the love of his life, his life depended on it as well.

He managed to land on his feet, and the moment
they hit solid ground he crouched down and looked
around. The property was shrouded in darkness. The
only light was from the stars and the moon overhead.
He had no idea where the assassin was, and he'd taken
a big chance in coming out on this side of the house.
But based on the trajectory of the missile, the bastard
was somewhere stationed on the other side of the house.

Suddenly a bright light whizzed overhead within

twenty feet of him. Another missile, this one through the living room window. Damn. As long as Margo stayed put, she was safe. For now. At least he now knew where the missile had been launched. Crouching down with his Beretta drawn, he headed in that direction.

MARGO PACED THE CELLAR that was stocked with bottles of wine. As a child, she'd loved hiding in her parents' basement and recalled a number of fond memories she had of being there. That space was a lot bigger than this one, and every once in a while her parents would join her when she hosted a tea party.

Those had been great times for her and now were great memories. Her parents had wanted more than one child, but after a couple of miscarriages they had decided she would be their only one. They had showered her with all their love and she thought about them often—a lot more than usual lately. Probably because, as she grew older, she wondered if they would be proud of the woman she'd become or disappointed that she hadn't followed in her father's footsteps by becoming involved in more of the day-to-day operations at Connelly Enterprises.

She drew in a deep breath, knowing her parents would have loved her enough to allow her to make her own decisions as to how she wanted to live her life. Murdock Connelly had been less of a traditionalist than her uncle Frazier. But her uncle had never tried pressuring her to take her father's place at the company. She smiled, thinking he was probably glad she hadn't. She loved her uncle immensely but could see how their opinions would clash.

She stopped pacing and sat on a stool. If she got

thirsty, there was plenty to drink with all the water and wine stored in here. She tightened her arms around her body as nervous shivers passed through her. She hoped Striker was okay. She wished there was something she could do to help but knew as well as he did that she would be a hindrance.

Striker hadn't left her a weapon, and she knew why. She'd made it clear she wasn't a fan of guns and would injure herself if left with one. Her greatest weapon was her belief that Striker would come back for her. That he would stay safe. But she couldn't discount the lunatic he was going up against. She hoped and prayed that the man she loved would come out the victor.

She was about to stand up when the ceiling overhead began to shake as if it was about to collapse on top of her. She quickly reached out to grab hold of a table as several wine bottles went crashing to the floor.

Margo knew the assassin had fired another missile into the cabin.

CHAPTER THIRTY-FIVE

DESPITE HIS DISCOMFORT, Striker darted between a number of low-hanging red oak trees, moving stealthily through the thickets. The temperature had dropped. Without a shirt he should have felt cold, but the anger radiating inside of him was keeping him warm.

He paused when he reached the area where he suspected the assassin was hiding. He was anxious but forced himself to wait, listening for any sounds. Time passed and he didn't hear anything.

The cut on his shoulder was hurting like hell, but he would deal with it. Right now there were more important issues he had to handle. A crackle of lightning lit the sky and he looked up and frowned. The last thing he needed was a downpour. Cold and rain weren't a good combination. Striker was about to move when he heard a click at the same time he felt the cold barrel of a gun pressed to the back of his head.

"Drop your weapon. Now!"

Striker did as he was told, dropping his Beretta while knowing he had backup with the knife in his boot.

"You fool. Did you not think I had all my bases covered?" a man's hard voice taunted. "I knew the moment your feet hit the ground. Now I'm going to kill you and then I'll find the woman and kill her too."

Knowing this was his only opportunity and he had to take it, Striker, in a lifesaving move, quickly shifted his body, missing the bullet from the man's gun by mere inches. Then, lifting his leg in a fast and firm kick, he knocked the gun from the man's hand, sending it flying into the brush.

Unfortunately, the kick didn't take the man down. Recovering from the blow, he lunged at Striker, his weight knocking Striker to the ground. The man went down with him and slammed a solid fist into Striker's chin. Then another. Pain nearly blinded Striker, but he pushed back and, using his weight and height, was able to gain the upper hand. Striker landed a couple of sharp blows that jarred the assassin before he sent a hard punch to Striker's abdomen.

Striker ignored the impact of the excruciating jolt to his gut and managed to get in a few more hard jabs that sent the man crumbling backward. Using that opportunity to his advantage, Striker landed on his feet in time to counter another punch and was able to knock the man back a foot or two with his own hard punch to the man's gut. By the time the man regrouped and was charging toward him, Striker had pulled the knife from his boot and threw it to lodge deep in the man's shoulder. When that didn't slow the man down, Striker quickly dived where he'd dropped his Beretta and in seconds he swiveled around to fire a shot, hitting the man in the chest.

The bastard didn't fall immediately. Instead a painful sneer showed on the bastard's face. And with blood spurting from his mouth, he said, "I preset the flame thrower. You won't be able to save her."

The man fell to the ground at the same time a fiery

missile was launched from twenty feet away. Its target was the cabin, and the moment it hit, the cabin was engulfed in flames.

"No!" Striker screamed at the top of his lungs and took off running toward it.

THE SCENT OF smoke alerted Margo that the cabin was on fire. She was suddenly filled with panic. Would her life come to an end the same way her parents' had? Where was Striker? Was he okay? She was certain he wouldn't want her to remain in a burning house. She raced up the stairs to the door and tried turning the knob only to discover it was jammed and wouldn't turn. She was locked in the cellar of a burning house.

Margo quickly moved around checking every corner, trying to find something she could use to force open the door. All the while, the scent of smoke got heavier. The room had no windows—just walls—and she could feel both smoke and heat overtaking her.

She tried the door again and when it didn't budge she moved away from it. Covering her face in her hands against the sting of the smoke, she had gone back down several stairs, intent on finding a corner of the room where she could feel safe, when suddenly she heard her name. She dropped her hands, wondering if she was hearing things. When she heard it again she knew the person calling her was Striker. She stood and raced back to the door.

"Unlock the door, Margo. I need to get you out of here," he shouted from the other side.

Clearing her throat against the smoke that was choking her, she said, "I can't, Striker. The doorknob is jammed."

She heard his expletives. "Go back down the stairs, away from the door. I'm bringing it down."

And he did. With a mighty force, he kicked down the door. "Come on!"

Margo raced up the stairs to him, and he gripped her hand. The moment he pulled her from the cellar, she saw the house was ablaze and fire was quickly spreading everywhere. How on earth had he made it inside the house to rescue her? There was no way they could get out alive. She was about to tell him that when he turned and swept her up into his arms.

"Keep your face buried in my chest, Margo."

And then he was moving, but she didn't know where to. Nor did she know how he was maneuvering around the fire since he'd told her to bury her face in his chest. But more than once she heard him curse and was jolted when he had to quickly change directions.

"Hold tight. I'm going to try to get us out through the living room."

She was tempted to lift her head and ask him if he was crazy. She'd seen the fire escalating from room to room. But from the way he was moving, jolting her every which way, she knew he'd decided to risk it. Suddenly she heard male voices holler, "This way, Striker!"

CHAPTER THIRTY-SIX

STRIKER KNEW THEY were safe when he breathed in the chilly air. Ignoring the feel of the blanket being thrown over them, he continued to hold Margo as he nearly collapsed to the ground. But he still held her, refusing to let her go, even when someone told him to release her because they both needed medical attention.

Through stinging eyes, he looked up and saw the place was surrounded by both FBI agents and police officers. It had been Stonewall's and Quasar's voices that had helped lead him out of their fiery hell. Also standing within a few feet of them were Roland, Frazier Connelly, Detective Ingram and others he did not know.

"We got here in time to see you run inside the burning cabin. Don't know how you did it without getting burned to a crisp," Roland said, crouching down beside him.

"Man, you okay?" Stonewall asked, also squatting down in front of him. "Damn. What happened to your shoulder?"

"Yeah, man, you look like shit," Quasar added.

Stonewall's and Quasar's observations had Margo scrambling around in his arms to stare at him. When she shifted, the blanket covering her shifted as well. Striker saw his T-shirt had risen up over her thighs, and he quickly pulled it down and tried to cover her with the blanket.

"Oh my God, Striker," she said, staring at him and seeing the assassin's handiwork from their fight. He probably looked like crap with his face bruised and all.

"I'm fine, Margo."

As if ignoring him, she leaned in and kissed a bruise by his eyes. "I hope the other guy looks worse than you," she said, as if her kisses would make the welts go away.

"He's dead," Quasar said. "Damn. It took both your knife and a bullet to bring him down. It's a good thing you're in great shape, Striker."

At that moment, a throat was cleared and Striker glanced up into Frazier's face. "You can release my niece now."

Striker wondered if Frazier hadn't noticed that Margo also had a tight grip on him. He looked at Margo when she placed a kiss at another bruise on his cheek and thought that even with smudges of soot on her face she looked so intrinsically sexy his entire body ached, which wasn't good since it was in pain already.

There was no doubt in his mind that those standing nearest had figured out that his and Margo's relationship was more than the bond between protector and client—something she evidently didn't have a problem exposing by kissing his face. That was probably the reason Connelly was frowning.

"Margo, your uncle needs to see that you're in one piece," Striker decided to say.

She twisted around in his arms and smiled at her uncle. "I'm fine, Uncle Frazier." And then, seeing Roland, she said, "And I'm fine, Uncle Roland." The shocked look on Roland's face was priceless, Striker thought. Margo, intentionally or not, had let out of the bag what had been a dark family secret for years.

"You need medical help," Frazier said to his niece.

She shook her head. "Striker needs it more than I do."

At that moment paramedics rushed forward, and Striker said, "We'll both get checked out. How about that, Margo?"

"Okay."

When Striker stood, she slid down his body and he quickly saw his T-shirt was rising up again. He practically wrapped her in the blanket.

"I'm fine, Striker. You're the one who needs to be covered. You're not wearing a shirt."

He didn't care about that, but he didn't like the thought of anyone seeing her wearing just his T-shirt. He leaned in and whispered those very words.

A blush touched her cheeks and the only response she could give was "Oh. Okay."

The moment the paramedics were finished looking them over—after adding drops to their eyes and making them breathe through some type of inhaler—the FBI and the police were there with questions. Striker allowed them to bandage the cut on his shoulder but refused stitches.

One of the paramedics had an extra jacket, which he let Striker use. That was a good thing since the temperature was steadily dropping. Law enforcement requested to take statements from Striker and Margo separately. Margo hesitated a second before being led away by a female FBI agent, Detective Ingram and some other woman.

"Ms. Connelly, I'm Special Agent Yvette Hines. To my right is Detective Joy Ingram and to my left is Dr. Randi Fuller."

Margo glanced around at the women and shook hands with all three. For some reason, it was Dr. Fuller whom she found most intriguing. She'd thought the psychic would be someone a lot older—in her fifties at least. However, the woman standing before her couldn't have been any older than she was. And Margo thought she was very attractive. In fact, all three women were, and she doubted the other two were even in their thirties.

"You're young," she said to Dr. Fuller, all but blurting it out.

Dr. Fuller didn't seem offended. Instead she chuckled. "There's not too much difference in our ages, but I've been doing this awhile. Even when I didn't want to acknowledge I had the ability to do so."

Margo wondered just how the woman knew her age and could only imagine how difficult it would be to live with psychic powers. "I'm surprised this place isn't surrounded by news reporters," she said.

"Only because they haven't been told what has happened yet. Since you were a juror on a federal case, your name had to be kept anonymous. We can't guarantee it will remain that way with reporters swarming around, which I'm sure they will be doing soon enough," Special Agent Hines said. "Even if they didn't get wind of your name, there's no way your face won't be plastered on the front page of tomorrow's paper. We don't want that to happen. We still intend to keep your identity anonymous. All the reporters need to know is that the assassin attempted to kill his next victim and that her bodyguard took him out."

"My *protector*," Margo corrected her, remembering the time Striker had set her straight.

"He was definitely that," Hines said. "When we pulled up, he was running back inside for you. I honestly didn't think the two of you would make it out alive. The entire house was engulfed in flames."

"I held my breath the entire time until the two of you came out," Detective Ingram tacked on. "And when Stonewall and Quasar Patterson ran into the building after Mr. Jennings, my heart nearly stopped beating."

Margo took note that Detective Ingram had referred to Stonewall by his first name, which led her to believe the two of them knew each other well. "How did you know what was happening here? The assassin blocked the phones so no calls could come in or go out."

"You can thank Dr. Fuller for knowing you were in danger," Detective Ingram said. She then proceeded to tell Margo about the package FBI agent Weaver had delivered to a private investigator and how it exposed the fact that, without their knowledge, a tracking substance had been applied to the hands of everyone in the courtroom that day. That meant no one was safe from the assassin since he was aware of everyone's location at all times. The mystery had been who he would target next.

"Although Dr. Fuller couldn't identify you per se, she knew the assassin was headed to a cabin near the Shenandoah Mountains," Detective Ingram added.

Margo turned to Dr. Fuller. "Thank you."

Dr. Fuller smiled. "Glad I was able to help. And it was really a team effort. Once I identified the location of the cabin, law enforcement didn't waste time getting here with the use of several choppers. One of those choppers, I understand, belongs to your uncle, and the others to the Charlottesville Police Department."

"Now for those questions we need to ask you so we can return you to Mr. Jennings," Special Agent Hines said, pulling out her notepad.

While Special Agent Hines was taking Margo's statement, Dr. Randi Fuller got the feeling she was being watched. Looking around, she saw a man crouching low on the ground, dressed in all black. Earlier, she'd heard one of the men call him Quasar Patterson. He was absolutely, spellbindingly gorgeous. With an intensity that made her stomach clench, his gaze was focused directly on her. To get control of the influx of emotions flooding her, she broke eye contact with him to glance over to where several police officers were taping off the crime scene. Temptation got the best of her, and Randi couldn't help but look back and found him still staring at her. She knew at that precise moment that the man staring at her was destined to be a part of her future.

That realization sent a shiver through her. She forced her gaze from his and tried to concentrate on the questions Special Agent Hines was asking Margo Connelly.

AN HOUR LATER, after law enforcement had finished their questions, three cars pulled up. Four men got out, and Striker recognized them. The Grangers. Sheppard Granger met Striker's gaze and quickly walked toward him, followed by his sons, Jace, Caden and Dalton.

Sheppard didn't stop until he was standing close to

Striker and Margo, who had rejoined him after giving her statement. "You okay, Striker?"

Striker nodded. "Yes, Shep. I'm okay."

Striker glanced at one of the men by Shep's side. "Sorry about your cabin, Jace."

Jace Granger shook his head. "Don't be. The main thing is that the both of you are okay," he said, switching his gaze to Margo and then returning it to Striker. "I can build another cabin, but you only have one life. Besides," Jace said, as a smile touched his lips, "it was time I did something with the cabin to make it more childproof."

"You're getting too good at saving lives, Striker," Caden Granger said, shaking his head. Striker understood Caden's comment. A year ago Striker had saved Caden's life.

Sheppard's youngest son, Dalton, said with a grin, "Glad you're in one piece. Hannah would have our asses if you weren't." Hannah, the housekeeper and cook at the Granger estate, had all but made it her business to adopt Striker, Quasar, Stonewall—and a few others—as Sheppard's *other* sons.

At that moment Chief Harkins came forward. "We kept this under wraps for as long as we could, but now the media are on their way. I suggest the two of you leave now. If we have any more questions, we know how to contact you."

"Come on, Margo, let me get you out of here," Frazier said, quickly approaching his niece.

Striker knew Margo was about to refuse to go with her uncle, so he said, "Go on with your uncle, Margo. I'll drop by your place later to check on you."

She opened her mouth to say something and then, as

if she thought better of it since they had an audience, she nodded. "Okay. I'll see you in a little while, then." Striker watched her walk away, knowing she was taking a piece of his heart with her.

"Hey, man," Quasar said, interrupting Striker's thoughts. "The SUV is probably toasted since it was parked in the garage. You can ride back to Charlottesville with us."

He looked at Quasar and Stonewall. "You two aren't going back on the chopper?"

"No, the Grangers offered us one of their vehicles. And I believe Roland will be riding back to town with them. It's bonding time for us," Stonewall said.

Striker knew that was their way of saying the three of them needed to do some serious talking.

"SO WHAT DO you guys want to talk about?" Striker asked a short while later, leaning this head against the headrest and stretching his long legs out in front of him. He would go home and clean up, soak his body in a tub of hot water. Then he would go check on Margo.

"We think you know. Why did you send Margo home with her uncle, when it was obvious she wanted to be with you?" Quasar asked from the backseat.

Striker frowned. "Doesn't matter. She needed to go with him." *While I get my head screwed on right.*

"The two of you hooked up. That's been obvious, but if there was any doubt in anyone's mind, I think Margo laid it to rest tonight," Stonewall said.

Striker pulled in a deep breath. "I wish she hadn't done that."

"Why?"

He glanced over at Stonewall. "You honestly have to ask me that?"

"Yes, he has to ask you that because I want to know as well," Quasar said, leaning forward between the two front seats. "The two of you have been an item for a while. I picked up on it. All that sexual chemistry and shit. So what's the problem?"

Striker didn't say anything for a minute. Finally, he said, "I could have lost her tonight, guys. If anything had happened to Margo, I don't know how I would have survived. That's why I've never allowed myself to get seriously attached to anyone. The thought of losing them the way I lost Wade and Mom is something I just couldn't handle." He knew they understood how he felt because he'd had similar conversations with them before. "And to be honest with you, I feel what went down could have been avoided. I should have been more on top of things tonight."

"You *were* on top of things, Striker. When we arrived, you were running into a burning house. You saved her life, man. You should be feeling good about that."

Well, he wasn't. He shouldn't have been caught off guard. "But had I known…"

"There was no way you could have known. The bastard blocked the phones so I couldn't get through. He still would have shot those missiles inside the house, even if you had known."

"How in the hell did the bastard track Margo here?"

Stonewall spent the next few minutes telling Striker about the package Weaver had sent to Jules Bradford Granger. "But I heard it was that psychic who let it be

FORGED IN DESIRE

known the next attempt would be on a woman hiding out near the Shenandoah Mountains."

"Thank God for that psychic," Striker said.

"Yes," Quasar said. "She's a beautiful woman."

Striker raised a brow. "You've seen her?"

"Yes. Tonight. She was there."

"I didn't know. There were a lot of people," Striker said.

"She was the one hanging with Stonewall's detective," Quasar said.

"I don't have a detective. We've talked a lot and met for drinks a few times, but we haven't had what I consider a real date."

Quasar chuckled. "In other words, she hasn't quite fallen under that Stonewall Courson spell."

When Stonewall didn't refute what Quasar had said, Striker knew there must be some truth to it. But he knew Detective Ingram was on Stonewall's radar, so it would only be a matter of time before the two hooked up.

At that moment Stonewall's phone went off. "What's up, Roland?"

A few minutes later he said, "Damn. I doubt he'll be missed. Yes, I'm glad the nightmare is now over."

When Stonewall clicked off the phone, he said, "Roland got word that they found Erickson dead in his cell a few hours ago. The last person who saw him was that US marshal they found dead earlier tonight when we were on our way to help you."

"What US marshal?" Striker asked.

"The one they believe is responsible for swabbing everyone with the tracking substance at the courthouse. His name was Leonard Small."

"Not that I have any complaints, but why kill Erickson?"

"I can only assume that US Marshal Small decided to take him out because he felt betrayed," Stonewall said.

"So, are you going to drop in on Margo tonight?" Quasar asked. "You told her that you would."

"And I'll keep my word," Striker said, feeling somewhat annoyed. When he went to see her, it wouldn't be for the reason they assumed.

CHAPTER THIRTY-SEVEN

It had taken an hour-long soak in the tub with Margo's favorite bubble bath to remove the stench of smoke from her body and hair. Now she felt clean, smelled good and, except for her eyes, which were still red, she thought she looked decent.

Margo had dressed in one of her favorite caftans and loved the feel of the silky material against her skin. Trying not to notice the time was nearly four in the morning, she reasoned that just like she had to clean herself up, Striker would have to do the same before visiting. After all, he'd been in far worse shape than she had. When she thought of how he had come back into that burning building for her, saving her life, she couldn't help but love him even more.

She left her bedroom to head downstairs. What if Striker didn't show up tonight? She shook her head, refusing to believe that he wouldn't honor his word. But for a minute she'd thought she'd felt him trying to put distance between them. Why? He'd admitted she'd become more than just a job to him. Although that admission hadn't equated to love, she wanted to think at least it was a beginning.

Her foot had touched the bottom stair when her doorbell sounded. Her heart leaped in her chest as she quickly moved toward the door. After looking through the peephole, she disarmed her security system and opened the door.

Striker stood there.

She could tell he had showered and changed, but because of the brightness of the porch light, the bruises around his eyes and chin were even more visible. And to think he'd taken the blows to protect her.

"I was beginning to wonder if you were coming," she said, standing aside to let him come in. Hoping that she didn't sound like the needy and desperate woman who she felt like at the moment.

"I told you that I would," he said, and when he passed by her she couldn't help but breathe in the scent of man and aftershave. She'd always found his scent so intoxicating. "I wasn't sure if your uncle had talked you into going home with him, to the Connelly estate."

"He tried, but I wanted to come here. To wait for you."

She closed the door and locked it, trying not to feel a little disappointed. Why had she hoped that the first thing he would do when he saw her was pull her into his arms? Was it because she so desperately needed to be held in his strong embrace? "I was about to make a pot of coffee. Want some?"

"Yes. On the way over here I got a call from Detective Ingram. They got a positive ID on the assassin. He's someone who's been wanted by both the FBI and CIA for some time. With him and Erickson dead, maybe things will get back to normal around here."

Margo figured Roland must have called Striker just as he'd called her and Uncle Frazier about Erickson's death. "Let's hope so."

He didn't say anything for a moment, just stood there staring at her. "We need to talk, Margo."

She preferred not talking. She wished he would just pull her into his arms and hold her for a minute. Then he could take her to bed, make love to her and help her forget about everything that had happened tonight. Besides, what did they need to talk about? From his too-serious expression, she had a feeling it would be a topic she'd rather not discuss but knew they would anyway. Besides, she needed to know what he was thinking.

"Alright, let's talk. Do you want to join me in the kitchen?" She led the way and he followed. They had made it halfway there when he reached out and took her hand, entwining their fingers. The moment he did, that all-familiar surge of desire swept over her.

She stopped walking, turned to him and didn't bother to ask what he wanted. Instead she just leaned close and lifted her mouth for his. She heard the low growl from his throat as his mouth lowered to hers. And then there it was. The wet-tongue, greedy-as-sin contact she wanted, needed and desired. The hunger she detected in his kiss was making her head spin. It definitely had her moaning.

Then just as quickly as the kiss had begun, it ended and he stared down at her. Was that anger she saw in his eyes? If so, why? Why was he upset that they had kissed?

"Go ahead and make the coffee so we can talk, Margo."

Nodding, she turned to continue on to the kitchen. Once there she prepared the coffee, fully aware he had sat down at the table and was quietly watching her. She'd discovered that Striker wasn't a talker per se. He was a man of action, and for him, action spoke a lot louder than words. But those times when he did talk, she would listen.

With the coffee brewing, she reached up into the cabinet to grab a couple of cups. When she turned back around, he was standing in front of her. Close. His body pressed hers against the counter. "Why do you have to be so sexy? So damn desirable?" he asked, and the question seemed to come out in a tortured groan.

She looked up at him. "I could ask you the same thing." Whether he knew it or not, *sexy* and *desirable* could be his middle names.

And then he was kissing her again, this time with even more hunger than the last. It was as if he had to convince himself that she was really here. Alive. And the fire hadn't harmed her in any way. For her it was very much the same thing. But it wasn't just that assurance driving her. For her there was also love.

Suddenly, she felt herself being lifted in strong arms and carried from the kitchen while their tongues continued to duel and tangle. When she felt herself being placed on the sofa, she was glad he didn't try taking her upstairs. She didn't want them to waste that much time. For some reason, the sofa seemed fitting since the first time they'd made love had been here.

She wasn't sure how Striker removed her clothes so fast. All she knew was that he did with an expertise that nearly overwhelmed her. She watched through a haze of desire as he undressed himself. She could tell from the penetrating look in his gaze that he wanted her just as much as she wanted him. They would talk later. Evidently whatever he wanted to discuss could wait.

When he had removed every stitch of his clothing,

she grimaced to see his bandaged shoulder and recalled
how he'd gotten the injury. Forcing those ugly thoughts
to the back of her mind, she decided to concentrate on
something else. Like how muscular his broad shoulders were and the thick firmness of his thighs. But
what really got her attention was the massive erection
that showed just how much he wanted her.

As usual, the air surrounding them was filled with
so many sexual undercurrents, to the point that she
could feel her nipples hardening and the area between
her legs get excruciatingly wet. He joined her on the
sofa, straddling her body and giving her a kiss that actually curled her toes.

She loved Striker's kisses. The depth of them always managed to set her on fire. Make her hotter than
she thought possible. At the same time, they managed
to make every cell in her body feel rejuvenated. She
heard herself groan as his kiss, slow and steady, suddenly took a turn to become deep and intense.

He broke off the kiss, leaving her disoriented and
more in a daze, while fighting to pull air into her lungs.
She lay there, stretched out beneath him and staring
up into the dark, penetrating eyes staring back at her.
He began placing feathery kisses on her face, starting on her forehead and slowly, methodically moving
downward. When his mouth reached her breasts, his
tongue latched on to a nipple and began teasing it with
his tongue, nibbling sensuously with his teeth, nearly
driving her over the edge only to snatch her back before she could fall.

She couldn't help noticing that one of his hands was
moving lower down her body. When it got to the area
between her thighs, she spread her legs open for him.

She felt his finger inch inside of her and fought back a guttural moan when another finger touched her clit. Then as if he wanted to show her what a great multi-tasker he was—like she didn't already know—he began fingering her at the same time his mouth on her breasts was driving her insane.

How was any man capable of giving a woman this much pleasure? Did he not know that he was almost killing her? Sending her mind spinning into one hell of a sexual frenzy? She figured that, even if he knew it, he really didn't care. His intent was to strike while she was hot, and she was definitely on fire.

His mouth let go of her nipples, and he used his tongue to trace a path down her body, greedily lapping her skin all the way down. When he began nibbling around her belly button, she thought she would go up in smoke then and there. And when he inched down farther on the sofa, he pulled back. Sitting on his knees, he lifted her legs over his shoulders.

"Your shoulder," she said, when one leg rested against the bandage.

"My shoulder is fine," he told her. Then he lowered his mouth to her. His tongue went straight for her clit, and he used it in ways that had her moaning and twitching around on the sofa, lifting her hips as pleasure ripped through every part of her body.

Sexual sensations she would never get used to tore into her, gripping her in a sensual tailspin. Then she came, screaming his name at the top of her lungs as her body erupted in one hell of an explosion. He didn't hold back. Instead he held tight to her hips, keeping his mouth firmly locked on her while lapping her up.

He finally drew back and lowered her legs before

moving his body upward to take her mouth, sharing the taste with her. Moments later he released her mouth to ease between her spread legs. The head of his erection was massive and slick and her body was ready for him. He held her hips steady as he slid inside of her. Leaning up, he took her mouth again, and as he began thrusting in and out of her, she noted that his tongue maintained the same rhythm as his body's thrust. All she could do was moan in pleasure. Over and over he brought her to the brink only to snatch her back with harder thrusts.

Suddenly her entire body splintered into a million pieces and she was propelled to sensuous oblivion. "Striker!"

She felt his body jerk hard once, then twice. When he called out her name, she knew he had joined her in what had to be the most intense sexual mating between them ever.

"You're quiet, Striker."

Striker glanced over at Margo as he eased back into his jeans. She was stretched out on the sofa, naked. It was taking all the control he could muster not to remove his clothes and take her again. But he couldn't do that. Nor could he forget that his weakness for her was his downfall and he was here to deal with it in the only way he knew how. And that was by imposing distance between them.

Instead of addressing her comment, he made one of his own. "Put your clothes on, Margo, and meet me in the kitchen."

She lifted a brow. "Okay."

If his tone and abrupt manner surprised her, there

was no help for it. Not now. What had just happened only reinforced his belief that Margo Connelly was more than a weakness. She'd become an obsession, and Striker Jennings didn't do obsessions. It didn't matter that he loved her. What mattered was that, for his peace of mind, he couldn't risk losing another person he loved. And because of his own lack of focus, he'd nearly lost her already.

By the time she made it to the kitchen, he had poured both of them a cup of coffee and was sitting at the table waiting for her to join him. Casting him a curious glance, she sat down, took a sip and asked, "So, what do you want to talk about, Striker?"

Before answering, he studied her features. Those belonged to the woman he loved to distraction. And that was the problem. *Distraction.* His lack of focus had nearly gotten them killed.

He took a sip of his coffee. "I failed you."

She lifted a brow. "And just how do you think you failed me?"

"I was hired by your uncle to protect you."

"And you don't think you did? Look at me, Striker. I'm sitting here, sipping coffee and breathing, because of you. You saved my life."

He shook his head. "If I had been more focused, I could have foreseen the danger headed our way. I could have devised a plan to get you away from the cabin and—"

"No, you wouldn't have foreseen anything. I'm sure you've been informed about the tracking substance. Moving me someplace else would not have mattered."

"I could have set a trap for him and made sure you weren't in any danger. I should have known my phone was blocked. The moment we got out of the shower I should have checked for calls. Hell, I shouldn't have been in the shower with you in the first place. I literally screwed up. Botched things up to the fucking nth degree. You could have died because of me. And if you had died…"

"I didn't die, Striker. I'm alive because of you. You risked your life saving me. That fire—"

"Should not have happened."

"But it did, and I'm alive. Why can't you accept that?"

Because he couldn't, and it was time he made sure she understood why. "I failed before protecting people I loved, Margo. First Wade and then Mom. I should have been there for Wade. I was his big brother and I was supposed to watch over him while Mom worked nights. She depended on me to do that. Instead, because I didn't want to miss any of my football practices, I encouraged Wade to go to that recreation center after school that had been established by cops. I thought it was a good way to make sure he didn't get involved with any street gangs. After all, the cops were there all the time and they were the good guys, right?"

He paused a minute. "And then with Mom, I should have been there for her. To make sure she took her meds. But I wasn't. And now there's you. I was supposed to protect you with my life, if necessary. Instead I placed you in even more danger."

MARGO SAID NOTHING as she stared at Striker, wondering if he realized he had just admitted he loved her. She'd heard everything he said, and her heart went out to him for all his misplaced guilt. She wanted to tell him that she loved him and that they could work out whatever issues plagued him together. But for some reason, she believed he had a plan. One that didn't include her.

"So what are you saying, Striker? Are you trying to tell me that all those times you held me in your arms, made love to me, kissed me, tasted me…that you wished you hadn't? That being with me wasn't good for you? That I was a mistake?"

"Yes." Then, just as quickly, he said, "No." He rubbed the top of his head and said in a frustrated tone, "Yes, I should feel that way, but there's another part that won't let me. And that's the part I have to deal with."

"And how are you proposing to deal with it?"

He paused a moment. "You no longer need protecting, so I plan to stay away from you for a while. At least until I can handle a few things."

Like your feelings for me? A part of her wanted to deny what he wanted. To say that staying away from her might be what he wanted but it wasn't what she wanted. That together they could work out his issues and that distance between them was the last thing they needed. What she wanted now was for them to do what they'd been robbed of doing and that was to behave like any other couple in love. She wanted them to spend time together without an element of danger lurking over them. Go out on dates, to the movies and dinner or do whatever they wanted to. She wouldn't crowd him. She just wanted to be with him whenever she could. But she knew that loving someone also meant giving them space when they needed it. Hadn't she explained that to her uncle when she'd left for college and then later when she'd relocated to New York?

Now she had to believe it herself. She had to believe

that Striker loved her as much as she loved him and that their love wouldn't diminish with distance. "Is that what you want, Striker?"

He shook his head. "No, but right now that's the only way."

Margo could see that his mind was made up and there was no changing it. "Okay. Then just know this one thing."

"What?"

"That I've fallen in love with you, Striker Jennings. And because I have, I'm willing to give you the time and distance you think you need. I hope that you'll realize that love can solve any issue."

She could tell by the surprise that lit his eyes that he hadn't expected her admission of love. Although he didn't say he loved her, as well, the important thing was that she believed he did and that their love was stronger than any of those issues he was battling.

He sat there for a minute and stared at her. Then, without saying anything, he stood and walked out of her kitchen. She held herself together until she heard the door close shut behind him.

It was only then that she allowed her tears to flow.

CHAPTER THIRTY-EIGHT

Two weeks later

STRIKER ADJUSTED THE aviator sunglasses on his face against the bright sun shining in through the car's windshield. He had returned to Charlottesville and the first thing he intended to do was go see Margo. He had needed time and distance, and she'd given him both.

Before leaving Charlottesville, he'd had a long talk with Sheppard, who agreed that he was carrying around misplaced guilt and, until he could let it go— all of it—he would always blame himself for what had happened while he'd been protecting Margo. As for his fear of losing someone he loved, Striker now saw, thanks to Sheppard, that life was a gamble, it wasn't meant to last forever, individuals should appreciate whatever time they had with the people they loved, and they should think of living and not dying.

Striker believed that returning to Little Rock had been the best thing for him. Visiting the old neighborhood had put a lot of things in perspective. He had visited the graves of his mom, Ray and Wade, and he had even stopped by his old high school, Little Rock Central. Coach Rivers was still there after all these years, and still had that old newspaper clipping framed on the wall, showing how Striker had led his football team to become national champions in his senior year.

He had enjoyed talking with Coach Rivers. The man was still a motivator and inspiration. Striker had never gotten around to thanking the man for standing up for him, being at the trial each day and becoming a character witness on his behalf. The testimony of Coach Rivers, some of his other teachers and a few of his neighbors had been beneficial in Striker getting a lesser sentence.

Thanks to Ray Jennings, they'd lived in a nice neighborhood and now a lot of the homes had been remodeled and were owned by a lot of preppies. He had walked his old neighborhood and was surprised to see many of the places he frequented as a kid were still there. Most had gotten a needed face-lift.

Last but not least, he'd gone to see Lamar Guyton, the father who had never acknowledged Striker's existence. It had taken him two days to find out the man had had a stroke a few years ago and was in a nursing home. Striker had gone to the nursing home to discover a man who couldn't even feed himself. Striker had apologized to Lamar Guyton for hating him all those years. After the apology Striker had left.

He had done a lot of soul-searching in Little Rock. He'd been able to walk away from his past and return to Charlottesville. To Margo. To his future. Sheppard had been right. Now he was ready to get on with his life, and more than anything, he wanted Margo in it. Of course, they wouldn't rush things. He wanted to date her properly. Find out all those things she liked to do. What helped tremendously was knowing she loved him. She had told him so, and now it was time that he shared how he felt about her.

He hadn't let anyone know he was returning to Charlottesville today and hadn't talked to Margo since walking out of her house two weeks ago. But he was back and he was more than ready to claim the woman he loved. He just hoped nothing had changed, and she still loved him as well.

"WHAT DO YOU mean you can't do it? I paid you," Liz almost screamed into the phone.

"Look, lady, I know you paid me, but I need to be careful now. I don't know who, but somebody is watching me. Possibly an undercover cop or something."

Liz didn't like the sound of that. Maybe she should just back off and forget her revenge on Margo. But she'd had almost three weeks to stew. And seeing that photo in the society column of yesterday's paper hadn't helped. Frazier had taken another woman to some big charity bash this past weekend. The two of them had been smiling for the camera. How dare he see someone else this soon? The more she thought about it, the more she wanted to hurt Frazier and knew the only way was by doing something to his niece.

"Fine. Just give me my money back." The resounding click in her ear told her the man had hung up. She began cursing to the top of her lungs, and she placed the blame squarely on Frazier's shoulders. First she would take care of his niece and then him.

Pacing her apartment, she came up with a plan, one she could handle herself. Crossing the room to her bedroom, she opened the drawer to her nightstand. Pulling out the revolver she kept there, she dropped it in her purse and left.

MARGO PUSHED AWAY from the sewing machine and
stood to work the kinks out of her neck. Claudine
would be arriving any minute. She had finally gotten
around to calling her yesterday and they had agreed to
meet today. As usual, Claudine sounded chipper and
said she couldn't wait to see the progress Margo had
made on her gown. Likewise, Margo was anxious to
see the material Claudine had chosen for the lining.

As she headed for the kitchen to pour another cup
of coffee, she tried not to dwell on the fact that it had
been two weeks since she'd heard from Striker. She
knew he was out of town; Roland had told her that
much when she'd asked about him. But Roland hadn't
said where he'd gone or when he would be back. She
thought about him every morning when she got up
and went to sleep dreaming about him at night. During the day she became enmeshed in her work, sometimes working from sunup to sundown on Claudine's
gown. She wished there was some way she could let
Striker know that whatever demons he had to face he
wouldn't have to do it alone. He had her and her love.

Maybe she should just leave well enough alone. Accept the fact that Striker had gone and there was a
chance he might not come back. That he thought his issues were bigger than their love and that he didn't love
her enough to even want to prove otherwise.

But she just refused to allow herself to believe that.
He was the best thing to ever happen to her. All she
had to do was think of the time she had wasted with
Scott. She'd had to make a trip to the police station to
give a statement regarding the attempted kidnapping,
namely her conversations with Freddie Siskin. Thanks
to Striker, both calls from Freddie had been recorded

on her phone. Scott had called last week trying to convince her that he had tried talking Freddie out of his plans. In the end, Scott had lost his job because of his alleged involvement. She'd told him he should choose his friends more wisely and to never call her again. To be certain that she didn't hear from him, she blocked his number. She wanted to put that part of her life behind her and build a future only with Striker. But it would have to be his decision.

Hearing the sound of the doorbell, she guessed it was Claudine, but she checked through the peephole to verify.

She opened the door and smiled. "Claudine, it's good seeing you."

"Same here," Claudine said with a bubbly smile on her face. "And I can't wait to show you the material for my lining."

Margo glanced past Claudine. "I don't see your car."

Claudine chuckled. "Stan dropped me off. We have a lunch date with his parents to go over the guest list and he figured if he controlled the time I'm here then we wouldn't be late meeting his parents. He gave me an hour and then he's coming back to get me."

Margo grinned as she stepped aside for Claudine to enter. "He sounds like a man who knows you have a problem with time."

"So he claims." Claudine then glanced around. "And where is that gorgeous hunk who was here the last time I came by? I believe his name was Lamar."

Margo told her the truth—at least what she did know. "He's out of town."

"Oh, phooey. I was hoping to see him again. I like him."

I like him too, Margo thought. In fact, she loved him. Instead of saying anything about that, she led Claudine to her workroom. "I think you'll like what I've done so far."

"I can't wait."

They had walked into Margo's workroom when suddenly there was a knock at her door. She looked at Claudine and smiled. "That's not your fiancé coming back for you already, is it?"

Claudine shook her head as if she was annoyed at the interruption. "I doubt it. He said he would give me an hour." She then looked at Margo accusingly. "You didn't book another appointment the same time as mine, did you?"

Margo drew in a deep breath, knowing how Claudine liked being the center of attention. "No, Claudine, I didn't double book. It's probably someone selling something. I'll get rid of them and be back."

"Fine."

Leaving her office, she closed the door behind her and headed toward the front, wondering who on earth it could be. She reached the door and looked through the peephole. It was Liz Tillman. Why would her uncle's ex-girlfriend be here? Striker had warned her there was a chance Liz would seek her out because Liz blamed her for her breakup with Frazier. Now was not a good time to have to deal with Liz, but she couldn't very well pretend she wasn't home, not when her car was parked in the driveway. Margo opened the door. "What do you want, Liz? I'm busy."

"We need to talk."

"Sorry, but a client is here and—"

"You're lying. There's no other car parked in the

driveway but yours," Liz said, taking advantage of the open door to push her way inside Margo's home.

"Now, wait just a minute," she said to Liz's fleeing back. "I didn't invite you in."

"Margo? Is everything okay?"

She turned to find Claudine had stuck her head out the workroom door. That was all she needed. "Yes. Everything is okay," she said, plastering a smile on her face. "Just a little matter I need to take care of. It won't take long."

"Oh," Claudine said, looking at Margo and then Liz. "I thought you said you didn't double book."

"I didn't. This is a personal matter."

"Oh. Okay."

Margo was glad when Claudine stuck her head back inside and closed the workroom door. She then turned a furious gaze to Liz. "I told you I had a client here, so please leave."

"I won't leave until you and I have a little talk."

Margo frowned. "We have nothing to talk about. You are interrupting my time with a client," she said, trying to keep her voice low so Claudine wouldn't hear them.

"You think I give a damn about your client after what you did to me?"

Liz opened her jacket, and Margo saw the revolver in Liz's hand. It was pointed at her. "Liz, what are you doing?" Margo asked, looking from the gun back up to Liz. "Are you crazy?"

Liz chuckled. "Yes, I'm crazy. Now let's go into your kitchen. If you refuse, I will shoot you right here. Then I'll go into your office and shoot your client, so as not to leave a witness."

Margo didn't say anything as she considered Liz's threat. She'd never thought the woman was capable of falling off the deep end just because Uncle Frazier had broken off with her. Hopefully, if they talked, she could make Liz come to her senses and see what a terrible mistake she was making.

"Fine," Margo said. "Let's go into the kitchen and talk."

CHAPTER THIRTY-NINE

STRIKER ROUNDED THE corner onto the main road that led into Margo's subdivision. As he neared her house, he saw another car besides Margo's car parked in her driveway, and the hairs on his neck stood up. The make and model matched that of Liz Tillman's vehicle. Striker recalled Frazier mentioning it when he'd warned him about Liz blaming Margo for the breakup. It could be a client's vehicle, but Striker decided not to take any chances and kept driving to the house next door, remembering it was up for sale. He pulled in the driveway and brought his car to a stop.

With his instincts roaring inside him that something was very wrong about this situation, Striker quickly got out of his car and circled around to the back of the house and then crossed the yard onto Margo's property. For once he appreciated all her windows, which gave him a good view inside her home. Pressing his body against the side of her house, he also appreciated she had her blinds open. He was about to cross the patio to her sliding glass door but quickly darted back to the wall when Margo entered her kitchen with a woman he could only assume was Liz Tillman. And he could clearly see that the woman was holding a gun on Margo.

He fought back his rage as he silently moved toward

the sliding glass door. He tried opening it and found it was locked. Pulling the pocketknife from his boot, he forced open the door, quietly slid it open and went inside. Quickly moving behind a huge potted plant that shielded his body, he crouched down to a position that gave him a good view of what was going on in Margo's kitchen. He could clearly hear their voices as well.

If Liz Tillman thought she would hurt a single strand of hair on Margo's head, the woman was sadly mistaken.

"HONESTLY, LIZ, IF this is because Uncle Frazier broke up with you, I had nothing to do with that."

"Didn't you?" Liz said, sneering. "I had plans for me and Frazier, and you ruined them."

Margo's cell phone suddenly rang. "Don't you dare think about answering that," Liz threatened.

Margo didn't know what to do. She could tell she wouldn't be able to reason with Liz. And whatever Margo did, she would have to be careful that Claudine, an innocent in all this, wouldn't get hurt.

"Liz, why don't we go somewhere else to discuss this? Away from here for more privacy."

"This place is just fine and we have all the privacy we need for you to tell me why you deliberately ruined things between me and Frazier."

"I didn't ruin anything," Margo said, hoping against all odds that she would get through to her.

"Yes, you did. Now everything I worked for over the past two years means nothing. I planned it all. I saw Frazier. I set my goal to have him, but, thanks to you, it's over. I paid someone to get rid of you just to see Frazier suffer, but the man I hired backed out."

Margo stared at Liz, not believing her admission. "You hired someone to get rid of me?"

A haughty Liz lifted her chin. "Yes. I suggested that he turn you over to human traffickers. I even paid the bastard a down payment. He was going to get the rest when the deed was done. Now I have to take care of you myself."

"You won't get away with it."

"Why not? I'll shoot you and make it look like a robbery. Of course that means I'll have to shoot your client, as well, and—"

"I don't think so. Now drop your gun before I shoot you."

Both Margo and Liz glanced at Claudine, who stood in the kitchen doorway holding a gun.

"I said drop the gun and don't think about trying something stupid. I'm a very good shot, lady, but if you want to call my bluff, go ahead," Claudine warned.

Liz stared at the woman and, as if deciding not to call Claudine's bluff, she dropped her gun.

WHAT THE HELL! Striker had been about to crash the little party in Margo's kitchen when he'd seen Claudine Bernard enter the scene. Where had Claudine come from?

He couldn't help but grin. It seemed Claudine wasn't just the it's-all-about-me bride-to-be he'd taken her for. The woman definitely surprised him. She was the last person he'd think would tote a gun, but in this case, he was glad about it. She had disarmed Liz Tillman.

He was about to come out from behind the plant and let Claudine know he would handle things from here when Claudine's next words stopped him cold.

"CLAUDINE, WE NEED to call the police," Margo said in a rush, inching away from Liz to pull her phone from the back pocket of her jeans.

"Don't move, Margo."

Margo blinked at Claudine's harsh command. "Why? We need to call the police."

Claudine smiled. "*We* don't need to do anything. In fact, this woman's timing is perfect."

An uneasy feeling settled in the pit of Margo's stomach. "I don't understand. What do you mean her timing is perfect?"

"Then let me explain things," Claudine said while still holding the gun on both Margo and Liz. "My plan all along was to kill you, Margo, and that was after I took care of your father's illegitimate brother, Roland Summers."

"Illegitimate brother?" Liz asked, speaking for the first time since dropping her gun. "There's an illegitimate brother?"

Other than flashing Liz an irritated look, Claudine ignored her question and then said to Margo, "The guy I hired to kill Summers botched up the carjacking, and Summers survived."

Margo's head began spinning. Claudine planned to kill her and had been responsible for Roland's carjacking? "But why? What did we ever do to you?"

"Your father and Summers drove my father to commit suicide."

Margo was convinced Claudine had come unhinged. "What are you talking about?"

Claudine sneered at Margo, as if Margo should already know the answer. "Summers was going to blow the whistle on his fellow officers, who were on the take. They set him up, and Summers went to prison."

"Prison?"

"Yes, prison. Then Summers's wife and your father were able to get him a new trial."

"And what was wrong with that when an innocent man had been sent to prison?" Margo asked, still having a hard time following Claudine. Uncle Roland had been a cop? He'd served time? What crime did they pin on him?

"Those bad cops forced my father, a good man and the fire captain in this city at the time, to falsify reports. They swore they would harm his family if he didn't follow their orders."

"And what reports did your father falsify?"

"The ones that said the cause of the fire that killed your parents was electrical."

Margo felt a lump in her throat, and the pulse in her neck began thrumming. "Surely you're not saying the fire that killed my parents was deliberately set."

Claudine rolled her eyes. "Of course it was. Don't be stupid. Did you honestly think five cops would willingly go to jail? They figured if they killed your parents and Summers's wife, that Summers would get the message and call off the investigation and the new trial. But he didn't."

Margo felt weak in the knees. Her parents and Roland's wife had been murdered?

"Those bad cops were eventually arrested and sent to jail. Fortunately, Dad wasn't linked to any of it, but the guilt he felt for falsifying that report eventually drove him to commit suicide. I was only fourteen and was the one who found him. He'd hung himself, leaving a note confessing everything. I never gave it to anyone. I kept the note all these years."

Margo just stared at Claudine. Did Claudine not understand that she wasn't the only person who'd lost someone because of those corrupt cops? Margo had lost her parents and Roland had lost a wife, a brother and sister-in-law.

"Your uncle Frazier Connelly is on my list as well," Claudine continued. "He will eventually get what he deserves."

"Good," Liz said.

Margo ignored Liz's words. "And what did Uncle Frazier do?"

"Nothing other than be related to you and Summers."

STRIKER HAD HEARD ENOUGH. He quickly moved from behind the huge plant.

"Drop the damn gun, Claudine!"

Startled, Claudine aimed the gun at him and he fired, hitting Claudine in the shoulder. She dropped the gun and fell to the floor. He rushed forward, kicking both Liz's and Claudine's guns away from their reach.

Suddenly, Roland, Stonewall, Quasar, Detective Ingram and two of her police officers stormed into the kitchen with their guns drawn.

"Call for medical attention for her," Detective Ingram said to one of the officers, pointing at Claudine, who was balled up on the floor moaning. "And handcuff Ms. Tillman. Read them both their rights."

After putting his gun away, Striker moved toward Margo and pulled her into his arms, placing a kiss on her forehead. "You okay?"

She shook her head. "No, I'm not okay. Claudine's father lied about my parents' deaths. They were murdered, Striker. It wasn't an electrical fire at all. And Claudine paid someone to set up a carjacking to kill Roland."

"I heard," Striker said.

"And I heard as well," Roland said, coming to stand beside them. "I was able to prove that those cops killed my wife, but I couldn't prove the fire that killed your parents had been deliberately set, although I suspected as much. I'm sorry."

Margo lifted a brow. "Why are you sorry? It wasn't your fault."

"In a way I feel like it was. Your father gave Becca the money she needed to hire a private investigator to get enough evidence to reopen the case. If Murdock hadn't gotten involved then—"

"How could he not get involved? Dad was your brother, and he had every right to get involved," she cut in to say. "What happened to them was not your fault. I don't blame you for anything any more than Claudine should blame us for what happened to her father."

She paused and then added, "I'm sorry for what they did to your wife. And to know you spent time in jail as an innocent man. That had to be awful for you."

"I survived."

"How did you know what was going down?" Striker asked Roland.

"We have Detective Ingram to thank for that. Earlier today, one of her men picked up a guy who's known as a 'criminal-for-hire.' He offered information in exchange for a plea. He said Liz Tillman had hired him to take out Margo. We tried calling Margo to warn her that Liz might do something herself, but when she didn't answer, we headed over here. We didn't know you were back in town." Roland's cell phone went off and he said, "Excuse me while I get this."

Margo turned her attention back to Striker. "I thought you were out of town too."

"I was. I got back today and came straight here from the airport. When I saw the car in your driveway, something didn't seem right."

"I'm no threat to Margo. I just dropped by to talk to her," a handcuffed Liz said, when the officer was about to lead her away.

Detective Ingram rolled her eyes. "Yeah, right, Ms. Tillman. And the next thing you're going to do is try to convince us that one of those guns isn't yours."

"B-but I don't know her," Liz said, indicating Claudine.

"You might not know her, but the two of you have something in common," Detective Ingram said to her.

"What?"

"Apparently you both hired the same guy to do your dirty work. Claudine Bernard paid Patrick Grooms to kill Roland Summers during a pretended carjacking, and you, Ms. Tillman, paid him to get rid of Ms. Connelly. He was picked up this morning and since then he's been singing like a bird."

"I don't know who you're talking about," Liz said. "I didn't pay anyone to do anything. I don't know anyone named Patrick Grooms. It will be my word against his."

"Um, not really," Detective Ingram said. "You see, Grooms also told us where the two of you met when you paid him to do the job. Unfortunately for you, it was a café with security cameras. You were captured on video making the payment to him. You and Ms. Bernard both were caught on camera at the same café." She then looked at the officer. "Now get her out of here."

As soon as Liz was walked out, paramedics arrived to take care of Claudine's shoulder. She continued to yell at the top of her lungs that Roland and Margo needed to die. Striker was glad when they finally finished dressing Claudine's shoulder and took her out.

Frazier Connelly rushed into the kitchen looking panic-stricken. "Margo? You okay? I got Roland's text about Liz."

"I'm fine, thanks to Striker," she said, reaching out to give her uncle a hug. "He saved my life once again."

Frazier glanced at Striker. "Thanks. And who was that other woman? The one whose shoulder is bandaged up?"

"You tell him everything, Uncle Roland. I'm too jumpy to do so right now," she said, snuggling closer into the comfort of Striker's arms. She wasn't sure where Striker had gone when he'd left town or whether he had begun to deal with all his issues. All that mattered was that he was here and had saved her life once more.

Striker tightened his arms around her, and Margo appreciated that. Hearing Roland retell the story for Uncle Frazier's benefit sent chills through her entire body. She hadn't looked into the barrel of just one gun today, but two. She was fine now, though. Striker was here with her.

CHAPTER FORTY

"YOUR BATH IS READY."

Margo glanced up as Striker walked down the stairs. Why now, of all times, did he have to look so damn sexy? Hot. So irresistibly male. "Thanks. And thanks for saving my life again. It seems to have become a habit."

Striker slid beside her on the sofa. "Hell, I hope not."

He took her hand in his, linking their fingers. "You'll never know how I felt when I saw Liz holding that gun on you. It reinforced my realizations about a few things."

"What?"

"Mainly, that you need a forever-protector."

A smile curved Margo's lips. "You want to apply for the job?"

His gaze locked on hers, his expression serious. "Yes."

She swallowed deeply. They hadn't had a chance to talk. More police officers had arrived asking for statements. Reporters had also shown up in droves. No doubt, the media would dig into that old case involving the police officers and their possible involvement in her parents' deaths. The media would also expose Roland's connection to her family, and she hoped he was okay with that.

Once everyone had left, except for the few members of the media who were intent on hanging around, Striker had locked up her home and brought her to his place. The news crew hadn't been allowed near his home since Striker lived in a gated community.

Margo had fallen in love with his town house the minute she walked through the door. It was spacious with a beautiful view of the mountains. And for some reason, she felt right at home. He had told her to get comfortable while he ran her bathwater because a good soak in the tub would work wonders for her. When she told him she had nothing to put on, he told her he had plenty of T-shirts. That reminded her of the last time she'd worn one of his shirts.

"Talk to me, Striker. Share your thoughts." Margo had a feeling she was asking him to do something he didn't do on a regular basis.

"I went home," he finally said.

"To Little Rock?"

"Yes. I haven't been back since I left. There was no need. Wade and Mom were gone and my mom's only sister, Aunt Gussie, died while I was locked up. I stayed away because I wanted to start a new life. Have a new beginning. I found that here in Charlottesville. I had everything I thought I needed. The only people in my life were those I wanted, and I didn't need anyone else."

He paused before saying, "And then…"

She'd been hanging on his every word. "And then what?"

"And then I met you."

Elation swelled Margo's heart. "I hope meeting me was a good thing."

He chuckled. "I didn't think so at first."

She could accept that. "But now?"

His hold on her hand tightened. "And now I can't imagine my life without you. But I had to come to terms with some things. I hadn't buried the past as deep as I thought. Not as deep as I should have. That's why I returned home, and I'm glad I did."

He paused again and then said, "Going home, visiting with people like my high school coach, who's still there, and walking the neighborhood and seeing the changes, good changes—all that made me appreciate how that town shaped me, molded me. Gave me values. I also went to visit the man who fathered me. He had a stroke a few years back and is in a nursing home. After seeing the condition he's in, I could no longer hate him for how shabbily he treated me and my mother. I even apologized to him for hating him so much."

He didn't say anything for a minute. "Whoever said you can't go back home didn't know what they were talking about. For me it was important to go back before I could move forward. I can do that now. And I want to do that. With you."

Margo swallowed. "You're sure of that? That you want to move forward…with me?"

"Yes, I'm sure."

He shifted so they were facing each other. "I love you, Margo. I knew I loved you when I left here that day, but I felt I'd failed you. And the thought of how close you'd come to dying—of how close I'd come to losing you—shook me up a bit. That's why I had to come to terms with some things. I've done that, and more than anything, I want you in my life."

"Oh, Striker."

Striker pulled Margo into his arms and held her

tight. Close to his heart. "But I want us to do this like normal people and not rush things. I want us to date, have fun, enjoy things together as a couple, and then when we're ready for that next step, we'll take it. Together. We won't be using anybody's timeline but our own. Okay?"

She smiled at him, fighting back tears of joy. "I wouldn't want things any other way."

Striker captured her mouth in a kiss that held so much love and promise. He didn't know that he could love a woman this much. At first the thought had been scary. Now it was wonderful.

When he released her mouth, he whispered against her wet lips, "I love you so much, Margo."

"And I love you."

He smiled before sweeping her into his arms and standing. "Now for your bath."

"Will you join me?"

"That's my plan," he said, heading up the stairs. "I don't intend to let you out of my sight for a while."

She smiled, tightening her arms around his neck. "Trust me, I have no problem with that. Like I said earlier, I want you for my forever-protector."

"Baby, you got me."

CHAPTER FORTY-ONE

DR. RANDI FULLER glanced up at the knock on her door. "Come in."

She smiled when Detective Ingram walked in. She was still baffled at the vibes she got whenever she was around the detective. She'd gotten the same vibes that night when she'd met Margo Connelly. For some reason that she didn't quite understand, her subconscious was saying that over the span of their lives the three of them would become the best of friends. She definitely couldn't understand the logic in that.

First of all, she'd met Margo Connelly that one time and didn't expect to ever see her again. And second, unless she returned to Charlottesville to work on another case, there was no reason her path would cross with Detective Ingram's either. Besides, as a rule, she'd made it a point not to have close female friends due to an incident that had happened while she was in college. Her older sister, Haywood, was all she needed. Randi considered Haywood her best friend and confidante. And then there was her mom, Jenna. She and her mother had always had a close relationship. In fact, she was close to both her parents. Very few people knew she was the daughter of world-renowned defense attorney Randolph Fuller.

"I was hoping to see you before you left, Dr. Fuller.

It's been quite a day and one of the cases I worked involved Margo Connelly again."

"What happened?"

Detective Ingram spent the next ten minutes telling her what had gone down at Margo Connelly's home. "I'm glad Ms. Connelly is okay," Dr. Fuller said.

"So am I. It's bad enough to have one person out to get you, but to have two others at the same time is crazy. I think she might need a full-time bodyguard."

"It certainly sounds like it."

"And I guess you heard about the medical examiner's report regarding Erickson's death," Detective Ingram said.

Randi nodded. "Yes. According to the coroner, Erickson had been dead a good two hours before Small's visit."

"Yes. So that means Small wasn't the one who killed him."

"Any leads as to who did?" Randi asked.

Detective Ingram shook her head. "Not a one. The FBI will have their hands full trying to figure this one out. Even the security cameras where Erickson's cell was located had been tampered with. We know it was an inside job, but by whom? Rumor has it that the mob replaced Erickson and it was decided that he would never leave prison alive."

Randi nodded again. "That doesn't surprise me. Erickson knew too much about the mob's business."

"I wonder who's in control now."

Randi smiled. "I hope you don't think that I know. And in case you're wondering, I also don't have a clue as to who killed Erickson. Usually victims come back to me wanting justice, but I doubt Erickson will. We didn't hit it off, and I warned him he would die before me."

"You did?"

"Yes. It was after he made a few veiled threats during our one-on-one meeting," Randi said, "although, at the time, I had no idea his life would end so soon."

"And now the mystery of Erickson's death is another murder to be solved."

"And it will be."

Detective Ingram glanced around. "Need help with anything?"

"No. I'm just packing up a few things. I wasn't here that long."

"But you were effective, and we appreciate it. So, you're headed back to Richmond?"

Randi had shared that much with the detective. "Yes, I leave in the morning. I'll be home only for a day or two and then I'm leaving again. To come back here, I canceled plans for a short visit to an island off of South Carolina. I plan to finally go there and spend at least two weeks doing nothing."

"What will you be doing later tonight? A gentleman friend of mine and I are grabbing a few beers and chips after work if you want to join us."

"Stonewall Courson?"

Surprise lit Detective Ingram's eyes and then she smiled. "Yes. How did you know?"

Randi chuckled. "I don't need psychic powers to figure that out. I saw your reaction at the cabin when you saw him race into the burning cabin to help save his friend."

Detective Ingram ran a few fingers through her hair, and Randi found the gesture telling. "Due to both our jobs, we've only had time to talk on the phone, text and meet to grab a few beers. We have our first official date this weekend."

"Good for you and thanks for the invite, but I'll bow out. I need to get back to the hotel and start packing if I want to be on the road first thing in the morning to avoid any rush-hour traffic."

"Okay, I understand. It was nice meeting you, Dr. Fuller, and you've made a believer out of me regarding a number of things," Detective Ingram said sincerely. "If you ever visit Charlottesville again, please look me up."

A huge smile touched Randi's lips. "I will, but only on one condition."

"And what condition is that?"

"That, from here on out, I'm Randi and you're Joy."

"Okay, Randi. That's a deal."

* * * * *

If you enjoyed Striker and Margo's story, don't miss the next book in the PROTECTORS *series, featuring Quasar and Randi, SEIZED BY SEDUCTION Coming soon from* New York Times *bestselling author Brenda Jackson and HQN Books!*

HARLEQUIN® DESIRE

Desperate to escape her sheltered life,
Hayley Thompson quits her job as church secretary
to become personal assistant to bad-tempered,
reclusive, way-too-sexy Jonathan Bear. But his kiss
is more temptation than she bargained for!

Read on for a sneak peek of
SEDUCE ME, COWBOY
the latest in New York Times *bestselling author*
Maisey Yates's
COPPER RIDGE *series!*

Hayley Thompson was a good girl. In all the ways that phrase applied. The kind of girl every mother wished her son would bring home for Sunday dinner.

Of course, the mothers of Copper Ridge were much more enthusiastic about Hayley than their sons were, but that had never been a problem. She had never really tried dating anyway. Dates were the least of her problems.

She was more worried about the constant feeling that she was under a microscope. That she was a trained seal, sitting behind the desk in the church office exactly as one might expect from a small-town pastor's daughter— who also happened to be the church secretary.

And what did she have to show for being so good? Absolutely nothing.

Meanwhile, her older brother had gone out into the world and done whatever he wanted. He'd broken every rule. Run away from home. Gotten married, gotten divorced. Come back to town and opened up a bar in the same town where his father preached sermons. All while Hayley had stayed and behaved herself. Done everything that was expected of her.

Ace was the prodigal son. He hadn't just received forgiveness for his transgressions. He'd been rewarded. He had so many things well-behaved Hayley wanted and didn't have.

He'd found love again in his wife, Sierra. They had children. The doting attention of Hayley's parents—a side effect of being the first to supply grandchildren, she felt—while Hayley had…

Well, nothing.

Nothing but a future as a very well-behaved spinster.

That was why she was here now. Clutching a newspaper in her hand until it was wrinkled tight. She hadn't even known people still put ads in the paper for job listings, but while she'd been sitting in The Grind yesterday on Copper Ridge's main street, watching people go by and feeling a strange sense of being untethered, she had grabbed the local paper.

That had led her to the job listings. And, seeing as she was unemployed for the first time since she was sixteen years old, she'd read them.

Every single one of them had been submitted by people she knew. Businesses she'd grown up patronizing, or businesses owned by people she knew from her dad's congregation. And if she got a job somewhere like that, she might as well have stayed on at the church.

Except for one listing. Assistant to Jonathan Bear, owner of Gray Bear Construction. The job was for him personally, but it would also entail clerical work for his company and some work around his home.

She didn't know anything about the company. She'd never had a house built, after all. Neither had her mother and father. And she'd never heard his name before, was reasonably sure she'd never seen him at church.

She wanted that distance.

Familiar, nagging guilt gnawed at the edges of her

heart. Her parents were good people. They loved her very much. And she loved them. But she felt like a beloved goldfish. With people watching her every move and tapping on the glass. Plus, the bowl was restricting her when she was well aware there was an entire ocean out there.

Step one in her plan for independence had been to acquire her own apartment. Cassie Caldwell, owner of The Grind, and her husband, Jake, had moved out of the space above the coffee shop a while ago. Happily, it had been vacant and ready to rent, and Hayley had taken advantage of that. So, with the money she'd saved up, she'd moved into that place. And then, after hoarding a few months' worth of rent, she had finally worked up the courage to quit.

Her father had been... She wouldn't go so far as to say he'd been disappointed. John Thompson never had a harsh word for anyone. He was all kind eyes and deep conviction. The type of goodness Hayley could only marvel at, that made her feel as though she could never quite measure up.

But she could tell her father had been confused. And she hadn't been able to explain herself, not fully. Because she didn't want either of her parents to know that ultimately this little journey of independence would lead straight out of Copper Ridge.

She had to get out of the fishbowl. She needed people to stop tapping on her glass.

Virtue wasn't its own reward. For years she'd believed it would be. But then...suddenly, watching Ace at the dinner table at her parents' house, with his family, she'd realized the strange knot in her stomach wasn't anger over his abandonment, over the way he'd embarrassed their parents with his behavior.

It was envy.

Envy of all he had, of his freedom. Well, this was her chance to have some of that for herself, and she couldn't do it with everyone watching.

She took a deep breath and regarded the house in front of her. If she didn't know it was the home and office of the owner of Gray Bear Construction she would be tempted to assume it was some kind of resort.

The expansive front porch was made entirely out of logs, stained with a glossy, honey-colored sheen that caught the light and made the place look like it was glowing. The green metal roof was designed to withstand harsh weather—which down in town by the beach wasn't much of an issue, but a few miles inland, here in the mountains, she could imagine there was snow in winter.

She wondered if she would need chains for her car. But she supposed she'd cross that bridge when she came to it. It was early spring, and she didn't even have the job yet.

Getting the job, and keeping it through winter, was only a pipe dream at this point.

She took a deep breath and started up the path, the bark-laden ground soft beneath her feet. She inhaled deeply, the sharp scent of pine filling her lungs. It was cool beneath the trees and she wrapped her arms around herself as she walked up the steps and made her way to the front door.

She knocked before she had a chance to rethink her actions, and then she waited.

She was just about to knock again when she heard

footsteps. She quickly put her hand down at her side. Then she lifted it again, brushing her hair out of her face. Then she clasped her hands in front of her, then put them back at her sides again. Then she decided to hold them in front of her again.

She had just settled on that position when the door jerked open.

She had rehearsed her opening remarks. Had practiced making a natural smile in the mirror—which was easy after so many years manning the front desk of a church—but all of that disappeared completely when she looked at the man standing in front of her.

He was… Well, he was nothing like she'd expected, which left her grappling for what exactly she had been expecting. Somebody older. Certainly not somebody who towered over her like a redwood.

Jonathan Bear wasn't someone you could anticipate.

His dark, glittering eyes assessed her; his mouth pressed into a thin line. His black hair was tied back, but it was impossible for her to tell just how long it was from where she stood.

"Who are you?" he asked, his tone uncompromising.

"I'm here to interview for the assistant position. Were you expecting someone else?" Her stomach twisted with anxiety. He wasn't what she had expected, and now she was wondering if she was what *he* had expected. Maybe he wanted somebody older, with more qualifications. Or somebody more…well, sexy secretary than former church secretary.

Though she looked very nice in this twin set and pencil skirt, if she said so herself.

"No," he said, moving away from the door. "Come in."

"Oh," she said, scampering to follow his direction.

"The office is upstairs," he said, taking great strides through the entryway and heading toward a massive curved staircase.

She found herself taking very quick steps to try to keep up with him. And it was difficult to do that when she was distracted by the beauty of the house. She was trying to take in all of the details as she trailed behind him up the stairs, her low heels clicking on the hardwood.

"I'm Hayley Thompson," she said, "which I know the résumé said, but you didn't know who I was... So..."

"We're the only two people here," he said, looking back at her, lifting one dark brow. "So knowing your name isn't really that important, is it?"

She couldn't tell if he was joking. She laughed nervously, and it got her no response at all. So then she was concerned she had miscalculated.

They reached the top of the stairs, and she followed him down a long hallway, the sound of her steps dampened now by a long carpet runner the colors of the nature that surrounded them. Brown, forest green and a red that reminded her of cranberries.

The house smelled new. Which was maybe a strange observation to make, but the scent of wood lingered in the air, and something that reminded her of paint.

"How long have you lived here?" she asked, more comfortable with polite conversation than contending with silence.

"Just moved in last month," he said. "One of our designs. You might have guessed, this is what Gray Bear does. Custom homes. That's our specialty. And since my construction company merged with Grayson Design we're doing design as well as construction."

"How many people can buy places like this?" she asked, turning a circle while she walked.

"You would be surprised. For a lot of our clients these are only vacation homes. Escapes to the coast and to the mountains. Mostly, we work on the Oregon coast, but we make exceptions for some of the higher-paying clientele."

"That's…kind of amazing. I mean, something of that scale right here in Copper Ridge. Or I guess technically we're outside the city limits."

"Still the same zip code," he said, lifting a shoulder.

He took hold of two sliding double doors fashioned to look like barn doors and slid them open, revealing a huge office space with floor-to-ceiling windows and a view that made her jaw drop.

The sheer immensity of the mountains spread before them was incredible on its own. But beyond that, she could make out the faint gray of the ocean, white-capped waves and jagged rocks rising out of the surf.

"The best of everything," he said. "Sky, mountains, ocean. That kind of sums up the company. Now that you know about us, you can tell me why I should hire you."

"I want the job," she said, her tone hesitant. As soon as she said the words, she realized how ridiculous they were. Everybody who interviewed for this position would want the job. "I was working as a secretary for my father's…business," she said, feeling guilty about fudging a little bit on her résumé. But she hadn't really wanted to say she was working at her father's church, because…well, she just wanted to come in at a slightly more neutral position.

"You were working for your family?"

"Yes," she said.

He crossed his arms, and she felt slightly intimidated. He was the largest man she'd ever seen. At least, he felt large. Something about all the height and muscles and presence combined.

"We're going to have to get one thing straight right now, Hayley. I'm not your daddy. So, if you're used to a kind and gentle working environment where you get a lot of chances because firing you would make it awkward around the holidays, this might take some adjustment for you. I'm damned hard to please. And I'm not a very nice boss. There's a lot of work to do around here. I hate paperwork, and I don't want to have to do any form twice. If you make mistakes and I have to sit at that desk longer as a result, you're fired. If I've hired you to make things easier between myself and my clients, and something you do makes it harder, you're fired. If you pass on a call to me that I shouldn't have to take, you're fired."

She nodded, wishing she had a notepad, not because she was ever going to forget what he'd said, but so she could underscore the fact that she was paying attention. "Anything else?"

"Yeah," he said, a slight smile curving his lips. "You're also fired if you fuck up my coffee."

This was a mistake. Jonathan Bear was absolutely certain of it. But he had made millions making mistakes, so what was one more? Nobody else had responded to his ad.

Except for this pale, strange little creature who looked barely twenty and wore the outfit of an eighty-year-old woman.

She was… Well, she wasn't the kind of formidable woman who could stand up to the rigors of working with him.

His sister Rebecca would say—with absolutely no tact at all—that he sucked as a boss. And maybe she was right, but he didn't really care. He was busy, and right now he hated most of what he was busy with.

There was irony in that, he knew. He had worked hard all his life. While a lot of his friends had sought solace and oblivion in drugs and alcohol, Jonathan had figured it was best to sweat the poison right out.

He'd gotten a job on a construction site when he was fifteen and learned his trade. He'd gotten to where he was faster, better than most of the men around him. By the time he was twenty he had been doing serious custom work on the more upscale custom homes he'd built with West Construction.

But he wanted more. There'd been a cap on what he could make with that company, and he didn't like a ceiling. He wanted open skies and the freedom to go as high, as fast as he wanted. So he could amass so much it could never be taken from him.

So he'd risked striking out on his own. No one had believed a kid from the wrong side of the tracks could compete with West. But Jonathan had courted business across city and county lines and created a reputation beyond Copper Ridge so that when people came looking to build retirement homes or vacation properties, he was the name they knew.

He had built everything he had, brick by brick. In a strictly literal sense in some cases.

And every brick built a stronger wall against all the things he had left behind. Poverty, uncertainty, the lack of respect paid to a man in his circumstances.

Then six months ago Joshua Grayson had approached him. Originally from Copper Ridge, the man had been looking for a foothold back in town after years in Seattle. He had a successful architecture firm, but he was looking to shift focus and go into business with his brothers. He wanted to mend fences with his family after the death of his father.

And so Joshua asked Jonathan if he would consider bringing design in-house, making Bear Construction into Gray Bear.

This gave Jonathan reach into urban areas, into Seattle. Had him managing remote crews and dealing with many projects at one time. And it had pushed him straight out of the building game in many ways. He had turned into a desk drone. And while his bank account had grown astronomically, he was quite a ways from the life he thought he'd live after reaching this point.

Except the house. The house was finally finished. Finally, he was living in one of the places he'd built.

Finally, Jonathan Bear, that poor Indian kid who wasn't worth anything to anyone, bastard son of the biggest bastard in town, had his house on the side of the mountain and more money than he would ever be able to spend.

And he was bored out of his mind.

Boredom, it turned out, worked him into a hell of a temper. He had a feeling Hayley Thompson wasn't strong enough to stand up to that. But he expected to go through a few assistants before he found one who could handle it. She might as well be number one.

"You've got the job," he said. "You can start tomorrow."

Her eyes widened, and he noticed they were a strange shade of blue. Gray in some lights, shot through with a dark, velvet navy that reminded him of the ocean before a storm. It made him wonder if there was some hidden strength there.

They would both find out.

"I got the job? Just like that?"

"Getting the job was always going to be the easy part. It's keeping the job that might be tricky. My list of reasons to hire you are short—you showed up. The list of reasons I have for why I might fire you is much longer."

"You're not very reassuring," she said, her lips tilting down in a slight frown.

He laughed. "If you want to go back and work for your daddy, do that. I'm not going to call you. But maybe you'll appreciate my ways later. Other jobs will seem easy after this one."

She just looked at him, her jaw firmly set, her petite body rigid with determination. "What time do you want me here?"

"Seven o'clock. Don't be late. Or else…"

"You'll fire me. I've got the theme."

"Excellent. Hayley Thompson, you've got yourself a job."

*Find out what happens when business
becomes very personal for
Jonathan and Hayley in
SEDUCE ME, COWBOY*
by New York Times *bestselling author
Maisey Yates,
available March 2017 wherever
Harlequin® Desire books and ebooks are sold.*

www.Harlequin.com

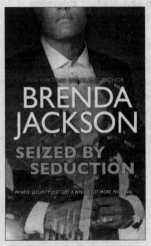

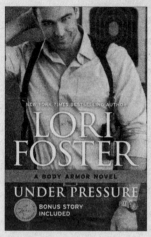

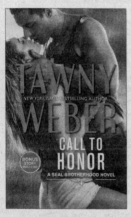

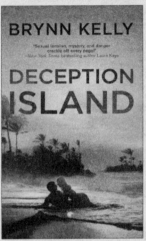

HARLEQUIN®
Desire

Powerful heroes…scandalous secrets…burning desires.

Save **$1.00**
on the purchase of
SEDUCE ME, COWBOY
by *New York Times* bestselling
author Maisey Yates.

Available wherever books are sold, including most bookstores, supermarkets, drugstores and discount stores.

Save $1.00

on the purchase of SEDUCE ME, COWBOY by Maisey Yates.

Coupon valid until April 30, 2017.
Redeemable at participating outlets in the U.S. and Canada only.
Not redeemable at Barnes & Noble stores. Limit one coupon per customer.

52614617

5 65373 00076 2   (8100)0 12263

HDMYCOUP0217

REQUEST YOUR FREE BOOKS!

2 FREE NOVELS
FROM THE ROMANCE COLLECTION,
PLUS 2 FREE GIFTS!

YES! Please send me 2 FREE novels from the Romance Collection and my 2 FREE gifts (gifts are worth about $10). After receiving them, if I don't wish to receive any more books, I can return the shipping statement marked "cancel." If I don't cancel, I will receive 4 brand-new novels every month and be billed just $6.49 per book in the U.S. or $6.99 per book in Canada. That's a savings of at least 18% off the cover price. It's quite a bargain! Shipping and handling is just 50¢ per book in the U.S. and 75¢ per book in Canada.* I understand that accepting the 2 free books and gifts places me under no obligation to buy anything. I can always return a shipment and cancel at any time. Even if I never buy another book, the two free books and gifts are mine to keep forever.

194/394 MDN GH4D

Name   (PLEASE PRINT)

Address   Apt. #

City   State/Prov.   Zip/Postal Code

Signature (if under 18, a parent or guardian must sign)

Mail to the **Reader Service:**
IN U.S.A.: P.O. Box 1867, Buffalo, NY 14240-1867
IN CANADA: P.O. Box 609, Fort Erie, Ontario L2A 5X3

Want to try 2 free books from another line?
Call 1-800-873-8635 or visit www.ReaderService.com.

*Terms and prices subject to change without notice. Prices do not include applicable taxes. Sales tax applicable in N.Y. Canadian residents will be charged applicable taxes. Offer not valid in Quebec. This offer is limited to one order per household. Not valid for current subscribers to the Romance Collection or the Romance/Suspense Collection. All orders subject to credit approval. Credit or debit balances in a customer's account(s) may be offset by any other outstanding balance owed by or to the customer. Please allow 4 to 6 weeks for delivery. Offer available while quantities last.

Your Privacy—The Reader Service is committed to protecting your privacy. Our Privacy Policy is available online at www.ReaderService.com or upon request from the Reader Service.

We make a portion of our mailing list available to reputable third parties that offer products we believe may interest you. If you prefer that we not exchange your name with third parties, or if you wish to clarify or modify your communication preferences, please visit us at www.ReaderService.com/consumerchoice or write to us at Reader Service Preference Service, P.O. Box 9062, Buffalo, NY 14240-9062. Include your complete name and address.

ROM15R

LARGER-PRINT BOOKS!
GET 2 FREE LARGER-PRINT NOVELS PLUS
2 FREE GIFTS!

HARLEQUIN

Romance

From the Heart, For the Heart

YES! Please send me 2 FREE LARGER-PRINT Harlequin® Romance novels and my 2 FREE gifts (gifts are worth about $10). After receiving them, if I don't wish to receive any more books, I can return the shipping statement marked "cancel." If I don't cancel, I will receive 4 brand-new novels every month and be billed just $5.09 per book in the U.S. or $5.49 per book in Canada. That's a savings of at least 15% off the cover price! It's quite a bargain! Shipping and handling is just 50¢ per book in the U.S. and 75¢ per book in Canada.* I understand that accepting the 2 free books and gifts places me under no obligation to buy anything. I can always return a shipment and cancel at any time. Even if I never buy another book, the two free books and gifts are mine to keep forever.

119/319 HDN GHWC

Name   (PLEASE PRINT)

Address   Apt. #

City   State/Prov.   Zip/Postal Code

Signature (if under 18, a parent or guardian must sign)

Mail to the **Reader Service**:
IN U.S.A.: P.O. Box 1867, Buffalo, NY 14240-1867
IN CANADA: P.O. Box 609, Fort Erie, Ontario L2A 5X3
Want to try two free books from another line?
Call 1-800-873-8635 or visit www.ReaderService.com.

* Terms and prices subject to change without notice. Prices do not include applicable taxes. Sales tax applicable in N.Y. Canadian residents will be charged applicable taxes. Offer not valid in Quebec. This offer is limited to one order per household. Not valid for current subscribers to Harlequin Romance Larger-Print books. All orders subject to credit approval. Credit or debit balances in a customer's account(s) may be offset by any other outstanding balance owed by or to the customer. Please allow 4 to 6 weeks for delivery. Offer available while quantities last.

Your Privacy—The Reader Service is committed to protecting your privacy. Our Privacy Policy is available online at www.ReaderService.com or upon request from the Reader Service.

We make a portion of our mailing list available to reputable third parties that offer products we believe may interest you. If you prefer that we not exchange your name with third parties, or if you wish to clarify or modify your communication preferences, please visit us at www.ReaderService.com/consumerchoice or write to us at Reader Service Preference Service, P.O. Box 9062, Buffalo, NY 14240-9062. Include your complete name and address.

HRLP15